TIME TO TAKE A CHANCE

DEBBIE HOWELLS

B

First published in 2011 as This is Your Life. This edition published in Great Britain in 2023 by Boldwood Books Ltd.

Copyright © Debbie Howells, 2011

Cover Design by Head Design Ltd.

Cover Illustration: Shutterstock

The moral right of Debbie Howells to be identified as the author of this work has been asserted in accordance with the Copyright, Designs and Patents Act 1988.

All rights reserved. No part of this book may be reproduced in any form or by any electronic or mechanical means, including information storage and retrieval systems, without written permission from the author, except for the use of brief quotations in a book review.

This book is a work of fiction and, except in the case of historical fact, any resemblance to actual persons, living or dead, is purely coincidental.

Every effort has been made to obtain the necessary permissions with reference to copyright material, both illustrative and quoted. We apologise for any omissions in this respect and will be pleased to make the appropriate acknowledgements in any future edition.

A CIP catalogue record for this book is available from the British Library.

Paperback ISBN 978-1-80549-241-2

Hardback ISBN 978-1-80549-239-9

Large Print ISBN 978-1-80549-240-5

Ebook ISBN 978-1-80549-242-9

Kindle ISBN 978-1-80549-243-6

Audio CD ISBN 978-1-80549-234-4

MP3 CD ISBN 978-1-80549-235-1

Digital audio download ISBN 978-1-80549-237-5

Boldwood Books Ltd
23 Bowerdean Street
London SW6 3TN
www.boldwoodbooks.com

In memory of my mum

PROLOGUE

I remember distinctly that crisp December day and how an early fall of snow brightened the greyness, crunching underfoot as we walked slowly from the car park. That day my life changed forever... Oddly, I felt elated when they told me. At last I understood those terrible headaches, the mood swings and why, from time to time, my legs would collapse from under me, without any warning at all.

And now that all these doctors and consultants at last knew what was wrong with me, they could get on with fixing it – at least, that was what I thought, back then. But it doesn't always follow. Particularly in the case of an aggressive tumour, like the one they've found, in my brain.

My euphoria had been short lived of course. I struggled to accept the truth. How could I possibly have a brain tumour? It had to be a mistake. My scan results had got muddled with someone else's...

But there was no mistake. Life in all its fullness had dealt me a rogue card, and in the blink of an eye turned everything I'd ever known on its head. But there was no time to be wasted, I was told. No putting off the inevitable. Not if I wanted to live... And so Lizzie accompanied me to the hospital, the last thing I'd want to put her through, waiting outside as I went for my treatment – such a small figure as she sat there, such a heavy weight on her shoulders.

I'd never envisaged anything like this. But does anyone? The future's always there in front of us, and even now, as I sit in my garden, I'm looking ahead. I catch myself thinking I'll plant a clematis to tumble through the Albertine rose for next summer or maybe I'll move that lilac, before it gets any bigger. There's nothing to stop me doing it, of course. Life will go on without me... But it'll be someone else who watches the vivid splash of purple amongst the tiny pale roses, or the lilac thrive in years to come because I moved it to where the soil is better drained.

It's not that I'm giving up, but I can't pretend any longer. The facts are there in front of me and through long wakeful nights, I've reached my own conclusions. I can't deny what's happening, my legs so weak I can barely walk, my balance worse than ever and those headaches... pain like I've never felt before, that refuses to go away. But I have to face the reality – that it's all coming to an end.

What is it like to die? Is it a drifting away into a dreamless sleep never to awaken, or an arrival, somewhere unimagined, carrying the story of a life like a backpacker... Would it be easier not to know it was coming? Not to have had the scan and to just have nature take its course, knowing what lies ahead... for me and Lizzie.

With her long, tawny hair and dark brown eyes, she's as beautiful on the outside as she is inside. There's a trusting gentleness about her, perhaps a little too trusting I think sometimes. She always expects the best from people, relies on them even, and every so often they let her down. Not that she isn't capable because she is, but she looks for reassurance, as though she doesn't quite trust her own judgement.

It's Lizzie's future I'm worried about. She needs the wind in her wings, light in her path and dreams to take her wherever her heart desires. She's forgotten what it is to stand on a beach in a storm and stare in awe as the waves curl over and crash onto the sand, or to laugh and *laugh until she cries, or to love so unreservedly you feel it in every cell of your body. What it is to truly feel alive...*

There's an inner strength buried somewhere inside her. When she finds it, it will change her life forever. I wish with all my heart that I was going to be here to see it, but of course here lies the irony: it's only when I've gone that she'll discover it.

I'm so tired... of this losing battle I'm fighting. Time is running out, and while the rest of the world lies sleeping, I think of Lizzie. Of everything I want for her, firing my one wish into the darkness, breathing the same words in my head.

Hoping someone, somewhere, is listening.

1

It had been the strangest day. As though fate itself had taken a hand, reaching into Lizzie's life, bombarding her with annoying trifles and odd coincidences tweaking her thoughts this way and that like some cosmic plaything, until finally it cut to the chase.

Sitting on the floor of her bedroom, she stared at the letter that had just fallen into her lap, a most peculiar feeling coming over her. The handwriting was unmistakeable – how come it had stayed hidden all this time? With fumbling hands she opened it, unable to think of anything else.

* * *

The day had begun with the kind of May morning that breathed promise.

But not for everyone. To Lizzie, the world was grey, like London in the rain in January, the worst month, with the sparkle of Christmas over and months before the first hint of spring. She didn't glance up at the brilliant, azure sky spun with threads of gossamer, or feel the heady warmth on her face – just closed the front door and began that walk she could have done with her eyes closed.

This was how it was – had been – for almost a year, her perceptions dulled by the fog that followed her around and the hole in her life her mother's death had left, like a gaping wound that refused to heal.

Logically she knew the painful part should be behind her, despatched to that part of her brain which holds even the haziest of memories. She'd read enough about brains to know that most of her life was stored there, a series of snapshots and recordings filed away in the depths of her temporal lobes. It had been a year now, hadn't it? Long enough surely, for the worst of her grief to have faded into a dull, aching kind of backdrop.

If there was time, she'd slip into Joe's. After another delay on the tube, she really shouldn't, but as she walked past, she lingered just long enough for an invisible hand to reach out and pull her in. Just for five minutes, of course... what was the harm in that?

Joe's was her sanctuary, blasting the sixties guitar music she loved out of oversized speakers – Hendrix and Santana this morning. A whole other world where she could lose herself and today her luck was in. The table in the window was empty and quick as a flash she slipped into the chair, still warm from the large fat man who'd just got up.

Safely cocooned and with a strong dose of caffeine flooding through her veins, Lizzie took a breath and sighed. It came from the heart, that sigh, though she barely knew she was doing it. She had too much on her mind – work, Jamie, *her wedding*...

* * *

It was hard to believe it was three years ago. New Year's Eve, one of the most romantic nights on the calendar, Lizzie had always thought. Though not when you'd just been dumped, most unceremoniously – and for a surgically enhanced, St-Tropezed nymphomaniac.

She'd had a talent for it – falling for the easy-come easy-go types, who'd leave at the drop of a pair of knickers, floozying from one bed to the next without caring.

Enough was enough, she told herself, as the countdown started. They were history. The second bottle of wine had done it – along with the sparkly lights and the schmaltzy music – and the cheer as Big Ben rang out. *Out with the old, in with the new*, she'd thought suddenly, gazing at Jamie through rosé-tinted spectacles. Maybe this serious-looking man, quite sexy in his designer suit, might it be he was *the one*?

It was the beginning of three years that changed everything – chiselling away at her, moulding the free spirit into someone grown up and organised. With a proper job and neat skirts and fitted jackets in her wardrobe, instead of her sassy minis of old as she flitted between temping jobs.

Jamie planned – everything. Considered and deliberated over everything. It was contagious too and spendthrift Lizzie who could never resist a bargain had been replaced by a most sensible girl, whose every purchase was calculated.

'Eliza... Look. It's frightfully good value, this Jaeger sale... You can save 50 per cent on your suits... You really ought to buy half a dozen now and put them away...' Not getting at all that Lizzie in Jaeger suits would be like dressing your maiden aunt in Vivienne Westwood. Lamb dressed as mutton, she thought, pretending not to hear him.

No longer did Lizzie wish on stars or gaze at the moon the way she used to – those hippy happy days were behind her and friends had drifted away. After all, that old life of riotous nights out with the girls, drinking until they fell over, belonged to a past she'd put behind her.

One person remained from Lizzie's old life. Katie – who never said *I told you* so when the iffiest of Lizzie's decisions backfired on her. Who'd mopped her tears when her mother died. Who occasionally winkled out the old Lizzie, who'd long gone to ground.

'*Cocktails at the Warehouse, just one or two... Come on! He'll never know...*' she'd added persuasively, and unbeknown to Jamie, they'd snuck off giggling and crawled home pickled after midnight.

It was Katie too who'd egged her on to buy that glorious dress for her thirtieth birthday party. Actually, it was more a dinner than a party – a dull affair, organised by Jamie, who, never one to miss out on a networking opportunity, had invited a bunch of work colleagues.

Wow, Lizzie! You're a goddess... like Titania out of A Midsummer Night's Dream...

A brilliant swirl of green and blue with a beaded halter neck, the dress had somehow clung in all the right places, reminding Lizzie of simpler, more carefree times. On the night, she'd had spent ages fiddling with her hair, pinning it up so that long strands here and there artfully tumbled down. She'd felt gorgeous – for all of five minutes – until Jamie utterly destroyed it.

How frivolous, Eliza... I rather imagined you'd wear that new suit...

It wasn't the words, more the way he'd spoken them. The disdain and disapproval on his face. It had hurt way beyond vanity. He simply didn't get it – that this was *her*, that colour and frivolity and sexy made her feel alive.

It had been downhill all the way after that, with her and Katie getting blitzed as the only way to survive such a deadly evening.

I can't believe you behaved so immaturely. Jolly embarrassing actually... I can't imagine what the chaps thought. Really, Eliza... I don't know why you're friends with that dreadful girl...

A pang of nostalgia struck her as she'd shoved the dress to the back of the wardrobe. *Oh what I wouldn't give to be footloose and fancy free and without a care in the world...*

But with her mother ill, it was no time to think about herself. Not the time either for Jamie's proposal. The last thing she expected – now, of all times, when she needed to be thinking about her mother. But knowing what lay ahead, she'd felt a sudden rush of gratitude, that he'd still be there after her mother wasn't. He'd produced the enormous diamond before she could change her mind.

'Oh... oh... it's beautiful...'

'Doesn't he get what's happening to your mum?' Katie could see what was happening, but then, this was Jamie after all. About as subtle as a brick, as always.

'I think he just thought it was a good idea, to do it now. So she would know before... I mean, we have been together for years...'

Jamie, of course, had thought no such thing but with her mother slipping away before her eyes, Lizzie's logic was more skewed than ever.

Katie had bitten her tongue. It was hardly the time after all.

If only she'd stopped and thought. About how wise it was, making such a huge commitment in the wake of losing her mother. That losing your cornerstone as she had sent ripples through your soul, changing you inside forever.

But a kind of numbness had moved in, clouding everything. And now, nearly a year had passed and the big day was almost here. Lizzie could barely believe there were just four days to go. Most things were now in place but without Isobel, nothing felt at all the way it used to.

Life goes on, Eliza... Jamie had said most firmly just a week after the funeral, wasting no time as he booked exclusive hire of a small-but-classy London hotel.

'We'll have the Hamachi tuna sashimi, don't you think, Eliza? Followed by roast poulet with blah blah blah...'

He hadn't wanted Lizzie's input, just as Lizzie hadn't wanted Katie's:

Lizzie! What's the hurry? Is he frightened you'll change your mind?

* * *

Lizzie rested her head in her hands. She'd like to hide here in Joe's all morning, Jamie's to-do list buried in her pocket – he'd emailed it to her after dashing off to some last-minute conference.

But with her latte finished all too soon, she couldn't put it off, and with a regretful sigh and a wave to Maria, who called a cheery 'ciao, Lizzie' from across the room, she reluctantly melted back into the madness on the streets. And out of nowhere, as she walked, the thought came into her head.

Why don't I feel excited? It's my big day. I have my designer dress, flowers to die for, a top chef, the best vintage champagne... Shouldn't my heart be thumping, my blood fizzing with anticipation, my cheeks aching from all the smiling at absolutely everyone I pass...

No, she told herself firmly, ignoring the irritating voice. It wasn't surprising at all. She was quite simply exhausted. It was all this rushing around trying to organise everything. Taking a deep breath, she tried to ignore the sinking feeling in her stomach. When Saturday came, and she put on that dress and her hairdresser had worked her magic, *then* she'd feel excited, she knew she would. *How could she possibly not?*

Meanwhile, there was today to get through. One last day, starting with this meeting she was late for, before she left as early as she could.

Ignoring the blast on the horn as a taxi driver swerved to avoid her, she darted across the road and in through the glass doors.

'Three minutes late, Lizzie! What time do you call this? *Come on...*'

It was Julian, standing there, tapping his watch. But then he started early, worked late and didn't have a life, she supposed, unlike the rest of them. Her heart sank into her boots.

'This really isn't good enough... They'll have started without you...'

He leaped up the stairs quite nippily – no mean feat in such obscenely tight trousers. It was definitely the ageing rock star look this morning, thought Lizzie, trying her tear her gaze from his leop-ard-print bottom.

But as the meeting had droned on and on, Lizzie's mind had drifted off – miles away, awaking with a jolt at the end. Slightly disbelievingly, she'd glanced at the clock – it couldn't possibly be that time already... But as she looked around, stars appeared before her eyes, then the room started to spin. Suddenly, she couldn't breathe.

I need some air, she thought in a panic, her heart racing errati-cally. Squeezing through everyone, she edged towards the door and slipped away.

Out of the building and in spite of the clouds gathering ominously overhead, she fumbled in her bag for the Ray-Bans. Safely camouflaged and lowering her head, she walked unsteadily down the street and across the road towards the relative quiet of Green Park.

Still light-headed, Lizzie kept going until, away from everyone, she found an empty park bench where she sat, rather heavily for someone so slight and sighed a shaky sigh.

Breathe, Lizzie, breathe... She sat, taut, ready for flight.

* * *

Something was in the air – but Lizzie dragged herself back to the office, still feeling at odds, staring at the clock. Since when did time pass so slowly? Her attempt to sneak away early again was scuppered by the odious Julian, whose earlier agitation had subsided into extreme good humour for some reason.

'Ah, Lizzie, do you have a minute?' He'd appeared from his office, a benign smile on his face.

But, well-meaning, he'd summoned everyone, and to Lizzie's intense embarrassment, had rambled on with his usual verbosity about what he affectedly referred to as 'the blessings of marriage' and 'lifelong commitment', words which sent a chill down Lizzie's spine, before opening a bottle of champagne.

It was warm but Lizzie gulped it. For the second time that day she fought an untimely desire to run, instead smiling blindly around the office at everyone as their voices echoed in her ears.

'I felt like that, doll!' Jude's red lipstick had transferred to the rim of her glass, and her teeth. Always grateful for a distraction, she was swigging champagne like there was no tomorrow. 'Only not like till the day before...'

'Like what?' Lizzie was flummoxed.

'Poleaxed! Shit scared... You know! It's a big day, isn't it, in front of all those people... But it'll be a good one. The best. Especially the wedding night! Oh, that was worth waiting for, I can tell you.' She winked at her.

'You're so lucky, Lizzie...' Little dark-haired Sammy looked enviously at her. 'I mean, you're getting married... it's just so romantic, isn't it?'

'Thank you. I mean, is it... I am...' Lizzie stuttered. *Lucky? Romantic?* She took another gulp of champagne.

* * *

Lizzie fled sooner than she should have but that was too bad. The tube was its chock-a-block worst, and she failed to notice the man who'd edged closer and closer until he was pressed up against her, breathing noisily in her ear. And that was when she lost it, a spark of anger flaring inside as she ground the heel of her boot into his foot. *How dare he...*

It flashed into Lizzie's mind how Jamie had bought them for her. *You can't beat a pair of good quality high-heeled boots...*

And for once, he was right. She'd cursed those heels many times but this was her reward for every uncomfortable step. Her assailant gasped, a contorted look of pain on his face.

But the strangest mood was upon her, the most restless of thoughts in her head. *Bring it on*, she silently challenged the universe, her nails digging into the palms of her hands as she clenched her fists by her sides. *Throw something else at me. Do your absolute worst...*

She'd stood stiffly after that, enduring the beastly tube as it jolted through the darkness, staring mindlessly at a pair of arms further down the carriage. They were encased in a rather damp coat. Nice though, Lizzie noticed – navy, wool by the looks of it, expensively cut, she thought, desperately trying to distract herself.

Unintentionally, her eyes wandered upwards, scrutinising purely objectively, of course, blue, smiling eyes with the skin slightly crinkled at the edges, and fairish windswept hair that would have looked more in place on a beach. *Brad Pitt's hair mixed with Jude Law's eyes*, she vaguely registered, before he smiled and winked at her then got off at the next stop.

How could she have... Lizzie's face flushed with shame as more sardines prised themselves in beside her. First she'd assaulted someone, then been caught red-handed ogling another. A wild, alien energy coursed through her veins as yet again she fought the urge to run anywhere, just to *escape* – from the heaving carriages, the mundanity and pointlessness of all of it.

* * *

Only with her front door closed behind her, soaking in a steaming hot bath, did Lizzie start to feel more like herself. But even submerged in the bubbles, she still couldn't fathom her thoughts. It niggled at her that her wedding felt such a chore. Tired or not, shouldn't it be the biggest day of her life, looking forward to the future that lay in front of them? For the first time she contemplated the enormity of what she was committing to... and that's when something shifted. Barely perceptibly at first. But it was that question, the one that she couldn't quite bring herself to answer. W*as Jamie really the man she wanted to share her life with*? It floated in the air, unanswered.

And even afterwards, in the huge, shapeless jumper she loved and which normally made her feel so much better and with the large glass of wine she'd promised herself, she was restless. She drifted through to the sitting room, but it wasn't a room to relax in. Like everything in this house, it was a 'but'. She ended up just standing there, uncomfortably, registering unhappily that her so-called 'home' was just imposing elevations stuck in a snobby post-code. She defied anyone to slump into the hideous beige sofas, or look around the stark white interior and feel snug and safe and comforted.

God... she missed Isobel. More than ever, with her wedding looming. Lizzie felt a tightness in her chest as a tear rolled down her cheek, but it was no good, was it – wishing for what couldn't be. But then she couldn't help herself and she shook with silent sobs.

Going to the bedroom, she pulled a chair over to the vast wardrobe, and climbing up, reached for the topmost shelf where pushed out of sight was a wooden box. Modest looking, its contents were priceless – at least to Lizzie – of photos, letters, precious bits of her life.

It was almost exactly a year since the last time, when she'd tucked away a few treasured items. Dragging it out now, Lizzie sat on the floor. Whether déjà-vu or just plain nerves, her hands were trembling as she opened it, finding her mother's old jewellery box and underneath it, a notebook, a journal her mother had kept until her illness prevented her from writing. It had been far too painful to read at the time and Lizzie had left it – out of sight, out of mind.

A whole year. How can that be?

Lizzie studied the notebook, taking in the daisies on the front – her mother had loved them. Then starting to turn the pages, before she got any further an envelope slipped out and landed in her lap. Picking it up, she turned it over.

And that was when she forgot all about the events of today. It didn't occur to her that if Jamie hadn't gone to his conference, she wouldn't even be sitting here like this. Nor that the events of the entire day had in some obscure way been tipping her off balance. All that mattered at that precise moment was the letter and with shaky hands she opened it.

2

_____

Dearest Lizzie

I hope that maybe the dust is settling – enough at least for you to start to move on. Because at some point, after all that's happened, that's what you have to do.

Think for a moment: here you are in the middle of your greatest adventure – your life! Or maybe somewhere along the way you lost sight of that... I know, you have to work, pay the bills, but...

You have choices. Never forget that. Imagine for a moment, if you were granted three wishes, Lizzie. What in your life is most in need of change? What do you most need? Freedom, maybe? What a gift that would be! Remember, Lizzie – you are as free as you choose to be.

There's a place in the West Country. It's known to the locals as Spriggan Point. You've been there before, with me, many years ago. I can't remember who told me about it, just that there's a magic to be found there which heals the broken spirit. And you can feel it, Lizzie, even when the fog rolls in off the ocean and you can't see one step in front of you, but it's in the wind touching your skin, the spray from waves crashing on the rocks, even the sand underfoot. It reaches into your soul until you, too, can't help but feel part of something bigger. What I found there never left me.

Maybe you need its magic too, Lizzie. I'll leave a map with this letter. There's a farm nearby, where we stayed – Roscarn, if I remember rightly. And don't let anything stop you. Let it weave its spell on you too, before you do something you regret.

Don't be upset when you read this. None of us go on forever! Life has been great! Make sure you have a great life too...

With love forever

 Mum

As Lizzie read it, pain like a knife stabbed at her. Barely taking it in, she read it again, her face wet with tears. And as she sat there not moving, she realised. It was all a mistake. Her mother had meant this for her a year ago, not now, just days before her wedding...

Rummaging through the box, Lizzie looked for the map but there was no sign of one. And as a knock at the door interrupted her, she forgot about it.

'Cheer up love, it might never happen,' quipped the delivery man with an annoying wink, as she opened it and signed for the large box he handed over.

Lizzie simply took the parcel and carried it into the house. The orders of service – it had to be. With a sinking heart she opened it, to find them beaming up at her.

Saturday 27th June

The Marriage of

James Archibald Mountford

And Eliza Rosalie Lavender

As Lizzie stared they seemed to mock her. He knew how she hated 'Eliza' and the 'marriage of' suddenly sounded like a prison sentence. And how come she was marrying a man whose middle name was Archibald? Then she thought of her dress, of its stiff, unyielding form like a straitjacket, hanging in the spare room waiting to deliver her to her warder.

Lizzie sat for ages, not moving, as a million thoughts filled her head. Then she rushed back to fetch the journal, scanning the page she'd just read.

It's made me think though. I've been muddling along with my life for so long now, never stepping beyond the safe and familiar. And I like how safe feels – but I've forgotten what I've been missing out on and the excitement of stepping into the unknown...

The book fell out of her hands and it was as if the fog started to lift, as Lizzie admitted to herself that everything was wrong. Those lines might have been written for her alone. The pompous husband, the beige house, the soul-destroying job – she didn't in all honesty want any of it.

It hit her like a blow, knocking the air out of her. But that was her life she didn't want. But she couldn't stay. Staying meant the end, giving up. But she had no one, nowhere to go to...

Lizzie sat there long after night fell, unwanted thoughts filling her head. She'd come this close to marrying the wrong man. Everything she loved, that made her feel alive, had gradually faded away, leaving a shadow of who she was.

It was there in her darkest moment that she found it. Just the faintest trace of strength like the furthest, dimmest star. But enough for her to do the only thing she could think of, and digging out her battered old suitcases from the loft, hurriedly, untidily, she packed

– only the clothes she liked, the dreaded suits being abandoned in the wardrobe with the hair straighteners. It was a pitifully small pile of possessions that she heaped by the front door – not much to show for three years.

But all done and ready to go, and oblivious to the moonlight beaming in through the window, Lizzie slept, dead to the world.

* * *

Under a canopy of ancient beech trees, a wisp of smoke spiralled above the embers of a dying fire. Nothing stirred, and when it did, it was as if the trees themselves were whispering.

'Are you sure we should be doing this?' The words were barely detectable.

'Oh shush yourself, it's fine! How could it possibly not be!' There was a rushing noise, the cracking of twigs underfoot, then quiet again. 'All that matters is it's done with love...'

The pungent scent of rosemary filled the air.

'Which it is of course! We agreed, didn't we! That if your heart is full of love, everything will follow...'

The air filled with more whispers. 'So, everything's in place then. Everything...'

'I only hope it's enough...'

'It's working this time, it has to be. All the signs are there...'

'Come on – we've nearly finished...'

The voices were hushed for a moment. There was no sound at all, but the faintest movement of the leaves.

'Such a perfect moon, isn't it?' Spoken like a wish.

A collective sigh filled the air, then the fire hissed as more herbs hit the glowing cinders, and the voices faded away leaving silence.

3

The sun was rising when, clearer in her head than she ever remembered being, Lizzie dragged her cases down the path and heaved them into her car. Then she went back inside, just to leave an envelope – against that Chinese vase she'd always hated. Then after leaving her door key and engagement ring beside it, she closed the door for the last time.

Outside, Lizzie paused, reaching for her mobile, willing her friend to answer, but instead getting the business-like recording.

Hello, you're through to the voicemail of Katie McDonald, please leave a message...

'Hi, Katie? It's me. I *have* to talk to you. I've done something... I'll tell you all about it later...'

* * *

As she drove along the South Circular, with the stop-starting and the honking because she wasn't paying attention, even the traffic seemed to be trying to stop her going. A frown crossed her face. *Was she really doing the right thing?*

She thought back to last night. Leaving now was the only way – before it was too late. Some might call her foolish... Well, let them. Years back, like Elizabeth McKenzie, she too used to *do* things, though you'd never know it now. She took a deep breath – if a middle-aged secretary could take flying lessons... What was she so scared about?

As she headed past Heathrow on the M4, she put her foot down just as her mobile buzzed. Katie? But she glanced over to see 'Jamie' flashing up on the screen. *God...* Panicking, she turned her music up. Then in a fit of impulsiveness she opened the window and hurled her mobile out onto the carriageways, narrowly missing a motorcyclist who swerved and raised his fist at her. Ignoring the aggressive toots from behind, Lizzie gave a whoop of glee as the burden suddenly lifted from her shoulders. And as she sped down the motorway headed who knew where, and with the windows down and the wind in her hair, for the first time it struck her that she was really, really free...

Lizzie drove non-stop for hours, her spirits high and her heart soaring, oblivious to the clouds that were gathering overhead the further west she drove. Forgetting all about Jamie and her wedding, she contemplated a vague plan that she'd stop at some point – it didn't matter where – and find a B & B for the night. And then tomorrow she'd get going again and just keep heading west. Cornwall, she'd decided, where she'd stop at the first small, quiet place she came to by the sea. She'd already pictured it in her head – the black, jagged rocks she'd clamber down to the sandy beach below, or a sleepy village nestled in a cove where she could sit or swim or walk a coast path, while she contemplated what to do next. *I can't wait...* she kept thinking excitedly, holding the image in her mind. *I just can't wait to be there...*

Wanting as many miles as possible behind her, Lizzie kept driving, imagining an invisible barrier keeping Jamie away. Of course, he wouldn't even know she'd gone yet, and by the time he did... even Lizzie didn't know where she'd be.

It felt like she was waking from a long sleep as the thoughts raced through her head. She'd clung to Jamie for all the wrong reasons, she could see that now. Afraid of being on her own, she just couldn't bring herself to leave him.

But life had another surprise in store. A warning light, which flashed on somewhere past Bristol. Lizzie's car had belonged to Isobel – an elderly Golf, which she'd never told Jamie about, because she'd known exactly what he'd say.

Really, Eliza, there's just no excuse these days for anyone running a car that's not environmentally friendly and green blah blah blah... Think of the environment...

She knew the rant off pat, just as she remembered her mother mentioning this light that used to flash from time to time. Lizzie ignored it. At some point it would stop, like it always did. And eventually, about ten miles further on it did, only instead of going out, it became continuous, at which point Lizzie got worried. It would rather take the wind out of her sails to go crawling back to London now. Then another light blinked at her just as a slip road came into view, and rather gratefully she took it.

Lizzie nursed the stricken Golf for another three or four miles before she saw it. An old-fashioned metal sign in a hedge proclaiming 'Garage', which had an equally rusty arrow swinging underneath, pointing in the vague direction of a winding, country lane. She looked in dismay. Miles off the beaten track already, she hadn't seen a road sign in ages, but the absence of any alternative swayed her and she swung her crippled car across the road.

The lane meandered for a mile or so, before she saw a faded old sign proclaiming 'Littleton' as a few scruffy cottages emerged out of the countryside. Then an old church, hidden away in the woods, then more cottages and then – was that it? A single ancient petrol pump stood proudly at the side of the road, in what presumably passed as a forecourt. It wasn't the most convincing of establishments, but if they could fix her car and get her on her way, it really didn't matter what it looked like.

She pulled over and got out, making her way over to the shabby kiosk which had a shelf full of dusty Coke bottles and not much else.

'Hello? Anyone there?' she called, tentatively venturing inside.

Nothing, then a hacking cough which made her jump, followed by a loud sniff, as an old man in filthy overalls shuffled out of the gloom.

'Mornin', miss? S'pose you be wanting some petrol like?' The accent took Lizzie by surprise.

'Actually, I was hoping someone could look at my car. There's a warning light... it's been on for about the last five miles...'

The old man started sucking his teeth and squinting out of the corner of one eye at her, shaking his head most disapprovingly.

'Should a brought it in right 'way, miss, could have all manner goin' on in there.' He shook his head some more.

'Well,' Lizzie started most indignantly, then sensing it was pointless to explain, stopped. 'Well,' she tried again, with deliberate calmness, 'do you think you can fix it?'

'Mmm, well, best I 'ave a look, right? And you give me your phone number see? That way I can tell you what it is.'

'Oh. Okay. Oh. I don't have one. And I can't go anywhere until I get my car back.'

The man gave Lizzie a funny look.

'Aaar,' he said knowingly. 'Aaar. Right. I see.' Then he paused. 'What you means is you needs somewhere to stay.'

'*Stay?*' Lizzie started to panic again. 'I don't want to *stay*, I just want you to fix the car so I can be on my way.'

He chuckled. 'Oh no no no. You see it won't be fixed till

tomorrow earliest. You best go down the Star, miss, they do rooms. Ain't nowhere else to go.'

So on the strength of that most heartening of recommendations, Lizzie gathered a few possessions, while Dave, as he told her his name was, just stood there, coughing and saying 'aaar' a lot. Then, resigned to her fate, she handed him the keys and wandered down the lane to find the Star.

The quiet was disconcerting. It had been bright and sunny when she left London, but here clouds had arrived menacingly overhead and heavy splats of rain were falling. Lizzie's footsteps seemed to echo, and she nearly leaped out of her skin as a crow cawed loudly in a nearby tree. She passed a few more old cottages but no people – it was like a ghost town. All she could hear was the wind rustling slightly in the trees, and what sounded like a tractor in the distance, but apart from that, absolutely nothing.

Her thoughts were rudely interrupted, however, when she wandered on round the next corner and nearly got mown down by an Audi TT doing at least seventy as it sped furiously by. And then she found the Star, which shattered some more illusions. Instead of being the quaint old-fashioned, thatch-roofed village pub she'd been expecting, its modern red-brick exterior looked grim. And the mother of all commotions was going on inside.

'I ain't havin' no bleedin' council bastards tellin' me what to do...' came an angry male voice, clear as a bell through the closed door. Farmer, Lizzie assumed from the yokel intonation with which he spoke with such passion.

'William. If we're going to get anywhere with this, you have to calm down,' came a female voice. Soothingly. Not quite so passionate, from what Lizzie could gather.

'S'all right for you, inn't it? You ain't got them marchin' through your land, leavin' friggin' gates open, chuckin' their crap in the 'edges...' He made a sound like spitting.

'Lord sakes. Someone needs to get this nonsense under control,' came another woman's voice, a well-spoken one this time, sounding more than a little exasperated. 'It's the traffic we're talking about surely, not the blasted ramblers. It's not that difficult. All we need to do is close the road, temporarily of course, and move the sheep every day for a month. At five o'clock on the dot. That'll fix the buggers!'

The voices faded to a rumbling discontent.

'It'll only work if we all agree,' said the first sane voice Lizzie had heard.

The exasperated woman spoke up again. 'Very well. All in favour, raise your hands...'

After much mutterings in the background, she added, 'Right. Monday morning – everyone?'

Feeling rain soaking into her T-shirt, nervously Lizzie went in, not sure at all what she'd find. But no one even noticed until she crept over to the bar and timidly enquired about a room.

'A room, miss?' bellowed the young barman, grabbing the attention of absolutely everyone there. 'You say you want a room?'

'Just for one night,' Lizzie added hastily, suddenly conscious of everyone's eyes turning to stare at her. 'You see, my car's being fixed up the road.'

'Oh,' said the barman, a wicked glint appearing in his eye. 'Not Dave? You sure you just want the one night? Could do you a deal if you decide to stay for five?'

'No,' Lizzie answered far too loudly, clearly showing her alarm. *Five?* 'No. Just the one. Thank you. It isn't going to take long,' she added firmly, ignoring his raised eyebrows.

'Whatever you say, miss...' He smirked, turning to rummage for a key.

Lizzie's stomach turned over. Dave hadn't exactly inspired confidence, and now, this cocky barman standing there grinning at her really wasn't helping at all.

Maybe she should go. Right now. She could hot-foot it back to Dave's, reclaim her crippled car and creep back up the road to civilisation. But she was interrupted by the exasperated female voice from earlier.

'I say, you better come and have a drink. You'll need one. Name's Antonia by the way. You're not from round here, are you?'

Lizzie turned to face Antonia, a slight figure with long fair hair which hung in unruly curls down her back. She was pretty in an unkempt kind of way and a bit older than her, Lizzie guessed. But in skin-tight jodhpurs and riding boots, might have come from another planet.

'Um, I'm Lizzie,' she said uncertainly, holding out a hand.

Antonia shook it heartily. 'Take no notice of these old farts. They're all up in arms because the roadworks on the main road mean our lane gets used as a rat run. Absolute flaming nuisance, of course. William blocked it with his tractor and let the tyres down but he never knows where to draw the line. Ended up getting arrested, the stupid arse... And you can't go out on a horse with all those bloody townies who think they own the road... Buggers hoot at you as they pass! God, I can't tell you. Poor Hamish nearly sat on a Porsche. Golly! Should have let him – that'd make them think. Anyway, the upshot of it all is the farmers start moving their sheep around. Spot on rush hour. That'll sort them! Can't run a bloody sheep over no matter what you're driving!' she hooted triumphantly, thumping a fist on the bar.

Just as Lizzie was wondering who or what on earth Hamish was, one of the men, in an unlikely outfit of a Stranglers T-shirt and a beany hat, wandered over and stared at Lizzie, the look on his face unmistakeably hostile as he pointed a grubby finger at her.

'You ain't one of them danged ramblers I 'ope...' he said menacingly.

'Lord's sakes, William. Do you honestly think she'd tell you if she was? Now clear off and leave her alone.' Antonia rolled her eyes at Lizzie, as William, clearly used to her bluntness, simply glowered at her, muttering obscenities under his breath as he shambled back to the others.

'Farmer,' said Antonia by way of explanation. 'Alpha male, though you'd never think so to look at him. Pity... he's quite sexy when he's not being such a cretin,' she added regretfully. 'Awfully good with horses, believe it or not. And I'd far sooner some mud and sweat than poncey pinstripes, wouldn't you? My ex wore them. Once was enough, I can assure you.' Her eyes wandered up and down the retreating view of the farmer.

Lizzie blinked disbelievingly. Mad and sweat? It didn't appeal in the slightest though she could understand an aversion to pinstripes. Surely there was middle ground – with scrubbed country types in nice, clean clothes rather than this lot who looked straight out of the fields.

But Antonia was on a roll. She clearly had a thing for the beany-hatted farmer who looked several years her junior, her eyes flickering lustfully in his direction every so often, a fact to which he seemed oblivious.

'So, where were you going before your car packed up?' she asked nosily, the long curls falling over one shoulder.

'Cornwall,' said Lizzie firmly. 'Just for a break.' Wondering where on earth that had come from.

'Jolly nice,' said Antonia cheerfully. 'Bit of a comedown I should imagine, finding yourself here, of all places. Oh well, could be worse.'

Could it? Lizzie wasn't sure how. If you were going to spend a night in the country, you wouldn't exactly choose the Star. Not unless you were desperate – like she was.

'Cripes, is that the time? I must shoot – riding lesson! Cindy'll be champing at the bit! Lord... can't even remember which horse she's on. Nice to have met you, Lizzie! Good luck with your car.'

The barman sniggered in the background as Antonia left, and feeling like a fish out of water, Lizzie sipped the rest of her drink as she listened to the conversation going on around her. Words like 'overdrives', 'wethers' and 'bleedin' bastards' floated around. It was obviously the nerve centre of the village in here. Then she crept out and headed for the privacy of her room.

Expecting the worst, she was pleasantly surprised when she opened the door. It wasn't *so* awful – not exactly luxurious, but not terrible either. Aside from the wilted rose on the dressing table, there was a kind of mismatched effect going on, with pea-green curtains that didn't quite close and clashed with the bedcovers, and peach and yellow towels folded neatly on the bed. But at least the sheets looked clean when she folded them back. Jamie would have been horrified... *Jamie*... it hit her like a thunderbolt. And by now he'd have read her letter.

The doubts were back again – bigger, more forbidding than before. Whatever had she been thinking, running off like that, only to end up in this godforsaken backwater. It was madness. So much for finding herself – she'd completely and utterly lost it.

She should have stayed, in the familiar surroundings of London and squashed into Katie's tiny flat, where she'd have faced up to all those wedding guests to cancel with her friend holding her hand.

It would have been better too, if she'd stayed and told Jamie in person. But told him what exactly? That she'd opened a stranger's letter and it had made her see the light?

It never would have worked, she knew that. He wouldn't have listened to a word. *You're not making any sense at all, Eliza, it's wedding nerves, blah blah blah...* She could hear him saying it. He'd have bulldozed over her and completely dismissed what she told him.

It wouldn't have made any difference, she thought sadly. There was no right way, no easy way. Not with someone like him. And somehow, in this small room in a terrible pub in a village many miles away, Lizzie could finally answer her question: Jamie wasn't the man for her.

4

Horses in the night... thought Lizzie sleepily, nestling deeper under
the covers until all that was visible was the top of her head. *Horses
in the night in the middle of London...*

But she was rudely awoken as a car went speeding past,
followed by hooting and angry shouting, and prising her eyes open,
saw that it wasn't the middle of the night and nor was it London
either.

As she lay drowsily in bed, the events of yesterday flooded back and
she was wide awake in an instant. Fending off the doubts, suddenly
back with a vengeance, persuading herself that actually, no, she hadn't
lost her mind, far from it. She'd been saving herself from a fate worse
than death. By beige... She got out of bed and pulled some clothes on.
She needed to talk to Katie, only that wasn't so simple without a phone.

Lacking the convenience of a phone in her room, when Lizzie
asked the barman where she could find one, he pointed to the one
on the bar. There, right in front of her and right in front of
everyone else too, though it had to be said, there was only one deaf
old man and his smelly dog in there, but Lizzie didn't like the leer

on the barman's face. In fact she didn't like anything about him, not least that her predicament seemed to be his entertainment. Well, he wasn't getting the sordid details of her personal life. Reluctantly, he pointed her in the direction of one outside in the car park, where at least she could close the door.

Feeding in her coins at an alarming rate, Lizzie acquired Katie's number and dialled, slightly apprehensively.

'Good morning, could I speak to Katie McDonald?'

'Katie McDonald,' came a crisp voice that didn't sound like Katie at all.

'Katie... it's me,' she said hesitantly.

'LIZZIE! Oh my God, oh my God! I've been calling you all night! Are you all right? Where are you?'

'I'm fine Katie, only...'

'Oh I'm so glad you called! You won't believe what Jamie's up to, you've never seen him so narked...'

'I can't believe I've done this... I'm really, really sorry, Katie,' Lizzie said sounding rather pathetic. 'I didn't mean to cause all this trouble. It was just so, well, it all happened so quickly. I will tell you about it. But the odd thing is, I know I've done the right thing. At least, I think I have...'

'Are you sure you're okay? I've been trying your mobile and worrying myself sick. I had visions of you ending up in a twisted heap of metal somewhere... Where *are* you?'

'I'm fine,' Lizzie told her, swallowing a lump in her throat. 'I am, really. I, er, lost my phone on the motorway... Jamie was calling me...You've heard from him then...'

'He's beside himself,' said Katie. 'He ranted and raved at me until I reminded him it wasn't my fault. He said, *I wouldn't be so sure about that...* Can you believe it? He's more upset at cancelling the wedding than anything else, what would everyone think, blah blah, you know how he is...' She broke off. 'Sorry, Lizzie, but you can just imagine...'

'He'll be furious,' Lizzie said. 'But I will offer to share the costs, surely he knows that...' She could just see him, stalking around the house, the frown worse than ever, letting rip at everyone he spoke to. It clinched it. There was no going back now. Her name was blackened for ever.

'Oh, I most certainly wouldn't do *that*,' said Katie unfeelingly. 'He told me his insurance will see it's all paid off...'

'What insurance?' *He'd insured their wedding?* 'He never mentioned anything about it to me...'

'Hardly surprising, is it? You know what he's like...' said Katie bluntly.

Lizzie was silent. What sort of man did that, sneakily, behind their partner's back. What else didn't she know about? Anger crept up on her offsetting some of the guilt.

'So, what are your plans?' asked Katie cautiously.

'I'm not exactly sure. I'm in a little village several miles off the M4. It's called Littleton. My car's off the road for who knows how long. Dave's garage hasn't started on it and I'm stuck in this rip-off pub because there isn't anywhere else. Oh, Katie – it's the middle of nowhere and I'm stranded!'

'Well, you need another mobile,' said Katie practically. 'And I don't suppose they sell them in the village stores round there. Or Dave's garage for that matter... At least I know where you are now, and if your car doesn't get fixed, I'll get one sent to you. In fact, why don't I do that right now?'

'Oh. No.' It came out all high-pitched. She wasn't staying another whole day. 'Katie, my car will be fixed. I won't be here.'

'Lizzie. I think you better go and actually ask that garage man what's happening. And phone me straight back.'

'Okay,' said Lizzie, able to put the moment off no longer. 'But, Katie, please, *please* don't tell Jamie where I am.'

'As if,' said her friend disbelievingly. 'Just so you know, Lizzie, even if this is all a bit spur of the moment, I think you've made the best decision...'

* * *

The sun was shining as Lizzie made her way back up the lane to the garage, the air full of the heady scent of apple blossom tinged with damp earth from last night's rain. This time it was an enormous shiny Discovery that nearly flattened her into the hedge, and she was starting to see what everyone was so heated about. She spotted the girl she'd met in the pub last night – Antonia – who waved at her before climbing onto a huge orange horse.

Lizzie's car was exactly where she'd left it, doors closed, bonnet down, looking to all intents and purposes like it was finished. Her hopes up, she went to look for Dave who she found watering his window boxes, which raised her hopes further. He must have finished, clearly.

'Mornin', miss! Lovely one, inn't it!'

'Hello, Dave. Is it done?'

'Oh, dear me no. What gives you that idea, miss?' Dave folded his arms and chuckled. 'No. See. I need Mick here to do that. Thought 'e'd be in today, see.'

Lizzie felt a wave of impatience. Couldn't he have mentioned this yesterday? Hadn't he understood that she needed to be on her way?

'Look, Dave, this is really urgent. Can't you call Mick? Because if he's not here soon, I'll have to make other arrangements. I need my car back because I need to be on my way... don't you see?'

But Dave just shook his head and gazed at her benignly.

'Trouble is, miss, that car ain't goin' nowhere. Tried to move it meself just this mornin'. Totally seized up like. Won't go at all.'

Lizzie took a step back, swallowing her disappointment. It was *too* unfair. This wasn't supposed to happen, least of all now, when she should be back on the M4 heading ever closer to the wilds of Cornwall.

'Dave, do you know when Mick *is* coming in?'

Dave considered for a moment. 'Well, see, mebbe tomorrow like, or mebbe today, later on. Mebbe next week... not altogether that sure.' He scratched his head with oily fingers.

Next week? Lizzie stared at the oil-streaked hair.

'*Please* can you tell me as soon as he gets here? Only I'm supposed to be somewhere else...'

'Oh aye, miss. Now don't you go worryin'. You just leave things to me. Real good bloke is Mick.'

She walked slightly dazedly back towards the pub, and this time, when a car came by at seventy and missed her by about an inch, Lizzie shouted aggressively and waved her fist like a local. And that's when she should have got worried.

* * *

Having returned to the Star, Lizzie called Katie and broke the news. After retreating to the privacy of her room and bursting into tears, she took up the five day deal on her room, the barman's snigger barely worth the pittance she saved, then for the first time Lizzie could remember, she had absolutely nothing to do.

I should have been at least as far as Devon, she thought sorrowfully, *with a cliff path to wander and waves to gaze in awe at...* But Dave had been right about one thing. It was a beautiful morning and she pulled herself together. There was no point sitting in the Star all day being annoyed by the barman. No point feeling sorry for herself, either. It was her fault she was here – well, sort of. And in the absence of a better idea, she'd go for a walk. She'd get some fresh air in her lungs and the sun on her face and make the most of it.

After pulling on a pair of old trainers, she ignored the questioning look on the barman's face as she slipped out. The birds were singing and a whisper of a breeze ruffled her hair as she walked further down the lane and found a footpath which took her through the leafy shade of a beech wood. Only dimly registering the cool earthiness filling the air and ground that was soft with leaf mould, she walked on until the trees ended in a vast expanse of grass the lush green of spring. Ahead of her the fields sloped gently up, and after the shade of the trees, the sun felt hot on her skin as she climbed. Her heart pumping faster from the exercise, she carried on until at the top, exhilarated and in the full glare of the sun, she sank onto the grass out of breath.

A swathe of fields spiralled away in a vast circle beneath her and the views for miles were spectacular. Not a single soul was to be seen, and there was an incredible kind of peacefulness that somehow seemed to seep into her soul.

Lizzie flopped back on the grass, thoughts whirling giddily in her head. Staring up at the cloudless sky, the sun's rays like hot pinpricks, she could feel her body relaxing. But her mind was another matter, tossing and turning this way and that. One minute everything seemed so *obvious* and the next about as clear as mud. Reading Elizabeth's letter had knocked Lizzie sideways. But as she lay there, a glimmering of understanding came to her as to how she'd come to be in such a mess. And at last, she allowed her mind to venture back, into the forbidden zone, to the day they'd found out about the tumour. That most gut-twisting, heart-wrenching of moments. Would it be easier not to have known? If one day, further down the line her mother had simply just not woken up?

Feeling the knot growing tighter inside her, Lizzie wiped away tears. More tears – where were they all coming from? Hadn't she done her crying a year ago? She might have, had it not been for Jamie who couldn't abide public displays of emotion. His words of comfort had been *Chin up, Eliza, don't let the side down.* She'd done her best to just carry on as usual, believing it was the best thing – but now, it was catching up with her. And there, on top of the hill with the brightness of the sun and the softness of the grass, albeit a little late, it finally got her.

As memories of her mother's last weeks came back, her body shook with sobs. Thoughts of the horrible funeral filled her head – more sobs. It had poured with rain on the day. After the briefest of services, with Jamie stiffly by her side, Lizzie had wished the flowers hid more of the coffin. Rigidly controlled at the time, now she wailed loudly.

Drained at last, Lizzie lay there. In the end it was details, all of it, she thought, wiping away the tears. And none of it was how she remembered her mother. What would she make of this? But the more she thought about it, the more obvious it was that her mother would have approved wholeheartedly. To the end, Isobel had embraced life. It was an adventure... Jamie wouldn't know one if it hit him between the eyes.

With the sun dipping down towards the horizon, Lizzie's step was a little lighter as she made her way back to the village. Her head was clearer too and she'd composed herself again by the time she turned into the lane towards the Star.

'COO-ee!' It was Antonia marching to catch her up, two small terriers trotting along at her heels.

'Hello!' Lizzie stopped to wait for her.

'Still here? Silly to ask. Nothing happens fast around here! No doubt old Dave's being as slack as ever! I hate to tell you but that place is useless.'

'I'm beginning to realise! How come he stays in business?' Lizzie asked.

'Oh, the old rogue's got it made. He's rented that place since the year dot for a peppercorn rent and every so often all of us misguided villagers buy a tank of petrol even though he's 10p a litre more than Tesco. All in the name of supporting local business. I ask you... Bloody man just exploits us if you ask me.' Antonia looked disgusted.

'Who are these?' Lizzie bent to stroke the dogs.

'Full and Bursting. I wouldn't touch them. Horrible little bastards rolled in fox poo,' said Antonia, continuing, 'Well, seeing as you're stuck here, fancy coming over for a drink later? It's Apple Trees, past the pub on the left. Just need to muck out a few stables first – six-ish okay? Jolly good, toodle-pip!'

Not waiting for Lizzie's reply, she strode off up the road, her golden curls glinting in the sun.

* * *

Back in the salubrious surroundings of her room, Lizzie flung the windows open and flopped onto the bed. She couldn't help dozing off, but was rudely awakened a short while later by a car speeding past, followed by another as a relentless stream of traffic started up. Closing the windows to the racket, Lizzie was beginning to think the villagers had a point. It wasn't really on, was it, to go blasting through some backwater just in the name of shaving a couple of minutes off your journey.

By now wide awake, she reached for Elizabeth's letter again as the unthinkable crossed her mind – that if she'd found it just one week later, she'd have been Mrs James Archibald Mountford by then and her beige fate would be sealed. Lizzie shuddered. Or would she somehow have seen the light... Fleetingly it crossed her mind about whether fate had had a fall-back plan just in case.

Lizzie read it again and a neglected voice in her head positively shouted at her. *You've got it all wrong! Yes, you work hard, but there's so much else! When did you last take a sickie because it's too lovely a day to be in the office? Or go running on the beach just for the joy of it? Or get blitzed with your girlfriends and laugh until you fall over?*

It was true. She had been this close to becoming Mrs Boring-without-a-life, married to Mr Serious-with-a-beige-house. Both with serious-but-boring jobs with prospects. Nothing in the slightest wrong with that, of course. Nothing. For other people. Not Lizzie.

Images of Julian in tight trousers and Jude filing her nails flashed into her head. And endless meetings about budgets and cost cutting – soul destroying when you were trying to be creative. But oh. OH. How could she possibly have forgotten? She might have run away but she still had that job and in two and a half weeks she was due back.

Even working out her notice would be unbearable. Could she call Julian? Did she dare? Just *maybe* talk him round? She knew for a fact that some of her workmates were being laid off... Lizzie glanced at her watch – five past six – might she even catch him now?

She was put straight through.

'Ah Lizzie!' Lizzie could feel the hairs on her spine prickle. How could someone be so nauseatingly smug, she thought, picturing him sitting at his desk, smelling the garlic breath coming out of the phone. 'What a pleasant surprise!'

'Hello, Julian. Actually, the reason I'm phoning, is to tell you I'm leaving the magazine... I'm... handing in my notice. As soon as I can. You see, er, I've had a slight change of plan.'

'Oh *no*,' he said in horror. 'Oh dear. I had, er, heard actually, Lizzie...'

How? But she remembered how Jamie had insisted on inviting work colleagues to the evening do, much against her better judgement.

Julian sounded worried. 'Now, Lizzie, I do hope it wasn't my speech that put you off was it?' he asked fretfully. 'About the blessings of marriage, which I must say is rather close to my heart. As you know,' he added, sounding unbelievably self-righteous.

'Oh...' Lizzie wracked her brains. 'Er well, actually, I do have to say it really made me think, Julian. Yes, I did a lot of thinking when I got home. It was very useful indeed.'

'Oh dear.' Julian was sounding even more worried.

Lizzie crossed her fingers. It wasn't ideal, but sometimes a lie was the only way. She instantly thought of the tea bags. 'Actually, Julian, what I was wondering, was there any chance, in the, er, *circumstances*, you might just consider accepting a shorter notice? Only this is all terribly difficult for me as I'm sure you can imagine and I would be so awfully grateful... and it would allow me to do more, er, *thinking* you see... I'm sure Jude would be happy to cover...' *Sorry, Jude...* She'd be no such thing, Lizzie knew that but how many times had Lizzie covered for *her*. She was desperate and Jude owed her.

She could hear him huffing as he thought about it.

'Well, it's not at all usual... and we'll miss you terribly...' he started, sounding more than a little put out. Lizzie held her breath. 'But, oh, in the circumstances... I suppose it would be all right. Just this once. But don't let this get out,' he warned.

* * *

Handing over the bottle of the Star's finest white vin de table she'd taken with her to Antonia's, her hostess looked less than impressed.

'Lord, they're not still flogging that old crap... Here, already opened this. It's much nicer.' She handed Lizzie a glass of something red, then enquired when her car would be mended.

'I've absolutely no idea! It's in the hands of the gods, and well Mick, whoever Mick is, whenever he deigns to turn up.'

Antonia snorted. 'I'm afraid your first mistake was leaving it with Dave in the first place. Mick shows up when he feels like it. I don't suppose he mentioned that. Doesn't appear for weeks sometimes. He's not a bad mechanic, just rather elusive. Hope you weren't going anywhere in a hurry.'

'I was... sort of, but I suppose it doesn't matter. Not really...' Lizzie was just wondering whether to inflict her sorry life story on Antonia, when a rotund black shape with hooves came galloping into the kitchen. It skidded to a halt in front of her, threatening her with a small pair of horns.

'Bloody animal.' Antonia glared at it. Through slitted yellow eyes, it glared just as furiously back.

'Bugger off, Dave,' she ordered, pointing over at the door. 'Get out...' The animal glanced over at Lizzie, shooting Antonia a look of pure venom before scarpering back outside.

'Bloody madhouse,' said Antonia, slamming the door behind it. 'Should have eaten it months ago. Now, don't happen to like horses do you? I've got one that's marvellous with beginners...'

Lizzie stared at her in horror. '*No* – thank you.'

As Antonia topped up their glasses, Lizzie looked around the homely kitchen, with the pile of dogs sprawled on the flagstones beside the Aga and bridles cluttering the table.

Old paintings hung on the walls, slightly crookedly and looking to Lizzie as though they might be valuable. The furniture also looked suited to somewhere grander, but Antonia clearly wasn't house proud. She'd left her boots over by the door where she'd kicked them off and dropped a bunch of carrots still covered with earth in the sink, but in spite of the untidiness the cottage was welcoming and homely.

Lizzie just had to ask her. 'So how did you come to be living here? And please don't tell me your car broke down...'

'I was far too young to tie the knot,' said Antonia, resting her feet on an empty chair so that the holes in her socks showed. 'I mean, golly – twenty-two and completely naive. You know how it is. Still, at least I got one thing right. Harry had money, which is always useful... Oh, and I have this daughter. Teenager – frightfully hormonal, I'm afraid – and quite touchy. Anyway, we separated,' she continued matter-of-factly. 'He wanted us to move to the States with him – completely out of the question of course. Insisted I leave the horses and when I told him he was being ridiculous, he went without me. But *so* much better this way,' she added heartily. 'I can't tell you! Anyhow, I came to Littleton about five years ago to look at a horse... Damned animal was bonkers. Bolted with me for miles and bloody nearly killed me but at least I came across the house! Well, Harry's less generous these days, and it's frightfully handy with all those stables out there...' She waved her hand towards the garden. 'Anyway, been here ever since!' Then without pausing for breath she asked, 'So tell me about you. What takes you to Cornwall?'

Where the blazes did Lizzie start. 'Okay. Until yesterday, I was engaged to be married, to Jamie.'

Antonia's eyes were like saucers.

'Only it was all a big mistake. God, such a big mistake...' Lizzie shook her head. 'And before that, my mother died.'

She shouldn't have had that second glass. Wine always did this to Lizzie – lowered her defences, heightened her emotions. Her voice wavered. In all this time, in a *year*, she'd never spoken those words out loud to anyone.

Antonia reached across the table and patted her arm, a little like she patted her dogs.

'She had a tumour. In her brain. And it was the most terrible thing ever watching her go through it. She was so brave...' Lizzie hadn't known there were any tears left after earlier and she mopped them gratefully with the tea towel Antonia pushed towards her.

'Anyway, then I got this letter,' Lizzie started to sob heartbreakingly. 'I only found it two days ago, and it made me wake up to myself, I suppose you could say. I've realised I needed to change things.'

'Starting with the boyfriend.' Antonia looked at her, suitably impressed. 'Golly! Awfully good place to start.'

'Okay. Let me tell you about him,' Lizzie said, blowing her nose and pulling herself together. 'He's sort of good looking. Well, I thought so. Obviously... And quite arrogant. Thinks he's superior to everyone else. And serious. He does work hard and makes a lot of money, which he likes to show off with. And buy expensive beige things for his horrible beige house. Our wedding was all about how rich and tasteful he is. I can't believe how close I came to marrying him...' Laughing and crying at the same time.

'You should have married him first, Lizzie, and set yourself up,' said Antonia entirely seriously.

'I'm surprised he hadn't made me sign some sort of prenuptial agreement... You know, he even insured our wedding. Without telling me...'

'Lord! Sounds as ghastly as mine was! No one ever tells you that men are such crap! Well, there's the odd one that isn't, like my vet for example. Lovely man, darling. Not my type at all though, sadly... There's always William,' she added thoughtfully. 'But stupid bloody idea isn't it, tying yourself down like that...'

'Well, Jamie'll probably finish better off than when he started, thanks to the insurance. Plus, his middle name is Archibald.'

Antonia hooted. 'That's nothing. Mine's was Cecil! Like something from the Dark Ages! Absolutely no doubt, darling, we're much better off without them! Cheers!'

Antonia poured out the rest of the wine.

'So, how long ago exactly did you lose your mother?' she asked more soberly.

'Just coming up to a year.' The lump was back in Lizzie's throat.

'Golly. He was in a hurry then, wasn't he? Awfully soon, I would have thought...'

Stupidly Lizzie was blinking back tears yet again.

'I'm so sorry!' she howled, her tears by now a torrent, 'but until now, I haven't really talked about it!' And with that she completely dissolved.

A rather shocked Antonia clattered off and came back with a loo roll, the tea towel by now well and truly soaked. Then after more clattering about in a cupboard and the sound of the top being taken out of a decanter, she stuck a small glass under Lizzie's nose.

'Scotch, darling. Just a teeny snifter. Awfully good I find, when you're a bit... you know...'

The snifter did the trick and fortunately Lizzie had gathered herself together before the door was flung open again, only instead of a sheep, this time it was a furious-looking teenager. With huge flashing eyes and hair flying out behind her, she was stunning.

'I can't believe you forgot.' She gave Antonia a look like daggers. 'What sort of a mother forgets her own daughter. Honestly. Sometimes I think you do it on purpose to save on petrol.' And she shook her red curls and flounced haughtily up the stairs.

Antonia looked guiltily at Lizzie. 'She'll get over it. I expect

Elspeth gave her a lift. Bloody woman. It's her mission in life to make me look like a rubbish mother.'

'That's not exactly difficult...' yelled the voice from upstairs, but Antonia ignored her.

'Cassie?' she shouted without bothering to get up. 'Scout needs mucking out. And Felix called – he'll be late. Can you catch Hamish while you're out there?'

'And this is Lizzie by the way,' she added as Cassie reappeared down the stairs in her jodhpurs. 'She's staying at the Star. Dave's fixing her car.'

Cassie looked across with interest. Lizzie's first impression had been right. She really was extraordinarily pretty, with golden skin and dark eyes fringed with the blackest lashes. And that hair was just glorious – waist-length Titian curls, now caught in a heavy plait that she'd looped over. Lizzie put her at about sixteen.

'Hello! Poor you,' she said sympathetically, then turned to glare at her mother.

'It was really, really embarrassing, Mummy. I was standing outside for half an hour until Mrs Hepplewhite came along. And on my own, all that time. I could have been kidnapped or mugged or anything... Think how guilty you'd have felt...'

'I'm sorry, Cassie. Honestly, darling. I promise to remember next time...'

'You always say that...'

Cassie was not to be placated, and was pulling on her boots when there was a knock at the back door. A tall skinny boy stood there looking awkward.

'Hello, Cass. Hi, Mrs M... er...'

Cassie sighed exasperatedly.

'Oh, Dylan, not now... I'm really busy. Felix is coming over and I need to warm Halla up. And I'm already late because my useless mother forgot to collect me…' Cassie glared at Antonia one final time before stomping out.

Dylan shuffled his feet and went pink. 'Okay, well, I'll, er, go then…'

'I really wish she'd put the poor boy out of his misery,' said Antonia after he'd gone. 'Truly. If it's not him hanging around looking lovesick, it's his brother and Cassie's not interested in either of them, thank God.'

'That's a shame, he seemed – nice.' Gentle, thought Lizzie, and clearly besotted with Cassie.

'Teenagers,' huffed Antonia. 'Emotional, hormonal and spotty – they're all the same. I'll open another bottle.'

But Lizzie got up to leave.

'Thanks, but I should get back. Thank you so much, for the wine and the shoulder, and sorry I needed it. I'm not usually like this!'

'Oh, better out than in,' said Antonia matter-of-factly. 'And God, if I'd been through what you have, I'd be a raging alcoholic by now. If you're still here on Friday evening, there's a quiz night at the Star. The highlight of the Littleton social calendar! We could show those old farmers a thing or two, if you're game?' Her eyes gleamed mischievously.

'I don't think I'll be going anywhere in a hurry,' Lizzie said resignedly.

As she walked down the path, Lizzie watched over the fence as, cool as a cucumber, Cassie cantered a feisty-looking horse around the floodlit school while a small, ferocious German barked orders at her. The horse and Cassie looked like one, as under her with its chin tucked in and its tail aloft like a flag, the little black horse pirouetted and waltzed as effortlessly as a prima ballerina. Whether you liked horses or not, it really was rather pretty, she couldn't help admitting.

By now getting dark, as Lizzie walked down the lane, in a weird sort of way she liked it. It wasn't the same as London where she'd found herself looking over her shoulder every five minutes or jumping at every shadow that moved. Here, she felt safer. It was turning out to be quite friendly – well, more or less. Even William, the ranting farmer in the Stranglers T-shirt had forgotten to mutter about ramblers when he stomped past in the opposite direction, glaring distrustfully instead. Antonia was right – he did have quite a nice bum – Lizzie took a sneaky look. And the Star didn't look quite so dismal either, as the sun dropped behind the horizon.

5

By Friday, Lizzie had fallen into a new routine. Deciding she might as well treat this like a mini-holiday, she was waking decadently late for her, and sometime before nine, she'd pull on whatever clothes came to hand and wander down for breakfast – only this morning, instead of the barman and his smart-alec comments, there was a tall, angular girl with bright eyes and pink spiky hair that stuck out in tufts. Over slashed jeans and a black lace vest, she wore a short orange cardigan that clashed horribly with her hair.

'Blimey! You actually staying here?' she said, looking as surprised as Lizzie. 'Kettle's on. I suppose I better get you some breakfast. Oh, I'm Tilly by the way.' She smiled widely showing the gap in her front teeth.

'Hi, I'm Lizzie. Tea would be perfect, and some toast if it's not too much trouble...'

Lizzie sat by the window and flicked through the local paper. There was the usual quota of speeding cars flashing by, and a particularly noisy one went past just as Tilly brought breakfast over.

'Noisy bastards, aren't they?' She looked cross, then sat herself down opposite Lizzie. 'Don't mind do you? Only I spend so much time on my feet. I'm a hairdresser. Well, I'm training to be one. Money's rubbish, that's why I work here too. Bloody knackering it is. Anyway, you wait till Monday! The word on the grapevine is that the villagers are going to revolt! Those cars will think twice once they've got stuck behind a flock of sheep... It takes William half an hour to move his lot from just over the road there to his fields up the other end of the lane. I think he's got about three hundred of them... They're so cute! Anyway, just think how many cars will be queued up by the time he's finished! I'm coming in specially to watch!'

Barely drawing breath she chattered on. 'And Mr Woodleigh's joining in with his cows. They've been everywhere, his cows – his fences are terrible. Last year they escaped and stormed the village fete! Mrs Hepplewhite was upset because they demolished the cake tent before the judging and she was determined to win... Everyone helped to round them up but there's no hurrying those heifers anywhere. Oh, I can't wait!' she squeaked and jumped up as the phone started to ring.

There was a special delivery after breakfast. A lifeline in the shape of a new mobile. Katie had charged it, put credit on it and programmed her number into the address book. There was even a text waiting, ordering her to call straight away which Lizzie did, from the privacy of her room.

'Katie! It's me! Thank you *so* much!'

'Lizzie! I've had a brilliant idea! Why don't I come and join you for the weekend? You're stuck there and I'm not busy now... You see, I had a wedding to go to until the bride did a runner... D'you think there's any chance of a room?'

Lizzie's heart leaped. 'There are plenty but you can share mine! It's huge! When can you get here?'

'Well, if I remember rightly, I took the afternoon off to go with a certain bride-to-be for a manicure and bikini wax, so if I finish here about twelve, I don't know... I could be with you by six I guess?'

'Well, bring your glad rags! Because you and I have a date. Oh, and Antonia, of course, to the Star's weekly quiz night. Tonight!' Lizzie said ecstatically.

'Quiz night? Oh God. You sound like you're looking forward to it,' said Katie, rather worriedly.

* * *

Lizzie found herself with yet another glorious sunny day at her disposal. With more enthusiasm than the previous day, this time she stuffed her mother's letter in her pocket, and heading in the opposite direction to last time, she followed paths through the fields to a sheltered spot by a lake.

Time really was a luxury. But an essential one, she'd decided. Too much rushing around made you forget that. She was lying in the long grass just feet from the water. The peace and quiet were exactly what she'd been looking for and even though she was miles from Roscarn and nowhere near the sea, she could feel it soaking into her.

How odd that she didn't miss Jamie *just a little bit*. After three years of sharing a home and a life and a bed – but actually that had been the least spontaneous area of their relationship. Friday and Saturday nights and not exactly earth-moving. It just went to show, didn't it.

At least she'd escaped – by the skin of her teeth. Screwing up her eyes, Lizzie thought about it. Jamie and his friends had the money and enormous houses, while she was homeless and jobless, but free. She liked how that sounded and, sighing, turned her gaze upwards, feeling slightly as though she was playing truant from some boring history lesson, waiting, any minute now for a voice to boom out and hand her a detention.

How utterly self-indulgent it was, just to lie staring at the heavens. When had she last really looked at the sky, or at the feathery wisps of cloud-like spiders' webs, twisting and turning on the blue. Lizzie watched the ghostly shapes drifting slowly, her mind emptying and that was when she felt the faintest stirrings of something else. Briefly, madly, she fancied she could hear a whispering, as if the trees were breathing their secret to her. Fleetingly as she lay there, a hint of breeze brushed her skin and suddenly she felt part of something much greater and more powerful, turning her ear to the ground for a second, listening for the drumming of nature's heartbeat.

A splash in the lake jolted her from her ponderings, and rolling over, Lizzie fixed her eyes on the clear water. A dragonfly flitted here and there over the glittering surface, catching the light as it went. Stalks of grasses waved slightly, barely moving. Here it was again, all around her – that sense of utter peace. Flopping over onto her back again, she dozed.

The sun was low when she awoke. She took a last look around as she got up. How beautiful this place was. All the handiwork of nature, but the grasses framing the lake *just so*, with clusters of wild flowers where the sun reached and wild garlic filling the shade. There'd be water lilies in the summer – Lizzie could see the first curled up leaves poking through the surface of the lake. It was as much a work of art as an Old Master. And suddenly, out of nowhere, an idea took root. Her pulse quickened. Was she mad to even think about it? But as she looked around and thought some more, a smile stretched across her face. She couldn't wait to talk it through with Katie.

* * *

Fortunately the rush hour brigade had dispersed before the familiar shape of the little MG drew up outside the Star, and Lizzie ran outside to meet Katie.

'Lizzie! You look – so different!' Katie studied her friend, lightly tanned and so much more relaxed in just days. 'Oh, it's *so* brilliant to see you!' She hugged her, smelling familiarly of her trademark CK One, before stepping back and looking at her quizzically.

Lizzie glanced down at the scruffy old jeans which she'd barely noticed. And what was wrong with an old T-shirt when all she was doing was walking and lying in the sun and daydreaming... Katie by contrast, was dressed in slick, elegant black as she always was. Every bit the city girl, Katie, not one shiny brown hair out of place.

Linking her arm through Katie's, Lizzie didn't even notice how odd it sounded when she said 'Perhaps we could walk up to Dave's to get my clothes...'

Then she showed Katie to their room.

'Now don't expect too much,' Lizzie warned, fiddling with the clunky lock. 'Are you ready? And here we are! Welcome to Littleton's finest!'

'Erm, lovely,' said Katie, taking in the tired wallpaper and the curtains that didn't quite meet in the middle. She slung her bag on the floor. 'Not exactly the Ritz but hey! Now what does a girl have to do to get a drink round here? I mean we are in a pub aren't we! Shall we order something on room service?'

Lizzie nearly choked. 'Er, round here? I'll nip downstairs and get a bottle. Red okay? It's slightly less horrible than the white.'

She disappeared and was back in no time with a bottle and two glasses. As she poured it, Katie took one and held it towards Lizzie.

'Here's to your new life... long may it last!'

'That, my friend, is up to Mick!' Lizzie clinked her glass against Katie's.

'Now, spill! I can't believe it but you still haven't really told me *anything*...'

'I'm not sure where to start... I suppose...' Lizzie thought back. 'It was that last day at work. Tuesday wasn't it?' It seemed a lifetime ago. 'Anyway, it was just another boring, tedious day, and suddenly I realised I wasn't excited about anything. Not about marrying Jamie, or the wedding – any of it. It had all become a chore. Isn't that terrible? Then I had this meeting to go to, and even now, I can't remember what it was about. It was like I lost two hours of my life that morning, and when it was over, I had a panic attack. At least I thought it was at the time, and I ended up leaving early... Actually the whole day was weird.' Only as Lizzie recalled it did she realise it was true. 'I'm beginning to realise Katie, I've been missing something for ages. Probably since before Mum was ill. I'm still not sure exactly what... Anyway, it all ended up with me finding this.'

She rummaged around for the letter and passed it to Katie.

'But Lizzie – who wrote it?' **? HER MUM...!**

'I've no idea.' Lizzie sat cross-legged on the bed. 'You see, the strangest thing is it was addressed to someone else entirely. But the postman made me keep it. He said once I'd signed for it, he couldn't take it back. And that evening, I had a glass of wine and opened it. I couldn't help it.'

Katie looked at her like she was mad.

'It's funny though... it's really *about* you, isn't it—'

'I know...' interrupted Lizzie. 'Jamie's ex was Miranda, I'm sure, and that stealing bit... I stole Julian's tea bags...' She giggled.

'I'm sure Jamie's ex was called Marla...' said Katie slowly. 'Anyway, it doesn't matter does it? It got you out of there! And it does kind of remind you what's important. Strange though, how you got it *this* week...'

'Imagine if I'd found it a week later,' Lizzie said.

'I never thought Jamie was right for you,' said Katie quietly. 'He sapped the life out of you. You stopped laughing and doing mad things. I know that was partly because of your mum, but I never imagined you'd marry him...'

'Oh Katie... I've thought about so much these last few days,' Lizzie told her. 'You wouldn't believe it! It's the crying I should have done a year ago! You should have seen me at Antonia's! It comes and goes.' Her voice wobbled again. 'But at last, it's a little easier. It really does help to talk about it. And I think I need to.'

'I always thought you coped so well,' Katie said softly. 'Just the same old Lizzie, life going on as usual.'

'Well, on the outside maybe. I only pretended I was fine because Jamie was so unsympathetic. The one time he saw me cry, guess what he said: *Now chin up, Eliza, don't let the side down.* Can you believe it? What sort of thing is that to say to someone whose mother's just died?' A tear trickled down her cheek.

'So what now?' said Katie, ever practical.

'I'm not really sure,' Lizzie said, 'beyond this evening. The quiz night starts in half an hour and I've promised to join Antonia against the farmers! And then, once I have my car back, I need to decide what comes next. I mean, I thought I'd head towards Cornwall, of course, but after that, I was thinking... maybe... about being a garden designer... but I'm not sure – it seems a rather big step...'

Katie's eyes lit up. 'Seriously? That would be perfect, Lizzie! You could advertise locally, have a website, start in a small way... it wouldn't be difficult at all. Where, though?'

'I haven't got that far.' *Small steps at the moment – one at a time...* 'I... I think I'll go to Cornwall first, and decide after that. But you think that maybe it would work?'

'Absolutely!' Katie said. 'You've been designing gardens on paper for years haven't you – it can't be that different...'

'Only that I'll be on my own,' said Lizzie slowly. 'I don't know... I

need to think about it. Look at the time! I think we should find
Antonia.'

* * *

Antonia was already halfway through her drink by the time they
went down to the bar. The farmers were gathered round a couple of
tables, leaning on their elbows and muttering amongst themselves,
throwing hostile glances in the general direction of the girls.

'Oh excellent!' said Antonia, her eyes lighting up. 'Had a
horrible feeling you'd had a better offer!'

'Not much chance of that! Antonia – this is Katie, my, er, matron
of honour and my best friend!'

'Oh Lord... haven't brought the boyfriend, have you?'

'No!' Katie grinned. 'I happen to think Lizzie made one of her
better decisions, even if her timing was a bit out...'

'Couldn't agree more.' Antonia nodded. 'I told her exactly that –
should have married the bugger first and got her hands on his
money.'

Katie looked at her – then, realising she was serious, hooted
with laughter.

'Now, Lizzie, have you met Tilly? *Tilly?*' Antonia yelled across
the bar making everyone wince. 'Come over here a moment... We
need another girl. What do you say?'

Tilly looked at them slightly uncertainly. 'I'm supposed to be
working...'

'Nonsense,' said Antonia. 'The old codgers'll drink much more
later once we've thrashed them. They'll be drowning their sorrows
for hours, just you wait...'

* * *

In the end, Tilly wangled the night off and both men's teams were annihilated. It was indecently easy. Four girls versus all of them, but they were rubbish, every last one of them. The trouble was they were all so preoccupied with the matter of the speeding rat-runners that they couldn't focus on anything else.

'What's with them?' asked an astonished Katie afterwards. 'Or are they always like that?'

'Mostly yes,' said Antonia dismissively. 'Unless you're talking about tractors, sheep or Series 2 Land Rovers, you can't get any sense out of any of them.' A couple of heads turned her way at the mention of Land Rovers. 'There! What did I tell you! Ah. This is more like it – Timmy darling! Cooeee! Over here...'

A large, brown-haired man in jeans wandered over and kissed Antonia on the cheek, before grinning round at the rest of them.

'Hello all. Tilly, just the girl! Think you could fit me in over the weekend? I'll buy you a pint?'

'Of course, Tim, you know me. I'll be chained to that bar as usual.'

'Darling,' interrupted Antonia. 'You must meet Lizzie, who's marooned while Dave fixes her car.'

'Dave? Up the road here? Oh bad luck,' he said sympathetically, a twinkle in his blue eyes. 'You'll probably still be here at Christmas.'

'And, darling, this is her friend, Katie.'

If Tim had been a stockbroker rather than a village vet in the back of beyond, Lizzie would have got it – that flicker of *something*, before Katie's lashes blinked and broke the moment.

'Lovely to meet you,' she said softly, holding out a manicured, lily-white hand towards his large, somewhat weathered one, her eyes holding his a little longer than necessary.

Much later, as the four girls and Tim trooped up the road to Antonia's, Lizzie discovered that he had the dubious pleasure of ministering to Antonia's equines. Antonia simply adored him – strictly on a platonic level, her strongest feelings being reserved for her horses, he assured her.

'Lovely girl,' he said with a grin. 'Don't get me wrong. Nice horses too!'

'Have you lived here long?' asked Lizzie, relieved to talk to someone other than a leering barman or useless mechanic.

'Funny you should ask! Now don't take this the wrong way, but I came here as a locum for a two-week stint – and that was, let me see, about eight years ago...'

Lizzie felt a stab of alarm. There was a pattern here, with people passing through though not quite managing to leave. First Antonia, then Tim and now her – so far, at least. Were there others? Was Littleton bewitched? Maybe Lizzie was being bewitched too...

Back at the cottage, Antonia ushered them into the sitting room where Cassie was spread along one of the battered leather sofas with three dogs on her lap, feeding crisps to the small sheep Lizzie had met before.

'Cassie! I've told you before. I don't want that animal in here,' said Antonia crossly as Tilly went skipping over.

'Oh, Antonia, you can't mean that. He's such a sweet little baby, aren't you?' Sitting down next to it, she tickled him between his ears and bent to kiss the little muzzle.

'It's not sweet, it's evil. And it craps. Everywhere. Get rid of it, Cassie. Now!'

Cassie rolled her eyes, looking scarily like a red-haired version of her mother for a moment, before dragging herself off the sofa. 'You're *so* mean, Mother. Phil and Kirsty do what they like and they're disgusting little animals.'

'Full and Bursting,' whispered Tim to Lizzie, who snorted with laughter.

'But he's not a dog!' yelled Antonia.

'Well, *he* doesn't know that,' said Cassie, stalking out.

Dave paused for a moment by Tim, who bent and rubbed the little head.

'Hello, mate, you're a fine chap.' Dave waved his budding horns impressively.

'He'd be a fine Sunday lunch,' muttered Antonia under her breath, opening the wine. 'It's high time that sheep was for the chop. I'm ringing the knacker,' she announced. 'On Monday...'

'Now hold on, you can't possibly do that. You already told me he's Cassie's,' Tim reminded her.

'Huge mistake, darling. Never thought for a moment she'd actually keep him. Let's face it, the only point of sheep is to eat them. And a Welsh Black too. They're awfully delicious you know, such a waste...' she said regretfully.

'I don't think anyone should eat sheep,' said Tilly carefully between hiccups. 'They're so sweet... Anyway, I'm a vegetarian.'

Lizzie had seen her tucking into a bacon sandwich earlier on and Antonia wasn't having any of it.

'Rubbish, darling,' she said. 'You love a nice bloody steak as much as the rest of us. And where would all the farmers be without us dedicated carnivores?'

She poured the wine into glasses and took a quick slurp from one before passing them round to her guests.

'Anyway, there's absolutely no other point in keeping them, is there?' Antonia was as about intransigent on the subject as she was about men. 'Which reminds me, Timmy darling, poor Lizzie has just escaped the clutches of the devil himself...'

'A man?' mouthed Tim silently, grinning at Lizzie who nodded.

* * *

It was far too late by the time they returned to the Star, which was in darkness. They'd left a snoring Tilly at Antonia's and taken her key. Tim had offered to drive them – much to Lizzie's amusement.

'So-o,' Lizzie teased a quieter-than-usual Katie later on, as they lay in the dark in their single beds, both a little the worse for wear. 'What about Tim? Awfully nice boy...' She mimicked Antonia's voice. 'I saw you, Katie McDonald! You can't fool me...'

Katie was quiet. 'Actually, I really like him,' she admitted, which was Katie-speak for saying she fancied the pants off him. 'But what's the point? Because once your car's fixed and you leave, why would I ever come back?'

6

Saturday dawned, and little did Lizzie know when she awoke on what was to have been her wedding morning that the cogs and wheels of the universe were revving up again, ready for the next instalment. But blissfully unaware, she lay there savouring the peace and the fact that her friend was here, until Katie yawned sleepily and stretched.

'I thought we'd go out for lunch,' she announced stifling a yawn. 'My treat. There's a place near here I've read about. The Old Goat, or something like that. It has to be better than this place. Actually it's quite famous – I heard it's won an award.'

'One condition though,' Katie added, yawning again as she sat up. 'You'll have to find some better jeans.'

After a late breakfast with Tilly, who'd returned with a covering of dog hair and a headache from Antonia's, they wandered off to retrieve more bits and pieces from Lizzie's car, and also to check on its progress. As they rounded the corner and the garage came into sight, Lizzie nearly fell over backwards. The bonnet was up and a young mechanic-type in greasy overalls was poring over the engine.

'Morning. Are you Mick by any chance? Only that's my car... And I was hoping it might be ready...' Lizzie stood looking hopefully at Mick, who scratched his head.

''Lo, miss. Well, 'fraid to say it's buggered.'

As he spoke, the bottom dropped out of Lizzie's world. Not having her car, this changed everything. How would she get to Cornwall now?

'Can't you do something? *Please?*' There was desperation in her voice.

'Well, on a car this age, it'd cost more than it's worth to put it right. Wouldn't make too much sense really. But it's up to you.'

'How much are we talking about?'

'Well, 'ave to get the parts on Monday, but rough figure...' Mick mentioned a sum that made both girls wince.

'Trouble is, it means I'm stuck.' Lizzie's voice had gone squeaky. 'I don't know what to do.'

Mick cocked his head like a sparrow. 'Me sister's selling her car. If you're interested, mind... Nice little jeep. Quite clean and tidy. I've been looking after it for her. Tell you what. I'll bring it over next week if you want to take a look at it. Tuesday say. Okay?'

What could Lizzie say. Only chances were, seeing as this was Mick, it would probably be Friday at the earliest and by then she'd have been here well over a week. It had already been quite long enough and Lizzie was restless for magical Cornish coasts and that bracing dip in the sea.

'Okay,' she said with great reluctance. 'I better give you my mobile number. But if there's any chance you can get it here sooner, I'd be really grateful...'

'Okey-dokey,' said Mick. 'You taking them bags now? Only s'pose you'll want me to get rid of it...'

'Oh!' Lizzie started. How could she, when it was her last link to her mother?

Katie elbowed her. 'It's a car, Lizzie. Just a car. It isn't important – not really. It's okay...' she added looking anxiously at her, as they gathered the last of her suitcases. 'Come on. Let's get everything back to the pub.'

A perplexed Mick watched them unload what was left and stagger back down the lane.

Safely back in her room, Lizzie dissolved into tears.

'Come on. Change,' said Katie bossily, never one to be sentimental. It was a car, for God's sake. 'We're going to be late for lunch.'

It was the next piece of the cosmic jigsaw as without a car, Lizzie was stuck here. For an indeterminate period, or until Mick turned up with another one.

* * *

The Old Goat wasn't far away and they sped along the lanes in Katie's MG with the roof folded down, slowing down for groups of horses and the odd cyclist. After a recent review in a national paper, the pub was crowded, word having spread far afield about its weekend roasts and locally sourced menu, hence lines of brand new Audis and BMWs crammed down the sides of the lane.

Unlike the Star, it looked just as you imagined a country pub should with a quaintly sloping thatched roof and window boxes brimming with flowers. Inside, the stripped wood and fresh white paint was a welcome sight, as was the starched linen and menus on the tables. Looking around, Lizzie was suddenly ravenous. Fortunately, Katie had booked – every spare table was taken.

She perused the menu for ages, trying to make up her mind.

'For goodness' sake, just order *something*,' said Katie, before suddenly jumping up. Then 'No!' she shrieked as two men came towards their table.

'Darling? Is that *really* you?' The resonant voice came from the more slender of the two, who was immaculately dressed in a white shirt and impeccably tailored trousers.

Katie stared disbelievingly before she flung her arms round his neck.

'Darius! It *is* you! I don't believe it! What are you doing *here* of all places?'

'I might ask the same of you, flower,' he mock-flirted back.

'And Angel too! Oh wow!' She kissed him noisily on both cheeks.

Katie's shrieks had got the attention of most of the restaurant, but Angel was not the least perturbed. Camp didn't describe the half of it. He looked as though he was wearing lipstick, and was flamboyantly dressed in a bright cerise shirt. He also wore the most gorgeous jeans Lizzie had ever seen, so soft-looking she had to stop herself reaching out to touch them.

'Boys, meet my friend Lizzie! She's marooned here! Her car broke down...'

After breathless gasps of 'no', and 'not really', the boys embraced Lizzie just as warmly.

'How's Sylvia, pet?' Darius asked Katie. 'I got her a darling little piece for her boudoir, did she show you?' Sylvia was Katie's mother.

'She loves it! I think the entire street's seen it! Darius's mum is her neighbour,' she told Lizzie. 'Why don't you join us for a drink? We haven't even ordered our food. Lizzie can't make up her mind...'

'Darlings, we'd love to... if you're absolutely sure...' The boys looked delighted.

'Goat's cheese salad, Lizzie darling – it's to die for,' said Angel, brushing against her arm as he sat down, giving her a feel of that denim. She'd been right. Soft as velvet. 'It's the house special – on the quiet. The Old Goat... don't you see? Anyway, it's divine, I assure you...'

Pulling up an extra couple of chairs, Darius proceeded to explain how they'd just bought a cottage nearby.

'We've relocated, flower,' he explained to Lizzie. 'Our little antique shop. From the King's Road to Rumbleford... sounds quite poetic, doesn't it? Angelus, it's called – after both of us – *An-gel-us*...' he enunciated. 'Anyway, we needed a little bolt-hole. A love-nest,' he whispered, just to make sure she understood.

'How exciting!' said Katie.

'Well it is...' said Angel. 'And what we really want more than anything is to sit outside in the evenings, petal. Have little cocktail parties—'

'You know how we *love* parties,' interrupted Darius theatrically.

'—and invite our new neighbours. It's the quietest place on earth there, darlings... like you just wouldn't believe... You can hear the flowers talking and almost touch those stars, I *swear*. So different to London...'

'It is,' said Darius, but you could hear the 'but' in his voice. 'I mean, it seems scandalous to whinge, darlings, but the garden's...' he looked over his shoulder furtively '... bombed. A war zone. There. I've told you.' He sat back looking disgusted.

'You know what we're like,' said Angel to Katie. 'We're just *not* DIY-ers. We shouldn't moan because, really, we're just *so* lucky to have found it, but I mean petal, just look...' He apologetically showed them his hands, as lily white and manicured as Katie's.

'Mmmm...' Katie was thinking. 'But you know, I've actually just had the most stupendously brilliant idea. You're just not going to believe this, but Lizzie's a garden designer. Why doesn't she do it for you?'

The boys and Lizzie stared at each other – the former in ecstasy, Lizzie in total horror.

'Oh, Lizzie. Please say you'll do it. We're desperate,' they pleaded in unison, each of them grabbing her hands.

Lizzie looked from one to the other in shock. It was way, way too soon. The idea was one thing, but she hadn't actually *decided*, had she, or got as far as the many practicalities. There was the small matter of a car, for instance. She'd have to say thank you, very firmly, but no. Maybe in a month's time, if they still wanted her, but at the moment, sorry, but it's just out of the question. A picture of a tiny cottage miles from anywhere crept into her head, with one or two flowerbeds that needed weeding and a patch of long grass to mow...

'Darius could collect you on Monday,' offered Angel, as if reading her mind. 'And don't worry about tools, darling, we've no end of those around the place...'

'Oh! Perfect!' Katie clapped her hands in glee.

* * *

The goat's cheese special did indeed look divine, but as the boys left, Lizzie was having doubts.

'Katie! What were you thinking? You'll have to call it off. Tell them it's all a mistake...'

'Oh, Lizzie, it's a great idea,' said Katie smugly. 'Wasn't I clever to think of it?'

Lizzie shook her head.

But as they ate, Katie was determined to talk her round.

'I don't see what the problem is,' she persisted. 'I mean, one garden, Lizzie – what will that take you. A couple of days? You'll have that long at least before Mick turns up with the jeep. Just do it! It's not as though it will stop you going to Cornwall...'

Lizzie had to admit she was tempted. And with any luck, she'd be on the road again by next week. As Katie said, she'd finish the boys' garden in a couple of days and be leaving Littleton for good.

What a day this was turning out to be, thought Lizzie, with new-found fragile optimism. Full of the strangest coincidences... bumping into Katie's friends like that, here of all places.

As more cosmic jigsaw pieces slotted into place, Lizzie was just adjusting to the idea when out of nowhere, came a thunderbolt.

'Excuse me a moment... I'm sorry to interrupt your lunch, but it's just that I think we know each other...'

Another of Katie's amours? Through a mouthful of the locally grown arugula and baby spinach leaves, Lizzie looked and looked again, realising with a shock that he was talking to *her*. Her heart did a hop and a skip – he was gorgeous. That tousled fair hair, faded jeans, the worn shirt... Her kind of man, most definitely. She gazed back shyly, trying not to choke as the last of the salad caught in her throat and made her eyes water.

After taking a sip of water, she swallowed. 'Um, do we?' There was something familiar about him. She'd seen him before – some-where – but for the life of her she couldn't remember.

As she wracked her brains, the hubbub of voices in the back-ground seemed to fade and the strangest feeling crept over her. It was like she knew him – yet she didn't. But on another level alto-gether, they recognised each other. Like soul mates, she pondered. *Twin flames. Matching halves...*

'I know it sounds like a really dodgy chat-up line,' he continued earnestly, which in all reality it did. 'But I'm sure we've met.' He looked at her intently. 'I just can't remember where.'

For a moment it was tangible as the goat's cheese on Lizzie's plate, this *connection* between them. But as they gazed at each other, just as quickly it vanished, leaving them wondering if they'd imag-ined it.

'Hey, look, I'm sorry I disturbed you! Actually I better catch my friends up. Um, have a good lunch.' He smiled uncertainly, his eyes crinkled at the edges as he turned away. Lizzie's stomach did a backflip. Katie looked equally as gobsmacked.

'Wow, Lizzie! Wow! How could you *not* remember *him*? As chat-up lines go, that was *good*...'

But it hadn't been a chat-up line, she knew that. It didn't occur to Lizzie for one second that he wasn't telling the truth.

7

By the time Katie had departed for London on Sunday, Darius had already called round to see Lizzie, desperate for her to start work. He'd found them eating breakfast and been most concerned as he looked around the Star.

'Really, sweetie, you could have stayed with us if we'd known... It's so awfully, well, *agricultural*... don't you think?'

He arranged to pick Lizzie up the following morning first thing.

'You'd never find it on your own, sweetie! It's out in the boondocks! The back of beyond, darling!' he'd added, seeing her look of bewilderment.

* * *

It would be a good experiment, Lizzie had decided. To see if garden design and her were a match. It was only one garden after all. She'd cut the grass and weed the flower beds – it would take two days, three at the most. And if it were a total disaster, well. She was leaving anyway, wasn't she...

With nothing better to do with the rest of the afternoon, she decided to do some more exploring. As she passed Antonia's, she paused to watch a dumpy woman bumping around the sand school on a rather stocky horse. The woman's face was red with exertion and the horse looked as though it was about to collapse. Antonia herself was standing in the middle, screeching like a sergeant major, as the horse broke into a rather lumpy trot.

'HUP, two, HUP, two – heels DOWN, hands STILL – no, no, NO – shoulders back, stick your boobs OUT... Like THIS... YES...'

Lizzie couldn't understand it. Why subject yourself and the poor horse to something that looked so uncomfortable. Then she glimpsed Cassie cantering a large white horse in the field next door, effortlessly clearing every huge fence she rode it at. Gripped, Lizzie watched. This was better. Incredible, yes, and absolutely terrifying.

Returning Antonia's wave, she continued up the road past the church. A cat yowled and Lizzie briefly glimpsed a ghostly figure flitting among the trees, but by the time she'd blinked and rubbed her eyes it had vanished, leaving her convinced she'd imagined it. Further on were a couple more cottages with neat flower beds and trim hedges, and then, what on earth was this?

It had to be the 'danged ramblers' that William had been so incensed about. A motley crew wielding ski-poles with plastic bags hanging round their necks, was marching purposefully down the lane towards her. Then, just before they got to her, they turned off the lane and started to climb a padlocked gate.

Ignoring the sign that clearly stated 'Private – Keep Out – no ramblers' with a skull and crossbones someone had added underneath, they waited until the last member of their group was over, then continued marching right across the middle of the field. Lizzie was astounded at such blatant disrespect for the landowner. No wonder William had been so irate – she was quite annoyed with them herself. The cheek of it! It just wasn't on doing that sort of thing, even a townie like her knew that.

Lizzie wandered on up the lane, peering in at every garden she passed, until she almost reached the end of the village. And then she saw it, on the opposite side of the lane, in all its dishevelled, rose-covered glory. An involuntary 'oh' escaped her. Facing her was a small, dilapidated cottage. With broken tiles and peeling paint-work, but she didn't see them, instead gazing unblinking at weath-ered stone walls festooned with the most glorious colour. A week or two earlier or later, she'd have missed it. As it was, she'd timed it to perfection.

Lizzie crossed the road and just stood, hoping no one was at home to notice the stranger snooping over their gate. But then something else caught her eye. The 'To Let' board in the drive. The house was empty. Lizzie's heart started pounding.

As if of their own accord, her fingers programmed the letting agent's number into her mobile.

* * *

And before she knew it, Monday had arrived. Darius had come to fetch her in his smart black Freelander, which ponged of Eternity for Men, and he chattered excitedly as he drove haphazardly along the lanes, slamming his brakes on and swerving every now and then to avoid flattening an overweight pigeon or panic-stricken rabbit that dashed out of the hedge on a suicide mission. Weaving along a maze of windy lanes, Darius slowed when they came to a small hamlet.

'Darling, I can't believe we're finally here! Do look! Welcome to our humble abode!'

He turned off between two ancient oak trees and Lizzie gasped. The cosy little love nest she'd pictured hadn't remotely resembled this. They swept up a rather smart gravel drive with neat lawn laid either side and parked outside the impressively glassed front of a fabulous, no-expense-spared barn conversion. Tall spiralling topiaries framed the door like sentries.

'Darius, this is stunning!' Lizzie was awestruck.

'Oh darling, come and see the inside. It's simply to die for!' Clearly pleased, he flounced theatrically up the wide steps, and flung the doors open.

Inside was just as awe-inspiring. Lizzie's eye was immediately drawn to the enormous fireplace which towered into the rafters, logs piled high either side. Huge soft sofas and a heavy coffee table were arranged facing it, and though there were priceless antiques throughout, it wasn't precious, simply hugging you from the moment you entered. To one end was a state-of-the-art kitchen from which clattering and hissing noises were coming, and straight across was another set of huge glass doors. Lizzie's heart sank – surely this wasn't it...

'I've got the coffee on. Or tea, darling, if you'd prefer... So lovely of you to do this Lizzie...' Angel appeared and embraced her.

The boys took in the look on Lizzie's face. 'We did warn you, didn't we, petal?' they said anxiously. 'Oh deary – are you *terribly* shocked?'

Taking each of her hands in theirs, they led her through the doors to stand outside, where together they surveyed the chaos. At the far end amongst a bed of nettles were fruit trees, but the rest was a complete muddle, with not too much else identifiable among the brambles, rubbish and overgrown grass.

'It has potential.' Lizzie tried her best to sound positive but her heart was in her boots. 'But, boys, do you have any idea how long this will take? There's weeks of work here... Or what it's likely to cost?'

'Darling,' said Angel. 'We *so* want you to do this. We just *know*, both of us—' he caught Darius's eye '—that you are just *perfect* for us. We *completely* trust you...'

Lizzie suddenly realised as she looked around the garden, just what she could do with this. How much she would love to be the one to tame it into shape. She looked at the faces gazing back at her.

'Putty in your hands,' added Darius with a sideway glance at Angel. 'Just name your price, flower...'

Cornwall would still be there and it would beat hanging around the Star. Feeling a flutter of excitement, Lizzie gave up fighting the inevitable.

'Okay.'

Back inside, Angel brought out a tray of coffee and fondant fancies in garish colours, which he presented to Lizzie with a flourish.

'I'm experimenting, sweetie! Absolutely nothing artificial! You must tell me what you think of them! Be honest now...'

Delicately flavoured with almond and elderflower, they were sublime and as they ate, the three of them hatched a plan. As the boys wanted to entertain outside, the focus was to be a paved dining area under an enormous cotton awning, and there were already piles of flagstones dotted about which the boys had sourced from a salvage yard. Business was clearly booming and money, Lizzie was discovering, simply wasn't an object. The focus was to be a massive table that they'd snapped up at some sale, which they proudly showed her. They also had grand plans for an elaborate system of raised beds.

'Angel simply *has* to grow his own veggies, darling...'

'And it just *must* be *organic*...'

'And we'll make our own compost, you see... oh, and what sort of worms should we order, flower... Dendroebaena or Tiger worms?'

'B-both?' Lizzie didn't have a clue.

The whole place cried out for colour against the stone and dark timbers of the barn. She'd divide up the garden and plant flowers in every corner, and against the old walls, which were just made for some roses to tumble over them. So much for a couple of days – there was weeks of work here if Lizzie wanted it.

'Contemporary cottage garden!' announced Darius flamboyantly. Then, anxiously, 'Oh goodness, flower, would that work?'

'I think it would be perfect,' said Lizzie, getting into the swing, imagining spiky phormiums and grasses with splashes of zingy orange and acid green.

'And when you've finished, we'll throw a Lizzie party to celebrate!' He beamed. Seeing her look of alarm, he patted her hand, adding, 'Don't worry, flower! It's just a little thing we do! We had a Harry party for the architect... Huge fun it was – all those Harry Potters and Harry Hills! Ooh, do you remember Dirty Harry, Angel? Sex on legs,' he whispered girlishly to Lizzie.

'Oh, we simply *love* parties, darling. We'll just have to have one,' gushed Angel. 'And we thought that in the summer, what better place?' He stood there proudly, surveying the bedlam.

8

Caving in to the invisible forces at work, Lizzie arranged to view the empty cottage. Just out of curiosity. There was no harm in looking, was there? She'd quizzed Antonia about it that evening, as they shared yet another bottle of wine.

'Good God, Lizzie. You're full of surprises! You can help at the horse show if you're staying – I need another pair of hands. With all those super-competitive mothers and their ghastly brats, it'll be chaos... Talking of which, William had his sheep out earlier. Bloody brilliant it was! When he eventually got the last one into the field and shut the gate, you should have heard those drivers! William stood there glaring at them and didn't say a single rude word, which was bloody astonishing for him. Think he rather enjoyed himself. Next lot's due to move at 8 a.m. precisely! Awfully good sport, don't you think?'

And at eight the next morning all hell was indeed let loose, as it wasn't only William who dutifully moved his flock three hundred yards back up the lane to the field they'd come from the previous evening, but at the other end of the village, his wristwatch perfectly synchronised, Mr Woodleigh's cows meandered unhurriedly in the opposite direction. Clearly this morning the traffic had built up both ways, with furious drivers yelling and hooting and it just happened to culminate in the mother of all pile-ups outside the Star.

Lizzie hid in her room and watched with amusement as the Hooray Henrys and Yummy Mummys waved fists and yelled in plummy voices about this being an absolute bloody disgrace before accelerating sharply up the lane and splattering their immaculate vehicles with cowpats. Ten minutes later all was quiet again, and Lizzie walked up the road to look at the cottage.

* * *

Like most cottages in the village, Rose Cottage was part of the Littleton estate, but had been empty for quite a while, so old Bert, the estate manager, told her when he showed her round. 'Bin in the Woodleigh family for generations', or so he told Lizzie.

'You prob'ly seen him earlier out with them cows. Nice family,' he said. 'But all them houses are the same. A bit basic, like. Not to everyone's liking.' He chuckled. 'But bit of a clean-up and a lick of paint, it'll look all right.'

There was a whiff of damp as Lizzie stepped into the kitchen. She wanted to throw open the windows and let the sunshine in so this poor, neglected little house could breathe. Then wash down the woodwork down and paint its walls... turn it into a home again.

'Still, it keeps the rents down,' he added. 'You want it, you can move in whenever you like. Think you'd be right at home.'

'Don't you want references? Credit checks?' she asked. 'What do you need?'

The old man shrugged. 'Always gone on gut feeling meself. Never worked against me in the past. No, don't you worry about that, miss, you'll be fine.'

All her objections were floating away. As she walked through the small rooms, the thick walls felt as impenetrable as the towering oaks outside. And as the cottage drew her gently to its heart, it propelled her up the stairs, waiting with bated breath for her to discover the view that lay in store. As she gazed at the fields that stretched for miles, an image of a beach flashed into her head.

'Can I just think about it? Only for a day or two, but it's just, well, I want to be sure...'

He chuckled. 'You take your time. I won't let anyone else round till I hear from you, you have my word on that. You know, I've a feeling it would be right perfect for you...'

Unbelievably it really was that simple. If she decided she did want it, he added, all he needed was a small deposit and a month's rent in advance, which astounded Lizzie, who remembered in the past supplying lists of references, embarrassing bank statements and a deposit worthy of a small mortgage itself, all for some soulless flat in deepest suburbia.

Undeterred by the strong aroma that remained in the air from the moving of Mr Woodleigh's cows, the quiet and space had crept up on Lizzie. The garden too, another neglected tangle, but hers to do what she wanted with...

A wave of sorrow engulfed her. Her mother would have loved this place... A single tear escaped and rolled unnoticed down her cheek. She'd have donned her gardening gloves and pitched right in there beside Lizzie and for a moment she imagined the familiar voice beside her.

Lizzie, isn't it just lovely? It would be perfect for you... Quite extraordinary how you came across it wasn't it? Perhaps it's meant to be...

Startled, Lizzie looked around. She could have sworn her mother was standing next to her. Would have put money on it, even.

And the very next morning, just an hour after she signed the lease in the estate office, the most surprising thing yet happened when she had a call from Mick, who had come up with the jeep earlier than expected. It was clean as a whistle like he'd said, and a very pretty turquoise colour. How Jamie would detest it, Lizzie found herself thinking, which is probably what clinched the deal.

9

The early days in her new home passed in a blur, as having hastily acquired some gardening tools of her own, Lizzie continued to work on Darius and Angel's garden. After months of a desk-bound existence, the work was both backbreaking and tiring, but in the evenings she was spurred on by an urge to feather her nest.

The cottage needed a good clean from top to bottom just as Bert had said and first she'd washed the worn brick floors, memorising their random patterns before moving upstairs to scrub the wide oak boards in the bedrooms. That done, she was ready to begin with the painting.

Antonia had helped her move in, somewhat horrified.

'God, Lizzie, you've hardly a damn thing in here...'

Shocked, she'd disappeared and returned with a mattress and some bedding, as well as a kettle and tea bags. And having most happily departed from the Star, it was heaven, Lizzie decided, to be lying in her own bedroom, gazing out of bare windows at starlit skies, while dim silvery moonlight filled her room.

Impatient to check out her new home, Darius and Angel too had been over complete with a cast-off sofa which was far superior

to anything Lizzie would have chosen. Angel had tutted at the state
of her kitchen and stared in abject horror at the old Rayburn.

'It's archaic, flower,' he told her firmly. 'From the Dark Ages.
Promise you won't cook on that thing – you'll probably *die* from
some horrible disease...' before absolutely insisting that they buy
her a cooker as a house-warming present. Her objections – Lizzie
had rather fancied giving the solid old Rayburn a whirl – fell on
deaf ears.

Tim too had stuck his head in, between clients, suggesting that
she and Katie should come for dinner, next time Katie was staying.
Noting with interest a slight flush as he mentioned her, as soon as
he'd gone Lizzie texted her friend to tell her.

Vet in my kitchen wants you in his kitchen x

Through it all, her mother's letter was never far from sight.
Every so often Lizzie reread it to remind herself. Already life was
taking shape in ways she could never have imagined, with doors
opening all around her, so that all she had to do was take a small
step through the right one. Like the one into Rose Cottage, for
instance. In every respect it was perfect for her – and all she'd done
was meet Bert up here that first morning, and now, here she was. In
the safe haven, the port in a storm, she'd always craved, where she
could batten down the hatches and shut herself away from the
world. Except she didn't want to shut this new, friendly world out.

Antonia appeared frequently, usually early in the evening
clutching a bottle of something which they'd start on before going
to the pub. As well as the mattress, she'd lent Lizzie some ancient
garden furniture – a table that wobbled no matter where you stood
it and three equally dilapidated chairs of various shapes and sizes.

'You're welcome to them, darling,' Antonia had said. 'Was only going to turn them into firewood. Don't let any fat people sit on them whatever you do...'

But the chairs were more than up to holding Lizzie and Antonia, neither of whom were very big and they'd sit outside in the evenings, ever warmer as June passed, putting the world to rights.

'This malarkey with the sheep doesn't seem to be working,' said Antonia distractedly, as she poured some wine. It was home-made elderflower that she'd found in a cupboard in her kitchen. 'And Lord only knows what else we can do...'

'I'm sure it's got a bit quieter,' said Lizzie. 'Erm, why don't you have a chinwag with William about it?'

'Tried that, darling... actually it was rather odd. He went awfully pink and didn't say much at all. Not like him...'

'Methinks our William has a crush,' said Lizzie wickedly. 'He's probably harbouring some secret fantasy about al fresco sex in one of your stables... After all, you're the only woman who can hold their own when it comes to talking about sheep and Land Rovers. You're perfect for him!'

'Bollocks, darling!' Looking surprisingly flustered for Antonia, she swiftly changed the subject. 'You know you really ought to go to Rumbleford. It's full of shops you'd probably love – you know, those so called antique shops that are full of junk. Think there's a Saturday market too... No offence, just you're not exactly an Ikea sort of girl, are you, darling?'

Lizzie didn't imagine Antonia was either, but then she didn't have any priceless antiques like Antonia did, and Lizzie wasn't proud – junk shops sounded just fine. And she'd indulge in some window shopping in Darius and Angel's emporium, if they were open.

'I'd come with you,' Antonia continued. 'But Hamish is having his physio... poor little darling jarred his fetlock.'

* * *

Occasionally an idle thought popped into Lizzie's head. What if she'd married Jamie... She shivered as she imagined herself, a manicured, over-styled corporate wife-types, hardly able to breathe without permission. They'd be on that honeymoon by now indulging Jamie's fascination for all things cultural, staying in a cheap and cheerful hotel in Edinburgh. Where was the romance? The excitement? When there was a whole big world out there... Lizzie had suggested a tiny island in the Caribbean, imagining a deserted beach at the ocean's edge and sipping cocktails with her hair in braids. Or going on safari, eating round a campfire to the haunting sounds of bongo drums. Hardly surprisingly Jamie had dismissed both. *We're just not those sort of people, Eliza...* was what he'd said.

* * *

That weekend Lizzie followed Antonia's advice and did indeed venture into Rumbleford. Belying its name, the Rumble trickled benignly through the town centre under the single arch of an old stone bridge, before meandering away into the distance. On either side, cobbled streets held a captivating array of little shops and cafés which Lizzie couldn't wait to explore.

She found the junk shops straight away. Antonia had been right and they were exactly Lizzie's thing. Almost immediately she spotted a large pair of old lanterns, perfect for her cottage. Next came a painted metal wall clock and a battered coffee table, followed by an old milk jug and piles of old flowerpots for her garden. Colour – everywhere! Nothing beige *ever*, she thought with satisfaction, paying without batting an eyelid.

After the first shop, she made for the next and so on,

completely absorbed and oblivious to the hours ticking by. She found some woven throws in vivid blues and greens, and a gorgeous vase of dark green glass, which she couldn't bring herself to leave behind. It instantly brought to mind one of Jamie's pompous little asides – *accent colours are so passé, Eliza...* Defiantly, she bought the lot.

After traipsing to and fro depositing her various acquisitions in her car, across the river something else caught her eye, irresistibly drawing her like a magnet. Above a dazzling window display, 'Sparkie's' was spelled out in artfully crooked pink letters which even at a distance seemed to catch the sun and twinkle right back at her. Only narrowly missing a passing car, Lizzie crossed the road towards it.

'Oh...' she exclaimed out loud, as she stepped through the door.

The walls inside glowed a soft gold, and as she looked around, her eyes took in the words stencilled intricately on them – '*the earth has music for those who listen*'.

This shop could have been put together with Lizzie alone in mind. It wasn't just the colours, the designs, the mix of vintage and new, it was the ambience, the decor, the hint of something in the air – like cinnamon or bergamot, guessed Lizzie, only more exotic.

Floral prints hung alongside bold Pucci-esque tunics and maxi skirts that looked as though they came from the sixties. Denim in every shade imaginable... Her eyes alighted on a rail of Bohemian style dresses and faded flared jeans – clothes she'd loved in the days before Jamie and the suits. It had been years since she'd even looked at such things.

Long having forgotten how the right clothes can make you feel, Lizzie perused everything with delight, touching with delight the soft, sheer fabrics, running her fingers through silken scarves, pulling things out and holding them against her – completely losing track of time, until ages later the salesgirls were starting to look concerned. Eventually, one of them came over.

'We wondered if you'd maybe like some help!' she said in a gentle sing-song voice. She wore a glittery name badge with 'Nola' painted on it, and was clearly dressed in clothes from the shop. Her long hair was streaked with green, which matched the striking eyes that looked anxiously into Lizzie's. 'Only Julia and I, we were getting a little worried about you. Weren't we, Julia?' she called over, her eyes not leaving Lizzie.

'Oh! I'm so sorry,' Lizzie blushed to the tips of her ears, then looked at her watch. 'That can't be the time! Have I really been here that long? Only these are the loveliest clothes I've seen in years. It's all just so... just lovely...' she added lamely. 'Sorry, I better go...'

Nola and Julia looked at Lizzie quizzically.

'You've been in here about two hours...' said Julia, just as gently, 'hasn't she Nola? And really, it doesn't matter at all! We were just a bit worried about you! Are you sure you're okay? We were just about to have some herbal tea – would you like some?'

This time Lizzie flushed beetroot. And then realised she'd had nothing to drink all day, and that herbal tea was really quite appealing.

'Thank you! And well, maybe you could help me...' she started hesitantly. 'I can't seem to decide. I used to love wearing clothes like this, only it was ages ago! I've been living in suits for years...'

The girls looked at each other, then led Lizzie over to a sofa she hadn't seen until now.

'Why don't you sit here? Your feet must be aching horribly,' they said sympathetically, which they had been for ages. Then, having brought her some chamomile tea, their favourite, they told Lizzie, because it was very relaxing, they quizzed her.

'Tell us a bit about you,' probed Nola. 'It helps us to find the right clothes... but only if you want to, of course...'

'Well, I used to work for a magazine. Now I'm a gardener. And I've just moved to an old cottage. From London...' She hesitated, not quite wanting to delve into the whole Jamie business.

'What do you do when you're not at work?' asked Julia.

'Oh, more gardening! My own, which is old and very neglected, unless my friend Antonia comes over with a bottle of wine. I've only known her since I moved here. My other friends are in London.' My other *friend*, she silently corrected herself. 'Oh, and I'm decorating my cottage...'

The girls looked at her thoughtfully, then at each other before springing efficiently into action.

There was no doubt they knew their clothes. Restored by the tea, Lizzie watched in awe as somehow every item the girls suggested was absolutely right. Uncannily so, and just half an hour later, she walked out ecstatically clutching half a dozen carrier bags of the loveliest things she'd ever owned. As she thanked them, they'd made her promise to call in again soon. Not to spend any money, they assured her. Not at all, but just come in and say hello. Sparkie's was already up there with Joe's in Lizzie's book, another oasis of calm, and she couldn't imagine ever shopping anywhere else.

'Now that you've found us, Lizzie, you must come back! For lunch, or just herbal tea! You know where we are if you need us.'

Assuring them she would, Lizzie completely missed the looks that they exchanged as they closed the door behind her.

'She looked so lost...'

'She's run away, hasn't she?'

'What from, I wonder...'

'Or who...'

'But we helped her, didn't we? Maybe more than she knows...'

'And she'll be back, I'm sure of it.'

'Now that she knows we're here...'

* * *

And then later on, just when Lizzie was happily engrossed in organising her accent colours and rusty lanterns, Bert, the estate manager, turned up, carrying a large box which he handed to her.

'Present for you, miss.'

'Oh!' Lizzie stood back as the top opened on its own and a furious, spitting head emerged followed by a long, tabby-coloured body that barged its way out and would have fled if Bert hadn't slammed the door in the nick of time.

'You'll be needing a good mouser. He was going spare, like... thought he might be useful, young Darren... He's about five now. Nice chap really. Take no notice of all that racket. Had him since a kitten – think he's one of Mrs Einstein's. Don't think he's ever bin in a box before...' Bert chuckled to himself, adding, 'Won't be any trouble...' which of course Lizzie believed implicitly.

He settled in right away, soon bringing her a present in the form of three dismembered mice and a large decapitated rabbit, before falling asleep sprawled on her new bed.

* * *

As well as creating what Darius and Angel described as 'simply heaven, darling' as they minced about the newly laid lawn and admired how far she'd got with the planting, Lizzie found she'd made two unlikely new friends. Soon she was being summoned out of the blue to dinner, breakfast on Sundays, and impromptu cocktails whenever the mood took them.

Darius, whose real name was actually Derek, Lizzie discovered when she met his mother, was the most incredible cook and took it upon himself to share his talents with her. The boys were nothing if not hospitable.

'*Lizzie sweetie, long island iced teas at six, petal.*' Or '*Darling, Bellinis after work. Darius is having an Italian phase,*' which was her absolute favourite evening of all as they sat outside until the moon shone high in the sky. But it was Angel, who was actually called Adrian, who winkled out of her the story behind her career move. He ground and gnashed his teeth and shed almost as many tears as she did as she told him all about losing her mother, and about how she'd only just escaped marrying Jamie. Then they'd both fussed around her, stroking her hair and mopping her tears before fetching yet another round of Bellinis.

'Darling, men can be *such* bitches, don't I just know it,' Angel exclaimed in his most diva-like fashion yet.

* * *

Lizzie's size fives barely had time to touch the ground in this whirl of activity that had become her life. Not sure whether this was entirely a good thing, she nevertheless embraced every opportunity that came her way. Her grief was still there, but more manageable now and somehow, with all her new friends around her, it felt different.

Thanks to Katie, her new website was finished and Tilly had pinned an advertisement in her hairdresser's. As she'd said most eloquently, 'Not all the old farts round here have computers.'

The trip to Cornwall was still on Lizzie's mind, but with a cat, a house and a fledgling business, she'd postponed it. Already her mobile was ringing and dribs and drabs of work were coming in. It was almost scary, the speed with which it was happening, as though she'd set something in motion that had taken on a life of its own.

After Darius and Angel's garden, she had a few commissions from clients nearby – a lawn needing manicuring here and there, or a corner of neglected garden that needed a facelift. Lizzie had found her element. And getting dressed for work was effortless too in just old jeans and whatever top came to hand. Tying her long hair in a ponytail or loose plait, she'd splodge on some make-up and be ready in no time. Jamie would have absolutely hated it!

Lizzie had yet to meet Antonia's bête noir, but she didn't have to wait long. In her oldest jeans with her paintbrush primed, ready to start on her stairs, there was a sharp knock at the door, then another, and Lizzie opened the door to a much older woman. Of a similar height to herself but dressed in tweeds, she had an unmistakeably schoolmistressy air about her. Tilting up her head, she'd frowned down her nose at Lizzie, inspecting her from head to toe. She'd then held out a dry hand, which she'd withdrawn at the sight of Lizzie's paint-spattered one.

'Elspeth Hepplewhite. I thought that, as chairperson of the local WI, I should come and introduce myself.'

The penny dropped. Lizzie stared.

Mrs Hepplewhite peered at Lizzie more closely. 'You were the one who was staying at that terrible pub.' She tutted disapprovingly.

'My car broke down,' said Lizzie apologetically. 'I'm Lizzie. Er, would you like to come in?'

'I know,' said Mrs Hepplewhite without a hint of a smile. 'And that won't be necessary. I've simply come to inform you about the WI. We meet on Tuesday afternoons. At two o'clock. Punctually. No doubt you will be joining us.'

Lizzie opened her mouth and closed it, dumbfounded. 'Mrs er...'

'Hepplewhite,' snapped the old trout.

'I'd, er, love to,' she started.

The thinly plucked eyebrows disappeared into her hair.

'But I-I'm not sure,' Lizzie faltered.

Mrs Hepplewhite drew herself up and bristled indignantly. 'Oh?'

Lizzie loathed confrontation at the best of times, but, taking a deep breath, she forced the words out.

'Thank you, and I appreciate you inviting me, but I work most days. I can't really commit myself. But thank you, *very* much,' she emphasised politely, 'for coming to ask me.'

Darren appeared, rubbing his lithe body against Mrs Hepplewhite's legs and almost knocking her over. Then he sat on the path in front of her, fixed her with unblinking green eyes and frantically started scratching.

'Hmmph,' the woman snorted, then looked with horror at her legs. 'Well, I assume you'll come to our Christmas fair at the very least. We rely on the locals to support it, you know.' She bent down and scratched her left leg. 'It's not one of Mrs Einstein's is it?'

The look on her face was one of horror when Lizzie nodded, and she marched briskly down the path, pausing now and then to reach down and scratch, without so much as a backward glance.

At which point Darren stopped scratching, winking at Lizzie, before sauntering in through the back door.

'Should have warned you,' said Antonia suddenly that evening. 'You're bound to get a visit from the village bat. No one escapes. Elspeth's a total pain in the arse – no redeeming features whatsoever I'm afraid. Puts the fear of God into everyone, well, does her best to... Think I told you about her – she's the one that scoops up Cassie when I'm late.'

'Actually, she's already been. I managed to wriggle out of joining the WI, but I think Darren gave her his fleas...'

'Gosh, well done.' Antonia looked impressed. 'I swear membership will quadruple the day that woman resigns,' she declared. 'We ought to set up a rival group. Instead of boring old lunches and knitting, we'll get pissed and talk about our sex lives and horses or something. It would be heaps more fun... Loads of the old girls round her would join us, you know they're all ravers on the quiet...'

And this was shortly followed by the Lizzie party that the boys had absolutely insisted on.

'Darling, you can be the Queen this time, I'm going to be Elizabeth Taylor,' announced Darius theatrically. 'You, flower, must come as yourself,' he told Lizzie. 'In your gardening clothes, with soil in your hair and mud on your jeans, like you usually have.' He paused for breath as he looked at her dotingly.

Lizzie ran her fingers through her hair – soil?

'And everyone else has to dress up too!' finished Angel triumphantly. 'Now, sweetie, the deal is that you invite half the guests and we'll invite the rest. It's your party after all.'

Lizzie's protests fell on deaf ears.

'Sorry, honey, it's the rules...'

Lizzie gave up. 'But what about the men?'

'Oh, flower, they have to dress as Lizzies too of course! Such fun! Oh we just love parties,' Angel told her. 'Be a pet. Indulge us.'

But being the new girl, Lizzie hardly knew who to invite. Antonia, Katie, of course, Tilly, oh and Tim... well, four wasn't bad seeing as she'd only just moved in. And just maybe Nola and Julia from Sparkie's, so one lunchtime, she decided to pay them a visit.

'Oh, Lizzie, we'd love to!' Nola clapped her hands together, then peered closely at her face. 'You look more peaceful,' she added. 'It's good. Won't you stay for lunch? We were just about to close...'

They'd led Lizzie through a door at the back of the shop into a small room flooded by sunlight. French doors opened on to a little balcony which overlooked the Rumble, where a wisp of smoke was coming from a recently extinguished candle. There was the oddest array of objects out there, Lizzie couldn't help but notice, like rocks and what looked like a bit of antler. Her attention swapped to the room, where the table was already set for three with prettily painted plates and another candle burning in the centre.

'Oh...' Lizzie looked at it. 'But I really don't want to intrude...'

Nola took her hand and led her to one of the chairs. 'It's for you, silly! We were expecting you. Didn't you say you'd be coming back?'

A baffled Lizzie didn't know what to say, so she just sat there as they talked away and produced home-made soup and crusty bread.

'Now you must tell us – are you happy in your cottage?'

'I love it! It's quite amazing really... when you think I found Littleton completely by accident,' she told them.

Nola gave her a sideways look.

'And then I was stuck without a car,' she went on, 'so Katie came to stay. We went out for lunch and bumped into Darius and Angel, you know, the boys who are having the Lizzie party, and that's when they offered me my first commission.' She stopped. 'Then I stumbled across my cottage and someone sold me my jeep.'

It was freaky. What's more, both the girls were looking quite unsurprised by what she was telling them.

'Everything's obviously as it should be,' Julia gently pointed out. 'You said yourself, it all seems to have worked out perfectly! But have you wondered, Lizzie... whether it's more than just coincidence...'

'Um – no,' she replied uncertainly. And she hadn't even got on to the fair-haired stranger.

Lizzie drove back home so deep in thought she completely missed the turning to Littleton. And it was only after she'd turned round she realised she hadn't seen the rusty sign in the hedge that had led her there, that day she'd fled from London. Even more curiously, when she reversed back to check, it was nowhere to be seen.

* * *

'They sound barking,' was Antonia's comment when she told her about the Lizzie party. 'Golly, well I could go as old Queenie – got a posh frock or two and a tiara hidden away somewhere. You better scrub up a *bit*, Lizzie, you are the guest of honour after all...'

Katie emerged down Lizzie's stairs looking every bit like Elizabeth Hurley, except for her boobs, which were on the small side, so they stuffed the dress with chicken fillets and stuck her in with tit tape.

Tilly, bless her, was in a quandary. 'I was going to go as Hilary Duff in *Lizzie Mcguire*, in a blonde wig I borrowed from the salon,' she said sounding perturbed, standing with her pink head on one side as she spoke. 'But it makes me look more like Lady Penelope in *Thunderbirds*, so then, I thought, well, you're the guest of honour, someone ought to go dressed as you... What do you think?'

'Um, be my guest' said Lizzie doubtfully. 'If you want some patched jeans and a second-hand T-shirt from the Oxfam shop, help yourself.'

'Mmmm.' Tilly thought some more. 'Cool. I think I will. Can I borrow your Hunters?'

* * *

Actually the boys were right, and it was a hoot, with half the guests thinking Tilly was Lizzie, which all added to the madness.

The barn had been decorated most tastefully with candles and flowers on every available surface, and Darius had the most divine cocktails lined up. He'd put on a trial run for Lizzie the previous weekend, inventing the innocuously named Frizzy Lizzie in her honour which was completely lethal, and had given her the worst hangover of her life. They'd decorated the modern scrap metal sculpture that Darius had bought with gardening tools and fairy lights, and the garden was lit with flaming torches which created flickering shadows as the sun sank over the hills, so that it all came to life with just the perfect amount of flamboyance. With the thumping music and the most curious ensemble dressed as various Elizabeths, the evening went with a bang.

'I do *so* love parties,' said Angel wistfully, clasping his hands in front of him as he looked around at the crowd. 'Isn't it wonderful to see everyone enjoying themselves? *Everyone* came you know... Well, nearly everyone...' he frowned. 'Tom Woodleigh's not here yet, darling, you'd love him, he's rather gorgeous... Oh, sweetie.' He clutched Lizzie's arm as Tilly drifted in from outside. 'She's off her head already.'

Floating serenely in from the garden, Tilly was followed by an unmistakeable waft of smoke, which along with the vacuous expression on her face, completely gave her away.

'Hi-i.' She drifted in towards the party. 'Oh, hi, Angelical...'

'Oh she is, isn't she,' whispered Angel, before adding, 'As a kite! Oh bless, what a lamb, no one's ever called me Angelical before! I think I might see if there's any left,' he whispered as he slipped out into the night.

Nola and Julia added a touch of class to the surroundings. Their Eliza Doolittle and Liza Minnelli rather stood out amongst the camp lunacy of the outrageous queens, and the boys fell completely in love with them.

'Aren't they just heavenly?' gushed Darius, gazing at them with wonder. 'Flower, you have the most blissful friends...'

And it was mutual. 'You have such good friends around you, Lizzie,' Nola said to Lizzie, taking her hand as she looked around. 'Just look at them. They love you – don't you see how you belong?' Which Lizzie found strangely moving.

It half crossed her mind that the handsome stranger from the Goat might be here, but she didn't see him though she did meet one or two of the boys' neighbours, who having failed to get any sense out of Tilly, asked her if she'd look at their gardens.

After downing Psychedelic Sunsets at the same rate she usually got through wine, Antonia was already three sheets to the wind and her tiara had slipped over one eye when Lizzie found her telling a girl she'd never met before all about the shenanigans with the rat-runners.

'Darling! Meet Sloozie! Golly, must have another one of these drinkies... Seem to be awfully thirsty this evening...'

As she tripped off to find one, the girl grinned at Lizzie. More sober than Antonia, she was striking looking, with long black hair and sharp, lively eyes.

'This is all in your honour is it? I'm Susie! The garden's amazing. Tell me, how did you come to meet the girls?' She nodded at Darius and Angel.

'Long story,' Lizzie said ruefully. 'I was a runaway, just passing through. I wasn't planning to stay but my car broke down. And I'm still here... How about you?'

'Ma and Pa live round the corner.' She indicated vaguely. 'I just visit at weekends now and then. Do tell me – is this thing about moving livestock doing any good?'

'It's hard to say – I should think a few of the drivers have given up and avoided it by now.'

'God! Only in Littleton! Daddy has a few cows, though I can't imagine he'd get involved... What did you run away from anyway – if you don't mind me asking?'

'Um, a fiancé, a wedding and a job that was destroying my soul?' Lizzie offered.

Susie looked impressed. 'Well, jolly good for you for doing it. That's quite brave. Oh, I've just got engaged actually...' She flashed a ring that was almost as big as Lizzie's had been.

But before Lizzie could ask her about her wedding, Antonia

rejoined them, bumping into Lizzie and spilling the contents of her glass down her front.

'Good thing you're wearing those scruffy old things,' she exclaimed, before muttering, 'Blast, have to go and get another one.'

It was all oddly surreal, with Lizzie in her work clothes and everyone else in fancy dress. And all the while, out of the corner of her eye, Lizzie watched Katie. Who'd have thought it – the city slicker and the country vet? She watched, as Katie played with Tim, luring him ever closer like a tigress seducing her prey. Someone really should have told him – his fate was sealed.

10

'Sorry this is such a rush,' said Antonia, who was looking extremely smart in a tailored suit and high heels – except for the dog hairs, that was.

'But I thought it would be best if you were secretary. I've put your address on the schedules and your phone number too. Then you just need to keep a note of who is entered for what. Now, you'll probably have trouble with Mrs Harper. She'll absolutely insist on you telling her who her daughter will be competing against and who the judge is and you absolutely mustn't. It's highly confidential and none of her business and she's a total pain in the arse. Anyway, I'll help you, don't worry. Golly, got to go. THANKS!'

As Antonia rushed out before Lizzie could protest, she glanced at the schedule her friend had left behind for the Littleton Charity Horse Show and Gymkhana. Being secretary wouldn't be too bad, would it? 'Proceeds to Hethecote Farm', she read. She'd have to ask Antonia where that was.

* * *

Lizzie's new surroundings were better than any therapy. Hard at work on her garden, she uncovered plants long lost under a blanket of weeds and tended the roses that had been left so long. And as she dug and pruned and cut and planted, she started to find a place in her head for the events of the last year, until gradually a kind of acceptance infiltrated where before there'd been the worst kind of emptiness and she could begin to look forward to the future. Even she could see that slowly, but surely, this place was working its magic.

Bert and his wife, Molly, lived just one field away up the lane. Lizzie had fallen in love with Molly, who was small and wide and lived in an old-fashioned floral pinny. She was frequently to be seen pegging out impossibly white underpants neatly and precisely end to end on her washing line and if she saw Lizzie she'd invariably wave and call, 'Yoo-hoo Lizzie! Come and have a cuppa!' Lizzie couldn't quite believe those pants – they really were straight out of the packet white too; no grey ones to be seen.

Molly's homely kitchen always smelt of cooking and made Lizzie imagine hordes of pink-cheeked grandchildren grabbing handfuls of home-made biscuits and scoffing them as fast as they could, before tearing off outside again.

'Sit yourself down, duck,' she always said, while she warmed the cups and made a proper pot of tea. Inevitably, Darren would accompany her, curling up on a chair as he kept an eye on proceedings.

If Molly had an opinion on the moving of the sheep and cows in rush hour, she kept it to herself.

'It'll bring naught but trouble, you'll see,' was all she said on the matter.

* * *

Work wasn't as forthcoming as Lizzie had hoped. There were plenty of smaller jobs and she was managing to get by, but only just, and she didn't want to dip into her savings unless she had to.

'What you need is a nice rich man,' Antonia had told her bluntly. 'Ideally one that's in town all week and only comes home for weekends...'

'With a big garden...' Lizzie said, briefly fantasising about a rambling old farmhouse and a big walled garden of her own.

'*Garden?*' Antonia looked horrified. 'No, no, Lizzie. A big *bank balance*. Much more fun than a garden! It's a frightful bore when the funds get low. Actually, I could do with a little extra myself...' She looked thoughtful. 'I was thinking about taking some liveries. You know, I think that would be rather splendid! I could charge loads of dosh round here for a stable, especially when the hunting season starts! And if they do all the mucking out themselves, it'll be easy... you know, I really think I'm onto something!'

But it didn't help solve Lizzie's problem. Darius and Angel had been full of suggestions.

'Oh, darling, you should have said... Leave it to us! We'll spread the word, tell everyone how perfectly *wonderful* you are...'

Driving back from the boys' barn that afternoon, Lizzie had been deep in thought about work and taken the wrong road. Cursing that there was nowhere to turn her car and with a sense of déjà vu, she carried on to the first driveway she came to and, pulling in, noticed the sign.

'Hethecote Farm' it read and the penny dropped. This was the farm that the horse show was raising funds for. Underneath was a smaller notice: '*Open Tuesday to Saturday 12–6 p.m*'. Stuck on the bottom with what looked like Sellotape was a scrappy piece of paper on which someone had scrawled, '*Casual workers wanted for weekends and holidays. Also gardener. Apply within*'.

A gardener. Why not her? On the spur of the moment, Lizzie

followed the drive between two fields, one with half a dozen small ponies in and the other a group of alpacas that watched her with beady eyes. At the top, beside a five-bar gate, was a small car park, where Lizzie stopped her car and got out.

A woman in dungarees was sweeping a huge stable yard which looked deserted. 'Terribly sorry, we're closed on Mondays!' she shouted, until Lizzie tried to open the gate, when she came over.

'Sorry. I didn't mean to bother you, but actually, it was about your advert. At the bottom of the drive!' Lizzie added, as the woman was looking vague.

Understanding dawned on the woman's face. 'For weekenders! Oh, you should have said! Come on in...' She held the gate.

'It's rather an assortment of animals, I'm afraid. I hope you like horses... To think it all started with two Shetland ponies and an orphan lamb... after too many gins, no doubt. Would you like to look around, or shall I take you through the job?'

'Animals?' Lizzie frowned. 'I thought you wanted a gardener!'

'Ohhh. That... Well, we do. I think. It depends, you see. I kind of put that sign up without thinking it through...' *After too many gins*, thought Lizzie.

'... and well, I have this idea. Let me tell you about it. I'm Miriam, by the way. Pleased to meet you...'

Miriam Kirby led Lizzie around her farm, explaining what she had in mind. The whole idea about opening the farm to the public had come about when her husband died and left her with a struggling farm, too many animals, and three children who were still at school.

'Nightmare, it was,' she said ruefully. 'I had to either do something quickly or sell up, which I couldn't face doing. And we had all these outgrown ponies that the children couldn't bear to part with which was when I thought. You see, even living in the country, there are so many children who don't have a pet, and never get to spend time with animals. So, for an entrance fee, their parents can bring them here and they can take a dog for a walk in the fields, or groom a pony and lead it round the paddock. No riding – we're not a riding school. I did think about it at one stage, but the insurance was unbelievable. So there you are. I'm not sure what you'd call us...'

Lizzie looked over the stable door to where two donkeys were pulling hay from a manger. One instantly turned its furry rump on her and farted.

'Oh that's Sid,' said Miriam. 'Take no notice – his manners are appalling. The other one's Johnny and he's not much better. Anyway, as you can imagine we get quite a few disabled children coming here, and it really seems to benefit them. Heart-breaking stuff I can tell you. We had a lovely little girl called Hannah who used to visit. So shy, she was – like a mouse, and so self-conscious about her poor, bald little head. Well, the first day, I took her in to see Arrow. He's a Welsh mountain pony – very small and long in the tooth and a bit of a know-all. We shave his mane because he gets sweet-itch. Anyway, it was love at first sight. Arrow fell in love with her and she with him, and she was a different child after that. Lived for her visits, her parents said.'

'How often does she come here?'

Miriam turned away. 'She died, I'm afraid. Leukaemia. Tragic.' Her voice wavered.

'Oh! I'm so sorry,' Lizzie was shocked. 'That's *so* sad...'

'The problem is,' said Miriam, recovering her composure, 'that we don't make anything like enough money, but how could we possibly close?'

'There's the horse show, isn't there?' said Lizzie. 'A friend has asked me to help.'

'Antonia? She's a marvel,' said Miriam. 'But when you've this many animals, it's a drop in the ocean. Which leads on to my idea about the garden...'

They walked across the stable yard towards a wall with ivy growing up it. Halfway along was an old wooden door which Miriam opened, and following her in, Lizzie found herself in the biggest kitchen garden she'd ever seen. This was far more her scene than the stable yard.

'This is yours?' she asked incredulously. 'It's fabulous!'

'Well, it used to be. Before I ran the animal centre, I grew all our vegetables and used to sell them locally. Now it's just a worry. It's going to rack and ruin because no one has time to tend to it. Shall I tell you my idea?'

Miriam outlined how she wanted to open it to the public. Ideally she'd have restored it to its former glory and charge people to come and see it, but she couldn't possibly afford either the time or money to get it done.

'What I need to do is somehow get outside people involved. I'm pretty sure that once it got off the ground, it would be just as popular as the animals! I'm just not sure where to start...'

'Well, just a tidy-up would be good. Those roses need pruning, and the vegetable beds need weeding and rotavating... Simple stuff, there's just a lot of it! You could do with an army of teenagers to come and work here. Do you know any?'

'I had thought,' said Miriam slowly, 'about renting it out as allotments. To families, who could bring their children here and have reduced entry to the farm or something... What do you think?'

'Maybe,' said Lizzie. 'But mightn't it work better if you could get some huge community project up and running? We featured one once in the magazine I used to work for. They got young offenders in, and actually, most of them really got something out of it. They got to grow their own vegetables and enter flower shows. There was only the odd problem, but it worked...'

They agreed they'd both give it some thought. It wasn't exactly the job that Lizzie had been hoping for, but it had fired her imagination. The question was how to make it pay.

* * *

It was still very much on her mind when she went to Antonia's that evening, where Tim had just finished giving Halla a check-up.

'He's been a little off colour,' explained Antonia. 'Cassie wants to compete him next weekend. Now, Timmy darling, I really do think it's time Lizzie learned to ride. Owly's simply wonderful, he's a doting aunt with novices. Safe as houses...'

The unfortunately named Owly had grey spectacles on his large, brown head and an air of immense wisdom. His bottom lip flapped comically and as far as Lizzie had ever seen, he never ventured faster than an amble.

'I haven't come to talk about horses, Antonia. I met Miriam. We were looking at how to make money from her garden. Like allotments...' She stepped back as Owly reached for her pockets.

'Allotments? Sounds a bit crackers if you ask me! Old Miriam's a good sort. Has this rather bold hunter. Jumps anything...' She sounded envious, her mind still fixated on horses.

'Actually, it's not as daft as it sounds,' said Tim, rubbing the brown head in front of him. Owly closed his eyes in bliss, his lip wobbling. 'Let's face it, that place is hugely popular. And animals are a lot nicer than most people. Present company excepted of course,' he added hastily. 'It's no wonder that kids are so drawn to them. It must cost her a fortune though. But the garden... maybe she should contact some schools and see if they want to get involved? For a fee? She could rent them each an allotment and hold a contest for the most original garden...'

'Like Chelsea Flower Show, you mean...' butted in Antonia.

'She could get the press to feature her, promote the farm...' he went on.

'I say, darling, you are clever...'

'And there must be grants she could apply for...'

'And don't forget fundraising, darling... Golly! I know I do the horse show, but I always fancied organising a ball! You know, a really posh one in a stately home or something... Be awfully good fun, don't you think?'

'You're completely brilliant, both of you!' declared Lizzie, her eyes shining with admiration at all these possibilities they'd come up with. She couldn't wait to go and tell Miriam.

11

The fiasco about the rat-runners had subsided somewhat, after a number of the Hoorays and Yummy Mummies had complained to the council about the untimely moving of the livestock, as Antonia filled Lizzie in that evening over their customary bottle of wine. This time she'd come to Lizzie's and she and Darren were ignoring each other as usual, as she told Lizzie what had ensued.

'Bloody arse from the council went to see William. Went to see the lot of them by all accounts. Anyway, basically they all said the same. That there was no grass and they had to keep moving the stock because otherwise they'd escape and be an even bigger nuisance. Load of tosh, of course! There's tons of grass this year. Anyway, old Woodleigh told the council bloke that it had being going on for years and none of the villagers ever minded the live-stock being moved, and that it was the influx of rat-runners that was the problem, not the animals. Don't think they've any plans to stop. Thought I might join in on Hamish!

'That cat of yours is evil,' she added. 'It hasn't blinked once the whole time I've been sitting here. One of Mrs Einstein's, isn't it? They're all over the village. You want to watch it Lizzie – it's a witch's cat. I've never met her but there are rumours – it's probably cursed! Now, I might have a new client for you. He's a pompous old sod. Friend of my ex-husband I'm afraid, but she's sweet enough. Got their number here somewhere, if you're interested...'

Antonia scrabbled in her pocket and pulled out a handful of bits of hay and pony nuts which she scattered on the floor, and a tattered scrap of paper came with it. Forgetting about Mrs Einstein, Lizzie took it eagerly, particularly as her association with Miriam wasn't going to be as profitable as she'd hoped.

'Here you are. Ginny and Edward. Talking of pompous gits, heard from your ex at all?'

Lizzie looked at her. 'He doesn't know where I am, what I'm doing or what my mobile number is either. I could be the other side of the world for all he knows.'

'Don't be too sure, darling,' said Antonia darkly. 'It's horribly easy to find someone once you put your mind to it...'

Lizzie's smugness was gone in an instant. No way would she ever be ready to face Jamie. 'He couldn't find me here,' she said nervously. 'There's nothing to link me to anything.'

'Your old car?' suggested Antonia. 'Bet anyone could track that down. Anyway, I'm just saying, don't be too surprised if at some point the bugger finds you.' She stared at the empty bottle in surprise. 'Lord, the wine's finished already... I suppose we better go to the pub.'

Lizzie couldn't help noticing William shift uncomfortably in his chair when they arrived and look rather pointedly in the opposite direction.

'Antonia!' she hissed in her friend's ear. 'I told you! There's definitely something funny going on!'

And there was, only it was the fair number of winks and nudges among William's little group until the poor man stood up, drained his pint and stalked out of the pub without a backward glance, at which point everything returned to normal.

'They really are a bunch of Neanderthals,' said Antonia. 'It's not like they don't have wives – though God knows how that happened. Would you fancy being hitched to one of that lot? Imagine the scintillating conversation – the merits of various fertilisers or inseminating cattle, all the while dealing with yet another set of clothes that stink of cows. I tell you it's the only reason they go to the WI – for something else to talk about. I will *never* marry a farmer...'

* * *

Lizzie's spare bedroom doubled as her office. Botanical drawings she'd found in a market filled one wall and a single shelf held the precious books she was accumulating, about all kinds of plants, wild flowers, herbs and the roses that she loved with a passion. She'd been torn about whether to put her desk or the bed by the window, with its breath-taking views over the back garden to the fields which lay beyond. The bed had won however, and so it was there where the ceiling sloped down, with a mountain of cushions piled on it and Lizzie's desk was in the corner.

Sitting at it, she was just dialling the number Antonia had given her when she heard saucepan-sized hooves clip-clopping down the lane, accompanied by a steady, rather odd grunting sound that appeared to keep in rhythm. Hamish.

Large and unpredictable, this morning he'd been ambushed by a bored Darren. Antonia had first coaxed, then ferociously threatened Hamish, but he couldn't stop goggling with huge round eyes as the cat stared back from its vantage point.

'Fucking horse!' yelled Antonia in the end, closely followed by 'Fucking cat! Couldn't move it could you, Lizzie? I swear it's doing it on purpose! Poor Hamish! Frightfully highly strung you know!'

Privately, Lizzie thought Hamish was thick, but she pulled on her Hunters and ran across to scoop up Darren, who yowled blood-curdlingly, sending the transfixed horse into orbit. Antonia brought her whip down with a resounding thwack on his well-rounded rump, and he accelerated into a staccato trot now that the danger had been removed.

'Oh jolly good show, thanks awfully!' she shrieked, not the slightest abashed.

As she disappeared round the corner, a familiar Land Rover drew up.

'Glad I've caught you.' Tim looked more than a little anxious. 'Only I've just called in on Miriam. She asked me to look at one of the ponies. There's nothing wrong with it, but actually, it's her I'm worried about.'

'Why? What's the matter?' asked Lizzie, long aware that while Miriam looked after all those animals, no one kept an eye on her.

'She was complaining of pains, in her stomach. Her colour was pretty awful too, and you know Miriam, always so healthy. I suggested she made an appointment to see her doctor, but she said she couldn't possibly, she had far too much to do. Talking of which, so do I. This locum's been delayed again and I've a long list of calls. Sorry, Lizzie, I just thought you'd want to know.'

'Thanks. Yes, of course I do. I'll try and call her now.'

Lizzie tried to call Miriam immediately but it rang and rang the other end, and she was forced to give up, calling the number Antonia had given her instead.

* * *

Ginny and Edward Plunkett-Mackenzie had moved to Oakley last summer, to an old Edwardian property, complete with acres of garden that had remained unchanged for years. The lovely house was typically large and spacious, with an impressive drive that circled around the front of it. Ginny, a tiny fragile figure, had huge eyes and perfectly highlighted hair. Dressed in spotless pastel pink jeans with creases neatly ironed down the front of them, she'd appeared the instant Lizzie pulled up and had excitedly taken her arm and led her through a gate in the hedge.

'It's *frightfully* scruffy Lizzie, I'm afraid...'

But an awestruck Lizzie had just stood and taken it all in. It wasn't at all the kind of garden she would imagine belonging to Ginny.

The rear of the house had a proper old-fashioned verandah which looked original, from which steps led down to the lawn. Rambling overgrown flower beds framed the path, from which more stone steps led to an ornamental pond. In a corner beyond, there was a rather crumbling statue that Lizzie thought was possibly Pan. It was probably worth a fortune... And that wasn't all. The lawn extended around the far side of the house to a more informal area where there was an old timber-framed greenhouse surrounded by apple trees. But utterly beautiful as it was, it was running riot.

Ginny had chattered away. 'You see, it's Edward's sixtieth... Not until next year, Lizzie – I *do* know this will take time... But what I want is to throw a really *super* party for all our friends, but I can't possibly of course until the garden is sorted out... Goodness, we couldn't possibly let anyone see it in such a state. But do you think you could do that for me? It would absolutely have to be finished by the end of May...'

Lizzie frantically scribbled notes as they walked.

'And...' added Ginny, a touch of steel entering her voice. 'There is just one proviso. I'm sure it won't be a problem for you, Lizzie! But absolutely everything must be pink... I don't mind what shade...' she'd added, as though making a grand concession, 'but

I've always wanted a pink garden. Maybe just the teeniest dot of lilac here and there would be all right, just in the background, of course...'

Lizzie kept quiet. It was, of course, totally absurd to have a tacky pink garden behind this gem of a house. The idea alone was a travesty.

But Ginny had jumped up at the sound of tyres crunching on gravel as a rather large car swept in to the drive. 'Oh, how marvellous! Now you'll be able to meet Edward! Come on, Lizzie!'

Lizzie followed her towards the house again as a squat, smug-looking man with terrible skin strode down the steps towards them. A toad, Lizzie instantly thought, stifling a smile.

'Darling,' squeaked Ginny, looking distinctly on edge. 'This is Lizzie! She's going to make me a lovely pink garden!' Ginny clasped her hands with an air of ecstasy etched on her tight face.

'Lizzie. Hi. Edward. Good to meet you.' He extended a large hairy hand, and clasped hers firmly, smiling widely to display a set of teeth that were far too white to be his own.

'Hello, Edward. You have a beautiful garden here,' she said, her eyes fixed on those teeth.

'Mmmm, yes, not too bad, is it?' Edward looked around him, an expression of self-satisfaction settling on his coarse features.

'The little wife here knows exactly what she wants, so I'll leave it all to you girls.' He winked lasciviously at Lizzie at the same time patting Ginny on her tiny bottom. She gave a tinkly, brittle little laugh.

'And, darling, don't forget, Jim's coming round at six for a gin. Have it ready will you, there's a good girl.'

Lizzie stiffened as she forced herself to smile back. She knew exactly why Edward disturbed her. In fact, fast-forwarded twenty years, this could have been her and Jamie, with Lizzie dressed in pastels and Botoxed to within an inch of her life and him boasting smugly about the impressive mansion he'd just bought… except he wouldn't have let Lizzie make any decisions about the garden. Give Edward his due, at least he was up for that.

Lizzie could cope with the most demanding clients if she fell in love with their gardens and in one afternoon she'd fallen hook, line and sinker for this one. Even in this state, it had a timeless beauty that you could never recreate from scratch. She'd cope with the owners. And Ginny wasn't too bad, it was just the dreadful Edward… Apart from him and the whole pink thing, this was a dream of a project.

She detoured home via Hethecote Farm just to check on Miriam, who was obviously feeling better than this morning when Lizzie tracked her down cleaning saddles.

'Just a tummy ache,' she reassured Lizzie. 'Nothing to worry about – really! I'm fine!'

* * *

It was like flitting between the sublime and the ridiculous as Lizzie alternated between Ginny's and Hethecote Farm, one with unlimited resources to pour into a completely self-indulgent project, and the other with the worthiest of causes but trudging around in her dead husband's boots because she couldn't afford to buy new ones.

Miriam's garden scheme was well under way, with half a dozen schools initially signing up to rent their own allotment within the garden. The local press had set a date for a photo shoot and interview, and some much needed funds were at last coming in. Lizzie was spending a couple of mornings there, helping the schools as they began to design their gardens. She was determined too that Antonia would organise this ball. It was exactly the support Miriam needed.

'When's a good time for it, do you think? Autumn maybe?'

'This year? Lord no.' Antonia was horrified. 'It'll take yonks to get it organised. We need to collect raffle prizes – tickets for Glyndebourne, air tickets, that sort of thing.'

Air tickets? Lizzie, who'd been about to offer her gardening services as one of them, was silent.

'So when?' persisted Lizzie, who wanted to be able to tell Miriam.

'Oh, I don't know... next summer? Don't worry about it. Anyway, you going to Bert's retirement do? A good old chap, Bert,' Antonia changed the subject. 'Very fair. Just as long as his replacement isn't some jumped-up little public school boy with ambitions, after all, we can't have the rents going up! Anyway, don't get too excited. I've been to these dos before. There'll be Mrs H.'s nasty curly sandwiches, naff old potato chipsticks and a cake. If I were you, I'd give the sandwiches a miss, they're always a bit iffy, but the cakes are another matter. Eucalyptus might be totally barking, but she's the creator of the most divine cakes you have ever tasted! Bound to be one of hers. She started making them years ago, to help her put on weight, and then got bored with the same old recipes, so she invented new ones. They're quite famous round here! Just turn up, oh, I know, we'll arrive together, have a bit of cake, toast old Bert and make our excuses. What do you think?'

Lizzie had yet to meet the infamous Eucalyptus, who lived next door to the church in a tiny cottage tucked away in the trees. By all accounts, she was a recluse, and so far, Lizzie knew her only by reputation as a painter of the abstract kind of art that Jamie used to rave over, but which had always left her cold.

* * *

Entries for the horse show were coming in thick and fast. Antonia had asked her if she'd judge the prettiest mare class.

'But I don't know the first thing about horses,' Lizzie objected.

'That's why you'd be perfect, darling,' said Antonia firmly. 'And it doesn't matter who the judge is, someone always complains. You've really nothing to worry about.'

Which didn't fill Lizzie with confidence.

* * *

Antonia hadn't been exaggerating about Bert's retirement do. Apart from a few nods, nobody paid them much attention. Mrs Hepplewhite had sniffed and pointedly turned her back on them, presumably for boycotting the WI, and they'd stood quietly looking at the modest party that had gathered.

'Over there,' murmured Antonia in my ear. 'By the window – long face, mouth turned down – avoid like the plague. Harriet Armitage-Brown. Brown by name, brown by nature...' she muttered bitchily, Harriet being dressed head to toe in dingy old clothes. 'Bit of a nightmare. She'll drag you along to her coffee mornings, which are okay because of the food, but she drones on like you wouldn't believe. Just don't catch her eye. If she comes over here we'll make a dash for it.

'Oh, and over there is Cindy, darling,' she added, nodding towards a pretty, fair-haired woman with a rather vague air about her. 'Does the church flowers when she can get past Mrs H., whose are dire. You wouldn't believe the rivalry that goes on over a few naff old geraniums. I say! Look at William... doesn't he scrub up awfully well...'

William did indeed look marginally cleaner than usual, in washed jeans and minus the beanie hat, revealing thick, tousled hair. Feeling Antonia's eyes on him, he turned and winked at her.

She jumped in amazement, clutching at Lizzie's arm. 'Did you see that? He winked at me!'

Bert was dressed in his Sunday best, a checked shirt and tie, his usually windblown hair combed neatly, faithful Molly at his side. Smiling and nodding at everyone, his cheeks were a little pink. Someone had covered the rickety table with a plastic tablecloth, and laid it with paper plates of food and drinks. Lizzie made the foolish mistake of nibbling the corner of one of the fish paste sandwiches.

'Warned you,' muttered Antonia in her ear. 'Which one was it – the salmonella special or a listeria tart? You mustn't miss the E. coli dip either, mmm, lovely...

'That's the Woodleighs over by the door,' Antonia told her. 'Well, of course you know him, from all that malarkey with the cows. But Lord—' She broke off. 'Now who, I wonder, is that...' Rendered speechless for the second time that morning, Antonia's jaw had dropped. Lizzie followed her gaze. A youngish man, good-looking in a rather schoolboyish way in a shirt and stripey tie strode in and confidently shook Mr Woodleigh's hand.

A voice behind them muttered, 'That's 'im, bit of a new broom. Fings all be different now, you mark my words...'

To which another glum sounding voice replied, 'Aye, bugger'll start puttin' rents up in no time, you mark my words...'

A skinny, worried-looking woman with stooping shoulders and dressed in shapeless black came scuttling over to Antonia.

'I was hoping you'd be here,' she whispered, as she peered anxiously into Antonia's face.

'Oh excellent! Eucalyptus! Meet Lizzie! She's moved in up the road from the church. Next door to Bert and Molly. I've told her all about your fab cakes. Which one is it today?' enquired Antonia greedily.

This was Eucalyptus? Lizzie'd built up a picture in her head of the cake-making artist: a plump bohemian, with titian hair, dressed in a riot of colour. A matronly kind of woman, not a timid, neurotic-looking stick insect...

'Hello, Lizzie...' Eucalyptus worriedly held out a small hand that was almost as limp as her hair. 'It's passion fruit and macadamia, with satsuma frosting,' she offered doubtfully, drooping even more as she stood there.

'Oh yummy,' said Antonia. 'Can't wait to try it. Don't think I've tasted that one before.'

Antonia and Lizzie exchanged glances between mouthfuls of cake, which in spite of its off-putting contents was sublime. Mr Woodleigh, the first time Lizzie had seen him without his cows, still looked as though he'd walked straight in from the fields which in all likelihood he had, and he made a brief speech about what a thoroughly all-round decent chap Bert had been to have working for them all these years, before everyone clapped enthusiastically.

They watched as the 'new broom' swept his way around the room, introducing himself to everyone as he went. Then he got to Lizzie, and held out his hand. A pair of friendly brown eyes smiled eagerly. Lizzie always noticed people's eyes. 'Windows to the soul' weren't they supposed to be, or so she liked to think... At any rate, they were a good indicator of character, she always thought, forgetting how many times she'd got this wrong.

'Toby Anstruther-Smythe.' He introduced himself with huge self-assurance, in rather clipped, public-school tones. 'I'm the new estate manager. I say, simply delighted to meet you both.' He was looked extremely pleased with himself. Antonia too looked rather chuffed.

'Antonia!' She grasped his hand and held on to it. 'And this is Lizzie. So how are you finding Littleton?'

'Hmm. Funny little place,' he said tactlessly in his rather booming voice. 'Might need to shake things up a little, you know,' he continued, oblivious to the surly looks of everyone standing within earshot.

'Good for you, darling,' said Antonia admiringly. 'What did you have in mind? I'm always up for something a little different...'

'There's nothing like change, is there,' he continued, beaming at her delightedly. 'Anyway, awfully sorry, but must move on. Need to get round everyone.' But then, looking straight at Lizzie, he took her completely by surprise. 'I say, old bean, you and I should get together one evening. You know, both of us being new round here and all that. Found a smashing pub the other night... how about it?'

Lizzie was filled with horror. Followed by panic, and an unsquashable conviction that this was a very bad idea. Absolutely no way was she going on a date with someone who reminded her of a Labrador.

'She'd love to,' Antonia answered quickly. 'Wouldn't you, Lizzie? Absolutely excellent idea. Here's her phone number.' She ferreted around in her pocket and quickly scribbled something on some paper.

* * *

'Antonia! I'm not going! You'll have to tell him! It's too soon and he's not my type. You go,' Lizzie was outraged.

'Nonsense. Do you good. High time you stopped moping about. It's only a drink for goodness' sake. Just go out for the sake of it, it'll be good practice. Hardly think he's an axe-murderer,' said Antonia bluntly. 'Now, let's get another slice of cake before this bloody lot polish it off.'

But Lizzie definitely wasn't going. She'd made her decision and this time, she was sticking to it.

* * *

Later, at a loose end, she wandered back up to Hethecote Farm. Miriam was looking weary.

'Just the girl,' she said, brightening slightly. 'Only I've a bit of a predicament on my hands. Mallow House have been in touch. Only they want one of our allotments... and I'm not sure what to say.'

'What's the problem?' said Lizzie, who'd never heard of them.

'Oh – of course. Sorry... They're a home for young offenders. Not serious ones – just children from poor backgrounds who shoplift and daub graffiti in the wrong places... Poor little things really. So misunderstood. Only I'm not sure our schools would be too happy about sharing the garden with them...'

'What if they came at different times?' suggested Lizzie. 'The schools come in the mornings mostly... what if the Mallow House lot came later on?'

'Possibly,' said Miriam. 'It might work... but I'd have to write to them all wouldn't I? And explain... Oh dear. There's too much to do.'

'Why not think about it?' said Lizzie. 'And if you think it's a good idea, I'll help. And can you leave these seeds somewhere for the schools to find? They're a gift from one of the garden centres.'

'Isn't everyone so kind?' said Miriam, then winced, clutching her stomach.

'Have you seen the doctor yet?' said Lizzie in alarm. 'You really ought to...'

'I will – when I have time...'

12

As they drove the few miles to the pub, Toby Anstruther-Smythe, it soon became apparent, had extremely Big Ambitions. Boasting to Lizzie about his grand plans for the Estate, and about how it needed moving into the twenty-first century, he of course, *ho ho*, was just the person to do it. Lizzie had the feeling that his overconfidence wouldn't win him many friends round here, but maybe there would be at least some changes for the better. Like dealing with the dreaded rat-runners for starters wouldn't go amiss.

It was a pub she hadn't been to before – The Coach and Horses – and on such a sunny summer's evening they sat outside in the garden under an umbrella that Toby insisted on leaving up, even though Lizzie had goosebumps in its shade.

'Awfully nice place, don't you think?' remarked Toby loudly. It was one of those pubs that had been modernised, which wasn't really to Lizzie's taste, but it was pleasant enough and at least the wine was well chilled.

'Funny old lot in Littleton,' he said bluntly, forgetting Lizzie was one of them. 'Could do with a bit of a shake-up, don't you think? Don't know anything about this nonsense with the farmers, do you? Even old Woodleigh seems to be joining in. Not much of an example to set to your tenant farmers,' he added arrogantly, reminding her horribly of Jamie for an instant.

'Well actually,' Lizzie said, 'have you seen that traffic that comes tearing through? There'll be an accident if no one does anything. They drive like maniacs. And it is a country lane,' she emphasised, before suggesting, 'Er, maybe you should get involved? Someone in your position might be able to do something...'

'You're right,' he agreed. 'I'll think about it, old girl.' He stared rather too obviously at her.

Toby, Lizzie soon realised, was totally naive when it came to the opposite sex. His version of flirting seemed to mean horribly suggestive glances, which she was finding rather off-putting and in spite of her best efforts to like him, there wasn't the tiniest spark of chemistry. But he was pleasant enough company, and as Antonia had rightly said, it didn't do a girl good to spend too much time brooding.

'So what brought you to Littleton?' asked Toby eventually, when he'd exhausted the topic of himself, his education and his some-what limited career as an upmarket estate agent flogging over-priced property in Chelsea.

'I walked out on my fiancé four days before our wedding,' said Lizzie brightly, and waited to see his shocked response.

'I say, old girl, that was a bit much, wasn't it? I mean, speaking for the chap of course.' Toby was flummoxed, but then she noticed a gleam in his eye.

A couple of glasses of wine later, Toby offered to drive her home, and as they walked across the car park, he casually swung an arm over Lizzie's shoulders. Mistakenly leaving it there instead of shrugging it, Toby obviously took this as encouragement.

If he'd shown just the slightest finesse at that point, just maybe it would have ended differently – or maybe not. But perhaps Lizzie should have been thankful that any romantic notions about him were well and truly squashed when he simply spun her round and clamped his mouth on hers.

Lizzie tried to disentangle herself, but Toby's arms were so tightly round her she could hardly move. Not believing she hadn't seen that coming, she had no wish to encourage him. Pulling away, she muttered none too tactfully that having just extricated herself from one disaster, it was too soon to be embarking on another.

Finally released from that grip, she backed off while she could. Toby wasn't so bad, but. She'd been right – he really was like a Labrador. Very eager but horribly drooly and best kept at arm's length. A timely flashback to the gorgeous man from the pub confirmed it.

But by the time they pulled up at Lizzie's cottage, Toby seemed to have forgotten he'd been rebuffed. Parking by the gate, he unfastened his seat belt and leaned towards Lizzie.

'I suppose there's no chance of a coffee?' he asked hopefully. Short memory span too, she noticed ruefully. Not a hope.

'Erm, Toby, I've got a really early start tomorrow, but thank you for a lovely evening.' She shot out of the car before he tried anything.

He visibly drooped, then brightened as he suggested, 'Never mind, old girl. Let's do it again sometime,' before speeding off down the lane.

Lizzie breathed a sigh of relief, listening until the sound had faded completely. It was a lovely night, she noticed, looking around in the darkness at the trees looming like giants, towering over her protectively as their branches swayed gently in the breeze. Lizzie fancied she heard a whisper of something, and a sharp crack like someone had stepped on a twig. She strained her ears, but hearing nothing more, decided she must have imagined it.

* * *

Lizzie knew Antonia would find the whole episode hilarious and she was right. Antonia had laughed loudly when she told her.

'It's your fault for making me go,' Lizzie told her sternly. 'In my fragile, vulnerable state you *made* me go out with him, and I could be psychologically damaged after that *assault...*'

'Crikey, Lizzie, it was only a snog! It can't have been that bad... Perhaps you should learn self-defence, I'll teach you if you like...'

It would take a brave man or else a very stupid one to ever try it on with Antonia. However, she'd taken a shine to Toby. 'Don't know what the fuss is about. You could do far worse you know...' she had mused thoughtfully, lips pursed in contemplation.

'I thought you fancied William? You've been ogling at him ever since I met you. Well, go for it. If you really want my cast-offs, Toby's an excellent idea,' said Lizzie. It was the perfect solution for everybody.

'Hmm.' Antonia was thoughtful. 'Haven't been on a date in yonks. Might be a laugh. Always had a bit of a thing for those public school types you know... Awfully sexy don't you think?'

'Ask him out then. Bet he'll say yes.' Trying to get her head round how anyone could find Toby sexy, Lizzie decided not to add that in all likelihood, he wasn't fussy and would probably leap on the first female of any description who showed the slightest interest.

'You know, I think I'll do just that. Might be jolly handy – got quite a nice car, hasn't he? I know, I'll ask him over for coffee, just being neighbourly, of course... You can be here too. Then you can pretend you have to go...' Her eyes lit up. 'Like candy from a baby! You free on Tuesday?'

Lizzie buried her head in her hands.

* * *

Tim had finally got round it. He'd turned up at Lizzie's looking awkward, eventually asking her. The date was fixed.

She was looking forward to Katie coming to stay again, but the beloved MG was off the road with three punctures, so she'd been forced to get a train.

'It's those bloody chavs,' Katie had raged on the phone earlier, incensed. 'Just when I needed it. And it's not the first time. My poor car. Someone ought to catch the little bastards and flog them,' sounding as though she'd be more than happy to do it herself.

Lizzie drove her jeep over to the usually deathly quiet little station at Boxton, which saw the arrival of only three trains a day.

Katie was already waiting outside when she got there, and the stationmaster was lurking furtively in the background, scratching his head until flakes of dandruff rained onto the shoulders of his ill-fitting uniform issue jacket, transfixed by those two lezzer-wotsernames hugging madly and kissing each other in front of the station. Shocking! He'd have to make sure and tell the wife.

Having promised to meet Antonia at the Fox for another round of the quiz night, Tilly joined them and yet again they blitzed the opposition.

'That was fucking brilliant,' declared Antonia, when it was over. 'I say, how about we carry on at mine?'

Taking another two bottles of the Fox's finest vin de table, red, obviously, they all decamped to Antonia's as seemed to be becoming a habit, leaving a bar full of disgruntled men muttering under their breath behind them. Cassie had raised her eyebrows at the four of them with an exaggerated air of resignation, and sloped off to bed, a trail of manky-looking dogs shambling along behind her.

Collapsing into Antonia's huge, shabby sofas, they consumed the rest of the wine.

'No sign of Tim then,' remarked Katie casually.

'Probably stuck in some God-awful farmyard somewhere up to his armpits in shit,' said Antonia brusquely. 'Told him years ago he should have stuck to horses. Far more civilised, darling. Actually, says he's getting a locum...' she added, getting up and disappearing out to the kitchen.

'Pity you weren't here for that rave last year,' said Tilly, going off on a tangent as she often did. 'Only it was really good. What I can remember. Come to think of it, I don't remember much about it at all...' she added vaguely.

'Tilly,' said Katie patiently, 'that's probably because you were stoned, don't you think?'

Antonia returned with some glasses. 'What party was that?' she enquired bossily, and when Tilly started describing the stage made of old trailers and the multicoloured flock of sheep, instantly said, 'You were at that rave? God, it nearly gave Elspeth apoplexy! Bloody brilliant, wasn't it?'

13

Tentative plans for the Hethecote Farm fund-raising ball were made that weekend. The self-appointed committee of Antonia, Lizzie and Katie paid Miriam a visit on Saturday afternoon, and sitting in her large untidy kitchen, outlined what they had in mind. A large black cat sat on the table near her, eyeing the others distrustfully.

'This is Navajo,' said Miriam stroking its head. The cat closed its eyes appreciatively, then slightly opened one, which it fixed on Antonia.

'Damned animal's giving me the evils,' she grumbled.

'Oh, take no notice... he's a sweetie,' said Miriam and the cat looked smug. 'One of Mrs Einstein's actually...'

'Really?' Lizzie's ears pricked up. 'Funny, so is mine...'

'Lord's sakes,' said Antonia impatiently. 'Sod the cats. Can't we talk about the ball? We just need to sell around two hundred tickets, for a black-tie bash with live music, that should do it,' she said. 'We'll get the Bozo Dog Doo Dah Band and give everyone loads of free champagne which we'll find someone to sponsor, and then food... I was thinking some of William's lamb or old Woodleigh's beef... and then when they've had a skinful, we'll hold the auction! It'll be marvellous, darlings!'

'Maybe the children could grow the vegetables...' said Miriam thoughtfully. 'Oh dear, it does seem such a cheek to ask all these people to put their hands in their pockets...'

'Nonsense!' said Antonia. 'They can afford it! Anyway, giving money to charity is a tax dodge! All perfectly in order!'

'You know, the people who buy tickets for these balls are the kind of people who always give money to charity,' said Katie. 'And Hethecote Farm is just as deserving as any of the others. You deserve it.'

Miriam was somewhat overwhelmed at their show of support.

'I don't what I'd have done if you hadn't driven up that day,' she said to Lizzie, dabbing her eyes with a grubby handkerchief. 'Anyway,' she sneezed, 'I'm more than happy to leave it to the three of you. You could always hold it here you know... in a marquee?'

Antonia opened her mouth to speak. 'Actually...' but Lizzie kicked her, and for once she shut up.

'That's so kind, Miriam, can we think about it?'

'What on earth did you do that for?' demanded Antonia once they were outside. 'I was only about to tell her that we couldn't possibly hold a posh black-tie do on a clapped out old farm like Hethecote...'

Lizzie shook her head. 'Exactly. Anyway, what would be so bad about it? The furthest part of the garden is just grass, and if you think about it, the house is quite imposing – from the outside, anyway. No one needs to go inside, except the caterers. And getting the guests to come here would make them see the place. We could do tours! It might actually be quite a good idea...'

'Miriam should auction Sid and Johnny...' said Antonia thoughtfully.

'Well, it's the only possibility at the moment,' said Katie sensibly. 'Unless you've had a better idea?'

'God. You're both as barmy as Miriam. Let's go to the pub.' Antonia stalked off towards the car.

* * *

Tim was a surprisingly good host, Lizzie only feeling slightly like a gooseberry as she sat round his kitchen table with him and Katie. Katie, however, seemed quite at home. Gone was the trademark black, replaced by some very tight jeans and a checked shirt and Tim couldn't seem to take his eyes off her. At the end of the evening, Lizzie stood on tiptoes and kissed his stubbly cheek.

'Thank you,' she said and glanced at Katie. 'I just need to check my mobile... I'll, er, see you in the car in a minute.'

* * *

Katie disappeared for the day on Sunday, having been swept off by a slightly bashful Tim, who promised to return her to the Star that evening, leaving Lizzie at a loose end. Deciding that she hadn't seen Nola or Julia for at least a fortnight, on the spur of the moment she drove to Rumbleford.

'Oh, Lizzie, we were thinking about you!' they said as they always did.

'I suddenly thought I hadn't seen you for ages! And Katie's gone out for the day, so I thought I'd call in... if you're not too busy?'

Nola took her hand, her green eyes gazing steadily into Lizzie's. 'Of course we're not! And we're always happy to see you, you know that! Come through to the back!'

'I'm not sure why I'm here,' confessed Lizzie. 'I mean, we're still getting together next week aren't we? It just came into my head to come over here, so I did...'

'You don't need a reason, silly!' teased Nola. 'No one does! We're a shop! Now tea? Or coffee? And how are the plans for the ball?'

'Apart from the fairly major decision about where we'll hold it, fine... We'll sort it out. I suppose I ought to let Antonia choose, seeing as it was all her idea.'

'So where's Katie today?' asked Nola.

'Out!' said Lizzie with a grin.

'Ah – Tim?'

'Of course! You guessed?'

'Oh Lizzie. Some things are just so obvious!'

* * *

As Lizzie walked back to her car, she stopped in her tracks, not believing her eyes. Here he was *again*, coming along the pavement towards her – the stranger from the Old Goat.

'Hello!'

'Hello again! I still haven't worked it out but I haven't given up!'

'Me neither,' admitted Lizzie.

They stood awkwardly for a moment, before he said, 'You know, I'd ask you for a coffee, but unfortunately I have to be somewhere...'

'Oh!' said Lizzie startled. 'Me too, actually...'

'Better go then...'

'Bye...'

Crossing paths with him always made Lizzie feel at odds. The rest of the day passed in a blur. Katie disappeared back to London, and on the Monday evening, she had just made it home from Ginny's before Mr Woodleigh started herding his cows down the lane. She'd become quite adept at avoiding the movement of livestock until now, but tonight, however, it all went horribly wrong, as with his hand pressed hard on his horn, one of the rat-runners in a huge BMW came speeding up the road and slammed through the middle of the cattle.

If Lizzie hadn't been standing right there when it happened, she wouldn't have believed it was possible. The cattle abandoned their orderly progression and started cantering all over the place bellowing their heads off, and over the top of all the commotion was this horrible, agonised sound.

Not knowing what else to do, Lizzie got on her mobile to Antonia who promptly called Tim. The BMW driver was stalking around furiously making calls into his mobile, well and truly immobilised now that he'd driven into a cow. A grim-faced Tim arrived within minutes and quickly despatched the mutilated animal.

'I'm leaving that cow for the police,' he said furiously. 'It's time those bastards did something.'

The driver marched over. 'I'm suing,' he announced angrily. 'High time someone taught those idiots a lesson. These bloody farmers think they own the place.'

'I think you'll find, sir, that they do,' said Tim through gritted teeth. 'And they're not the idiots from where I'm standing.'

The driver rounded on him. 'What did you just call me?' he spluttered. But in the nick of time a police car turned up. Followed by another.

The driver pointed his finger at Tim. 'I'll have you...' he said nastily.

'Oh I doubt that,' said Tim calmly. 'I hope you're insured, only the police are over there looking at the cow you just killed.'

The next day, peace was restored, at least temporarily. 'Road closed – local traffic only' signs were placed at either end of the lane. The only pity was it took a dead cow to do it. Two police arrived on Lizzie's doorstep, a middle-aged village bobby and a younger one with twinkling eyes who looked slightly more on the ball and she told them everything she'd seen.

'Was there, um, any particular reason why the animals were being moved around so often?' he asked. 'Only, it seems there have been a number of complaints, though I have to say, not from anyone who lives here, about cattle and sheep on the road...'

He looked at Lizzie most quizzically while the older one fiddled with his notebook.

'Oh well, it's the grass you see. There's not very much about. If they don't keep moving the animals, they escape and that's even worse.'

The policemen just looked at her. The other one scratched his head.

'You see it's odd,' the younger one said, sounding puzzled. 'Everyone we speak to says the same. Only, what I don't get is it looks like there's plenty of grass to me.'

And it was clearly not Lizzie's lucky day, because shortly after their departure, there was another knock at her door.

'Harriet,' she told her deadly seriously. 'Armitage-Brown,' she added in the same flat monotone. 'Now I've been meaning to come round for ages, only I'm just so busy. I'm having a coffee morning. For charity. All the ladies in the village are coming. You'll want to bring a cake. Don't make a coffee one, they never sell and you better not put butter icing on it because I think people watch their cholesterol levels. I do, since I've been ill, my doctor says...'

Harriet rambled on and on delivering her tedious monologue until Lizzie's eyes were glazing over. She was one of those people that didn't stop to draw breath, and every time Lizzie tried to say something, she got louder. Having given up trying, Lizzie waited. And then Darren appeared. Sitting directly in front of Harriet, he started to cough, but in full swing by now, she ignored him. Darren, not used to being snubbed, gave Lizzie one of his winks, then proceeded to vomit up bits of mouse all over Harriet's boots.

There was silence – but not for long, as Harriet stood saying 'Oh, oh dear...' over and over as she stared unhappily at her boots.

Lizzie quickly hosed them clean, but it was too much even for Harriet.

'Oh, well I better let you get on, it looks as though you have rather a lot to do...' she said, beating a hasty retreat down the path.

Lizzie bent down. 'You really are a superstar,' she said to her cat who was looking smug. As she stroked her hand along his back, which he arched with appreciation, Lizzie realised Harriet hadn't even asked her name. Rubbing himself possessively around her legs, Darren was purring like a motorbike.

* * *

'Has Harriet been to see you?' Lizzie asked Antonia that evening.

'Ghastly old trout turned up this morning,' said Antonia conversationally. 'I opened the door and there she was. Jolly bad timing really, didn't have a chance to escape so I told her one of the dogs had crapped in the kitchen. Seemed to do the trick. Did say she'd call some other time though...' Antonia looked far from happy at the thought. 'Nightmare.'

'Darren threw up on her boots, but not before I'd been roped in to her next coffee morning. *Couldn't* you come with me? *Please?* You can make cakes, can't you? It's next Friday...'

'Phew,' said Antonia with relief. 'Farrier's coming. Love to, darling, but I can't.'

As luck would have it they bumped into Darius and Angel at the Goat.

'Boys, I need your help,' Lizzie begged them. 'Only I've just been signed up for the most tedious of all tedious coffee mornings,' she wailed.

They looked at each other.

'Oh dear no, not one of Harriet's, sweetie?' asked Angel, looking dismayed.

'You know her?'

'Oh, darling, we all know Happy Harry, don't we?' said Darius with delight. 'Rather well as it happens. Don't worry, she lightens up when she's had a few. We had her round for cocktails. Only the once mind.' They looked at each other and giggled. 'Doesn't know when to stop! She got absolutely *blottoed*, darlings...' whispered Darius. 'Had to send her home in a taxi.'

'Oh how fab,' said Antonia with glee. 'I absolutely must remember to put tons of sherry in my next cake.'

'Er, well, going back to this coffee morning,' said Lizzie. 'It's a charity thing... I have to take a cake.' She glanced apologetically at Darius. 'I don't suppose...'

'Oh, of course, flower – ooh, chocolate rum cake, or amaretti cheesecake? Or tipsy walnut cake? We might as well have some fun,' he added wickedly. 'Why don't I come with you, pet? There's safety in numbers after all. We should suggest she gives her donation to Hethecote Farm... And I'll bring a little hip flask just in case,' he added confidingly. 'If all else fails, we can sneak it into her coffee when she's not looking. That'll get things going.' He winked.

* * *

The horse show was looming and Antonia was tearing her hair out, writing long lists which she kept losing.

'Portaloos,' she said to Lizzie. 'Ropes, stakes and a beer tent. Rosettes. Golly! I mustn't forget to collect those...'

But offers of help were coming in from all over the place.

Darius and Angel had volunteered as stewards and Tilly as a car park marshal, roping in the Star's bolshy barman to help her.

* * *

It had to be said, the horse show was a success. Everyone had gathered at the crack of dawn, huddled in jackets against the chilly autumn air. But another fine day had been promised and the mist soon lifted, as they waited for the competitors to turn up. In spite of appearances to the contrary, Antonia had everything under control. Darius and Angel made efficient, if comical, stewards.

'Now, darlings, if you'll all just listen... This is the running order. Lucy? Are you here? Oh, it's you, is it, sweetie – divine jacket darling, quite stunning... then it's India – is your pony all right, petal, only he looks awfully hot and bothered, poor lamb...'

And so it went on. Tilly did a sterling job in the car park until everyone started ignoring her directions when she gave up, retiring to the beer tent. Lizzie found her there later when it was over.

The judging of the prettiest mare went without a hitch – or so Lizzie thought, until later she was accosted by two mothers.

'It really is most unfair,' said the first, waving a finger at Lizzie. 'My daughter hasn't won a thing today.'

'I agree,' said the second. 'And everyone knows the prize-winner had mane extensions just last week. She cheated! I demand you eliminate her!'

'Disgraceful,' agreed the first. 'I'm going to object.'

But Lizzie had slipped away and hidden.

The highlight had been watching Cassie win the open jumping. After the countless horses and riders that had struggled round the course, it was pure magic to see her take each enormous fence in her stride, the beautiful white Scout clearing them effortlessly. She was in a league of her own. And no one could possibly complain, thought Lizzie. You couldn't cheat at showjumping.

'Bravo!' called out a voice from behind her.

'Yeah, but that's the show organiser's daughter. Bet she was round here yesterday practising...' muttered another.

14

Later that week at Antonia's, tucking into her own personal version of pasta Bolognese which Lizzie tried to forget was basically road-kill rabbit with a hefty slosh of red wine, it was Cassie who told her about Bonfire Night.

'Oh Lord,' said Antonia hastily. 'Completely forgot to tell you. You have to go. It's the social event of the year. Bit of a wheeze, actually. Old Woodleigh usually barbecues a few of his sheep. There's oodles of home-made cider from good old Pete, and a dodgy band or two, but by then everyone's too plastered to notice how awful they are – or how cold it is,' she added as an afterthought.

Cassie raised her eyebrows at her mother. 'Actually, the band this year is cool. Some friends of mine are in it.' She screwed up her face as she thought. 'Kind of like Joan Jett or early Avril Lavigne... they happen to be really good.'

'Cassie particularly likes the drummer, don't you?' said Antonia slyly.

'Don't be so horrible, Mummy,' said Cassie furiously, turning pink. 'Anyway, you're far too old to understand...' she retaliated, before stomping off.

So Cassie had a boyfriend at long last...

'God. Don't know what she sees in him. Typical youth with acne and an aversion to eye contact. Can only manage monosyllabic words such as "like", "well" or "um". Or maybe "dunno" on a good day. Still, I suppose it's better than the wrinkly rockers we usually have to put up with...'

* * *

Winter arrived overnight that year, breathing an icy blast which brought the mild autumn to an abrupt end. Lizzie awoke to find the world transformed by a glistening coat of frost. It was beautiful in an icy, other-worldly kind of way. The trees took on an ethereal air, every twig looking as if it had been dipped in icing sugar. But in her cottage, in the absence of central heating, the temperature barely ventured above freezing, and Lizzie stood in her kitchen huddled in layers of sweaters, watching her breath form clouds as the kettle took longer than ever to boil. Then suddenly remembering and not waiting for the kettle, she pulled on some more clothes, scraped the ice off her car and headed up to Hethecote Farm, terrified that the frost would have wrecked the schools' gardens.

Miriam helped her drape fleece over each of them, then they went inside to the kitchen in the big house, which was almost as cold as Lizzie's, and huddled next to her Aga drinking tea.

'I can't be too long,' said Miriam, looking more pale and drawn than Lizzie had ever seen her. 'All the animals will be hungry. The ponies will be all right – they're inside – but it's everything else I'm worried about. Oh heavens, I hope it's not going to be a hard winter. I'm worried I'll run out of hay...'

'Don't worry,' said Lizzie firmly. 'I can stay and help you for an hour or so. Don't forget, there's still donations coming in from the newspaper article... And didn't Mr Woodleigh offer you a deal on your hay...'

It was true. There was more money coming into Hethecote than there had been in ages, but poor old Miriam was so used to being worried, she was struggling to kick the habit.

Carrying armfuls of hay to all the animals had soon warmed Lizzie up, but when she got back to her cottage, she was only able to get warm under layers of blankets. She was rather worried about Miriam. She'd caught her sitting on a bale of hay with Navajo. Though she looked terrible, she'd got up and tried to put a bright face on as soon as she'd seen her.

Lizzie hadn't minded the cold initially, but the novelty was fast wearing off. And though she could light a log fire, and keep a good blaze going in a fireplace, up to now the ancient Rayburn in the kitchen had defeated her. Dimly trying to recall Bert's instructions about how to light it, to her horror all she succeeded in doing was filling the place with smoke. She'd have asked him to help her, but she knew that he and Molly had gone away.

By now desperate, and after leaving at least a dozen messages, she had eventually got hold of Pete, crossing all her fingers that he wouldn't start having one of his elusive phases. But eventually he turned up, and Lizzie watched through a small hole she'd scraped in the ice on the kitchen window as the battered van parked in the lane, and the stooped, balding figure made his way slowly and dejectedly up the path. He looked more like a funeral director than a handyman.

Having lingered over the mug of coffee Lizzie offered him, Pete reluctantly got down to business. 'Better 'ave a look-see then.'

Spreading a dust sheet in front of the Rayburn, after much sighing, fiddling and muttering about bloomin' grate's being buggered and new riddlin' arms, Lizzie's heart sank to the bottom of her furry boots as all thoughts of heat being restored faded. Pete got creakily to his feet and wiped his sooty hands on his trousers, then scratching his belly, revealed too much flabby white flesh and the top of his maroon Y-fronts.

'I'll have a word with that young Toby. Tell him see, how you needs this going swiftly-like, on account of it being that chilly...' He looked at her, frowning, seeming suddenly to notice her strange attire of several sets of clothes layered on top of each other, all topped off with a woolly hat.

'Mebbe you needs to get one o' them fan 'eaters or sommat...' He nodded at Lizzie. 'I'll let you know when your parts are 'ere.'

Meanwhile, Lizzie spent as much time as possible with Antonia, who didn't believe in roughing it and whose oil-fired Aga was turned right up, meaning her cottage was toasty warm. One evening, however, when Lizzie got there, she was looking distinctly unhorsy and was even wearing make-up. Lizzie was just about to ask why when there was a loud knock at the door.

'Now act casually, darling,' she muttered. 'I don't want him getting suspicious.'

It was the long awaited date with Toby, who looked delighted when Antonia greeted him with a kiss on both his cheeks. Lizzie was more than happy to settle for a 'Hello, old girl' from the far side of Antonia's kitchen table, as if she was one of her smelly old dogs.

'Um, this is jolly nice,' said Toby enthusiastically, looking around at Antonia's hastily tidied kitchen, where only one bridle was spread across the table instead of the usual half a dozen, and the boots were all standing neatly in pairs instead of kicked off and left where they fell. 'I say, jolly nice indeed.'

'Would you like a glass of wine?' Antonia had schmoozed back with a glass which she handed to him to hold, while she carefully topped it up.

'Lizzie?'

'Just a tiny bit,' she said, not wanting to stand in the way of true love. Usually Antonia would fill her glass up to the top no matter how she protested, but tonight she got about half an inch.

'There you are, darling. I know you're busy this evening, so I won't give you too much.' She caught Lizzie's eye and winked.

* * *

Bonfire Night arrived, another cold, clear evening with the temperature already plummeting and Lizzie walked with Antonia down the lane to the appointed field. Already, there was what she guessed was a soundcheck going on, as guitar strings twanged and Cassie's friend drummed. Lizzie was dying to hear what happened with Toby.

'Golly, darling, he was frightfully keen once he got started,' said Antonia candidly. 'There's a lot to be said for a younger man. Far more energetic than the old husband ever was. Jolly keen to learn, too... Must see if he's on for an action replay...'

Lizzie tried to banish the disturbing images from her head, but fortunately they ran into Cassie, her arm through that of a nice-looking boy, taller than she was, with long dark hair.

'Mother.' She glared at Antonia. 'This is Liam. And this is Lizzie,' she told him in a completely different tone of voice as she turned to smile at Lizzie.

'The drummer,' said Antonia disapprovingly.

'We're really looking forward to hearing you play,' Lizzie said to him, to make amends for Antonia's rudeness. 'Cassie says your band is really good.' She winked at Cassie, who shot her a look of gratitude.

'Cool,' the drummer managed, as he was dragged away by Cassie before her mother could embarrass her.

'You do realise he could have been so much worse, don't you?'

Lizzie told her sternly. 'Like with a drug habit, a criminal record and so many piercings in his head that he looks tortured?'

'All I keep thinking is it won't be long before my daughter has a better sex life than I have,' replied Antonia glumly.

The bonfire was spectacular – the biggest Lizzie had seen, sending sparks soaring into the sky, and belting out so much heat that everyone backed away. The fireworks that followed were no less impressive, though she did wonder what all the sheep in the surrounding fields would make of it.

Pleasantly warmed by a plastic cup or two of Pete's home-brewed cider, they'd managed to bump into Toby, and it was looking increasingly likely that Antonia would get her action replay. Lizzie had only just stepped back and left them to it, when a familiar figure bounced up beside her.

'Lizzie! How brilliant to see you again!'

It was Susie, who she hadn't seen since the Lizzie party.

'What are you doing here?' Lizzie asked delightedly. 'It's really good to see you!'

'Oh no, is that what it looks like?' she giggled nodding towards Antonia head to head with Toby. Lizzie sighed.

'Afraid so. New romance. He's smitten by the looks of things, poor Toby.'

'Oh he'll cope,' said Susie airily. 'Men love an older woman. Actually, I did want to introduce you to my big brother only he seems to have gone AWOL. Oh well, another time. He's wandering around nursing a broken heart that his bitch ex-girlfriend inflicted. It's been ages now, but he seems to have sworn off girls completely. Awful waste... he's quite handsome and he's very nice, for a brother...'

Lizzie loathed set-ups. Susie raised a speculative eyebrow at her, but fortunately she was saved from answering by the appearance of

Tilly, looking somewhat the worse for wear, propped up by Darius and Angel on either side of her.

'Oh darlings! How divine!' said Angel delightedly when he saw them. Then more quietly, 'Thank goodness! Shall I get us all some cider? Except maybe not for this one,' he added in a whisper, looking anxiously at Tilly.

'Oh but please, Angelical, just a teeny one,' she pleaded, as Darius grabbed her to keep her upright. Then she spotted Susie.

'Oh Susie! I think I'm in love with your brother...' she slurred, before her legs completely gave way.

'You and half the county,' murmured Susie with amusement, as they bent to pick her up. Lizzie's ears pricked up. Oh yes? Definitely not her type then.

Actually it was all rather romantic, especially after another plastic cup of Pete's cider. With the massive fire burning down now, the last of the silvery fireworks zipped through the skies, illuminating the faces of Liam standing with his arm round a pink-cheeked and radiant Cassie, of Darius and Angel hand in hand as they gazed spellbound, and then Lizzie caught a glimpse of an enthusiastic Toby nuzzling a delighted Antonia's ear and was so very glad that wasn't her... While all the time keeping her eyes peeled for signs of handsome strangers, of whom sadly, there wasn't a hint in sight.

* * *

True to his word, Pete returned just two days later, complete with the parts for the Rayburn, and an hour's fumbling and swearing later, not to mention a bit of bashing with a rather large hammer, he soon had a fire going. This time Lizzie listened carefully to his instructions and took notes, determined to remember every important word.

And with its cosy heat soon permeating through the cottage, she was at last able to take her coat off again when she came in. This was more like it, though Antonia would undoubtedly still declare it bloody arctic compared to her house.

* * *

Before Lizzie knew it, December was here, and with it Christmas, a time that would forever carry memories. Last year it had passed Lizzie by – she barely remembered any of it, but this year she wanted it to be different.

Tempting though it was to lock herself away, Lizzie knew she'd should keep busy, and as it happened, she wasn't given the choice. Antonia swept her along mercilessly, to Christmas carol concerts and mince pies at the church, endless boozy drinks parties with the other villagers and festive outings to the Old Goat, accompanied increasingly it seemed, by Toby, who was now well and truly and quite willingly under her thumb.

'Quite a sweetie, Tobes,' Antonia let slip. 'Think I might invite him for Christmas too...'

Toby, most curiously, seemed equally enamoured and had accepted the invitation with alacrity.

'Oh Lord, I suppose I better ask Euc,' said Antonia, with great reluctance. 'Only, she asked us last year. On the upside, she could always bring one of her cakes,' she added, sounding more cheerful about it. 'Do you think we could bear it?' she asked. She'd already invited Lizzie. 'You know, she's not so bad underneath that batty exterior. Had the most disastrous exhibition and never got over it. God, I'll have to remember to hang up that ghastly painting she gave me last year. Can't stand the thing, but don't want to upset the old girl.'

Then a few days before Christmas, Lizzie's phone rang.

'Miriam's collapsed,' came the hysterical voice at the other end. 'I don't know what to do... She won't let me call the doctor or anything...'

'I'll come over now,' said Lizzie, already jumping to her feet and pulling on her boots. 'Can you stay with her till I get there?'

'Okay, only can you hurry, she's making these awful noises...'

Lizzie drove as fast as she dared, calling Tim along the way because she didn't know what else to do. Leaving him a message when it went to voicemail, she hoped he'd pick it up. It was one thing looking after a person, but Lizzie didn't have a clue about the animals.

A girl who looked about fourteen came rushing over to Lizzie, looking frightened out of her wits.

'She's in the haybarn. She looks terrible... she keeps going on about the pain...'

Miriam did look terrible. Her face was ashen and she was convulsed in pain. Lizzie helped into a more comfortable position and looked around for a horse blanket which she gently placed over her. Then she pulled her mobile out of her pocket, and ignoring Miriam's protests, called an ambulance. Then she sat with her as they waited.

'I'm so sorry about this, Lizzie,' Miriam gasped, closing her eyes in pain.

'Sssh,' said Lizzie quietly. 'You mustn't worry. Everything will be taken care of.'

After she'd been rushed off to hospital, suddenly it seemed very quiet. Then a cow bellowed, and Sid and Johnny started to bray. It hit Lizzie. She'd thrown hay in mangers many times but what about everything else?

Fortunately, Ally, the girl who'd alerted Lizzie in the first place, had been helping Miriam for years and together they brought the ponies in from the fields, put hay down for the goats and sheep and fed the dogs and chickens. It was dark by the time they finished and Lizzie was astounded at how long it had taken. Then the welcome sight of the lights from Tim's Land Rover appeared, and his voice called across the yard.

'Lizzie? Everything all right?'

'No! Oh, Tim, it's Miriam! They've taken her to hospital. She's in a terrible way. Ally's helped me feed everything, but I'm going to the hospital now to see her. And there's all this to look after tomorrow...'

Hearing the panic in her voice, Tim took her arm. 'Look, it'll be fine. As long as the animals have hay and water, they'll survive. Ally? Can you ring around and see if you can drum up an extra helper or two for tomorrow? And I'll get on to Antonia – maybe she and Cassie will come over. And let me know what you find out about Miriam, will you?'

* * *

Lizzie drove towards the hospital, only slightly reassured by Tim's words. What if Miriam ended up staying in for days? Or weeks? Or never came home at all? Then, getting a grip, she stopped herself. Somehow or other, they'd manage.

If the approach of Christmas was difficult, wandering the corridors of the hospital brought back altogether more painful memories. Of pushing her mother in a wheelchair, waiting for the results of her latest scan, hearing their worst fears voiced by the consultant... Lizzie shook them from her mind.

Eventually locating A & E, she enquired about Miriam, and after a short wait someone showed her through. Miriam was lying in a cubicle, looking only marginally more comfortable than earlier, with a nurse who was taking her blood pressure.

'Lizzie,' she rasped, trying to sit up. 'I'm so worried about the farm...'

'Don't worry, everything's fine,' Lizzie reassured her. 'Between us, we fed everyone. But do they know what's wrong?'

Miriam sighed. 'They think it could be an ulcer. They're about to do some tests...'

Just then a doctor appeared. 'Mrs Kirby? I'm Dr Ruskin. We're taking you through now.' He looked at Lizzie. 'Are you family?'

'It's fine,' said Miriam in a whisper. 'You can tell her.'

'Well, we think you have a perforated ulcer. How long have you been in pain?'

'Not long,' said Miriam, just as Lizzie said 'Weeks.'

The doctor raised an eyebrow. 'No time to lose then.'

* * *

And so it was just as she'd wished for. A Christmas unlike any other. The show of help to look after the farm was staggering. Not only from Tim and Antonia and Cassie, but Ally had rallied an army of helpers and Miriam's eldest son had turned up. Miriam was recovering from surgery and no one knew when she'd be home, but meanwhile there were more than enough volunteers to cover everything. Her main concern was Boxing Day, which she anxiously told Lizzie that night, was one of their most popular times.

'Can you put a notice up?' she asked her. 'Just explaining that we've had to close due to unforeseen circumstances, and will be open as soon as possible.'

15

On Christmas Eve, they all crowded into the little church for midnight carols, trying not to giggle at Mrs Hepplewhite's truly dreadful renditions on the organ, which was almost impossible after the mulled wine they'd consumed after the evening feeds at Hethecote. Cassie even dragged her favourite dog in, at which no one batted an eyelid. Pete was there, of course, bellowing surprisingly tunefully at the back, and Toby had squeezed in at the end of their pew, so that he could get up easily to do a reading. Eucalyptus skulked in the shadows, ready for a spot of bell ringing as the service came to an end and everyone trooped back out again into the cold with cries of 'Happy Christmas' and 'Who's got the hip flask?' It was all jolly festive.

For just a brief moment, amongst the crowd Lizzie caught a glimpse of *him*. It was that fair hair, she was sure of it... but once again, he'd vanished. She told herself she was seeing things. What would someone like him would be doing here, in Littleton of all places, on Christmas Eve...

Later that morning, the other side of a few hours' sleep, Lizzie had collected a sleepy Cassie and they'd headed up to Miriam's again complete with an enormous bag of carrots – a Christmas present for the animals. Then with stables mucked out and all the hungry mouths fed, they returned to Antonia's to drink a toast with glasses of the most potent eggnog.

It was certainly the most eclectic Christmas gathering Lizzie had ever been part of. And with all the usual dramas... Everyone ate too much and drank too much. Eucalyptus, her straggly hair scraped into a bun and her tall, angular frame draped in black taffeta that had clearly seen better days, brought a very strange-looking Christmas cake with her, which everyone ate regardless. Wafting around looking rather vacant, over the course of the day she sank an entire bottle of sherry after which she became quite weepy, inflicting the tale of her doomed exhibition on one and all.

A captivated Toby leaped around attentively after Antonia, at her beck and call. Willingly, he topped up empty glasses and handed round full ones. Having made a sterling job of carving an oversize turkey, Antonia muttering about how it should have been a lamb and a Welsh black one at that, he lit the Christmas pudding with aplomb, singeing his eyebrows and nearly setting fire to the holly hanging decoratively from the beams. Undeterred and leaping up when Antonia yelled, 'Fucking dog's thrown up,' he finished the day keener than ever.

Cassie meanwhile happily unwrapped the heaps of presents that everyone had bought for her. Lizzie had bought her a make-up set and some perfume, and Eucalyptus had knitted her a fluffy pink scarf with silver threads in. Her grandparents had also come up trumps much to Antonia's annoyance, giving her vouchers from a well-known high street store instead of the new saddle that her mother had been counting on. Even Toby had bought her a CD. Cassie, clearly lacking in all things girlish, delighted in each one of them, her mother having bought her yet another pair of jodhpurs. They were even joined by a Christmas Dave – which for once Antonia allowed – complete with baubles hanging from his horns.

Later, collapsed by the roaring fire, after a riotous game of charades in which poor Eucalyptus had entertained everyone far more than she realised with her atrocious acting skills, it was with a sense of relief that Lizzie mentally ticked another box, at another milestone endured. Christmas on her own... and actually, she hadn't endured it at all. She'd really enjoyed it.

It was a cold, clear evening, with a million stars twinkling above and the ground already crisp underfoot. Lizzie had a warm, fuzzy feeling as she wandered up the lane, as much a result of the last sloe gin as the camaraderie of the party. She was carrying the presents she'd been given – a woolly hat from Antonia, chocolates from Cassie and a tiny framed painting from Eucalyptus which Lizzie had to admit she wasn't keen on, but she'd been greatly touched by the gesture.

As Lizzie unlocked her back door, she jumped as something shot inside in front of her and yowled. And as she switched the lights on, the ghost of Christmas past caught up with her. There, on her answerphone was a message from the last person in the world she wanted to hear from.

'Eliza? It's me, Jamie.' Silence. 'Er, Happy Christmas.' More silence. 'Wondered how you were. Thought I'd see if you'd like to go out for lunch tomorrow. I'll call you back.'

Lizzie was in shock. After all these months, she'd assumed that was it. She'd have to put him off. Tell him she was already busy, which she was – up at Hethecote. But a small part of her hesitated. It would be so... so *satisfying* to show him that she was fine, just fine, without him. She crossed her fingers. Maybe he wouldn't ring back.

But he did.

'Eliza? I thought it would be civil to wish you a Happy Christmas,' he said stiffly.

'Jamie? Oh God. I don't know what to say.'

'Maybe an apology would be a good start?' he suggested haughtily.

'Oh, yes, of course... oh, I am sorry, Jamie. About how I left. It wasn't the right way to do it, but at the time...'

'Yes, yes,' he said impatiently. 'I'm well aware that you didn't want to marry me. You don't have to spell it out. You left some things behind. Those suits of yours. Quite expensive they were. Thought you'd want them. I could bring them over if you like.'

There was a silence. No way did she want those suits. But Jamie as always bulldozed right over her, and she found herself lapsing into her old ways.

'Thank you...'

Before she knew it, she'd agreed to go out for dinner with him, but even as she put the phone down, Lizzie was regretting it.

* * *

Next morning, as she drove over to Hethecote, she still was. She'd been going to talk to Antonia about it, but when she arrived, the notice she'd drafted had been taken down and a large crowd of Miriam's helpers had gathered.

'We've decided we're going to open,' said Ally, her eyes shining. 'There's more than enough of us and we all know what we're doing. You don't think Miriam will mind do you?' Slightly anxiously...

'I think she'll be thrilled,' said Lizzie. 'What would you like me to do?'

* * *

The yard was spotless and all the stables pristine when the gates opened at midday. A steady stream of visitors kept arriving and Antonia stood by the gate, welcoming them heartily and collecting the money. Some had obviously been before and were happy to wander around unescorted, while others wanted a tour. Astounded at how the children and animals responded to each other, Lizzie understood why Miriam worked so hard.

She had ended up taking a new family around. The little girl was like a fragile bird with stick-like limbs and stayed mostly in her wheelchair, her head leaning to one side. The mother had been dismissive right from the start, looking at her watch and pointedly avoiding any contact the animals. It was the father who'd helped his daughter out of her chair, leading her slowly by the hand towards one of the ponies.

Lizzie had watched how Hairy Mary, an elderly Shetland pony, had turned and studied the child with the wisest kindest eyes, before reaching out and gently nuzzling her and the expression of joy on the girl's face would be etched on Lizzie's mind forever. It was the smallest, simplest gesture yet priceless. Even the mother had been won round by the little pony, her earlier impatience vanishing as they huddled closely, stroking her.

Antonia came and found her later, leaning over the door to the donkeys' stable.

'Got to hand it to her! Miriam's a marvel... She's really onto something with this animal thing. Can't wait to get cracking on that ball... I was thinking September – what do you think?' Then looking at Sid and Johnny added, 'Those two are ghastly, aren't they? Why the devil doesn't she shoot them?'

A day Lizzie would remember always was nearly over. It had been a huge success and they'd taken a record amount in donations. Miriam's son was off to the hospital to report back to his mother. It was like popping a balloon when she remembered the evening that lay ahead of her.

There was nothing for it at this late stage but to steel herself and, rebelliously, Lizzie washed off the smell of the farm and dressed in her new Sparkie's clothes. Just to make a point. This was definitely not a date. They were two mature adults and it was closure. Absolutely nothing more than that.

If Lizzie had only stopped and thought. How far she'd come in such a short time. Offered Jamie a coffee, told him quite reasonably that actually she'd had a busy day and was too dog-tired to go out...

In his shiny shoes and what looked like a new suit, Jamie picked his way carefully up the uneven path to her door looking like a fish out of water and before she knew it, she'd opened the door just as she'd known she would.

He looked just the same, but then what had Lizzie expected? The neatly ironed shirt, that air of tension, that perpetual frown, as if everything constantly fell short of his expectations – nothing had changed.

Except Lizzie clearly had. Her long hair hung in glossy waves and her skin was flushed from a day in the cold air. The faded jeans that fitted her perfectly and printed tunic in shades of soft green and turquoise harked back to the Lizzie of old – pre-Jamie. Not his style at all, but he nevertheless looked twice, with a faint expression of approval even as he bent to kiss her cheek.

'Jamie, I won't offer you a tour. It's not your kind of house at all.' Lizzie spoke firmly. 'But I do know a pub that you *will* like. Shall we?' And pulling on her huge furry coat, she closed the door and walked down the path, leaving him standing behind her with his mouth open. It felt good, Lizzie thought with a thrill, silencing the little voice in her head which was seriously questioning her motives.

Boxing Day at the Old Goat was always going to be impressive, and Jamie wasn't disappointed. He was highly enthusiastic about the locally sourced menu just as she knew he would be, waffling on pretentiously about how rare breeds such as Gloucester Old Spot really did produce extremely superior pork, *blah, blah, blah*. But he wasn't *so* bad, in small doses. Foolishly, she sipped her champagne and started to relax, forgetting entirely that was how the trouble had started in the first place.

So when Jamie ordered more champagne, a particularly expensive vintage, it was only polite to drink some of it, especially when he raised his glass and wished her well with her new life. After her day at the farm, Lizzie was feeling on top of the world, but then suddenly across the crowded restaurant, there he was again. The man.

Hit by the same sense of recognition as before, she looked over to meet his eyes fleetingly, just before he glanced at Jamie and looked away. After that, she sat there not taking in a word that Jamie was saying, not thinking straight at all. When she next looked over, he'd gone.

Why it didn't hit her there and then that she was with the wrong man, Lizzie never knew. After that, they got a taxi back to her cottage – mistake number one. Then Lizzie produced a bottle of sloe gin that she'd bought at the farmers' market in Oakley – her second mistake. Collapsed in the comfy armchairs, with a roaring fire in the hearth, and ignoring Darren's best attempts to warn her as he deliberately stuck his claws into Jamie's thigh and then bit his hand – drawing blood. Half a bottle later, the alcohol had kicked in. Lizzie was definitely muzzy, and her judgement was looking shaky. More than usual, as she tipsily looked at Jamie who suddenly seemed rather attractive. And what was the harm in one little kiss after all those years of living together? *Oh, that was quite a nice kiss*, she thought, her body traitorously responding to his out of pure habit. It was all in the spirit of Christmas wasn't it, the season of goodwill to all men...

She forgot what she disliked about Jamie. That voice of reason that had been whispering at her all evening had finally shut up. Lizzie'd had enough of whispered doubts tonight and had long stopped listening anyway. Going to bed with Jamie seemed like a perfectly reasonable idea and she hadn't protested. It was a long time since she'd felt a warm, naked body against hers and she realised she'd missed it, even though, as always, the earth didn't exactly move. Nice, she thought afterwards, but at last she knew what's wrong! It's an anti-climax, instead of a climax! She giggled to herself at her discovery, just as the room started to spin, her eyes closed and she fell into a drunken sleep.

16

All was quiet as Lizzie lay drowsily in bed the next morning – apart from the sounds of breathing from next to her. As it came to her that, in fact, she wasn't alone, she was instantly awake. A wave of utter dismay engulfed her, as it dawned on her what she'd done.

Leaping out of bed far too quickly, Lizzie's head thumped vengefully. She'd been saving that sloe gin too. For a special occasion. Slowly the events of the previous evening were all too painfully coming back. Oh God. She felt terrible.

Creeping downstairs, she drank two large glasses of water and put the kettle on. Sitting at her table, waiting for what felt like an age for it to boil, she rested her pounding head in her hands. They hadn't, had they? Surely not. But she hadn't drunk quite enough to forget that unfortunately, yes, there was no getting away from it. She was very much afraid they had.

A little while later, there were heavy footsteps on the stairs, and Jamie appeared in the doorway. Sighing, with that familiar frown back in place, Lizzie realised how much he irritated her. Somehow it made it worse.

'It's bloody cold...' he muttered.

'Jamie...' she started, but he put a hand on her shoulder.

'Don't, Eliza,' he said apologetically. 'It was the champagne. I think we both know it was a mistake. It would never work between us. Can we just leave it at that? I should never have come here.'

Relief flooded through Lizzie, but she knew she wasn't blameless. 'Let me make you some coffee before you leave,' she offered, thankful he wasn't going to argue.

'Where did you get that?' he said suddenly, picking up the tiny painting Eucalyptus had given her.

'It's a Christmas present. The artist lives in the village.'

'Very fluid... Rather like an early Kandinsky... Fascinating...' Jamie remarked pretentiously, studying it closely.

This time when they said goodbye, there was a finality in their words. Lizzie stood in silence as Jamie put on his shoes.

'They've got water in,' he said irritably, picking one of them up and disgustedly shaking it out onto the floor. 'Honestly. I only bought them a week ago.'

It was only after he'd gone when Lizzie went to mop it up, she caught the distinctive smell. Darren had left his mark.

Not at all liking the way she was feeling, Lizzie pulled on a fleece and, in need of a distraction, drove slowly up to Hethecote. Seeing that everything there was under control and not feeling very good company, she drove home again and went to dig her vegetable garden, but the bitter, damp cold did nothing to purge what remained in her head of last night. On this occasion, she didn't need anyone else to tell her she'd made a mistake. It hung over her like a black cloud and swamped her. Since moving here, she hadn't had a good word to say about him and yet she'd just had sex with him. What did that make her? *Tart, slut, easy lay...* She tortured herself with the words, refusing to entertain anything to the contrary – that she was none of those things, of course she wasn't. Yes, she was vulnerable still, more than she realised perhaps, and a little confused, most definitely. But she'd made a mistake, nothing more, nothing less.

Lizzie hid away, kept herself to herself, until a few days later, there was another celebration as she, Katie and Antonia joined the merry crowd at the Old Goat to see in the New Year. Still reeling slightly from the night with Jamie, Lizzie was coming to terms with the realisation that she still had a way to go. All it had taken was Christmas, closely followed by Jamie who'd timed his visit to perfection, and she was still as vulnerable as ever. Throw in the alcohol... It could have been much worse, she kept telling herself, struggling to imagine how.

Katie had been astounded to hear that Jamie had been here. She'd guessed immediately that there was something she wasn't telling.

'Lizzie... are you absolutely positively sure that there's nothing else I should know?' she'd demanded.

The silence had said it all. Lizzie cursed the way that Katie could always tell. Silly to imagine she could hide it.

'Oh Lizzie...' Katie was for once, dumbfounded.

As had been Antonia, who'd just stared at her appalled. 'But, Lizzie. Thought you couldn't stand him. What made you change your mind?'

So having thoroughly confounded her friends, this evening she kept a low profile. Amid the frivolity and shenanigans at the Goat, Lizzie quietly sipped her one glass of wine, for this, she'd decided, was her penance. Staying sober and very much in the background, she watched as everyone else threw themselves into the party. Katie and Antonia were by now having a whale of a time, sharing another bottle of wine magicked up by an ever-attentive Toby, and dancing flamboyantly to the cheesy music being belted out by Dickie the DJ, with his shirt open to the waist and his dated collection of seventies hits from the Bee Gees and Donna Summer.

Eucalyptus was there, jollier than Lizzie had ever seen her, with a much younger, very handsome man in tow. Antonia informed them that his name was Mac. The drummer had been given the boot and Cassie fancied him like mad. Lizzie could quite see why... Mac was lean, mean and very handsome, with dark eyes and thick brown hair, and about the same height as the lofty Eucalyptus. Poor Cassie. It seemed she'd set her heart on Euc's toy boy.

'He's wasted on her,' muttered Antonia disparagingly in Lizzie's ear. 'Fine young specimen like that hooked up with a lanky old fossil like Euc... Oh golly, more champers... how lovely, darling! Oh, we *must* dance to this!' she added, whisking Toby away to the mellow sounds of the Little River Band's 'Reminiscing'.

Pete was there, actually enjoying himself for once, smiling broadly at everyone in his best beer goggles, and Bert and Molly came early and wisely left early, before the party got too rowdy.

Tim, on a rare reprieve from his duties, also joined the fray – quickly homing in on a delighted Katie. Then Darius and Angel arrived together, recently returned and most prettily tanned from a fabulous skiing holiday in St Anton, glammed to the nines and ready to party.

'Darling wallflower,' said Angel theatrically, kissing Lizzie, when he discovered her hiding in a corner. He smelt wonderful. 'Why aren't you strutting your stuff with the other tarts?'

'Oh, Angel, if I told you you'd never believe me,' Lizzie said sorrowfully, just about to divulge all, when he leaped up. 'Darling, I'll be right back. Now don't go anywhere...'

She sat there and watched, part of it and yet... Tonight she wasn't – not really. It was just after eleven when she left the merry crowd and slipped quietly out of the side door. But as if she didn't have enough on her mind, fate had a final shocker for her and timed to split-second perfection, Lizzie collided with her mystery man. He stood there, holding the door for her.

'Leaving so soon?' he asked, an unreadable look on his face.

She nodded, feeling that pounding in her chest again, wishing she knew what to say. But wit and humour had deserted her tonight and all she wanted was to escape.

But he stood, not quite letting her past. 'I saw you in here on Boxing Day.'

'I was with a... a friend... I have to go,' she said frantically instead.

'Happy New Year.' He looked at her uncertainly.

'Thanks.' Then she added, 'Um, you too,' and smiled a small smile, before running out into the dark.

* * *

Lizzie counted away the last minutes of the year with a mug of hot chocolate and her cat, minutes that ticked slowly by as she sat alone watching the flicker of flames in the hearth. A year that had been good in so many ways now seemed less so, and who knew what the coming one would hold. Certainly no drunken flings with frowning ex-boyfriends. But as midnight approached, Darren stood up and paced around, then yowled at her and the air filled with a strange sense of expectancy.

17

The festive season was soon over, much to Lizzie's relief. Her mood was still low and the night with Jamie still hung over her completely out of proportion.

It was good to be engrossed in work again too, even though the weather stayed cold and bleak for the rest of the month. Lizzie kept busy nonetheless, spending as much time as she could up at Hethecote Farm, which went some way to restoring her sense of self-belief, as she tried desperately to bury the Jamie episode for good.

Miriam had discharged herself from hospital, though was having to take it easy, and was enormously grateful to all her extra helpers who were continuing to bear the brunt of the work needed to keep the farm running smoothly.

'You should go home,' said Miriam one morning, seeing Lizzie's pinched face and blue hands, as she mucked out one of the donkeys.

'But you still need my help,' protested Lizzie. 'And I haven't finished Sid's...'

Miriam stood leaning over the door. 'Whatever it is, it can't be that bad,' she said gently.

Lizzie stopped what she was doing and stared at the straw. 'It is,' she mumbled. 'It honestly, truly is...'

Miriam was quiet for a moment. 'You know, you can tell me if it would help... Not much surprises me... You've been through such a lot...'

Lizzie had told her about losing her mother. 'I'm fine, really – it's just... sometimes it just comes back and hits me out of nowhere. I can be busy doing something else, and then when I remember, it still shocks me... like it's just happened...' Once she'd started, the words tumbled out.

'I know what you mean...' A look Lizzie hadn't seen before crossed Miriam's face. 'I think it just takes time... Much longer than you might expect it to. But it does get easier, if it's any help to know that.'

Lizzie looked at her. 'I did something stupid and now I feel like an idiot. It's my fault, I can't blame it on grief or anyone else. And I really don't like what I did.'

'Oh Lizzie... Well, if it's any consolation, I've made mistakes too. Huge ones, especially after Andrew died. I was a mess – honestly. Couldn't see straight about anything. My poor children... You wouldn't believe the decisions I made. We all do it, you know. You shouldn't be so hard on yourself.'

* * *

But aside from the feeling that she'd let herself down, worst of all was that her shiny new life seemed tarnished, her weakness illuminated with frightening clarity.

Lizzie started running again, punishing herself, running further than usual whatever the weather, her trainers sodden and fingers blue, her legs plastered in mud. All this to prove to herself that she had a shred of self-discipline. And then one day, a while later, she woke up and understood. Miriam was right and she'd simply made a mistake, no more, no less. And it was time to put it behind her.

* * *

The next few weeks passed uneventfully. Antonia was busy with her horses. She'd taken in a couple of liveries and was out hunting every daylight hour, Cassie too when school permitted. She was also still helping at Hethecote, much to Lizzie's surprise.

'Well, poor old Miriam can't do it all. And you know, darling, she does need someone to ride that hunter of hers…'

Katie hadn't been to stay since the New Year, though she'd let slip that Tim had been up to London. Once or twice… Lizzie tried to picture him there in his Land Rover, dining in the kind of restaurants that Katie went to – and failed, wondering instead who was looking after his sheep.

Like the surrounding countryside, the village itself seemed dormant, and Lizzie threw herself into her work. Then, deciding she needed some company, she invited herself to brunch with Darius and Angel and planned to pay a long overdue visit to Sparkie's.

'Come late,' Nola had said mysteriously. 'We'll close up and have some time to chat. Anyway, we've added something and you're the perfect person to show it to.'

It was one of those dreary Saturdays that Lizzie finally got there – a grey one where the sun never showed, the temperature barely lifting. The shops were quiet after the usual madness of the sales and the bell gave its familiar tinkle as she opened the door and went in.

'Lizzie!' Julia kissed her on both cheeks and took her hand. 'oh,

I'm so glad you've come! Here – come and see what we've been working on. You wouldn't believe how quiet it's been, but we've been busy, so busy... Look!'

She led Lizzie through a door into a small room Lizzie hadn't seen before, where Nola was halfway up a ladder finishing the last letter of the words she was painting on the wall – '*so may it be...*'

'What's that?' Lizzie stared at the entire sentence, trying to grasp its meaning.

'*May the circle be open and never unbroken, so may it be...*'

'Oh, Lizzie! Come and sit down. Let me explain...'

There were armchairs and a sofa with cushions in warm shades of pink and lilac. On the windowsill were candles, one of which had just been blown out, with an odd-shaped stone and a single rose in a bottle. The lighting was soft and the walls muted shades with the faintest silhouettes of trees painted on them. It was like sitting in the middle of a forest. Lizzie sank into one of the armchairs, opposite a large curtained area with spotlights and mirrors.

'To those who know, it's a sign,' said Nola, slightly hesitantly, 'and to those who don't... You do know, don't you, that many of our customers come in here searching for far more than just clothes. Something more elusive – like an identity... Clothes make a huge difference, of course, but that's only part of it.'

'Do you remember,' added Julia gently, 'the first time you came in here? You were looking around for ages, and in the end we helped you choose things. How did you feel when you left?' she asked anxiously.

Nola took her hand.

'Fantastic,' Lizzie answered honestly. 'Because you found things I'd never have chosen and they were wonderful to wear. Not one of them was a mistake.'

'But it didn't solve everything, did it, Lizzie?' said Nola gently.

Lizzie looked at them, wondering what they were getting at.

'There was an emptiness in you. A sadness – something that needed to heal...'

A flabbergasted Lizzie just gasped. That sentence described exactly how she'd felt.

'You see,' said Nola slowly, 'we can help with more than just the right clothes. So many people who come in here are lost.'

'We just thought,' said Julia, looking at Nola uncertainly, 'that if we could give them *something* just from being in here, they could go away changed. Renewed, if you like.'

Lizzie frowned. She couldn't see what they were getting at.

Nola took a deep breath and took one of Lizzie's hands. 'Everything is about consciousness, Lizzie. It interacts with the energy of the universe. All most people want to do is live in love and joy...'

'...in perfect love and perfect trust,' added Julia mysteriously, almost as if part of a ritual.

They both looked at her. Julia took her other hand, then Nola's and closed her eyes.

'It's just that they've forgotten *how*...'

It didn't make sense. What was all this holding hands and 'energy of the universe'? It sounded like some new age poppycock, but Lizzie knew Nola and Julia well enough to believe they had their reasons.

'What's really going on in your life, Lizzie,' said Nola so quietly, 'goes way beyond what you can see...'

But discomfited though she was, as Lizzie sat there listening to them, imagining shadows flickering on the walls and hearing the sound of the river outside, there seemed an odd sort of resonance to their words.

* * *

January passed, then most of February. Lizzie spent long, grey days at her desk when the weather was at its worst, working on her design for Ginny and Edward. Then a weak March sun reappeared, and after hibernating since the New Year, the village slowly stirred back into life. And as it awakened, Lizzie felt something in her awaken too, as Nola's words came back to her. As she watched the smallest buds miraculously appear on the trees and daffodil bulbs poke their brave shoots through the chilled earth, she had to concede that perhaps there really was something in this energy of the universe hokum.

Eucalyptus, an unlikely vision in floaty dark grey, was fleetingly seen as she flitted up to the church by dusk, a diaphanous ghost on a mission to free the bells. Wednesday evenings were well known throughout the village, as it prepared to be subjected to the pealing cacophony that was the amateur bell ringers club. Quiz night restarted at the Star, and after barely ticking over since Christmas, the WI were back in full force, discussing recipes or listening to Betty's account of her lunch party, or whatever it was that they did over there.

And Antonia too re-emerged from all that hunting, bouncing down the lane on a very much larger-than-life Hamish, breathing smoke through his nostrils like a dragon.

Having started running, Lizzie was determined to keep it up, venturing further through the fields as the days grew longer. The ground still squelched underfoot in places, and flocks of massively expectant sheep patiently awaited the arrival of their unborn offspring. It was in one of these fields that she stumbled across Tim in muddy wellies and overalls, on his knees with a stricken ewe.

He nodded. 'Hi, Lizzie. Sorry, bit busy here. She's got the third one stuck...'

Fascinated and horrified at the same time, Lizzie found herself transfixed as the stuck lamb slowly emerged. 'Three?' she asked. 'I thought they only had one or two...'

The farmer who had the ewe in a stronghold, nodded at her.

'Blinking nuisance it is. Means he'll be bottle fed if he makes it at all. Already got half a dozen of 'em in the kitchen.' Glumly, he added, 'Like a blinking stable it is. Bloomin' stinks. Wife won't be too happy to have another. Really don't think I can take this one back too...'

The farmer and Tim exchanged glances.

Lizzie, who had always imagined lambs coming into the world in cosy barns onto a soft bed of clean straw, couldn't bear this unceremonious arrival into the wet mud, only to be unwanted.

'Want me to take it, Brian?' Tim asked the farmer.

'Aye. Got no use for it. And you may as well be off, lad. Don't think there's much more action round here tonight.'

Meaning the farmer didn't want to be billed for another second longer than was necessary. Holding the little creature under his arm, Tim looked over at Lizzie. 'Want a lift?'

To start with they walked in silence, but Lizzie absolutely had to ask that burning question, about the fate of unwanted third-born baby lambs, such as this one. It was tiny and so weak, and was making the most heart-rending bleating sounds.

Tim sighed, as he tucked the little creature into a blanket in the back.

'I'll probably end up keeping it with mine if it survives,' he said. 'Though in the interest of maintaining professional appearances, I try to keep this sort of thing quiet. The farmers would never look at me the same way again if they knew. All my sheep were unwanted of course. Acquired just like this one. It's how Cassie came to have Dave...' He raised his eyebrows. 'Farmers would think I was mad.'

And then Lizzie had a brainwave.

'Do you think Antonia would let Cassie have another?'

* * *

That Saturday, Katie had driven down again, quite possibly to do with Tim being up to his elbows in lambing, Lizzie suspected, and Antonia too had popped in en route to meeting Toby for another night of unbridled passion. The cottage was filled with the smell of the soup simmering on the cooker and a half drunk bottle of wine was on the side. Topping up Antonia's glass to the very top and waiting until she'd drunk at least half of it, Lizzie took the bull by the horns.

'Don't you think, Antonia, that Dave would be so much happier if he had another little sheep keeping him company?' she started.

'Have you been talking to Tim?' she enquired. 'Only strangely enough, he asked me the exact same thing. So there's another orphan going is there?'

'It's tiny. Tim's got it at the moment, but Cassie could raise it to live with Dave. You've got plenty of room out there... and it might keep Dave outside,' she added persuasively.

Antonia snorted. 'More likely I'll end up with two of the damn things in the kitchen. I'll think about it. Anyway, could we go please? Tobes probably got there yonks ago.'

Fully reinstated back in the heart of her friends again, Lizzie felt gathered back in to the fold. She'd punished herself enough. Toby was eagerly waiting at the Goat, as besotted as ever with Antonia and hanging on her every word. Tim joined them a little later. Finally under pressure from all sides and after several large glasses of wine, Antonia had caved in and agreed to take the lamb, and Katie and Tim were soon head to head deep in conversation. Everything seemed just as it was meant to be.

But Lizzie's feeling of quiet complacency was extremely short lived. Jumping to her feet, she only just made it to the ladies' before she was violently sick.

18

Dragged out by Katie to Rumbleford the next morning, Lizzie was still feeling wobbly. They wandered around some of the junk shops before stopping for brunch at a café overlooking the river. The usual picturesque stream had become a raging torrent after all the rain, bearing branches and all sorts along with it.

As they waited for the bacon sandwiches they'd ordered, Katie sat back and drank her coffee, and then said something quite unexpected.

'You know, I really could live somewhere like this! It's civilised enough that you can go out for breakfast on a Sunday, like we are, but still feels peaceful somehow. A million miles from London...'

Lizzie felt a smile creep across her face. 'But, Katie... you're a born and bred city girl... you wear black and high heels and go out for sushi and to the theatre...' she teased.

Katie grinned. 'I know! Okay. I really like him,' she said, slightly sheepishly. 'But don't go getting any ideas. It's not as though it's been that long. But... well...' Her brown eyes laughed back at Lizzie. 'You never know...'

Later on, as Lizzie waved Katie off outside her cottage, an unfamiliar sports car came speeding past. One of the occupants raised a hand, but with the sun reflecting brightly off the windows, Lizzie missed it. As she turned to go inside she heard it slow, but as she glanced back towards the lane, the car had driven off.

That evening, Lizzie hung her latest bargain, a big, old, white-framed mirror that she'd found that morning in Rumbleford, on her bathroom wall. It was exactly what she'd been looking for, its battered-looking frame perfect for the cottage. But catching sight of herself in it, she frowned at the weight she'd put on. And that night, she was further perplexed when, catching sight of her naked reflection, she noticed a pattern of prominent blue veins snaking across her boobs. The next morning as she dressed, suddenly out of nowhere, Lizzie realised. She hadn't had a period in ages.

Her heart was in her mouth and her legs turned to jelly as the thought sank in, because if she *was*, only one person could possibly be the father. The last person on earth she'd want a baby with. Jamie...

Lizzie scrabbled dizzily through her diary looking for the last little circle she always noted it with, feeling sicker and sicker as she searched. Lizzie thought about the sickness, and how hungry she felt, and she'd definitely put on weight... And all since that night with Jamie. Eventually she found the tiny circle – three months ago back in December.

One of the downsides of living in a small village is that word travels extremely fast, and Lizzie knew that if she went to buy a pregnancy test within a radius of about five miles, the village would know the results before she did. For now, she didn't want anyone to know, so she drove the ten miles to Pratt's Bottom, where she didn't know a soul, and slunk self-consciously into Boots with her collar pulled up, after a quick scout around for familiar faces. Afterwards, Lizzie couldn't recall the drive home, only sitting on the loo gazing at the blue line which confirmed the answer she'd been dreading.

* * *

Antonia was speechless when she found out, the only time Lizzie had known it happen. Sitting in her kitchen, absent-mindedly she poured Tropicana into her tea instead of milk, eventually managing ,'Good Lord. Thought you'd just got fatter. Won't ask how that happened.'

And in her next breath, faintly disapprovingly, 'Your ex I assume?'

And then Lizzie had to tell Katie.

'Oh, *Lizzie*... what are you going to do?'

'Please, Katie, please do *not* tell Jamie,' she begged. 'I really don't want him to know. Okay?'

But from there on, it wasn't long before she was getting knowing nods from Pete, and Bert, and the entire village somehow knew. Mrs Hepplewhite gave her a ferocious stare and 'hmmphed' most disapprovingly. But one person who took the whole thing in her stride was Cassie, who seemed to think it was cool.

'Are you religious?' she asked inquisitively, twisting a lock of her long red hair, 'because I had this idea. You see, I thought I could arrange like a naming ceremony in your garden, with a cake and everything. We could get Eucalyptus to make one, or I could make a Victoria sandwich... And I could put flowers and fairy lights everywhere...'

'And then...' Cassie twirled around in her jodhpurs '... we could have music and dancing. I know what I'm doing, you don't have to worry. I've organised loads of these for the dogs.'

Aware that things had spiralled out of control again and altogether in rather a daze, Lizzie carried on working, not able to think as far ahead to how she would manage when the baby was born. The thought was completely terrifying. Overwhelmed by the idea that there was a tiny bunch of cells multiplying inside her, growing into what would become a whole separate person, she was struggling to get her head round this at all.

'I've got a few things put away,' said Antonia. 'They were Cassie's, but you might as well have them. I can't imagine I'll get round to having another,' adding rather pointedly, 'I mean, there are hardly any suitable men round here, are there?'

She'd produced a bag full of tiny outfits, but try as she did, Lizzie couldn't feel the slightest bit maternal. She'd barely adjusted to her new life, and here it was changing again, scarily beyond recognition.

'I'm sure you'll cope wonderfully,' said Miriam gently. 'It's a shock, though, isn't it? I couldn't imagine being a mother until I actually *was* one. Then all of a sudden, you forget what it was like before.'

'That's exactly how I feel!' said Lizzie. 'I just can't imagine it at all...'

'It's hard work,' said Miriam. 'Especially on your own. All the time mine were home I never had a moment, but now... I miss them terribly.'

* * *

It was true that she was still becoming used to the idea of being a mother, and a single one at that, when Lizzie felt a familiar warm wetness between her legs. Which rapidly became a flood. And in the blink of an eye, a whole mishmash of emotions hit her before she consciously and quite calmly registered that in fact what was happening must be a miscarriage. And all her fragile dreams that had barely begun, melted into nothing.

Antonia and Katie between them stayed with her, feeding her, cocooning her and wrapping her in their love. But Lizzie was far from distraught, just numb. Unable to feel a thing, until suddenly, hating that her poor lost baby would have had a father that didn't really care, who wouldn't really have wanted it even, then that made her cry. And then part of her felt relieved, which made her feel guilty and then she cried even harder.

Angel called in to see her, and sat with her, mopping his own tears as well as Lizzie's.

'You'd have been the most perfect mother ever,' he said emotionally, making her cry yet again. 'But I'll tell you what, sweetie, one day I just *know* you will be...'

Nola brought her a present, which was uncalled for as her presence alone was enough, exuding the quiet strength that calmed Lizzie deep inside.

'Clear quartz,' she explained, her green eyes serious, 'to heal your soul, and realign your energy with the universe.' She looked earnestly at Lizzie. 'It will help you in many more ways too... It was just one of those things you know,' she added sympathetically. 'You do know that don't you, Lizzie? That it just wasn't meant to be.'

Lizzie believed her utterly. From that point she suddenly stopped feeling sorry for herself, and unwrapping the blankets, got up to make some tea.

* * *

Cassie's planned naming ceremony on a beautiful summer day with the first of the roses coming into bloom, became a bittersweet tribute to a soul yet to be born, shared as it was with an eclectic little group made up of Antonia, Katie and Cassie of course, but also Eucalyptus, draped head to toe in funereal black, complete with hanky which she sniffed noisily into, dear Bert who'd even put on a tie for the occasion, and Nola, who had quietly crept in and stood slightly apart from the others.

As Cassie read a poem and threw handfuls of rose petals into

the wind, in the background Lizzie could hear her mum's voice –
clearer than she would have believed possible, all but feeling the
familiar arms round her as she echoed Nola's words, telling her
that yes, it was *so terribly* sad wasn't it, but some things just aren't
meant to be.

19

But in the way that it always does, life went on. Though she knew she'd always think about the miscarriage as the baby that she never knew, Lizzie also knew it would do no good to wallow in it and she was trying to keep herself busy. She looked at her watch – already it was later than she'd thought. Pete was due round at nine to examine her kitchen window. It looked unquestionably terminal to Lizzie, but nothing had changed and it would probably take a year to get it replaced. Toby showed no signs of putting as much boundless energy into galvanising his workforce into action as he did into his sex life. Seriously distracted and as besotted with Antonia as ever, still nothing happened in a hurry.

As she buttered herself a slice of brown toast, Pete did indeed arrive, his sad eyes brightening at the sight of a cup of coffee, which as always he drank slowly, putting off the moment he might have to actually do something.

'What you need's a few 'ens,' he said suddenly after a while. 'Me and the missus, reckon we've got an old coop you could 'ave. Know that farm t'other side of Oakley? They sells off their 'ens after a laying season, only 50p. I allus gets a few for the freezer. Not pretty they're not, mind. Bin kept in a batt'ry.' He shook his head and took another swig of coffee. 'But feed 'em well and they'll come good. Keep you in eggs most of the year,' he added through a mouth full.

'Oh, Pete, I'd love some.' Lizzie meant it. There was plenty of space behind the cottage, and romantically she pictured fluffy, gently clucking birds laying their warm brown eggs in a nest of hay. The generosity of the villagers could be quite heart-warming.

Pete drained his cup, looking hopefully into it as if waiting for it to magically refill. Realising no more would be forthcoming, he cleared his throat.

"Bout that window,' he said, a touch indignantly. 'Freed it myself I did, only two winters ago,' as he looked at Lizzie slightly accusingly. 'Can't understand it. Better 'ave a look, I s'pose.'

'Well,' he reflected, quite sorrowfully after trying and failing to lever it shut, 's'pose it'll have to be replaced then. Best I go back to the office, sees what they want to do. I'll have to get back to you.'

As she waved him off, Lizzie didn't get her hopes up. But, today it didn't matter. All the windows were thrown open anyway, filling the cottage with the wonderful scents of honeysuckle and newly cut hay in the fields.

Making more coffee, Lizzie started to think about how she was going to talk Ginny out of her pink garden. And tonight, she and Antonia were going out. Tim's long overdue locum had at last turned up. Antonia had already met him and unusually for her had blushed bright pink, describing him as jolly hot totty, which had rather put Lizzie off, having seen Antonia's taste in men.

* * *

Driving back from her meeting with Ginny, Lizzie's mind was on anything but the road ahead of her. It didn't look as though she was going to sway Ginny from her vision of pure pink. Lizzie had produced two sketches, one based purely on pink, with mop-head hydrangeas, roses, phlox, delphiniums and so on. Ginny had loved it, her heavily mascara'd eyes glittering unnaturally as she'd rubbed her hands in glee. Then Lizzie had shown her the second, still with the pink flowers, but set amid a background with some white and purples here and there, and which looked so much more subtle and classy, but Ginny hadn't been convinced.

'You see, Lizzie – oh dear, it's just not really *pink*...'

In the end, Lizzie had left her promising to think about it. Narrowly missing a pheasant as she swerved to avoid it, she made it home with only twenty minutes to spare before Antonia was due.

* * *

Looking astonishingly unhorsy for once in a wrap-around dress and make-up, Antonia was early. There was even a waft of Chanel No. 5 instead of the usual eau de muck heap. This Leo must really be something.

'Don't tell me you're going out like that?' Antonia asked with her usual bluntness. 'Bit scruffy for dinner, isn't it?'

Lizzie's skin prickled. 'Antonia, this is *me*, just like you normally wear jodhpurs.'

Besides which Lizzie loved her tie-dye tunic and faded jeans. Sparkie's finest, no less. 'Shall we go?'

At the Goat, the table Tim had reserved was unoccupied, which came as no surprise, vets being notoriously bad at timekeeping.

'Red or white?' asked Antonia. 'We'll start a tab. And I've simply got to tell you. Remember Euc's toy boy? Well... Now, don't spread it around, but rumour has it that Mac's her son! Seems she had a love affair with a complete bastard about twenty years ago, and Mac was the result! Cassie's thrilled! Never got over it, I suppose, knowing poor old Euc. Frightfully fragile... Obviously put her off for life!

Golly! Come to think of it, I don't think I've seen her with a man even once...'

But the gossip was interrupted with the arrival of Tim and with him one of the sexiest men Lizzie had ever clamped eyes on. It wasn't just that he was tall and muscular, with the thickest mop of dark hair. That was just the wrapping. This man oozed sex appeal from every pore of his tanned skin. Every slight movement he made, whether the blinking of an eye, a self-deprecating shrug, or that calculated playful smile, had her hormones buzzing like she'd never known possible.

'Lizzie, I'd like you to meet Leo! He's here for a few months I hope, seeing as the practice has me working all hours of the day and night. Leo, I think you've already met Antonia?'

Antonia giggled coyly and batted her eyelashes, which on her looked faintly ridiculous.

'Lizzie! A beautiful name for a beautiful girl,' said Leo smoothly, dazzling her with a full wattage, heart-melting smile.

Lizzie spluttered the mouthful of wine she'd just taken all over him.

'Sorry,' she choked. Was he for real?

'No worries,' he said amiably. 'You okay? Sounds like you've a bit of a cough going on...'

'Fine, I'm fine...' She composed herself.

Never one to miss an opportunity, Antonia turned to Tim as he came and sat own to join them.

'Darling, about that blasted lamb. Bally thing keeps trying to hump me every time I go outside. Think you'll have to take his balls off after all. Personally, I think we should just eat him, but I don't suppose Cassie will allow it,' she finished, looking rather dolefully at him.

'Orphan lamb?' asked Leo, with a knowing look. 'Thought so... Cassie, did you say?' he added with interest.

'Far too young for you, darling!' said Antonia sharply.

'Don't worry, I'll sort him out,' said Tim. 'Leo will help me, won't you, mate? Now let's order – I'm famished. Er, roast lamb all round everyone?'

Leo was highly entertaining, full of stories about his last job and how he had to leave because his boss's wife had a crush on him. He clearly enjoyed the attention he was getting and Lizzie soon realised that the self-effacing manner he assumed was all part of a well-honed act.

'Honest,' he'd said, holding his hands up. 'I did nothing to encourage her. But it was just a little embarrassing...' His eyes twinkled wickedly making Lizzie's pulse race dangerously high.

It was Leo who drove her home. Tim got waylaid to 'have a quick peek at Hamish, darling. Seems a touch off colour,' or so Antonia had said, but then Lizzie never could spot a set-up.

Unlike Tim's utilitarian Land Rover, Leo drove a shiny new Audi estate, and on the way back, he didn't hang about.

'So how about we go for a drink? I need someone to show me around...' he said extremely casually.

'That would be... cool...' Lizzie tried to sound just as casual, in spite of her body reacting shamelessly to this glorious specimen of maleness just a few tantalising inches away.

'Well, you better give me your phone number then.' He grinned, those mischievous eyes twinkling, as they parked outside the cottage. 'Looks like your chaperone awaits!'

Darren was perched on the wall, staring most indignantly.

'So then, Lizzie...' His eyes flickered lower then held hers. 'I'll call you!' And with no indication of when or anything else, he sped off up the lane.

20

Ginny's garden was proving to be a headache, or rather not so much the garden but its owner, who was proving rather demanding, standing over Lizzie while she was working and making impractical suggestions. The evenings were busy with demands of another kind – Leo's. He'd called, but not for several days. He wasn't long-term material but he was fun, and Lizzie was quite proud that she hadn't been taken in by him. In fact, as a flirtation, it was fine. And everything was going a little *too* well, she should have realised.

It was lunchtime when Lizzie noticed a sports car parked across the lane in the lay-by. Undoubtedly one of those few remaining rat-runners, even though the main road had been opened up some time ago. A girl was sitting in it, chatting on her mobile, and still talking, got out and stared at Lizzie's garden.

Expensively dressed in tight black jeans and boots, even in the middle of summer, her sunglasses were perched on top of her head pulling back her shiny dark hair so it hung down her back like a curtain. She had that aura of confidence that Lizzie always envied, and suddenly she realised she recognised her. It was Susie.

She stepped into the road without looking and nearly got flattened by a speeding motorist.

'Wanker,' Lizzie heard her shout crossly. Just then her mobile went off inside and before she had a chance to talk to Susie, she heard her car roar off again.

But only a little later, as Lizzie was pulling out the weeds that were growing as abundantly as her vegetables, she heard a voice call, 'Hello?'

'Lizzie?' said the voice with astonishment as Lizzie appeared out of her flower bed. 'You live *here*? Oh, this just gets better and better!' Susie was practically jumping up and down with glee. 'Um, are you busy, I mean can I come in? I am sorry to just walk in like this only I couldn't help but notice your lovely garden. I was just about to come and see who lives here! To ask for help with something... But this is even better! I can't believe it's you!'

'So what kind of help did you mean?' Lizzie asked, slightly puzzled.

'Oh... Where do I start... well, I told you I was getting married didn't I! The reception is in a marquee in my parents' garden, which is lovely.' She floundered for a moment. 'I suppose the problem is decorating it. Mummy is about to spend a fortune on the most boring wedding flowers ever. It's my fault – I didn't know what I wanted. But I just drove past your cottage and saw this...' She indicated the arching boughs of roses in bloom on the front of the cottage. 'Anyway, it suddenly struck me that it would be amazing to have flowers like that in my marquee! You know, big branches of proper roses that smell like they ought to smell, with thorns and petals dropping off...' She tailed off. 'Do I sound mad?'

'Um, no...' It sounded fantastic – but Lizzie was wondering where this was leading.

'I mean, these are so gorgeous... not at all like the ones you get in shops!'

'They have names! The little creamy-coloured one is Madame Alfred Carrière, and the deep purpley one is Violette. It's really special because it's so very old.'

Susie's eyes widened. 'I had no idea... And they do smell heavenly...' It was true – the air was heavy with their heady fragrance.

'Look, why don't you come and have a drink with me? I was about to have one anyway...'

She led Susie round to the back, squeezing between the apple tree and the honeysuckle bush that grew over the water butt, to where Antonia's rickety table and chairs still were and Susie stood and looked around.

'I just love it,' she said. 'Absolutely all of it,' she added as Lizzie placed two glasses of lemonade on the table. 'You're so clever – it's not just the roses, it's how it all looks wild yet it doesn't. I love how things are just growing everywhere you look.'

Daisies and herbs sprung out of crevices in the old stone, and Lizzie had mowed either side of the flagstone path which imposed enough order on what was otherwise a wilderness.

'Oh Lord.' Susie looked at her watch. 'It's just that my mother is meeting the florist as we speak, and if I don't get over there fast, I'll end up with those vile stiff looking roses and that old-fashioned white blobby stuff. Um, it's a terrible cheek, but could I possibly bring her over to look at this? Only it really would be so helpful...' she wheedled.

'Of course,' said Lizzie. 'I don't mind at all... um, when?'

But Susie had jumped up and was striding back down the path. 'Later today? I won't be long...'

And as the little sports car zoomed up the lane, suddenly Lizzie felt a fluttering of trepidation at even the tiniest involvement in Susie's wedding.

* * *

True to her word, Susie was back in just half an hour. Lizzie recognised the car this time and when she appeared around the back of the cottage, Lizzie's stomach lurched. The person walking with her was none other than Mrs Woodleigh.

Holding out a manicured hand that rivalled that of her daughter, she introduced herself. 'It's Bella, please. And you're Lizzie, aren't you? My dear, this garden does you proud. I remember only too well how it used to look. Poor old Mr Roper, he had such terrible arthritis, it upset him awfully when he couldn't look after it any more. I think it must have been him who planted the oldest of the roses. You've made it beautiful again.' She paused to look around, before adding, 'Now, I understand my daughter has browbeaten you into creating some of your magic at her wedding?'

Lizzie glanced at Susie, who at least had the grace to look embarrassed, and then noticed Darren had appeared and was surveying the visitors with interest. Lizzie glared at him, daring him to vomit on anyone's feet and he winked slyly, as he rubbed against Susie's boot.

'Isn't he sweet?' she exclaimed, leaning down to stroke him as Darren fawned. 'He looks like one of Mrs Einstein's...'

Darren had fixed his beady eyes on Lizzie, then skipped over to a pot of lavender and sat in it.

'I'm really not sure I can help you.' Lizzie was struggling to find the words. 'I'm a gardener, I work with plants and design gardens. I've never done anything with cut flowers. You probably want a florist...'

'Oh.' Bella looked thoughtful. 'But wouldn't it be possible to decorate with plants? Better even? Like those lavender plants for example...' She glanced at where Darren was sitting – he preened. 'You clearly have an eye for it... And I've an area of my garden I badly need to rethink, and after the wedding, we could plant them all there. I would simply love a corner to look just like this, my dear. It's utterly charming.'

Lizzie was flattered, though when it came to a wedding, and probably not exactly a small one, she'd be completely out of her depth. But the words came out without thinking.

'I don't know... But you'd still need some flower arrangements for the tables, and a bride's bouquet. And I definitely can't do those.'

But Susie had already noticed Lizzie's green vase. Full of open roses, she'd placed it in an open window just that morning. They were a mix of different colours, scattering their petals as they opened. It was intended for her bedroom, but she'd forgotten to take it up there.

'Isn't that so perfect? On the tables, and a bunch like that for me to carry. It would look amazing with my dress... Oh, Lizzie, if you could do it, that is exactly what I want. Please, *please* think about it?'

There was a silence, quite a long one. Then Lizzie felt her head slowly nodding. 'Okay.'

Susie let out a delighted whoop. 'Lizzie! Oh thank you... It's going to be the best day ever now and all because of you...'

Bella just looked relieved. 'I'll be in touch next week, once you've had a chance to think about it.'

When they left, Lizzie breathed out and the enormity of the task sank in. She'd never been good at saying no and look where it had got her this time. But it was too late now. It didn't look as though there'd be any getting out of this.

* * *

Whether it was the full moon or the universe up to its old tricks again, it was a day for unexpected visitors and the next car to speed up the lane and park in the lay-by was an Audi. Leo. On a mission.

Dead-heading her roses in the back garden and preoccupied with Susie's wedding, Lizzie was too engrossed to hear him arrive, just felt two strong arms round her waist, which made her scream with fright, before he spun her round and kissed her firmly on the mouth. And what a kiss too... Taken by surprise, Lizzie felt herself sinking into his arms, her body forming to his and it took every ounce of self-control she possessed to pull away. The dark eyes looking down into hers were puzzled. Leo wasn't used to being resisted.

'Leo, I'm really busy,' she told him breathlessly. 'And surely you must be too?'

But Leo was quite used to juggling his schedule to build in a little extra-curricular activity here and there.

'I can't go yet,' he said, huge wounded eyes looking back at her. 'I've got at least ten minutes before my next client...' He glanced at his watch. 'Actually I could stretch it to fifteen,' he added wickedly, looking around at the long grass.

But Lizzie stuck to her guns. Leo was exciting, but she wasn't having any of it. She shoved him out of the garden towards his car.

'Maybe I'll see you this evening?'

It was all too much, and Lizzie fled to the safety of Sparkie's, where surely none of this would follow her.

'You won't believe the day I've had,' she told Julia. 'I've agreed to help with Susie's wedding...'

'Susie Woodleigh? Oh, Lizzie, how exciting...'

'And Leo's been making the most improper suggestions! I sent him away, of course...'

'Did you, Lizzie?' Julia looked surprised. Leo's reputation was legendary.

'Of course! Leo's terrible. He's a serial womaniser...'

'He has great... energy,' said Julia carefully. 'He draws people, especially women. He makes them feel good. Actually, Lizzie, you could say he does a lot of good...'

Lizzie was puzzled. 'But? You were going to say...'

'*Do whatever you wish as long as it harms no one,*' quoted Nola from the kitchen. 'You see, that's the problem with Leo. He's got part of it right, but it's the trail of devastation he leaves behind him. He collects hearts, Lizzie, but with no thought for the consequences. Elderflower or blackcurrant?' she added.

But Lizzie was staring at the latest addition to the walls.

People only see what they are prepared to see, which one of the girls had painted on since she was last here.

'Oh, do you like it?' Julia watched her read it. 'Don't you think it's so true, Lizzie? We thought it was rather fitting – in a shop that sells appearances!'

But that wasn't what Lizzie was thinking at all. It was the question it posed – about what she *wasn't* seeing.

It always seemed to happen just when she felt she had her life worked out. It kept changing, Lizzie was thinking as she drove home from Rumbleford. Things had this way of *happening*... and try as she did, she couldn't control *that*. Not Susie turning up unannounced for example, or Leo stopping by for a quick flirtation, or going back further, even her car breaking down in the first place.

Though convinced she was still missing something, the only thing that occurred to her was that the random collection of people filling her life here, pushing her in previously unthought-of directions, was exactly what she needed.

Lizzie had an entire blissful half-hour of peace before Leo returned all too soon. It wasn't that she hadn't been pleased to see him, but it was just that Leo liked either to be talking about Leo, or to be flirting or scheming about his next conquest, and that she couldn't just sit there with him, relaxed and just *be*.

Right now, he sat across the rickety table from her in the garden, Antonia's chairs just about bearing up, when they were joined by Darren who obviously recognised a kindred spirit in Leo to whom he could boast about all the sexy she-cats he'd been shagging.

Beer in hand, Leo colourfully recounted his narrow escape from a bad-tempered boar that morning. He waited for the incredulous expression that wasn't forthcoming, or at least for some show of concern for his safety, but was distracted when another car drew up. Susie was back again, looking pink-faced and rather apologetic.

'Lizzie? Hello? Are you there?' Sounding slightly more sober than earlier. 'I came to apologise! Only I got carried away and rather bullied you into it... Are you sure you're okay about the marquee? You can say no... The florist's still available...' Her voice tailed off as she noticed Leo.

'No, it's okay,' said Lizzie. 'I'll do it! As long as you remember I'm just a humble gardener... Come and have a glass of wine... Um, do you know Leo? He's one of the local vets...'

Lizzie went inside to find another glass, completely unaware that she was leaving Susie the object of Leo's rather speculative gaze.

'Have a seat.' He gestured to another chair. Suddenly the evening was getting interesting. 'But mind yourself, they're a little rickety...'

Susie, however, was less worried about the chair than she was about Leo, who was making her feel most unnerved, his eyes gleaming wickedly as he sat back with his arms folded watching her. No woman was out of bounds as far he was concerned.

As Lizzie came back out, she handed Susie a glass. 'Cheers. Here's to your wedding!'

Leo shifted slightly in his seat. A wedding? Well, it hadn't stopped him in the past... He remembered Miranda Holbrook, with whom he'd enjoyed some highly satisfying encounters in her stables, even a couple of times when she was married. Anyway, he enjoyed a challenge, and Susie wasn't married yet. Hmmm. Definitely interesting. He drank his beer thoughtfully.

'I wanted to ask,' said Susie tentatively, 'if you could decorate the church too. Otherwise I'm stuck with Mrs Hepplewhite...'

Lizzie still tried to avoid her ever since that memorable meeting when she'd tried to bully her into joining the WI...

'Anyway, she desperately wants to do my flowers, and I desperately don't want her to. Honestly, Lizzie, they're awful. I mean her nasty flower arrangements are. I don't want flowers like that, I want the church to look sort of, wild. Like a forest. D'you think you'd be able to do that too? Only I have to go and meet her in a minute... I don't suppose there's any chance you'd come with me?'

Leo was feeling excluded, and rather obviously clearing his throat, stood up and stretched.

'Babe, I'm going to leave you to it! I have to admit that wonderful though your company is, flowers are not a subject I can really contribute much to. So how about you both join me in the Goat later on, and if you promise to talk about something else, I'll buy you a drink!'

'Actually, I've promised to meet my brother. At the Goat, as it happens.'

'Cool,' was the lazy response from Leo. 'I'll see you there.'

Susie watched Lizzie's cheeks take on a tinge of pink as Leo bent and brushed his lips against them, catching Susie's eye as he did so. She'd come across his type before. Disconcertingly sexy and full of charm on the surface, but as boyfriend material, the worst. A womaniser and a commitment-phobe to boot, she wouldn't mind betting... the archetypal bad boy, definitely the kind to run a mile from.

Leo winked at her. Oh how he just loves himself, thought Susie. He annoyed her, not least because he was having such an unsettling effect on her. Oh she had the measure of him all right, and unlike Lizzie, Susie was a fairly shrewd judge of character. But she didn't like how he made her feel one bit.

As Leo left, Lizzie turned back to Susie, looking very pink and sparkly still. It's too late, she's smitten, thought Susie. For some reason she felt disappointed.

Ten minutes later, Lizzie changed into the only short skirt she could find which clashed somewhat with the top she was wearing and hastily put on some of her favourite orange lipstick before she and Susie walked down the lane. Elspeth Hepplewhite's shiny Skoda was already parked at the roadside.

'We're late,' muttered Susie. 'And you know what the old bag's like.' Though so far it seemed Susie was more than a match for Mrs Hepplewhite, whom it seemed may well have met her Waterloo.

They walked swiftly up the path to the church door where Elspeth waited, her finger poised on the light switch.

'Young lady, I was about to leave. You. Are. late.' Each word spat out in her most intimidating fashion. She spoke like this to everyone, except Father Sim and Susie's mother.

Susie caught Lizzie's eye. She'd already decided that to grovel apologetically would be the best course of action.

'Mrs Hepplewhite, I'm *sooo* terribly sorry, I was waiting for Mummy, but she got held up... I'm really so very sorry,' she repeated placatingly.

'Hmmph' snorted Elspeth, then swivelled her eyes to look frostily at Lizzie. 'And what are *you* doing here?'

'Lizzie's very kindly helping with my flowers, Mrs Hepplewhite. She's, er, decorating the marquee.'

The frosty look swung back to Susie again.

'Well, we may as well get down to business. Next month, isn't it? Father Sim of course? No point asking him about organists and flowers and what-not, won't be able to tell you a darned thing. You'll be lucky if he manages to get himself there. You'll have to remind him the day before. Now, as I've already told your mother, *I* will play the organ for you.'

Lizzie's heart sank for Susie. At Christmas, she'd been terrible.

'I can also do some flowers, just a nice little pedestal over here, white carnations I think, yes, perfect for a traditional village wedding.' Mrs Hepplewhite swung her beady eyes round at Susie. 'I always do the flowers here actually,' she announced imperially.

Susie swallowed and cleared her throat slightly nervously. 'Mrs Hepplewhite, that's very kind of you, but, actually, I'd really like Lizzie to do my flowers, and that way everything would match. Do you see?'

For one ghastly moment, it looked as though Mrs Hepplewhite was going to insist on doing the marquee flowers too, but instead, she drew herself up even taller, and stared down her long nose at Susie.

'I really am not sure about this,' she hissed, then glared at Lizzie again. 'I hope you are a professional, young lady. Do you have liability insurance? We can't allow just anyone in here you know, oh no...'

As Susie opened her mouth to speak, Mrs H. marched down the aisle, continuing, 'You need something there, by the altar.' She pointed at a sad, decaying effort on a rickety stand. 'I always think chrysanthemums look nice. They're jolly good value – I've known them go for five weeks. Five weeks... You'll need two little vases on the altar, and another by the pulpit, see where that arrangement is?'

Another stiff, triangular creation appeared out of the gloom. It was hideous. Susie nodded and smiled. The only place for that monstrosity was the compost heap.

'Now, especially.' Mrs H.'s tone sharpened as she fixed Susie with her sternest gaze yet. 'You. Absolutely. Must place something under the memorial – there.' She pointed to a plaque on the wall near the back of the church. Sounding positively angry now, the lecture continued. 'If it wasn't for those brave young men, God rest their souls, you wouldn't be here today.'

Did she really have to be quite so tyrannical? No wonder everyone chose to get married at St Oswald's in the next village.

'Kindly ask your mother to speak to me about the organ and that will be all. Good day to you.' And with that, Mrs H. abruptly switched off all the lights and swept out of the church, leaving them alone in the gloom.

Listening until the click-clack of her heels had definitely died away, Susie breathed a huge sigh of relief and collapsed into the last row of pews.

She giggled. 'Sorry about that. I didn't dare tell her that she wouldn't be playing the organ either. Rory's already booked such a cool string quartet... I might ask Mummy to break it to her gently! Anyway, tell me what you think, and please, not a chrysanthemum in sight...'

* * *

The Goat was quiet when they arrived, and Leo was already there, making no attempt to hide the fact that he was chatting up the tight-skirted blonde behind the bar.

'What will it be then, ladies?' Leo's eyes twinkled wickedly. 'How about a bottle of that pink wine you like so much? Er, you go on outside...' he obviously hadn't finished '... and I'll be out in just a minute.'

Linking her arm through Lizzie's, Susie said in a low voice, 'He's *such* a flirt! Oh, he's not your boyfriend, is he?' She looked apprehensive for a moment, but when Lizzie shook her head, carried on. 'It's just that I know his type. Oh you must know it too – drop-dead gorgeous isn't he, but you could never trust him an inch...'

'Actually, he has tried it on but that's all! Nothing happened...'

'Oh, there they are... Over here!'

She followed Susie across the garden to a table in the shade of an apple tree, where two men sat with their pints. A strange feeling came over her. Then Susie spoke.

'Hey guys, this is Lizzie!'

At that moment, the world seemed to grind to a stop. Even as Lizzie set eyes on the man whose back was towards her, a sixth sense was telling her she knew him. And as he turned to face her, she froze.

'Lizzie, this is Tom. My brother.'

She couldn't believe it. It was *him*...

'Hello...' An incredulous look spread across his face as he saw who his sister had with her.

'Um, have you met before, you two?' Susie's puzzled voice seemed to come from miles away.

'Not exactly,' said Lizzie just as Tom said, 'Well, we have, but neither of us can remember where...'

The other man looked resigned as he held out his hand to her. 'I'm Rich.'

'Hi!'

'So how do *you two* know each other?' asked Tom.

'Darius and Angel had a Lizzie party...' said Susie.

'Ah. The one I missed. So what part of the lovebirds little hide-away are you responsible for?'

'The garden,' Susie butted in. 'And now she's doing my wedding flowers!'

Tom pulled out the empty chair beside him. He'd seen the garden and it was cool. Just then they were joined by Leo, tucking the barmaid's phone number into his pocket. And suddenly next to Tom and Rich, it became glaringly obvious what was wrong. Leo was a lightweight. Glamorous, but completely lacking in substance.

Rich grinned at her across the table.

'So you don't remember how you met him? Well that's a turn up for the books, mate,' he teased Tom. 'You must be losing your touch...'

'I'll remember eventually,' he said amiably. 'Maybe it was a bar, or a party or something like that...'

In the middle of a conversation about the rat-run drivers, Susie suddenly shrank in her chair, as another group of people wandered across the far side of the garden.

Tom leaned forward. 'Don't worry, sis, its only Mrs Hepplewhite and her family. I know, let's ask her to join us!'

Susie thumped him. 'God, her daughter's ghastly too. Looks more like a horse than her mother if you can imagine it,' she muttered. 'Tom, we can't stay here, not like this! She's such a bully, she'll be over as soon as she spots us, just you wait.'

'Good God, you're right.' Tom's eyes grew rounder. 'She is, too.' He winked at Lizzie.

'Stop it,' giggled Susie. 'Oh she's not, is she?'

But Mrs Hepplewhite had indeed marched over and she bent to hiss in Susie's ear.

'Young lady, what's this I hear about a string quartet? Most untraditional I must say. I don't know what Father Sim will have to say about this. You have asked him I take it?'

Tom let his sister squirm a little longer than strictly necessary, before stepping in to the rescue.

'Hello, Mrs Hepplewhite! It was a terribly difficult decision, but you see, our cousins play in that quartet, so we had to ask them. Susie really wanted you to play the organ for her, but for the sake of keeping the peace in a rather, er, tricky situation, she didn't have much choice. I *do* hope you, er, understand.'

Almost falling for Tom's charm, which he used to far greater effect than his sister, with a loud 'hmph' she turned and stalked back to her family, who were all watching with looks of disapproval on their sour faces.

'You shouldn't have said that,' said Susie, looking at him. 'I forgot to tell you – they're called BlackJack...' She giggled uncontrollably. 'They're Nigerians!'

The Hepplewhite contingent looked over as the table erupted into laughter, all, that was, except for a neglected Leo, to whom feeling marginalised and overshadowed was not his idea of a good time. Susie was ignoring him and he'd picked up on the vibe between Lizzie and that Tom bloke, so it wasn't a surprise at all when he stood up and made his excuses, terribly apologetically of course.

'I'm on call first thing,' he explained. Always a good excuse, he found, reminding everyone of his impressive professional standing, which he followed with 'You ready, Babe?' twenty-first century cave-man claiming his woman.

After much manly hand shaking, they left – Lizzie more reluctantly, tossed and turned by the most unfamiliar sensations, feeling Tom's eyes gazing after her.

* * *

Once home, Lizzie hadn't planned to ask Leo in, instead wanting to sit in the quiet dark, alone with the maelstrom of thoughts that was raging in her head. All those times they'd run into each other by chance and now this... Tom. She couldn't stop thinking about him. But she hadn't bargained on Leo being so devious. Completely without scruples and knowing exactly how to play it, he wasn't going to let the opportunity go.

Uninvited, he followed Lizzie in through the back door. Lizzie could sense him standing close behind her as she put the kettle on, and as she reached for the mugs, he turned her to face him. Slowly and deliberately, he kissed her lips, very softly at first, biding his time until she started to respond, when the kissing became more urgent until Lizzie pulled back and tried to push him away.

'No, Leo.' Lizzie's words surprised both of them. She looked into those imploring eyes, which must have got him what he wanted so many times in the past. And very nearly relented. 'It would be very easy...'

'Then why stop now...' Leo nuzzled her neck and kissed her teasingly behind her ear, before finding her mouth again, kissing it softly, light, butterfly kisses, while pinning her against the wall.

But the moment had passed and anyway, Lizzie had made up her mind. She tried to break away from his grip. He certainly wasn't making it easy for her.

'Go home...' she protested, before he could change her mind, then when he ignored her, more firmly, 'I meant what I said...'

It killed the mood. Leo blinked as he realised that she really *did* mean it. He knew when he was beaten and after kissing her chastely on the forehead, left.

Good thing he didn't look back. Lizzie slumped weakly to the floor, too muddled to separate the traitorous feelings of lust that Leo had ignited from anything she might feel for Tom. Leaning back against the wall listening to his car go speeding up the lane, she waited for her heart to steady.

But that night, as she lay in bed with her mind wandering this way and that, she knew her decision was the right one, falling deeply asleep to immensely disturbing dreams of being endlessly, passionately kissed in her own rose garden, by a tall, familiar man. When the kissing eventually paused long enough for Lizzie to see who he was, she awoke instantly with a shock, her heart thumping for real. It wasn't Leo she'd been kissing – it was Tom.

22

'You're seeing an awful lot of Leo, darling...' Antonia was digging for gossip.

'Not as much as he'd like – and not so much now at all, really...'

Antonia was puzzled. 'Lord, Lizzie, why the devil not? I certainly wouldn't say no to *him*...'

Lizzie rolled her eyes. 'You have Toby, and that would be extremely unfair. He adores you.'

Antonia looked worried. 'Oh God. Don't say that. He's awfully sweet, but it's nothing serious. Surely he must know that...' She frowned.

'You do take advantage of him,' said Lizzie. 'And you can hardly blame him when you spend so much time together...'

'Golly. And I thought it was just for sex,' said Antonia, aghast. 'Shall we go to the pub?'

Antonia thought like a man. She'd be the perfect match for Leo, if he didn't need his ego stroked continuously. Antonia only ever stroked her horses.

Tim was already in the Star deep in conversation with William, who winked at Antonia as they came in. She blushed – just slightly.

'Hello, darling! William – lane's so much better, don't you think, sweetie? You farmers did a marvellous job...'

No one had ever called William 'sweetie' before and a reddish colour tinged his ears.

'We'll leave you to it, darlings! Come and join us when you're talking about something more interesting...' she added tactlessly.

'You're terrible!' giggled Lizzie as they found a table. 'Did you see the look on William's face?'

'Hilarious wasn't it? Golly, but he is bloody sexy...'

* * *

Lizzie had had a brainwave about Ginny's ghastly garden. Actually it was a rather inspired idea of how to make it pink without making it horribly, luridly garish, and in the event, Ginny had been thrilled at the idea of coloured uplighters among her plants, which would give everything a pink glow by night, while allowing it to revert to a much more tasteful mix of shades by daylight.

'*So* clever,' Ginny had enthused, clapping her hands together and smiling as widely as the Botox would allow. 'And so original! I can't think of anyone else who's done that! I'll buy pink fairy lights for the party, oh, and pink garden umbrellas... Oh, Lizzie, I knew you were just perfect for this!'

And Lizzie had escaped with both her professional integrity and the dignity of the garden intact, safe in the knowledge that Ginny's unerring instinct for the kitsch couldn't in any way be blamed on her when it came to organising the party.

* * *

Hethecote was on her mind. Now that she was spending less time up there, Lizzie was conscious of Miriam's workload, and drove over to see how she was. With summer round the corner, the farm was looking green and inviting and Miriam herself was looking better than Lizzie had ever seen her.

'You haven't seen the garden for a while – come and have a look,' she said mysteriously to Lizzie.

As they stepped through the door in the wall, a huge smile stretched across Lizzie's face as she looked around. She'd never imagined anything quite like this. Every allotment was different, each with its own identity. One of the schools had made a vegetable garden, complete with the most imaginative scarecrow ever topped off with an old mortar board, and lots of handmade labels marking each row of seedlings. There was an old blackboard with a list of tasks that they were ticking off as they completed them, and on the bottom in a childish hand was written, 'Piss off, Crows'.

Another was elaborately floral, with the initials of the school picked out in tulips that were just beginning to go over.

'Awfully clever idea,' said Miriam. 'They're planting flowers and vegetables only in the schools colours – maroon and white for everything. And they've found all these old-fashioned varieties.'

And so it went on. The detail that the schools, and the pupils of course, had gone into was astonishing. But one stood out in particular. The centrepiece was an arch, intricately constructed from wood. Climbing plants were creeping their way up it – but not flowers. These were vegetables.

'Cucumbers and red runner beans,' said Miriam proudly. 'Just think how it'll look in a couple of months.'

'But who made the arch?' asked Lizzie. 'Truly – I could sell those to my clients.'

'Ah. Well, it's the young offenders who've done this one. I thought about your idea – about staggering times. They come in after two in the afternoon. It works perfectly! It was a bit of a slow start, but then they really got into it – as you can see!'

'These are truly amazing,' said Lizzie. 'Really, I think that they should be photographed.' Then she had a real flash of inspiration. 'It would be wonderful publicity. I don't know why I haven't thought of this before, but I used to work for a gardening magazine. I could call them if you like – they might just be interested...'

'Well,' said Miriam. 'If you think so... Goodness!'

* * *

It was many months since Lizzie had even thought about Julian's greasy hair and tight trousers. She steeled herself to make the call.

'Ah... Lizzie.'

In an instant she was back in that office, suffocated and stifled and dreading the journey home. But this wasn't about her and her future – it was for Miriam and Hethecote, and quickly she filled him in.

'Hello, Julian. I'm involved in something rather interesting. I thought I'd run it by you before I go anywhere else...'

She put the phone down and sat there for a moment. *Buds and Blooms* were coming to see Miriam's gardens! If this went well, it would put Hethecote Farm well and truly on the map. Who'd have thought she'd be calling Julian after all this time... But Lizzie knew without doubt he'd love this and it would make a brilliant feature for the magazine.

* * *

'I've found a venue!' announced Antonia as she opened a bottle of wine. 'Friend of Harry's, darling! Got a crumbling old pile a few miles away. He's a lecherous old sod but we can cope with that – the house is sensational from the outside with a very impressive drive... He says he'll stick a marquee out the back in return for a couple of tickets! He'll probably only end up using one of them – no one will want to go with him...'

'Should we go and take a look? Before you decide? Only – well, just in case there's a landfill down the road or something... This weekend – I think Katie's coming down...'

'I suppose...' Antonia was thoughtful. 'I'll call him. Actually, I'll do it now. Won't be a mo.'

Picturing a balding, bent old man with a monocle, Lizzie listened in as Antonia buttered him up and arranged for them to go round later that week.

'Oh that's so fabulous, thanks awfully, sweetie,' she was saying. 'And I'm sure we can come to some agreement.'

'Oh God,' she said as she put the phone down. 'He only wants me to go away with him. To Marbella... jolly nice actually, and I know it's all in a good cause, but, darling... he is eighty-three...'

* * *

There was another party on Lizzie's mind – Edward's – and the next day, she checked through the list of plants Ginny had ordered and emailed it to the supplier. She'd dug the borders and started adding the mountain of compost that had been delivered, and Lizzie was looking forward to planting, with all the arduous preparation now behind her.

As always, her client was immaculately coiffed with brand-new highlights and dressed in pastels – palest pink and lilac. Lizzie's ancient patched jeans were covered in earth as usual, but Ginny, to be fair, didn't bat an eyelid as she invited her into the conservatory for a much needed coffee break.

Chatting over a large cafetière of coffee, Lizzie told Ginny about how she'd got involved with Susie's wedding.

Ginny clapped her hands with glee and squeaked, 'Golly, how

frightfully marvellous! Of course you must do it! I have no doubt you'll do it beautifully, no doubt at all. Now.' Leaning towards Lizzie, she lowered her voice conspiratorially. 'Have you met that brother of hers? Bit of a heartbreaker I'm told,' she said, the flush in Lizzie's cheeks answering her question.

A gleam came in to Ginny's heavily painted eyes. 'My older daughters, when they're home, are always at that pub with the terrible name,' she rolled them dramatically, 'desperately hoping he'll be there. It's "Tom this, Tom that..." Honestly, Lizzie, they drive me insane! He rarely is there, of course. I'm sure he's far too busy for village life these days. In any case, they're *much* too young for him!' She gave a slightly manic, high-pitched giggle as her face stretched into a grimace of a smile.

Botox, Lizzie thought instantly. Ginny had overdone it this time and it wasn't a good look.

'These girls, dear me, they're *that* age, and just will *not* be told. They go off to *that* pub, all dolled up, ready to throw themselves at him. No subtlety whatsoever.'

Subtlety wasn't exactly one of Ginny's strengths either. Lizzie had seen her daughters from a distance, drifting around the house, pretty girls, delicate as fawns, with their blonde flowing hair, long limbs and dewy skin, though much too young for Tom, thankfully.

'Anyway,' continued Ginny more brusquely, 'enough of all that. Back to business. When will these divine plants be arriving? In the meantime, you must come here any time you like, Lizzie! Don't worry if I'm not here! You just carry on what you need to do, but I would so love to be here when the plants are delivered. I'm so excited, I just can't wait!'

Ginny's eyes glittered slightly madly. Lizzie could just imagine her daughters doing the same over Tom.

But then the eyes turned just slightly steely. 'And you are quite,

quite sure that it will all be finished for Edward's birthday party? It's only a few weeks now, but I so want everything to be perfect...'

* * *

That afternoon Lizzie got to Hethecote just minutes before Julian swung up the drive in a very swanky Jaguar. Nothing had changed – the trousers were tight as ever, and he was wearing what looked like a Gieves & Hawkes jacket with a particularly snazzy handkerchief poking out of his pocket.

'Ah, Lizzie!'

She narrowly avoided being air-kissed as Miriam came over.

'Julian, meet Miriam Kirby, the force behind Hethecote Farm!'

'Delighted.' He smoothed a strand of lank hair off his face then offered his hand. 'I must say, this is frightfully... um... *agricultural*...'

As they made their way over to the garden, Lizzie gave him a potted history of the farm, and how they needed to become more profitable simply to survive.

'There are all these animals, you see,' she added as they passed Sid and Johnny's stable. As he always did, Sid farted noisily and Julian jumped backwards.

'Quite, quite... ahem... This is all very well, but it's not the animals I'm here to see, is it now, Lizzie.'

'No...' They'd come to the door in the hedge. 'This, Julian. This is why you're here.'

Give him his due, he responded exactly as Lizzie hoped. And looking around, she tried to see it through his eyes. Okay, it was hardly the Chelsea Flower Show, but the whole garden was alive and the characters of the individual gardens clearly apparent. Lizzie felt almost choked with pride as she stood with Miriam and watched him.

'And all these... have been made by schools?' he asked incredulously. 'My, my... I can see exactly why you called me. It's most innovative. Absolutely right on trend...' he blustered.

'And some local young offenders.' Two were out there now – thin and pale looking, glancing suspiciously at Julian. 'It's all organic, Julian. As much use as possible is made of recycled items. But, as you know, there are costs. Schools have to rent the gardens in the first place, and that provides funds for the farm. But it means that poorer schools are excluded... I suppose ultimately what we'd hope for is some sponsorship... And maybe, a feature or two in the press would help... Anyway, surely your readers would be interested to see what a class of children can achieve on a severely limited budget...'

'Absolutely...' Julian was nodding so enthusiastically his glasses nearly fell off. 'It's a marvellous idea, Lizzie! Marvellous! But...'

Here we go, she thought...

'Let's just say the magazine were to sponsor one of the gardens...' he said pompously. 'Nothing definite, of course, but just say it did... then I imagine we would receive some kind of *exposure*, shall we say...'

'My plan is to open a small shop,' said Miriam unexpectedly. 'Manned by volunteers the way the entire farm is. We'll sell the farm's produce, but inside we'll dedicate a wall to all our generous sponsors. And we could sell your magazine... er... for a commission...'

Lizzie held her breath. Julian looked slightly taken aback, then beamed at her.

* * *

Katie had taken a long weekend off and driven down to Littleton. 'We need to get going with this ball,' she told Lizzie. 'Antonia really needs booting up the bottom...' Which, reading between the lines, meant that she hadn't seen Tim for a while.

Antonia was wasting no time and had them all invited for drinkies at Harry's mate's pile. As they turned up the drive, Lizzie had to admit that as a setting it was unbeatable. There were tall, austere-looking cedars set amongst the neatest, most manicured lawns – a little different to the ponies and llamas in the untidy fields that flanked the bumpy drive at Hethecote. The house was impressive too – a sprawling brick and stone mansion, which could have passed for a country house hotel.

Obviously enjoying herself, Antonia swung her car noisily round on the drive and braked hard sending gravel flying every-where. The front door immediately opened and the man who stood there was tall and upright, with thick white hair and a forbid-ding look on his face.

Antonia marched over. 'Aubrey! Darling...' He kissed her cheeks resoundingly.

'By golly, Antonia, what a jolly fine-looking woman you are! Harry's a damn fool you know... Told him so myself... Brought some friends, I see.' Aubrey stared at an amused Katie and Lizzie. 'Good, good, well come on in... Fraser can serve us sherry.'

The house was just as imposing inside, though very slightly shabby. Apparently Aubrey had pots of money in the bank, which according to Antonia, he refused to spend on the house because he had an illegitimate son to leave it to.

'Probably got more than one, darling... Was always sowing his oats as I remember... Probably still is... Shocking old bugger when you think about it. His legitimate brats are after everything of course, but Aubrey's frightfully stubborn...'

By the time the girls left, Antonia had sweet-talked Aubrey into putting up a massive marquee. She'd also managed to avoid the trip to Marbella.

'Got to go into hospital, darling,' she'd confided to him. 'Women's problems, you know...' and whispered something in his ear.

An expression of shock had crossed Aubrey's face. 'Ahem... of course...' He cleared his throat. Nothing more was said.

23

An ominous-looking sky blanketed the village the following morning, releasing oversize raindrops which soon became a downpour. Katie was out with Tim, who'd pulled rank and taken a weekend off. Leo wouldn't be pleased, out in this deluge. It was even too much for Antonia, who called in by car.

'I must say, really can't be doing with this rain. Haven't ridden today... Doesn't usually stop me, have to say,' she told Lizzie, sounding somewhat perplexed. Then she added that she'd thought she'd take Cassie shopping, seeing as there was nothing else to do.

'Thought I'd treat her to a ghastly lunch at that American diner. Dreadful place but Cassie wants to go there. Fancy joining us?'

Lizzie declined. As much as anything she had a lot to catch up on. And there was another reason why she would rather be alone.

'Another time?' she suggested.

'I'll let you know how bad it is first,' retorted Antonia. 'Lord. Is that window of yours still not fixed?'

'I jammed it shut for the winter, and now that's as closed as I can get it.' In the end, Lizzie had bashed at the frame with a large hammer then managed to lever it shut.

Antonia's view was uncompromising. 'Typical of this estate,' she said, adding more firmly. 'Withhold rent. Had to do it myself once. That got them moving,' she said with satisfaction. 'Shall I have a little word with Toby for you? I'm sure he'll be frightfully helpful...'

She looked at her watch.

'Awfully sorry, better shoot. Fancy a drink at the Goat later? I'll phone Timmy and see if he's free. Haven't been there in yonks. Why don't you see if Leo's around?'

After Antonia had left, the rain continued to fall and Lizzie gave up on the idea of digging Ginny's beds. Instead, after making herself some coffee, she sat by her fireplace. It was two years to the day since her mother had died – which also meant she'd been here about a year. And what a year it had been. Some sadness still lingered, but Lizzie felt just a hint of pride as she thought about everything that had happened. As the fire crackled and the rain beat against her windows, she almost missed the quiet knock at her door.

'Nola? Come in! You must be soaked!'

Nola came in and handed Lizzie an odd-looking bunch of flowers before taking her coat off.

'For you! You've lit a fire – it smells glorious!' she exclaimed. 'Apple wood?'

Lizzie nodded. 'Tea?'

'Of course!'

'I know what today is,' said Nola as they sat by Lizzie's fire. 'Is it *two* years now?'

Lizzie nodded. 'It's hard to believe at times. So much seems to have happened since then.'

Nola frowned. 'It's a little more complicated than that...' she said.

'What do you mean?' Lizzie didn't understand.

'Well, you've *made* things happen. You've made big changes, Lizzie...'

'Mostly it feels like I'm caught up in a whirl of events,' said Lizzie truthfully. 'Things just seem to come along and carry me with them...'

'Oh no, no. It's not like that at all...' Nola shook her head. 'You've attracted everything in your life, Lizzie. Look at all your friends! Your work too,' Nola went on. 'It's *far* more than random. What were you looking for when you decided to stay here?'

'I-I'm not sure I can remember. I was just putting one foot in front of the other at that point. I'd escaped from a life I wasn't happy with as you know. I'm not sure I knew what I wanted. I had the letter my mother left. I'll show you if you like...'

Nola's eyes lit up. 'Would you mind?'

Lizzie went and fetched it. 'Here.'

Silently, Nola read it. 'When did she give you this?'

'She meant me to find it after she died, but I only came across it a year ago – it's why I left Jamie!'

She continued reading until the end when she looked up, her eyes shining. 'It's all in there! Everything you could ever need to know! Your mother must have been extraordinary, Lizzie...'

Slightly puzzled by Nola's words, Lizzie silently replaced the letter. Was it all really so obvious, or was there *still* something she was missing...

After Nola had left, Lizzie put her flowers in a vase. They were an unusual mixture – she identified sage, rosemary and hawthorn but the flowers themselves looked tight and withered up. Until it got dark, that was. When Lizzie looked again much later, they'd unfurled into stars of pink and lilac, filling the cottage with the sweetest perfume.

24

The heavy rain of the previous day had given way to drizzle and Lizzie put the finishing touches to the plan for Susie's flowers. She planned to hire lots of olive trees and flowering shrubs, and hopefully arrange them to make a kind of tunnel into the marquee. A quick search on the internet had come up with supplier of cut roses, and she'd found somewhere local to hire the vases. Picking up the phone, she called Susie's mother.

In the Woodleighs' huge farmhouse kitchen, Lizzie's hair frizzed spectacularly, as next to the enormous Aga, her dampness quickly evaporated. Bella perused the plan set out in front of her while Lizzie sipped her tea.

'I'm really most impressed,' Bella said to her. 'It all sounds quite perfect, for the church too I see. Susie's going to be over the moon! You do know, until she saw your garden she showed no interest whatsoever, so I'm quite glad she's chosen this herself. Now, I need to write you a cheque straight away, as you're going to have some quite huge costs to cover, and well, if I add a little something on,' she mentioned a figure that wasn't little at all, 'could we go just a little bit mad on the roses and make it even more special?

'Now,' continued Bella, 'I thought on a more practical note that you could borrow the gardeners. When you start setting everything up, it'll be far too much for you to carry, and they won't be able to get on with their usual jobs with a marquee in the middle of the garden. And don't forget, I was hoping that when you have time, you might come and give me a little advice about mine...'

It was two hours later by the time Lizzie finally left and at last the rain was stopping. The clouds were beginning to part, and here and there glimmers of brightness poked through the gaps between them. Lizzie filled her lungs with the scent of the rain-soaked earth . Her frizzy hair fell in rat's tails again, but she didn't care – in her pocket her hand clutched the rather large cheque, lest it fall out and be lost amongst the puddles.

And as a watery sun came into view, so did Pete with an archaic-looking chicken house on the back of his van, which he dragged round to a corner behind the cottage. And later still he returned with a large box that was making clucking noises.

'Rang the farm on the off chance – they sold me a dozen so I thought you might as well have some...'

Lizzie tried not to think about where the others in his van were destined for.

'Erm—' Pete coughed a bit embarrassedly '—took the liberty of gettin' you some supplies like, 'ope yer don't mind. Weren't too expensive, and them'll see you through for a bit.'

'Oh! This is brilliant! Thank you, Pete... Shall I put the kettle on?'

Pete's eyes lit up, but her excitement turned to dismay as she opened the box. They were the baldest, scraggiest birds she'd ever set eyes on, as well as agoraphobic, resolutely refusing to leave the hen house.

* * *

Later, Leo had called in, still a regular visitor, though not as frequent as before, having tactically withdrawn to reconsider his options. Besides, he'd met a rather pretty little blonde with a severely lame horse, who was rather grateful for his help. Actually, she really was tremendously grateful... he smiled to himself. He was headed over there shortly. She'd invited him for dinner, and hopefully much more, thought Leo happily to himself...

'I'll give you some wormer for them,' he offered. 'Just put a few drops in their water. But I'm sure they'll be okay,' he added as Lizzie handed him a beer.

Relieved when Leo didn't hang around, she'd just decided to wander down to Antonia's when yet another visitor turned up, and this was one she was not pleased to see – at all. She'd hoped never to see him again. It was Jamie, and he looked cross, even for him.

Lizzie folded her arms defensively. 'Jamie. This is a surprise! I didn't expect to see you...'

'I know I should have called you,' he said, 'but I also knew that you wouldn't want to meet. Look, can I come in for a minute. It won't take long, but we should talk. In private.'

Mystified, Lizzie led him round the back of the cottage, and gestured to the chair that Leo had just got up from, wishing for once that he'd hung around.

'I heard,' Jamie said then, more grimly, 'about you being pregnant.'

Lizzie gasped. 'I'm not now,' she told him. 'I lost it.'

'Don't you think you should at least have told me? Instead of me hearing second or third hand from some indiscreet friend of a friend of Katie's?' He really sounded angry.

Lizzie looked horrified.

'Yes,' he continued. 'That's exactly what happened,' he said, before adding, slightly more calmly, now that he'd said what he'd come to say, 'It was just a shock to hear it from someone else.'

Lizzie felt terrible and could completely understand him being upset. 'Oh, Jamie, I honestly didn't think you'd want to know, though I'd had the miscarriage before I'd decided whether to tell you or not... And then, when that happened, there didn't seem any point. I never, ever, dreamed you'd find out...'

Jamie sighed heavily. Those dreaded sighs that always dragged her mood down to the level of his.

'Well, I did,' he said flatly. 'Now you know. For your information, I would have done the right thing as an absent father, and I wouldn't have interfered. Just for the record.'

And he left Lizzie in stunned silence.

* * *

Darius and Angel were at the Goat that evening. Lizzie hadn't seen them in ages.

'Darling dizzy Lizzie,' said Angel effusively. 'I can't tell you how much we've missed you! SO much work, darling... I hate to say but the garden's the *teeniest* little bit overgrown...'

'But can you tidy it for us?' begged Darius. 'Pretty please... we'll wait...'

'I'd love to,' said Lizzie. 'But it won't be for a while, I'm afraid... I've Susie's wedding, Ginny's garden, Hethecote Farm which is really getting busy...'

'And don't forget the ball, darling... there's that to organise too...' Antonia chipped in.

'Ooh, how exciting! You must tell us *all* about it,' said Darius. 'And we must buy tickets, flower...'

'Yes. Er,' said Antonia. 'I'll let you know, darlings. They're at the printer's at the moment.'

* * *

Work was catching up with Lizzie. Not only was there Susie's wedding, but she'd just received an invitation to it, which had thrown her into a quandary knowing that she'd be seeing Tom again. To top it all, the scrawniest of the chickens had eventually tiptoed out, terrified out of her wits. It was a massive breakthrough and Lizzie had christened her Pete. The others had soon followed, Cassie suggesting Toby for the next and Tim for the third, but Lizzie drew the line at Antonia, and they plumped instead for Leo. All was well until Darren joined in and leaped amongst them, scattering them far and wide until Lizzie had grabbed him by the scruff. Darren had sworn and spat ferociously at her, but he seemed to have got the message.

Lizzie hadn't planned to go back to Ginny's that afternoon. Actually, she was heading for Sparkie's to try to find an outfit for the wedding, but suddenly she remembered she'd left her notebook in Ginny's greenhouse. Filled as it was with all her sketches for the wedding flowers, she didn't want to risk losing it. It was still early afternoon. She could call in to Ginny's with enough time to get to Sparkie's.

The house was quiet when she got there, and Lizzie let herself in through the side gate. She could see her notebook on the table round by the greenhouse, but as she went to pick it up she heard a muffled sob. Looking around, Lizzie couldn't see anyone, but following the path around the side of the house, she found Ginny sitting in the shade, in the furthest part of the garden.

Tentatively, Lizzie walked towards her. Ginny looked a small, sorry shadow of her usual self, her hair unbrushed, her pastel shirt smudged, and mascara in streaks down her cheeks. She blew her nose as she saw Lizzie coming towards her and hastily pinned on a false smile.

'I came by to collect this,' Lizzie explained apologetically. 'I didn't mean to disturb you...'

'Oh, don't take any notice,' Ginny tried to say with a heroic attempt at her habitual brightness. 'I'm sorry, Lizzie. You've just caught me at a bad moment...' And to Lizzie's horror, Ginny's face collapsed in a hideous grimace as more tears rolled copiously down her cheeks.

'Ginny...' Lizzie sat down beside her, quite worried by now, placing a hand on Ginny's hunched shoulders. 'What's wrong, what's happened?'

Feeling the sobs racking Ginny's body, Lizzie felt alarmed, uncertain what to do. Had someone died? And where was everyone else? 'Ginny, would you like me to call someone for you? Family or something? Edward?'

At the mention of Edward's name, the sobs turned to wails. 'Not Edward...' Ginny's body tensed as she regained control and at last the sobs subsided.

'Oh, you may as well know,' she said, blowing her nose noisily. 'It's Edward that's the problem... I shouldn't really be telling you this.' She wiped her face. 'He's having an affair.' Then seeing the look of incredulity on Lizzie's face, added, 'Oh, and it's not the first time. There've been several...'

Lizzie was flummoxed. Short, smug unattractive Edward, with those dreadful teeth, was having affairs? Lizzie struggled to imagine how anyone could find him remotely attractive in the first place. But then she looked at Ginny, who'd spent all these years married to him.

Wiping more tears away, Ginny continued, 'I think it all started when the girls were quite tiny. You know, there's what seems at the time like an endless period where your every waking moment is taken up looking after them. Wonderful though they are, life becomes just an endless routine of cooking, cleaning, washing and driving around to various activities... Everything revolved around the girls. And I suppose Edward is just one of those men who can't take second place. Even to his own children, even for a little while... So when someone else came along and paid him the attention he was missing, that was it. And now, the girls are older and I'm starting to get my life back. They need me less, and he's off dallying with his – his floozies...' Her voice croaked.

'Oh I know what you're thinking. That I'm stupid to stay with him. I suppose I am...' Ginny sighed through her tears. 'I nearly left him once. Three years ago... He was sleeping with his secretary. Honestly, it was disgusting. That brainless creature was young enough to be his daughter – she's only a couple of years older than Persephone – my eldest. God only knows what she saw in him. Power maybe? I really can't imagine what else. He's not the most attractive man, is he? I confronted him about it, he promised to finish with her, and we agreed we'd try to make our marriage work. That was just before we moved here. It was supposed to be a fresh start... I know it's very shallow, but this house and all of this...' Ginny gestured at the garden. 'This was what I always wanted for the girls, and I do love it so... and in about five years, they'll have grown up and gone. It's not long, so I told myself I could endure his behaviour just for a few more years, for *them*...' The tears had started again. 'He had another affair, of course, which didn't last long, and I turned a blind eye, but now he's told me he's seeing someone else. He says that this time it's serious, and he's not breaking it off with her. So, it's up to me, if I go on living with him knowing this, or whether we break up...'

Ginny had run out of tears, and sat there, slumped, staring at the ground.

'At the moment, I don't know what to think. I'm too shocked. And I need to think of the girls, and he is their father, even if he is a despicable bastard. So—' she smiled a watery smile at Lizzie '—I really do need to sort myself out, don't I?'

Lizzie looked at her, her heart full of sympathy. 'You know, you really don't deserve to be treated like this. It just isn't right. I don't know how you've carried on this long, not letting it show. Your daughters really don't know?'

Ginny shook her head with a degree of pride. 'I don't think so...'

'But,' Lizzie added slowly, 'there are worse things than growing up just with your mother. Mine brought me up. She was wonderful...' she said wistfully.

'Was?' asked Ginny with curiosity, then more calmly, 'Did you lose her?'

Lizzie nodded, suddenly unable to speak. 'Two years ago. She had cancer. She was my family you know,' Lizzie said quietly. 'I never knew my father, he died when I was four, and she didn't remarry. But it was good. She was a great mother. The best.'

Ginny was silent, then she raised her eyes towards Lizzie. 'Oh Lizzie. I'm sorry, I had no idea.' She took her hand and they sat in silence for a moment.

Then she added in a normal voice, 'This pink garden of mine. It's a silly idea, I know that. I don't mind what you do with it really. I know you'll make it look wonderful.' She went quiet again.

'Nonsense,' said Lizzie firmly. 'Your pink garden is going to be a sensation, don't you imagine for a moment it's not.'

* * *

A confusion of thoughts filled Lizzie's head as she drove to Sparkie's, in desperate need of some retail therapy. Poor, poor Ginny. How could she even bear to look at that awful man, let alone share a bed with him? And how did men like that get away with it? Edward's arrogance was outrageous. Lizzie shook her head, hoping that Ginny would come to her senses and kick Edward firmly into touch, exactly where he belonged.

After Ginny's bombshell, Lizzie needed Sparkie's more than

usual. Nola was up a ladder painting again when she got there, adding another line.

'For our customers who've lost their way...' she called down to Lizzie.

Everyone is beautiful... had been painted on a previously bare section of wall. Lizzie liked it.

Julia made herbal tea, and they showed her all the wonderful new clothes that they felt sure were here especially for Lizzie.

'Lovely, isn't it, that one?' said Julia admiringly. 'Oh Lizzie, you really *do* look beautiful, doesn't she, Nola? And some of these only came in this morning...'

Nola nodded in agreement, her feline eyes watching Lizzie.

Eventually, she'd chosen a dress that she'd instantly fallen in love with, wonderfully flattering in softest, sludgy blue dotted with flowers. It was a flowing kind of dress, the perfect length for showing off tanned legs and, of course, she had to buy the pretty beaded sandals that went with it.

The girls had given her a faded silk rose on a slide to wear in her hair as a present, which Lizzie would never have chosen for herself, but Nola and Julia were right. It was the finishing touch. Between them, they had brushed her hair and pinned it up at one side, and shown her how to pin the flower just above her ear.

'Oh,' they said, beaming at her with delight. 'You look stunning, Lizzie. Look.'

They'd pushed her in front of the enormous mirror and Lizzie did a double take. She barely recognised the person staring back at her – these girls were just incredible.

'Do you have time for a drink, Lizzie? Only there's a new cocktail bar just opened. Just round the corner, and Nola and I were going to treat ourselves. We'll treat you too! Kinky Pinks all round!' She'd taken her hand. 'Come and join us!'

Ginny would just love this place, thought Lizzie! Ice-cream

coloured tables and chairs with matching cushions, and a long list of cocktails with the most exotic names she'd ever heard. Lizzie eventually got round to telling them about meeting Tom, and Nola and Julia had exchanged very knowing glances.

'What?' Lizzie asked them, looking from one to the other. 'What is it?'

'Fate,' said Nola. 'Or call it destiny. You see, if you hadn't moved here, you wouldn't have met Susie, nor would you have met Tom. But you'd already met him, hadn't you? Oh, that's even more amazing. Surely you can see, Lizzie, it's meant to be...'

But Lizzie was confused.

'And,' added Julia, 'he recognised you, didn't he? It definitely means something, think about it.'

'It's karma,' said Nola.

'Kismet,' added Julia, nodding.

'Destiny. You can't avoid it.' And they were both silent, looking at her lovingly, their eyes sparkling with excitement.

It all sounded double Dutch to Lizzie as she waited for them to start on about the universe again. But it set her was thinking... In fact it startled her to realise just how much thinking she was doing these days, all about Tom Woodleigh.

'But...' she faltered. 'But it's not as though he's asked me out or anything...'

'Oh Lizzie.' Nola shook her head, a knowing look on her pretty face. 'You are a silly.'

'He thinks you're with Leo,' added Julia. 'Someone like Tom is far too much of a gentleman to go moving in on someone else's girlfriend.'

'Oh.' Lizzie was dismayed. They were right. How did they know these things? And why couldn't she figure it out for herself? And what was she supposed to do now?

25

The week of Susie's wedding was here and Lizzie's nerves were getting the better of her. It was going to be a huge affair. Over two hundred guests, top-notch caterers, and a band who were 'completely awesome', according to Cassie at least. Lizzie was wishing with all her heart that the Woodleighs had employed a society florist, leaving her free to spend the week as she usually did, digging flower beds and covered in earth, which though tiring was infinitely less stressful.

But then she might not have been invited... And Lizzie's heart was a-flutter as she thought about running into Tom, though she wasn't sure what, if anything, she was expecting. Rather rashly she'd invited Leo, though after what Nola and Julia had pointed out, she was beginning to wish she hadn't, but Leo had sauntered into her kitchen and seen the invite and before she knew it the words had popped out.

But she'd also had the best piece of news. Julian had called her first thing.

'Ah, Lizzie... I'm emailing you. Now. Copy of the article on the farm... You know... erm... well, could you just run your eye over it and make sure it looks all right?'

Astounded, Lizzie agreed, and called him back half an hour later.

'Julian – it's perfect. The photographs too... It really looks incredible!'

'Ah, well, glad to hear you say that.' He sounded pleased.

'Oh and Julian? Thank you, *so* much...'

* * *

It was Lizzie's last morning at Ginny's until after the wedding, and the plants were being delivered. After unloading what felt like endless trays of plants on the drive, the driver carried the heaviest shrubs over to the back of the garden, where they would be kept until after the wedding, before he drove off, leaving Lizzie alone with the rest, in pots, in the middle of Ginny's drive. Lizzie began the arduous task of moving it all, and as she carried yet another armful of plants across the lawn, she noticed the slight figure of Ginny's youngest daughter standing forlornly by the greenhouse.

'Hello. You're Alice, aren't you?' She'd noticed her before, the youngest and least flamboyant of the girls, but with brown eyes like a deer's and skin dusted with freckles, possibly the prettiest.

Alice smiled back shyly. 'I just wondered,' she asked quietly, 'can I stay down here for a bit? If I'm not in your way?'

'Tell you what,' Lizzie said, wondering if Alice *knew*, 'I've got tons to do here. You could help me for a while if you like? There's all this to move into the shade, and then we need to water it all. What do you say?'

Alice's face lit up. She followed Lizzie out to collect some more plants.

Lizzie soon discovered that Alice didn't share her big sisters' obsession with clothes and make-up, not to mention boys of course. She'd also divulged that actually, yes, she had met Tom. More than once actually... There was a twinkle in Alice's eye as she'd told Lizzie what a stupid crush her sisters had going on! If only she knew, thought Lizzie, mortified, that she herself wasn't much better.

And it seemed that Alice was also genuinely interested in the garden. She'd already asked if she could help with the planting. Maybe there was a gardener in this family yet.

'I could help you again if you like?' volunteered Alice shyly as Lizzie was leaving. 'I mean, I don't want to be a nuisance, only if it's useful...' Her voice tailed off.

'Do you know,' Lizzie said slowly, 'I might just take you up on that. I could really do with an extra pair of hands this week, with the wedding flowers. Obviously I'd pay you. It would be hard work though,' she hastened to add.

'Thanks!' beamed Alice. 'I'll just check with Mummy...'

* * *

Antonia had stopped as she rode past Lizzie's cottage on Hamish.

'I say, Lizzie... Tobes has asked me to the wedding! Going to be a frightfully posh do... Hope you've got a frock?'

Lizzie ignored her. 'You know we need some ideas for the ball! Have you got the tickets yet by the way? Shouldn't we be selling them?'

'Oh, darling, you're way behind! Yes, I do have them and I've already sold a hundred and twenty! Without even trying! Miriam's thrilled of course. And you'll never guess, but Eucalyptus even bought a couple... but she wouldn't tell me who she's bringing! I asked of course, but she went a bit pink and wouldn't say! Golly – I'm intrigued! I wonder if it's anyone we know?'

'I've seen the article for the magazine!' said Lizzie. 'It's perfect! The headline is "Gardens for a New Generation". We just have to hope that loads of people read it and want to send Miriam their money...'

'Stand still, darling,' Antonia said to Hamish who was bored and starting to fidget. 'I tell you,' she said to Lizzie. 'She'll have more visitors than she knows what to do with by the time we've finished.'

* * *

Susie's hen weekend had passed in whirl of sunshine, surfing and seafood, with some serious wine drinking thrown in for good measure. Rock had been at its picturesque best, with iridescent turquoise waves crashing onto the pale sand, and hot – gloriously so. Susie had found herself driven to waste not a single second. A sense of recklessness had her running for the sea, urging her further out to catch bigger waves than usual, pushing her usual boundaries.

Now on her way home, she was gripped by a sense of panic as she at last acknowledged what was eating her. Because just days before her wedding, Susie was having second thoughts. What if Rory wasn't the one? And she didn't feel enough for him? How did she know she wasn't making the biggest mistake of her life?

* * *

That evening, Lizzie had collapsed in the shade of her apple tree with a large mug of tea, with Darren perched on her lap. Her chickens clucked serenely as they scratched in the long grass, and Lizzie tried not to think about all the to-do lists in her head, as she gazed into the blue sky and felt the tension in her muscles ebb away. She breathed in wafts of the honeysuckle that was just coming into flower and that's exactly where Susie found her, when she wandered around the side of the cottage.

'Hey, Susie! You okay?' Susie looked tired – not her usual sparkly self at all. 'How about some tea, or a proper drink?'

'I could murder a glass of wine. I'm sorry, Lizzie, I should have brought some, but I didn't know I was coming here. I was driving by and well, I just thought maybe I could pop in, if you're not busy, of course...'

Something was definitely up, thought Lizzie. She looked most subdued – not a trace of that boisterous excitement.

'Of course I'm not – come on, I'll find some wine.'

Susie sat on the brightly cushioned seat of one of the chairs which were still in one piece but only just, and leaned her elbows on the table, quiet, after hours of driving too fast. Lizzie sat down opposite and poured out two glasses of white wine.

'How was your weekend? It must have been great! What did the girls have in store for you?'

'Actually,' said Susie, 'it was surprisingly uneventful. Oh, don't get me wrong, it was lovely – we sunbathed and surfed, and had some fantastic food. But, oh Lizzie, I've been feeling quite funny...' Susie couldn't stop once she started.

'You and Leo,' she asked tentatively. 'Is it, you know, anything serious?' She watched Lizzie's cheeks blush under her tan, as she studied her wine glass.

Lizzie looked up, a quizzical look on her face. 'Honestly? I don't think so. It could never be. He's just not my type. I do think he's gorgeous looking and I did wonder to start with, but...' She broke off, not wanting to tell Susie that meeting her brother Tom had put a stop to that; that Tom put Leo in the shade...

But tears had starting to trickle down Susie's cheeks, and Lizzie reached out a hand to her.

'I'm glad you said that. You know, that bloody Leo... I hate myself Lizzie... but I'm more attracted to him than I've ever been to Rory... sorry, I hope you don't mind me telling you, only I don't know what to do... I was hoping that if he was your boyfriend it would snap me out of it. You know, girls code and all that...' But Lizzie wasn't upset in the slightest, it was just that *Leo*, of all men... it was ridiculous. He wasn't worth it.

'Susie. You can't seriously be considering breaking up with Rory? I don't know Leo that well, but I can't imagine him ever settling with one person. He's attractive, yes, but he's a serial flirt,' she said firmly, adding, 'and he plays games. He's never there when you need him and turns up when you'd rather he didn't, out of the blue, and probably only because he hasn't had a better offer. It's funny really, when you meet someone like him, it's a challenge! You think you're going to be the one to change him, help him see the error of his ways and save his soul! Of course, the truth is people like Leo don't change. Not really.' Lizzie shuddered, as she thought of Ginny's husband Edward. 'Just imagine being married to such a... a... philanderer! You know, when I first met him, I wondered whether Mum would have liked him. I think she would have, though she definitely would have warned me off him. But, for once, I didn't need her to. I actually managed to figure it out for myself.'

In spite of herself, Susie wiped her face and attempted a wobbly smile. Lizzie was a better judge of character than she'd thought. It seemed she'd got the measure of Leo on her own, far better than Susie had imagined.

'The wedding was going to be so perfect, and now...' Susie looked downcast. 'I know I sound like a spoiled brat, and I really don't mean to. So much trouble has gone in to organising it. You know it's literally taken months to plan and oodles of money, and here I am, considering giving it all up just like that...'

'When you first met Rory,' Lizzie asked her. 'How did you feel then?'

Susie sighed. 'Oh, it was exciting and fun, and Rory always looked out for me. Still does. He's a good person, Lizzie, he doesn't deserve this.' The tears were starting again.

'And Leo is exciting and dangerous... You'd have great sex and he'd leave you as soon as the next girl batted her eyelashes at him. You've known Rory ages, of course it's not exciting like *that*.'

But Susie looked exhausted.

'Sleep on it,' said Lizzie. 'Try to put it out of your mind, and see how you feel tomorrow...'

'Do you often do that? Think what your mum's advice would be?' Susie asked.

Lizzie gave a small smile and swallowed. 'I used to hear her voice often. It was uncanny at times, as though she was standing right beside me,' she told Susie. 'It freaked me out to start with, especially when I couldn't believe she'd died. Now it happens much less often, but I can nearly always imagine what she'd say about something important. It's almost like she's still there...'

'What do you think she'd say to me?' asked Susie in a small voice.

Lizzie thought. 'You know, she left me a letter. About having freedom and choices... I'll show you sometime. I guess you have a choice, right now...'

They talked on into the evening, until the blue sky took on a wash of faded orange and pink which almost matched Lizzie's T-shirt as the sun slid down out of sight.

It was well past midnight when the girls made their way inside. Lizzie showed her guest to the spare bedroom. The little bed under the eaves looked to Susie like the most inviting place in the world, with fresh white cotton pillowcases, and the faded blue duvet, and all those colourful cushions. Susie decided she'd leave the curtains open, so that she could lie in bed and look at the stars. So much for that idea. As soon as her head hit the pillows, she was sound asleep. So soundly that she wasn't aware of Lizzie sneaking back in, nor that she left the crystal that Nola had given her on the table beside the bed before tiptoeing off to her own.

Next morning, Lizzie was up with the lark, but wondering if the wedding would still be on, thinking she'd better uninvite Leo very swiftly. She had to go and collect the vases she'd hired, and had left a note for Susie. The air was still cool, and some early morning riders trotted down the lane, making the most of the morning before the sun and flies got too much.

Stopping off at Ginny's on her way home, Lizzie wanted to check if the plants needed watering, and to make sure Alice was still free to help her over the next few days. Alice was out for the day, but Ginny assured her she was very happy, if Lizzie was really sure... And no need to collect her, Ginny would be delighted to bring her over, lowering her voice to say that if she didn't get out of the house, she might end up killing someone, nodding her bouffant head jerkily as she spoke, in the direction of her mother who was visiting. Poor Ginny – plagued by so many difficult relatives... She'd said nothing more about the Edward business but her face was stretched tighter than ever.

Back at the cottage, Susie's car had gone. She'd obviously tidied the kitchen before leaving a note, which slightly cryptically said, 'Thank you, dear Lizzie. Please don't worry about me, think I've sorted myself out! Lots of love, S x' written in big curly letters. Did that mean the wedding was on?

26

In London, Tom and Rich had decided to take Friday off, Bella having begged them to come down early.

'Darlings, I really could do with you two lovely strong boys. You wouldn't believe how much there is to do. We've got all the wine and champagne to set up, and car parking to organise. Your father's still tied up with the farm... you know what it's like when the weather's good. And your sister,' Bella added wearily, 'is rewriting the table plan yet again, honestly. Please. I'd really be grateful...'

Noticing more than the slightest hint of anxiety in his mother's voice, Tom agreed they'd be there Thursday night. It was a bank holiday on the following Monday too. They'd make a long weekend of it, he thought. He couldn't wait to get out of London... The heat was getting to him. When the air didn't move, it wasn't a good place to be. He found himself longing for open spaces and a cool lake to dip in, and maybe too, he'd see Lizzie... Then he reminded himself that she was out of bounds, already spoken for, belonging as she did with that tosser Leo, to whom he'd taken such a dislike.

But Tom had gathered himself together. No mooching around being preoccupied with someone else's girlfriend, he'd decided. It was going to be a great party that the folks were throwing for Susie, and he didn't get to see all of them that often. He was looking forward to it... Rich was, too. Rich, however, for his own reasons.

Last week, he'd unexpectedly bumped into Shar after finishing work, and they'd gone for a drink together. Best friends with Susie since childhood, Shar knew the Woodleighs as well as Rich did. They'd found a bar on a barge on the Thames, and sat outside drinking cold beers, gossiping about the forthcoming wedding.

And then, fixing his lovely brown eyes on Shar, Rich had held his nerve, taken one of her hands and asked her – if she was still in love with Tom.

Shar had given a quiet gasp that she hadn't been able to stifle, then turned pink with embarrassment.

'How do you know about that?' she'd asked, horrified at the thought that her unrequited crush might be common knowledge. Then, 'So, who else knows? How embarrassing...' Oh no. What if Tom knew too...

She'd rolled her eyes and Rich hadn't been able to stop himself laughing at her.

'I know he'll only ever see me as the spotty twelve-year-old with pigtails who used to come and stay in the summer holidays,' she eventually admitted. 'But a girl can dream, can't she?'

Rich nodded, still laughing at her loss of composure.

'Anyway. Let's talk about you! There must be a guilty secret somewhere, Richard Carter! Come on, tell me...' she'd insisted.

Several beers later, they'd decided to order some food, and it was dark by the time Shar looked at her watch. And then it only seemed right that he walk her home. It was dark after all, and far too hot to get the tube, he said. And as they walked, chatting easily, giggling at so many small things, Shar realised how much she'd enjoyed herself. She'd known Rich how long? Almost as long as she'd known Tom, and all the time it was as though she was wearing blinkers...

Well, now they were off and when Rich stopped on her doorstep, saying he'd see her in Littleton for the wedding, she'd taken his surprised face in her hands and kissed him on the lips, firmly, just so there could be no mistaking that she'd meant it and when Rich had kissed her back, it had been spine-tingling. They might have been slow getting started, but it was worth every second of the wait.

But neither waited until the wedding to meet up again. The next night, they'd met in a swanky fish restaurant, Rich being in the mood to celebrate. Shar had looked beautiful in a short skirt and boots, her chestnut hair shiny and falling all over the place. Wondering if it had all been in her imagination, as soon as she saw him, she knew.

As they sat sipping expensive wine, Rich was starting to wonder why she didn't order. Eventually, when he pressed her, Shar had blushed a deep shade of beetroot, and admitted, highly embarrassed, that she was very allergic to fish, and that it made her puke. Rich couldn't believe it.

'You completely daft girl!' he told her. 'Why didn't you say so?'

'I so wanted to see you,' admitted Shar, 'I probably would have eaten sheep's scrotums if it meant we spent the evening together.'

She covered her face with her hands, laughing at herself. What an idiot she felt, but for once she didn't mind.

Rich was grinning. He couldn't believe that this had been under their noses.

'Come on, let's just go...'

Giggling, they left more than enough money on the table to cover the wine, and scarpered like naughty children. Hand in hand they made their way down towards the Thames again, finding a bench to sit on where they ate chicken and chips out of newspaper.

And afterwards, Rich had kissed her, still giggling at first, then increasingly passionately until suddenly he stopped.

'What is it?' Shar's big green eyes questioned his.

Rich looked at her for a moment. 'You, this, us,' he tried to clarify. 'Only, we've been friends for such a very long time, are you sure? We could stop now, and still just be friends – very, very good friends...'

Shar gently touched his cheek. 'You darling idiot man, it's far too late for that,' she murmured, as she wound her arms tightly round his neck.

27

'Oh Alice...' wailed Lizzie. 'Sorry, but I can't do this! I don't know where we start...'

'Nonsense,' said Alice, with a sternness that belied her years. 'Of course you can...'

Lizzie walked around the marquee in circles, her stomach churning, feeling sick and dizzy all of a sudden. This space was simply massive. And all those guest who'd see it. And she'd never done anything like this...

Then she heard Bella's voice. 'Lizzie? Dear? Do you have a moment? Only the plants and trees are here.'

Oh, thought Lizzie, still in a panic and wanting to turn and scream and run a million miles away. This was insane.

She went through her list of what they were taking to the church, and the wonderful, long-suffering gardeners loaded it all on a trailer for her. Not only that, but those brilliant men actually volunteered to help the other end. Secretly, they were staying out of the way at the house, and Lizzie didn't blame them. Even Bella, normally so calm and unruffled, was looking stressed.

And so it was, two hours later, amidst a veritable forest outside the door to Littleton church, Lizzie and Alice got started. The gardeners had already begun shifting the largest of the trees inside. The ivy needed to go up first though, great long trails of glossy, dark leaves which Lizzie wound around the ancient stone columns. Four columns later, Lizzie had worked up a sweat. Between them, she and Alice then packed the windowsills with candles, covering the ledge behind the altar with the ones left over. Already it was transformed... They'd bring the plants in tomorrow, she thought, trying to envisage how it would look.

'Alice,' she called. 'Come and see!'

They stood at the back of the church together, and Alice grinned. 'It's *so* cool! Oh Lizzie, it's going to look amazing!'

But at the marquee, the tranquil scene had descended into chaos. Someone had left a gate open, and at that precise minute, two dozen greedy sheep were rampaging around Bella's perfect garden like hungry children in a sweet shop. And with a flower bed to tempt them, they weren't remotely interested in the grass.

Lizzie and Alice could hear the shouts and 'baaing', and they started to run. Bella and the gardeners were endeavouring to round up the small flock, now in full flight, aided ineptly by the marquee men, who far from helping seemed to be making matters worse. Two sheep stuck their heads up from deep in Bella's prized perennial border, chewing on mouthfuls of flowers, while several more could be heard galloping around inside the marquee itself.

Lizzie clapped her hands to shoo them and the woolly vandals demolished a mass of daisies on their way. Alice, meanwhile, had deftly slipped inside the marquee and sent the offenders packing out of there. Then Lizzie spotted a bowl and shaking it so it rattled noisily, a trick that Antonia did with Dave, she'd caught the attention of most of the flock who started to trot towards her. Making her way out of the garden and onto the drive, she looked back to check that they were still following. With the stragglers being herded out by Bella and Alice, Lizzie was relieved to see a very scruffy-looking farmer in an equally scruffy old Land Rover, making his way towards them. Parking at the side on the grass, he whistled to a couple of collies who took over. Bella was fuming. It was Mr Woodleigh.

'Darling. I simply can't believe you let that happen. The garden is ruined, you wouldn't believe the mess in there...' Bella looked close to tears.

Lizzie hardly dared go to look at the carnage that lay in the garden. The gardeners were already on their hands and knees, cursing as they collected the sheep droppings that had been scattered absolutely everywhere, and while there was no permanent damage to the marquee itself, the flower beds were decimated. What had been the most impressive spires of white delphiniums had been trampled to the ground, and how quickly those treacherous sheep had made inroads into what had been a showpiece.

Lizzie cast her expert eye around. The delphiniums were trampled and smashed to pieces, but the rest could be tidied up. It wouldn't be quite the same but at least there were more than enough plants in pots for the marquee, which she could easily fill the gaps with. She went in search of Bella.

'It's okay,' she reassured her. 'I can make your flower beds look fine.' She glanced at Bella. 'Though there's not much I can do about your delphs.'

A little more composed by now, Bella looked sad. 'We planted them just for this weekend, you know,' she said. 'Timed it to perfection too... They were *so* heavenly, the best we've ever had.' She sighed resignedly. 'Well, there was bound to be some kind of a hitch. Let's just hope that this was it, and that everything else goes as planned.'

Lizzie hoped so too. A couple of hours later, she'd done her best – patching the gaps up with a few carefully camouflaged pots among what remained of the plants, the flowerbeds at least looked respectable. Alice had cleaned up the inside of the marquee, and the pair of them collapsed on the grass. It was the end of a very long day. Susie had appeared about an hour ago, fortunately no earlier, and thought it all sounded hilarious, which it was, Lizzie supposed, now that the damage had been repaired.

'Poor Daddy,' she'd said, before hooting with laughter. 'Those sheep of his are notorious for escaping, it doesn't matter where he puts them. Mind you,' she added grimly, 'he better double lock them in until Saturday's over. I really don't want them at my wedding.'

Then came Thursday. Boxes and boxes of freshly cut roses had been delivered. After carrying them over to the old stables, which were shady and cool, Lizzie and Alice began the laborious task of unwrapping each bunch and cutting every single stem before placing them in buckets of cold water.

Susie was back to being her old excited self, with no further mention of her jitters. She'd raved about the roses. The old-fashioned cream-coloured one was Lizzie's favourite, with its extraordinary scent, but the rest were equally stunning, and in shades of deep reddish pinks and purples, massed together in the mismatched assortment of buckets, they looked perfect as they were.

Lizzie and Alice returned to the church. As the door creaked open, Lizzie was relieved to see that everything looked as fresh as yesterday as they moved the plants into position. She'd have to remember to water them. The poor trees particularly – they were shouting to have their roots buried in the ground, where they could stretch them out in comfort.

Huge white hydrangeas were placed either side of the altar, with taller, more subtle olive trees placed just beyond. Further pots of roses, and tall climbing jasmines and honeysuckle were grouped here and there against columns and under arches. Small bunches of herbs tied with raffia bows lay among the candles behind the altar, and the larger trees were grouped in the corners and along the side walls.

They hadn't been there long when they heard the door open and someone come stomping in.

'Good God, Lizzie! It's bloody amazing!'

Lizzie looked round from behind a huge hydrangea.

'Antonia! Sssh... You're in a church!'

'Oops, forgot for a moment. I say, it's frightfully swish... Not at all like when Harry and I got hitched... think we just had begonias or something.'

Then behind her, someone else crept in.

'Eucalyptus!' boomed Antonia. 'Should Lizzie decorate the bells?'

'Oh Lizzie... oh dear, it does look very beautiful...' Euc looked as anxious as ever.

'Oh Lizzie,' she said again. 'I really do have to talk to you sometime.' She looked around worriedly at Antonia and Alice. 'But not now... No – it can wait.' She scurried out of the church.

'What was that about?' called Lizzie.

'Haven't a clue. Seems odder than ever, just lately. Think she's losing the plot... Now, brought you some coffee.' She waved a flask in the air. 'Shall I pour some?'

The coffee was strong and black, and Lizzie drank it gratefully as someone else appeared. The trail of visits from nosey villagers seemed never-ending, and was taking up a lot of Lizzie's time. This time it was Cindy, who she'd only met in passing, looking very pretty, as Cindy always did.

'Cindy!' Antonia jumped up. 'Not quite like your flowers is it?'

Cindy gazed around slightly shell-shocked. 'Um... no... But it's truly lovely...'

'How's your book coming along?' asked Antonia. Without waiting for an answer, she continued 'Cindy's writing a novel, darling. She's promised I can be the first to read it, haven't you?'

'I've nearly finished, actually! I'll drop it over next week if you like...'

'Jolly good! Can't wait! Love a good old romance... Tell me, darling, is it raunchy?' Her eyes glittered.

Cindy frowned slightly as she thought about it. 'Well, I'm not sure you'd exactly call it a romance...'

Eventually, Lizzie and Alice were left in peace. Fortunately, neither of them noticed Mrs Hepplewhite stick her head round the door, then leave without uttering a single disapproving word. Only when they'd sprayed every last leaf with a fine mist of water, did they close the church door and leave.

Friday passed in much the same fashion only minus all the visitors, as they decorated the marquee, festooning tent poles with swathes of ivy, and massing the trees and rose plants like a beautiful, instant garden.

Bella had popped her head in, unbeknown to Lizzie, secretly delighted with what she had seen. She'd somehow keep Susie out until Lizzie had finished.

Susie had wanted a rose walkway into the marquee, which wasn't easy to build in a day, but the gardeners had come up trumps and produced a set of black garden arches, which they assembled to create a sort of tunnel. Draped with more ivy, the remaining climbing roses carefully woven in, when Alice added twinkling fairy lights, the result was spectacular. They'd then retired to the cool of the stables, where they filled the dark green vases until, finally, they realised they'd finished just as Bella poked her head round the door.

'Oh Lizzie,' she said... 'And Alice... I just had to come and say what magic you've worked... It all looks, well, perfect – more than perfect! And she's going to love those...' She stood looking at the vases. 'I left her jumping all over the place.' She raised her eyebrows. 'Please *do* go and see her. She's in the marquee. Needless to say, she's over the moon.'

Closing up the stable, they heard Susie long before they saw her. Walking through the tunnel, Lizzie and Alice were almost flattened by her, the most hyper Lizzie had ever seen her, her panda eyes evidence that more than a tear or two had been shed.

'Liz-zie!' She ran and flung her arms around her. 'This is a dream! I never imagined in a million years it would look as incredible as this! I can't believe what you've done.' Then she added more quietly, 'If it wasn't for you, none of this would be happening. You know what I mean.'

Suddenly Lizzie was mortified. 'Oh Susie, I'd asked Leo to come as my date... before, you know... I've completely forgotten to cancel him...'

'Don't!' said Susie. 'Honestly, there's no need, I promise...' Then she leaped up again. 'Oh, I can't wait, I can't wait for tomorrow...!' And to Lizzie's heartfelt relief, she jumped and danced around the marquee.

'Hi! I'm Shar,' said a small chestnut-haired girl with enormous green eyes, holding out her hand. 'Chief bridesmaid! I'm so happy to meet you, she hasn't stopped talking about this! And she's right, it's amazing! It really does look magical.'

At that moment, out of the corner of her eye, Lizzie noticed two more figures appear. Tom. And Rich. Shar's eyes lit up when she saw them, and she grinned at Lizzie. 'You've met these two before I think?' She raised an eyebrow quizzically at Lizzie.

'I have!' Lizzie was feeling awkward. Conscious of how scruffy she must look. 'Hello again!'

Blushing as they congratulated her on how the marquee looked, Lizzie found herself grabbing Alice's arm, then saying, 'We really must be going, it's lovely to see you again,' before dashing off, leaving three pairs of eyes following her hasty departure with amusement.

'That's twice now, Tom! You're losing your charm, mate,' teased Rich, as he hung an arm over a giggling Shar's shoulders.

Tom watched Lizzie leave. Feeling a touch deflated. He'd hoped to spend longer with her. Well, tomorrow he would, he decided. Leo or no Leo. And away from the scrutiny of his so-called friends.

Alice couldn't make it out. She couldn't understand either quite why Lizzie had dragged them both away so suddenly.

'You are funny,' she told Lizzie. 'I thought you liked him. Why didn't you stay and talk to him?'

* * *

Later on, bone-numbingly weary, Lizzie collapsed on the grass in her front garden with a rather stroppy Darren, who was rubbing against her knees and telling her how neglected he was feeling.

'Evening all, um, am I interrupting...?'

Lizzie leaped up. 'Tom?'

She loved how he looked. Kind of a bit scruffy, in those worn faded jeans, and an equally faded T-shirt and his skin had caught the sun in just a couple of days – it suited him.

'Fancy some company?' he asked, slightly awkwardly. 'Of the human variety that is?'

'Oh sorry... um... come in!' Tom was still standing on the other side of the gate.

Lizzie dithered. 'Would you like a drink of something? Tea? Beer?'

'Beer would be great...'

He followed her into the little kitchen with Darren stalking watchfully behind, and looked around appreciatively. It was basic inside. All the estate cottages were, but it was quirky and homely where Lizzie had added her touch, and felt fresh and welcoming – he liked it.

'You wouldn't want to be up at the house right now,' he offered, as if by way of explanation for his being here. 'Ma is a little stressed because two of the cousins had cancelled and now they've changed their minds. They're trying to reorganise the table plan or something. For about the twentieth time I think. Susie's running around tying black ribbons on all the trees, and the old man's forgotten to unearth the fairy lights. Haven't a clue where Rich is.' He frowned.

Come to think of it, Shar seemed to have disappeared too. Weddings. Was it *really* worth it? He just didn't get what all the fuss was about. Lights and ribbons and all that malarkey...

Weddings, Lizzie was thinking at the same moment. If I ever get married, she thought, it'll be on a beach, barefoot in the sand a stone's throw from the ocean...

'Shall we take these outside?' she suggested, holding two beers.

As they sat on the rickety chairs, which Tom had looked at somewhat dubiously, Lizzie tried to explain how she'd left London and come to be living in Littleton, while Tom told her about the business that he and Rich had started, selling once in a lifetime holidays in exotic locations. Neither had noticed the time passing, until Tom looked at his watch.

Draining the last of his beer, he stood up. 'Rather reluctantly, I think that my conscience is telling me that as the bride's brother, I really should return to the madhouse, and help with tying black ribbons on sheep or something. Tell me, am I the only one who thinks black is odd for a wedding?'

Lizzie laughed. He obviously didn't appreciate his sister's inner goth. 'It's not black, it's dark green and you must know by now what your sister's like...'

They walked down to the gate together.

He turned to look at her. 'You're coming tomorrow, aren't you? I'll see you then.' He kissed her on the cheek. 'It should be quite a party. It usually is when you get all our lot together. See you there!' He loped off up the lane, leaving Lizzie standing, touching her hand to her cheek.

28

Lizzie awakened as the rising sun filtered through her curtains.
Lying sleepily for a few moments, with a start, she sat bolt upright
and was out of bed like a shot. Pulling on jeans and a T-shirt, she
rushed downstairs to put the kettle on.

As it boiled, she quickly brushed her hair and put on a little
make-up, thinking of Tom. Reminding herself of every detail of last
night. It was only a drink, she told herself, so don't go getting
excited about him. Just a beer in the garden. That's all. *Oh, but there
was more. There was that kiss, of course. Don't forget the kiss...*

Up in the Woodleighs' stables, Lizzie had a posy to make for
Susie. Picking the darkest of the roses, she tied them all together
with a velvet ribbon which matched Susie's dress, and then started
on a smaller version for Shar. Setting aside another dozen roses for
buttonholes, she gathered what was left to take to the church.

The village was still asleep as Lizzie drove as quietly as she
could down to the church. Tying bunches of roses into the ivy that
framed the door, doing the same to the ivy-covered columns inside,
she threw the loose petals she'd collected down the aisle.

Without stopping, she was back at the Woodleighs again,

arranging the vases on the tables in the marquee. Yet more petals were scattered on the tablecloths, and as in the church, she tied bunches of roses everywhere until every last one had been used. And that was it. She'd actually finished...

Just then, Lizzie heard voices, and then Bella appeared through the caterer's entrance. She stood there in silence just looking at it all.

Oh no, thought Lizzie, a sinking feeling in her stomach. *It's not what she wanted, she doesn't like it...*

Bella's walked over to Lizzie and kissed her on both cheeks. 'It's lovely,' she said quietly, 'just beautiful. And *so* Susie... I really don't know how to thank you. It's just, well, a million miles from what we were going to have before you got involved. Thank you, Lizzie, thank you very much.'

'And now,' she added, 'I better go and find the bride. She was just a *little* overwrought at breakfast...'

Left alone in the marquee, Lizzie looked around with relief. She agreed – it did look good, but this was most definitely a one-off and next time a mad bride asked for help, she already knew what she'd say. Gardens were one thing – weddings another altogether. *God, she was looking scruffy...* time to get out of here before she ran into Tom.

She'd gone by the time Tom snuck in to the marquee. Great, no one here yet. Now, where *did* they put that table plan... Oh. So Lizzie was bringing Leo after all... He felt a flicker of disappointment.

* * *

Lizzie had two hours. As she lay soaking in the hot scented water, the faintest breeze floated in through the open bathroom window. She could just imagine the mayhem at the Woodleighs – an overexcited Susie, a stressed Bella and everyone else wondering what the fuss was about as they dressed in their finest. Including Tom... Closing her eyes, excitement rippled through her.

By the time she'd dried her hair, pinning up half of it in a messy knot and leaving the rest cascading down her back, and put on the Sparkie's dress and sandals, when she caught her reflection, it surprised her as much as the first time.

* * *

Up the lane in the bride's boudoir, Susie had been on her second glass of champagne when Shar, in her friend's best interests of course, firmly removed the bottle from her dressing table.

'As chief bridesmaid,' she'd announced, completely soberly of course, 'it's my duty today to save you from yourself. Susie! You've had enough!' And with that, she'd disappeared. Trapped by the stylist, protesting loudly, but unable to move while her hair was being transformed into a mass of pre-Raphaelite curls, there was nothing Susie could do.

Shar danced down the landing and knocked on another door a few rooms down. Shutting it quickly behind her, she grinned at Rich and kissed him firmly on the mouth. Then she brought out the bottle from behind her back.

'Surprise!' she giggled. 'I stole it from Susie, I told her she didn't need any more! No glasses, though, sorry! Want a swig?' She giggled again. But Shar didn't need it either – she was high enough already, on love and life. But hey, today they were celebrating. He took the bottle and put his arms around her. He had plans of his own. This was definitely going to be a good day.

* * *

Leo wolf-whistled. He could never bring himself to completely give up on a girl and he grinned with amusement as she blushed.

'Babe, you look sensational...' Lizzie could feel his eyes scrutinising her approvingly.

'You don't look so bad yourself...' she retorted, which was true. The white shirt showed off his tan and he looked too bloody sexy for words in his morning suit. Okay, so she'd sworn off Leo but her body hadn't quite got the message. Make no mistake, he'd be breaking hearts thick and fast before the day was out.

'Shall we?' He offered her his arm.

There was a certain magic in the air as Lizzie and Leo walked down the lane to the church. Cars already lined the sides of the lane and more were roaring up and down looking for somewhere to park. There were Jags and Land Rovers, old and new, and quite a few Porsches. Everyone was dressed just as Lizzie had imagined in posh frocks and morning suits with more than a few outrageous hats, she noticed, as she and Leo slipped into one of the pews near the back. All the candles had been lit, and the scent of the roses filled the church. As the guests filtered in, it looked more and more like a fairy tale – all you could see were the people, the candles and the ivy and trees towering over them. It was like an enchanted wedding in the middle of the woods.

The music was beautiful too, and when Susie arrived in her deep green dress which clung to her tiny waist and billowed out behind her, everything was perfect. Lizzie couldn't help but feel a bit sorry for Mr Woodleigh, squashed uncomfortably into a suit that looked at least two sizes too small for him. Shar looked stunning as the only bridesmaid, her green eyes glowing as she followed Susie down the aisle, stopping only to wink at Rich as she passed him.

And afterwards, the bells rang out joyfully in the anxious hands of Eucalyptus, while everyone filtered out of the church and handfuls of confetti fluttered over the newly-weds as umpteen photos were taken. There wasn't a cloud in the sky. It was just how a village wedding should be, thought Lizzie, if you didn't mind the fact that the bride's dress was almost black and her roses were darkest blood-red. The merry crowd eventually trooped up the lane to the reception and though Lizzie looked, she'd only glimpsed Tom in the distance.

Fortunately, there were no errant sheep, nor would you know there ever had been as the guests crowded onto the lawns, sipping champagne. And as they found their way into the marquee, all around Lizzie could only hear the 'oohs' and 'aahs' as people looked admiringly around.

'Shall I tell them,' whispered Leo in her ear. 'That it was your fair hands that created this masterpiece...'

'Don't you dare!' said Lizzie.

'But hey, Lizzie, honest, it looks cool...'

* * *

As she studied the table plan, Lizzie felt someone close behind her, then the hairs on the back of her neck prickle as a voice said in her ear, 'I was rather hoping to see you—'

But he was interrupted by one of the guests. 'Tom, darling! How simply marvellous to see you...'

Lizzie stood back as the speaker, a thin woman with a hooked nose, monopolised him and she drifted away to find Leo, who was already sitting at their table, deep in conversation with the pretty brunette to his right.

'Babe, meet Honey! She's one of Susie's cousins...'

Leo had obviously wasted no time. Honey stared at Lizzie, slightly confused.

After a sublime meal of the Woodleighs' home-grown lamb,

and the most delicious white wine Lizzie had ever tasted, she was enjoying herself. Watching the master at work was amusing – Leo was on fine form. And every so often Lizzie felt her eyes flicker towards Tom, a couple of tables away.

Even from where she was sitting, it was obvious there was *something* going on between Rich and Shar. You'd have to be blind not to have noticed. He couldn't take his eyes off her, and her eyes shone with love, Lizzie was sure of it, as she leaned in to listen to him, then fell about laughing. You just knew, that if they'd been the only people there, they'd have still had the best time ever. *Was that how it was*, wondered Lizzie, *when you found that person you belonged with?*

Then it was time for the speeches, when Susie's father's words brought a tear to Lizzie's eye and everyone raised their glasses yet again as Susie and Rory cut their funny cake.

What a rip-roaring party it was; Lizzie couldn't remember the last time she'd laughed so much. Leo was at his entertaining best, and had both her and Honey in stitches with his various hilarious anecdotes. As Leo disappeared in search of another bottle of wine, Lizzie seized her moment.

'Honey! He isn't worth it! He's the worst flirt ever! After being a vet, it's what he's best at...'

'So he's *not* your boyfriend?' There was a glimmer of what looked like hope in Honey's eyes.

'Absolutely no way. He's a health hazard. Damages hearts,' she added hastily, watching Honey's eyes light up.

As Lizzie mingled among the guests, she heard a voice beside her. 'More champagne?' It was Tom holding two glasses, one of which he offered to her.

'Thank you.'

'You seem to have been deserted...' He nodded towards where Honey was sitting, head to head with Leo.

'How can I put it... Leo can't resist a flirt... He's quite good fun and he's sort of a friend, I guess, but that's all...'

Tom was still frowning. 'So, you're not...'

'*With* Leo? Oh no, quite definitely not...' Her eyes twinkled at him. It seemed Nola and Julia had been right.

'Oh...' The truth was dawning on him. 'Well, er, would you like to join us?'

She followed him over to a half-empty table, where he pulled out a chair for her, taking one close beside her. His arm brushed momentarily against hers, sending little electric shocks flying between them. It felt inevitable somehow. Like Lizzie couldn't have stopped it if she tried.

'I didn't know,' confessed Tom. 'I always thought you and Leo were a couple, otherwise I'd have switched the seating plan and you could have sat here instead of my deadly cousin Dora... Susie's idea of a joke, putting her of all people next to me...'

'Anyway, I'll fill you in about some of this crowd that I'm lucky enough to count as family...'

As Lizzie looked around, this eclectic mix of the oldest and oddest of the Woodleighs seemed among the most extraordinary collection of individuals she'd ever come across. They had a certain style too. Grand but in a mothballed kind of way.

'Stay well away from old Jasper. Over there, in that ancient suit...' Tom nodded towards an angular, bony-looking man of about fifty-something, who was cruising around the marquee, a shifty look in his eyes.

'He's a notorious groper with terrible breath I'm reliably informed, to be avoided at all costs! I've never got close enough to find out!'

Urghh, thought Lizzie, quite revolted.

'Oh,' Tom continued, 'and over there's another cousin, Rebecca, known as Bex, absolutely without doubt out off her head on some illegal substance or other.'

Lizzie looked disbelievingly at the expensively dressed, regal-looking blonde weaving around the dance floor with a vacant look in her wide blue eyes. It reminded her immediately of Tilly.

'Now—' Tom grinned '—here comes Auntie Melons, so named for two obvious reasons. We don't actually call her that, though I don't think she'd notice,' he added in a whisper.

'Auntie Melanie.' He stood up and offered her his chair. 'Can I get you a drink? This is Lizzie. I'll be back in just a tick, and don't you dare tell her any of your stories about my misspent youth!'

He winked at Lizzie, as Auntie Melons leaned towards her, squashing her ample bosom against her, and taking her arm conspiratorially. She was probably in her late seventies, guessed Lizzie, and was wearing a tailored dress and jacket in Queen Mother blue, with the ubiquitous pearls. Her pale grey hair was carefully curled and her face powdered, but her pencilled-on eyebrows didn't match at all, giving her a permanent air of surprise.

'Dear,' she said to Lizzie, 'isn't it *such* a lovely wedding? I do love weddings,' she added wistfully. 'Quite something isn't it, little Susie married. Only seems like yesterday that she got stuck up the apple tree and wouldn't come down. Oh, dreadful business it was... had to call the fire brigade. Very odd dress though... I mean, black... Fancy!' The eyebrows frowned comically for a moment, as she thought about what she'd said.

Then she patted Lizzie's hand. 'Now, how about you and young Tom... You make a lovely couple, just like me and my Alfie. Such a nice boy he was... Don't you go leaving it too long, dearie...'

Just as Lizzie was thinking what a sweet old lady she was, Auntie Melons moved closer and lowered her voice.

'Someone's stolen my jewels,' she almost whispered to her, a frown making the eyebrows even more lopsided. 'See these earrings?' She touched her little hands to the enormous diamonds in her ears, adding conspiratorially, 'They're not real you know, they're fakes... Someone put them there. They probably thought I wouldn't notice... But they're plastic you know, I can tell. You have them... They're not much good to me...' And to Lizzie's horror, she started taking them off.

Fortunately, Tom reappeared at that point. 'Dance, Auntie.' Melons giggled slightly flirtatiously, forgetting about her ears, temporarily at least.

'Oh, I doubt you'd keep up with me, young man, but why not? And then you simply must dance with this lovely young lady.'

Turning to Lizzie, she whispered, 'He's such a nice boy,' and winked at her.

And then there were the young cousins, and Susie and Rory's London friends. Gorgeous young things, all of them, and so friendly. The exception, Lizzie soon noticed, were the teenage girls, who were regarding her with a degree of hostility.

More of the villagers joined the party for the evening, and Lizzie could see Toby, who was a bit of a groover as it turned out, whirling an unusually glamorous Antonia around the dance floor. Even Mrs Hepplewhite made an appearance, and after a large glass of sherry took to the dance floor for a quick boogie with Mr Woodleigh. Lizzie kept well out of her way.

Shar was having the *best* time. After all, this was her best mate, the girl she'd grown up with and shared every rite of passage with. Susie's family felt almost like her own, she'd known them so long. And this wedding was head-to-toe fabulous, from the frocks to the flowers, with the most divine food and the most delicious men. And having someone to share it with had brought everything more sharply into focus.

She could see Rich and Tom across the marquee. Curiosity got the better of her and she pulled a chair up beside Lizzie.

'So...' she said teasingly. 'What's with you and Tom, then?'

Lizzie blushed hopelessly. Shar was intrigued. She wasn't at all Tom's usual type. Historically, his girlfriends were quite glamorous, dull and extremely short term. Lizzie was very pretty, but you'd never call her glamorous. And all that long tawny hair was beautiful but bore no resemblance to his usual shade of blonde. Lizzie was interesting – not at all what she expected.

'And you and Rich... I mean, you are together aren't you?' retaliated Lizzie.

Shar giggled. 'You know, I think I'm in *lurv*,' she confessed reluctantly. 'And actually, you're the first person I've told!! Cheers!' They chinked glasses.

'Do you know,' she confessed, 'until a few weeks ago, I'd had the worst crush on Tom forever! He used to make my knees knock, seriously, every time he walked into the room. So loudly I swear everyone heard them! Can you imagine how excruciating it was for years, spending school holidays with my best friend in a perpetual state of embarrassment because I fancied her brother?' She shook her head, laughing at herself. 'Anyway, it doesn't matter now, but that bloody man is the sole reason I stayed single for about five whole years you know...' She shook her head in Tom's direction. Well, that was *nearly* true, single except for the odd fling as she'd tried and failed to conquer her obsession.

'Oh.' Lizzie swallowed. She hadn't known this, but quickly Shar added, 'Go for it! He really is as lovely as he looks. Just clueless! On another planet! Doesn't see what's right under his nose, as I know from bitter experience!' She looked at Lizzie and they both giggled. 'In fact, I'll let you in on a little known secret. So far in his choice of women, he is a total disaster. He seems to go for a particular type – you know – the obvious kind, with trowel loads of make-up, tight clothes, high heels and all that. And you've probably realised by now that Tom mooches round in faded jeans and old shoes all the time. He doesn't even think about what he looks like. Anyway, there was this girl who was crazy about him... very pretty and not altogether that bright... We were all going out on Rich's boat and one of her Jimmy Choos broke as she climbed on board and she fell in. I don't think he even noticed...'

They were engulfed in laughter by the time Tom and Rich returned with even more champagne, exchanging mystified looks, especially when a slightly sloshed Shar raised one finger towards Lizzie, saying, 'Not one word, don't say I said...'

Seconds later, Antonia collapsed into the chair next to them. She was wearing the most gorgeous dress, which looked horribly expensive and showed off her toned figure and seemed utterly at home as she kicked off her high heels.

'Simply marvellous bash, isn't it? Pass me some champers will you, darling, I'm parched...'

Lizzie passed her a glass, and looked at Shar. 'Antonia, this is Shar, she's Susie's bridesmaid. Shar, this is Antonia. She lives down the road with her daughter Cassie, and Hamish. Her horse... And Dave, who's a sheep...'

Shar looked at her curiously. Antonia extended a hand in front of Lizzie towards Shar.

'Good to meet you. Golly! Haven't danced this much in yonks. Tobes is simply inexhaustible, darling!'

'Antonia's man,' explained Lizzie. 'Toby. The estate manager. You've probably met him.'

'Aah.' A look of enlightenment dawned on Shar's face. 'He does seem, erm, rather dynamic...'

Antonia snorted. 'He certainly is. I say, Lizzie, have you seen old happy Harry? She's looking frightfully jolly...'

Harriet was indeed twirling around with a nameless man, resplendent in tangerine taffeta. Antonia hid behind Lizzie. 'I'm hiding, darling – don't move... Oh Lord, hope he doesn't spot me. Really could do with a rest.'

'It's the age difference,' teased Lizzie.

'What is?' enquired Rich, pulling up a chair to join them.

'Toby and Antonia. She was just saying she can't keep up with him!' Lizzie glanced at Antonia.

Antonia glared at her.

Rich and Shar had danced and danced, lost in the music and each other, and before long Tom had persuaded Lizzie to join in. He was a great dancer, whirling her around until, laughing and out of breath, Lizzie told him she needed to stop. He took her hand and led her outside.

Apart from the odd bleat from a hidden sheep, peace permeated the garden and Lizzie followed Tom down to the furthest part, where, from under an old oak tree, they looked across the fields to where the sun was sinking slowly in a glorious sky that was a similar shade of orange to Harriet's dress. The air was still warm, and if you could have painted your perfect summer evening, this would be it. In fact, the whole day had been perfect, every second of it. And it was about to get even more so, when hesitating only briefly, Tom gently pulled Lizzie close. Looking down at her, he stroked an errant strand of hair behind her ear. Her heart was pounding so hard Lizzie thought he must hear it, but then he bent his head towards hers and kissed her. And as their lips touched, for one blissful moment it was as though they too had melted into the landscape as everything – the music, the people, the marquee – all of it faded into the background.

'I've had a wonderful day,' she said softly when they came up for air, looking up at him, her hands linked tightly with his.

'Me too,' he replied. 'But... it's far from over yet... You, young lady, have a whole lot more dancing to do!' he added mock-sternly as he swept her back towards the marquee. 'And while we're at it, how about some more champagne? The night is young...'

* * *

It was well into the early hours of Sunday morning with the glimmer of dawn breathing life into the new day, when the last of the die-hard party-goers called it a night. The dog-breathed Jasper was still stalking the marquee in hot pursuit of a victim who'd luckily given him the slip, and Susie and Rory had long since departed in an ancient Jaguar, rattling the usual assortment of tin cans tied on with baler twine along with a muddy pair of Hunters. A distinctive aroma of sheep pooh had filled the air when Rory eventually started the engine, and Susie had refused to throw her bouquet, insisting instead that her mother should dry it so she could keep it forever.

The party mood subsided slightly after that, and after declining the invitation for a skinny-dip in the Woodleighs' pool, a slightly awkward Tom muttered something about walking Lizzie home.

Ha ha! thought Shar triumphantly. *I just knew it! See her home indeed...*

And it seemed at last that this wonderful day was over, unless, Rich whispered suggestively in her ear, she might like to come to his room, just for one little nightcap...

29

It was with some surprise that it dawned on Lizzie as she awakened later that Sunday morning, that she wasn't in her bed. In her sleepy, semi-conscious state, she registered the fact that she was lying on her sofa in her party dress, extremely warm and comfortable, apart from the slight thumping in her head and a mouth that felt like sandpaper.

Dimly aware of sounds coming from the kitchen, she prised one eye open and wriggled into a more upright position just as Tom appeared carrying two mugs.

Lizzie blinked disbelievingly at him, as he sat himself on the floor next to her, and passed one of them to her. And then it all came flashing back, how they'd giggled and danced and kissed their way down the lane last night, talking some more as the sun came up. And once back at the cottage, there'd been more talking, and much more kissing, which ordinarily might have progressed to something had an exhausted Lizzie not fallen fast asleep in Tom's arms. Tom, though, who would happily have continued kissing Lizzie for a whole lot longer, was sleepy too, but had felt strangely peaceful lying there with this girl in his arms. Eventually, he too had drifted off to sleep.

'Thank you, this is the best cup of tea ever.' She tried to sit up but winced. 'Oh... I think I have a hangover...'

Tom laughed. 'I should think you're exhausted after working for my sister, even without some thoughtless man forcing you to dance all night. Great sofa though...'

'Darius and Angel gave it to me... can you tell?'

He grinned and then a muscle twitched in Tom's cheek. A frown crossed his face. 'I'm glad you said you're not with Leo. He's not good enough for you...'

But it wasn't just that... Crap. Tom knew he was useless at these things. He wanted to tell her that he thought that *they* could be good together, that he'd like to see her again, often... but the words just wouldn't come to him. The risk of another rejection hung over him. It was complicated. And he couldn't imagine how he could have a relationship with a girl who lived just down the road from his parents.

Tom leaned over and kissed her again before getting to his feet.

'You know, I better get back and change. There'll be pandemonium at the parents' and they could probably do with some help. But do you fancy an early supper, if you can drag yourself out of bed by then, that is?' he teased.

Once he'd left, Lizzie gratefully collapsed back on the sofa. She wasn't entirely sure what Tom had been trying to say, if anything and anyway, she was too tired to think about it. Her whole body ached. All she wanted was orange juice and sleep, and the instant her eyes closed she was out.

Next time she awoke, she was horrified to see that it was four in the afternoon, and her phone was ringing. When she answered it sleepily, she found it was Bella, wanting to thank her. No sooner had she put the phone down when it rang again, only this time it was Antonia.

'I say, awfully jolly party, wasn't it? Must say I'm pooped though... Tobes has only just left... Has Miriam spoken to you? Only she left me the strangest message...'

The next call was indeed Miriam.

'It's been the most astonishing day,' Miriam told her rather excitedly. 'We had more visitors than Boxing Day! I had to call in extra helpers and there were all these people who wanted to look at the gardens... Lizzie? Are you still there?'

'Sorry! Had a late night! But that sounds fantastic! The magazine article isn't out yet... I wonder what caused it?'

'Some of the schools sent notices home... but oh, Lizzie, I don't know if we can cope with much more...'

* * *

Tom took Lizzie to the Goat, predictably, where a number of yesterday's wedding goers were already tucking in to sandwiches, and quite a few glasses of mineral water, Lizzie noticed, with a slightly more subdued air than the previous day. All except for Darius and Angel, who were larger than life and full of their usual enthusiasm.

'Lizzie flower!' They both kissed her. 'And with Tom Woodleigh... *darling*...'

Darius swooned and Angel gave Lizzie an exaggerated wink.

'We were simply *devastated* to miss yesterday,' Darius said sadly. 'I can't tell you, flowers. Auntie Marigold has just the *worst* timing. It was deadly, darlings. Feel sorry for us...'

'*Lethal*...' added Angel. 'And she's so doolally she'd never have missed us... Anyway! Do tell! It must have been simply *wondrous*...'

* * *

After an evening reliving the previous day with the various occupants of the Goat, it wasn't until they returned to Lizzie's much later on that Tom and Lizzie actually had a chance to talk properly.

'I still haven't figured out where we met before, you know,' said Tom as they went to sit outside, the back garden still warm in the evening sun.

'Nor me,' said Lizzie. 'And you know it's funny – I remember every bit of the wedding, but after that, it's a little blurry...'

'Are you flirting with me, Lizzie Lavender? Maybe I need to jog your memory...'

'Perhaps you could try...' Lizzie gazed innocently back at him and her insides did a backflip.

'What did you have in mind?' But before she could answer, he leaned over to kiss her and it was just like before. All Lizzie could feel was his lips on hers, his hands in her hair as everything faded around them.

'I'd say you remember rather well...' he muttered, gently kissing her neck then moving up to her mouth again.

* * *

Still in those earliest days and a little uncertain of what they were to each other, Tom took Lizzie out for lunch on the Monday. Away from Littleton and Oakley. Somewhere where they wouldn't know anyone and could blend into their surroundings. He knew just the place.

They drove in Tom's Boxster with the roof down so that Lizzie's long hair flew out behind in the wind. Tom had always liked the Spotted Pig. It was a proper pub. He'd first ventured in here underage, secretly thrilled at getting away with buying a pint, and had been back over the years with various girlfriends. It was part of his history. And unpretentious and untrendy, with red velvet seats inside and wooden tables alongside the canal, it was just his kind of place.

The food was tasty. Not as fancy as the Goat, but good plain pub fare – steak and kidney pie, ploughman's... that sort of thing. And after the last few days, Lizzie liked that they were alone. Tom was good company but so far, she hadn't gleaned much more about him than the nuts and bolts everyday stuff rather than the deeper, more soul-searching meaning-of-life type of talking. *Everything I'm so good at myself...*

Further along the canal bank sat a couple. A rather sleek, polished girl with shiny bobbed fair hair and high heels, who raised one eyebrow as she spotted Tom. She watched quietly for a while, her eyes not leaving him for a second, then she spotted the girl he was with. Then absolutely couldn't resist any longer just walking casually by, jogging his shoulder.

'Oh I'm so sorry...' spoken in such soft, lady-like tones, followed by, 'Goodness! Tom? What a surprise! Oh how *lovely* to see you! After all this time! Simon? Look who it is! It's Tom! Tom Woodleigh...'

Silenced, dumbfounded, Lizzie found herself deliberately snubbed. The intimate mood was shattered in an instant as she sat back and watched with disbelief as 'Lucy', as Tom had introduced her, completely took over.

The fish that Lizzie had carefully chosen earlier was suddenly bland and tasteless, and the French bread stuck in her throat, threatening to choke her. Tom himself was looking most uncomfortable. The atmosphere of just minutes ago, that air of unspoken promise, that hint at seduction, it had all just vaporised leaving Lizzie overshadowed in every sense, as she watched the old friends catch up.

'What brings you here of all places?' Tom had asked her.

'Oh, Simon and I were in Cirencester for the weekend,' she replied airily. 'And you?'

'Susie got married on Saturday... Lizzie did her flowers actually...'

With barely a glance at Lizzie, Lucy had raised those neatly arched eyebrows and said casually, 'Of course, you had the family wedding... I'd heard about that. How is Bella by the way?'

Her words were just a touch *too* familiar, and in that split second, Lizzie was on to her. This was no accident. Suddenly she had no doubt whatsoever that Lucy had carefully engineered the whole meeting, staking out the pub, biding her time, waiting for Tom to show. The gleam in her eyes said it all.

'She's well,' said Tom. 'Actually, we were just about to eat...'

'Oh, then we'll join you, won't we, Simon... we've so much to catch up on...' And that was that.

Lucy dominated. Holding his attention, as she chatted away, with an 'Oh you must remember this, Tom', and 'Oh, Tom, remember that time...'

There was no stopping her. Lizzie could feel Tom gradually becoming distanced, as he didn't meet her eye. Such a very different Tom to earlier. Simon too was less than impressed. Making only half-hearted attempts to join in, he eventually gave up and stared miserably into his pint.

It was the longest lunchtime ever before 'last orders' was shouted for the final time. They'd all wandered out to the car park together, where Lucy had hugged him far too closely, before she kissed him goodbye. Lizzie had felt slightly sick. And Lucy had smiled coldly at her, the smile not reaching her eyes, as she offered a limp hand in Lizzie's direction.

On the way home, Tom had tried to make light of Lucy's presence. 'Nice seeing her again,' he remarked casually, before lapsing into silence.

Back in Littleton, the kiss that they'd both anticipated earlier was reduced to a dry brush of lips on cheeks, as Tom stayed in his car.

'I'll call you,' he said, not quite looking at her, before driving off up the lane.

30

But he didn't.

'It's timing,' Julia had told her. 'There's something in his life he's holding on to... All you can do is let him go, Lizzie. If it's meant to be, he'll find you.'

'But it just seemed so... right,' said a baffled Lizzie, struggling to find the right word.

'Oh, Lizzie... not if it isn't for Tom...'

* * *

Life was definitely back to normal again, Lizzie thought to herself. Well, almost... She still felt let down – she couldn't help it. What she thought she'd sensed between her and Tom was unresolved, but the last thing she needed was another screwed-up man. *Get over him*, she told herself, *he's no different. They're all the same...* And actually, amazingly, it seemed she had.

Work had very briefly quietened, but not for very long. No sooner was one party over, than the next one loomed. Edward's. Ginny had been on the phone, double-checking that the garden was on schedule. Lizzie had hastened to reassure her, hiding the sudden sense of panic because actually, the party was next weekend. Since finding Ginny an emotional wreck, Lizzie had become quietly admiring of her stoical brightness, and the smiling, if Botoxed, face that she always presented to the world. So many women simply couldn't do that, thought Lizzie, though somehow she suspected that Edward hadn't heard the end of this.

* * *

After Miriam's anxious phone-call, Lizzie had driven up to Hethecote to see her. Even midweek the farm was busy and Miriam was looking flustered.

'Oh, Lizzie, it's awfully good of you to come, but I'm afraid I can't stop.'

'Don't worry – I'll help for a bit. What would you like me to do?'

Despatched to a distant field to catch Hairy Mary and another small pony, as Lizzie wandered back she was thinking. Supervising loads of people interacting with the animals just wasn't practical – there weren't the staff. But they badly needed the income... they had to think of something.

'Gin, Lizzie?' asked Miriam when they'd closed. She poured herself a double.

'Just a small one,' said Lizzie, who knew Miriam's gins. 'You see, I've been thinking...'

Miriam listened carefully as Lizzie outlined her idea. Her suggestion was that Miriam should keep two or three days a week where people had to book and offer unlimited, escorted access to the animals. That way she could plan the number of helpers available. The rest of the time anyone could just turn up and wander around the farm on their own like before, gardens included.

At the end Miriam sounded doubtful. 'I just don't know... It's quite a change... We'd have to make sure everyone knew... Would we charge more for the bookings?'

Lizzie nodded. 'But you could still offer discounts to your special cases...'

'I don't know... I'll think about it.'

On the way home, Lizzie called in on Antonia to run the idea past her, and noticed not only Tim's but Leo's cars, parked outside on the lane. And as she walked into Antonia's kitchen it became clear it was the fateful day.

'Darling! Everyone's here, isn't it marvellous? Have a glass of wine and come and watch!' Antonia was full of enthusiasm.

Tim was washing his hands. 'Hi, Lizzie!'

Leo stood in the corner of the kitchen and winked at her, as sexy as ever, even in filthy jeans and smelling like a farmyard. He gave Lizzie one of his self-effacing smiles which utterly failed to impress. And in another corner stood Dave, glaring suspiciously at all of them.

'Um, Antonia, I can't believe this is really happening in your kitchen...' said a disbelieving Lizzie.

'Why the devil not?' said Antonia utterly perplexed.

'Anyway, this isn't why I came round,' said Lizzie. 'Look, it's Miriam. There's been an influx of visitors at the farm! She's worried about coping with them all. I had this idea that she could open for two days the way she used to – you know, showing people around and helping the children handle the animals, and the rest of the time, anyone can just turn up. What do you think?'

'Golly, darling... is she really that busy?'

'It's a good idea, Lizzie,' called Tim across the kitchen. 'If she wants to make more money, something's got to change. I'll call in tomorrow and have a chat with her.'

'Antonia... what's this?' Lizzie had spied what looked like a manuscript spread across the end of the table.

'Oh, darling, you absolutely have to read it! It's Cindy's book! It's a thriller – frightfully exciting! About a serial murderer called Kevin. Her ex-husband's Kevin! I bet it's about him! It's really quite deliciously scandalous...'

* * *

After it was all over, Dave came to, lying groggily in a corner of the kitchen on an old blanket, minus two rather impressive attributes.

'I may as well have them for the dogs,' said Antonia casually. 'They'd love them. No point in them going to waste...'

Leo obediently fished them out of a bucket and passed them to her as if they were apples, as Lizzie looked on appalled.

'Thanks awfully,' said Antonia, taking them and putting them in the fridge. 'Gosh, jolly big aren't they?' she added.

'Now, shall we all go to the pub? I'm meeting Tobes... Shall I see you all down there?'

'Leo? Any plans?'

'No. Just been stood up actually...' He looked up from his mobile, puzzled. Lizzie and Tim laughed.

'It's something that happens to us mere mortals, mate,' said Tim. 'Though judging from your face, I guess not to you?'

Leo's face was indeed a picture. 'Her husband got home early. Oh well, plenty more fish in the sea.'

Lizzie gasped, just as Leo winked at her. 'Don't look so shocked! Actually I'm worth the trouble... as you'd find out if you gave me half a chance...' he added, his meaning adequately clear.

'Look, I think I better stay and keep an eye on Dave for a bit,' said Tim. 'Just until Cassie gets home. I'll see you down there in a while.'

As they walked outside, Leo turned to Lizzie, grinned lascivi-ously and waggled his eyebrows at her. She gave him a stern look.

Now that she no longer harboured obscene fantasies about him, she refused to put up with his nonsense.

'No funny stuff. Or I'll tell everybody about your escapades with Matilda Blenkinsopp. Oh yes, I know who stood you up. I've been doing her garden for the last six months and you're not exactly discreet... Ha! You didn't know that did you...'

Leo held his hands up in a gesture of surrender. Some girls were no fun at all, he thought, but actually Lizzie was all right. Rather like one of his sisters.

'In that case, if you're really not going to succumb to my manly charms, can I at least buy you a drink?'

He wasn't all bad, thought Lizzie. At least he seemed a good vet. Then she had an idea.

'Leo? Are you free next weekend?' Leo's ears pricked up. Had she changed her mind? But any licentious thoughts were soon crushed, as Lizzie continued. 'Saturday night? To come to a party with me? As my guest? It's a client of mine, so you would have to promise to be on your absolutely very best behaviour...'

Famous last words. And Leo never could resist a party.

Dave was very quiet for a couple of days, barely baa-ing at all. And walking with his back legs spread very wide apart, he looked like a cowboy from an old John Wayne film, which Antonia found hilarious.

* * *

Ginny's awful mother had thankfully long since departed, and thanks to some assistance from Alice, Lizzie had nearly finished the planting. Ginny, however, had gone missing.

'I'm not sure where she is,' said Alice. 'She was being quite mysterious. I think she's up to something – Mummy doesn't do mysterious very well.'

Ginny rushed back in due course, the highlighted hair slightly dishevelled and with what looked like a damp patch on her lilac jeans. Her face was looking a lot less taut, noticed Lizzie and she was carrying a small, ginger bundle which she held out to her daughter.

'Oh, Mummy...'

'It's yours, my dear little Alice...'

'Oh...' Alice gently stroked the little creature, which stared back at her out of the widest eyes. 'Thank you, Mummy! So much! I've always wanted a kitten...' She frowned. 'But what will Daddy say? Isn't he allergic to cats?'

'Nonsense,' squeaked Ginny dismissively. 'Complete poppy-cock. All that twaddle about allergies is nothing but a load of old codswallop. He doesn't like the hairs on his trousers, that's all.'

So the gloves were off then. Edward better be watching his back...

'She's all yours, darling,' said Ginny, practically purring herself. 'She was bred by a woman with a funny sounding name... Mrs...'

'Einstein?' said Lizzie. Her cats seemed to be all over the place.

'That's it! Now how did you know that! You'll have to think of a name for her...' she said to Alice.

But Alice had a grin on her face. 'Tom,' she said, giggling. 'I'm going to call her Tom.'

'Don't be silly, darling, that's a boy's name.' Ginny looked confused.

But Lizzie got it. Alice was about to drive those annoying sisters of hers completely up the wall.

* * *

Much later that afternoon, Lizzie called in on Bella Woodleigh. The marquee had been dismantled and there was little to indicate the wedding had ever happened, except for the missing delphiniums.

Lizzie found her in the garden, looking more lady of the manor than she usually did in a long linen skirt and battered floppy hat, wandering around slightly distractedly as she did the last bit of tidying up.

'Lizzie! How lovely! Honestly, if I'd known how tiring this would all be, I might just have thought twice... Come and have a drink. I have the first photos from the wedding. Would you like to see them?'

Bella couldn't help but notice how Lizzie's cheeks flushed with pink as she handed her the pictures of Tom. How handsome he looked in that morning suit... but then he was her son. She'd also with great interest noticed them together at the wedding. With surprise too, given Tom's usual type of girlfriend. But perhaps now was not the time to mention anything, so instead, ever diplomatic, she got onto the subject of her next project.

'Now, Lizzie dear, what I'd really like you to do is come and look at my favourite corner of garden. No one else in the family takes any notice of it, but I think that perhaps you might understand...'

They wandered back outside and through an arch in the wall that Lizzie hadn't seen before. 'It's in here. Horribly neglected, I'm ashamed to say, but please tell me honestly what you think...'

Lizzie took a deep breath as her eyes took it all in. It was beautiful – and crumbling. But an air of derelict grandeur had remained, with a small pond built of stone in the centre, its walls collapsed in places, but careful planting would both draw the eye and compliment the decay. It needed to stay a bit wild, thought Lizzie. Perhaps Bella was right when she had imagined making it look a bit like her own garden at home.

'I absolutely love it, and I think I know exactly what to do...'

Bella nodded. She'd guessed Lizzie would feel the magic of her own favourite corner of these enormous gardens. Listening enthralled as Lizzie outlined how she'd plant this rose here, and that particular one over there because it was low growing and would thrive where the wall was tumbling down. How she'd throw wild-flower seeds to flourish where it suited them and place a bench in the furthest corner where it would catch the evening sun.

As they walked back to the house, something was puzzling Bella.

'It's none of my business, Lizzie, but how did you end up living in Littleton? It's barely on the map and you have to admit, it is a little odd...' She broke off and looked at Lizzie.

Hesitating only briefly, Lizzie told Bella about Jamie. It seemed ridiculous now to think they'd been a couple. She even told her about her mother, and Bella's heart went out to her. She described how she'd decided on a career change, and uncannily, how she'd stumbled across Littleton completely by accident before she knew she even needed somewhere.

'One minute I was passing through, then I saw the cottage... I wasn't even thinking about staying, but suddenly it just felt right...' she said thoughtfully.

Bella touched her arm. 'Just the right place at the right time by the sound of it.'

Lizzie frowned. Everyone kept talking about timing... was it really so important?

'Actually, I think I know what you mean...' she continued. 'It was a long time ago but before I came here, I was engaged to someone else – a wealthy banker, as it happens. I very nearly married him... It would have been a privileged life in some respects, but I could never quite see myself like that... And in the end, well, Harry made the decision for me and swept me off my feet.' A reflective look crossed her face. 'And then, when I first came here, I fell in love again, with this glorious old house, with all its draughty windows and shabby curtains. But from the minute I walked in, I felt at home. I've never had a single regret. It's as though some things are just meant to happen...'

Before she left, Lizzie agreed that as soon as Ginny's garden was finished, Bella's would be top of her list. How long would she stay, Bella wondered, watching her walk down the drive. After all, once she'd finished putting together the pieces of her shattered life, and she was well on the way to doing that, what else was there for her here?

* * *

There was a disagreement going on in the Star when Lizzie got there.

'Anyway, Antonia,' Tim was saying. 'Hold on a moment. Have you ever stopped and thought about what you spend on all Hamish's titivating? That is the most pampered equine I've ever come across, even round here. Remember last year when he was daft enough to climb into the hedge and ripped himself to shreds on some barbed wire you didn't know was there? You couldn't ride him for weeks and he cost you a small fortune in vet's bills...'

'She's moaning about the cost of castrating Dave,' said Leo. 'Tim's hardly ripping her off. Of course, if it were a horse, she wouldn't bat an eyelid...'

'Horses are completely different,' retorted Antonia. 'Intelligent, affectionate, clever...'

It was Lizzie's turn to smirk. If Hamish was a human, he'd have flunked out of school at the first opportunity and ended up hanging around the streets. Personally, she thought Dave was far smarter.

'Anyway,' added Antonia bossily, changing the subject before anyone else said anything against her beloved Hamish, 'we're off to the Goat to meet Toby. Fancy joining us?'

'Got a date actually,' said Leo with a self-satisfied look on his face.

'What he really means is a shag,' said Lizzie brightly.

* * *

In the Goat, Lizzie spotted Ginny's older daughters, who nudged each other and stared rather obviously at her as she came in.

'Drinks, ladies?' asked Tim.

'Oh, red wine for me,' said Antonia. 'Lizzie?'

'Same – please...'

They sat down at an empty table, and Antonia leaned towards Lizzie. Not one for being discreet, she asked with her usual frankness. 'Now, simply got to ask... what's going on with you and Tom Woodleigh? Seemed you spent a jolly lot of time together at that wedding... Nice enough chap, but a bit clueless if you ask me. But, if you're not, seeing Tom that is, I'll have a think. Sort out a blind date or something.'

'No, Antonia, please don't... I won't go.' The idea alone was terrifying.

'It'll be such fun... Oh darling, here comes Tobes. Darling...' Antonia seemed to have completely forgotten all about not encouraging him.

'Evening, Lizzie, evening, Tim! Excellent! All got drinks I see. Be right back...' Toby was as chipper as ever.

'I think you should let Lizzie sort out her own love life! Worry about your own! Do you know, Lizzie, she can't resist matchmaking! Not in all the years I've known her, since she had her first horse...' Tim was at her defence.

'That was Willy, darling. Magnificent creature... Never should have sold him you know. Went round Badminton last year.' She looked quite downcast. 'Biggest bloody mistake of my life. Far worse than the divorce.'

Maybe she should get away for a bit, Lizzie thought. Spriggan Point and Roscarn were in her thoughts. She could do with a bit of magic right now. Wonderful though life here was, she needed space. Away from well-meaning blind dates and stressful parties. From worrying about Hethecote Farm and from everything that reminded her of Tom. It was the right *time*... She made a mental note. After Ginny's party, she'd take a week off and disappear.

31

The day before Edward's party, Lizzie drove over to check on Ginny's garden.

Ginny's face had got definitely got tighter – stress, most likely. It was a scene of pandemonium, with a half-built gazebo and Ginny flapping around like a little pink butterfly, making the marquee men take it down and start again because that awning had to be just a tiny bit further over or it would look simply terrible... The men were tearing their hair out.

'Oh Lizzie, I'm so behind... The weather forecast isn't good, so I had to organise *this*... And now I'll need to decorate it, oh goodness, I hadn't thought of that...' Lizzie's heart sank. She wasn't going to get talked into that side of things. 'And you are coming, aren't you? Excellent networking opportunity for you,' said Ginny sharply.

'Of course I am,' said Lizzie. 'I wouldn't miss it for the world.'

* * *

Lizzie hadn't seen Antonia since the last night in the pub. Not even bouncing into the distance on a horse, which was fairly unusual.

Wandering round the back of Antonia's cottage that evening, she called out 'Helloooo, anyone home? Antonia?'

Eventually, Antonia emerged from her study, with a flurry of barking canines who flung themselves at Lizzie. She rubbed her eyes. 'Oh golly. Friday isn't it! Seem to have lost track... Had a tad on my mind...' She looked a bit vacant.

Then, seizing upon the bottle under Lizzie's arm, her eyes lit up. 'God, I could really do with a drink. Let's open it.' She took it and made for the kitchen, rustling up two glasses and a corkscrew as she cleared the usual array of old *Horse and Hounds* and bridles to one side of the big old table.

They sat in unusual silence, sipping wine, or in Antonia's case, gulping it, until she took a deep breath, announcing, 'That's better.'

Topping up their glasses, she explained. '*Bloody* Harry is getting hitched. To *bloody Marla*.' Spoken in an exaggerated American accent. 'Bitch woman. So, out of the blue, he wants a divorce and a financial settlement, a pretty *bloody* mean one at that. So, although he's filthy rich and my extremely competent lawyer will undoubtedly take him to the *bloody* cleaners, which is no more than he deserves, in the meantime it leaves me with the teensiest little cash flow problem.'

She was silent again, before adding, 'Meanwhile, I am supposed to just sit here, while she hopefully earns the ridiculous amount she's charging me. I tell you, you wouldn't believe what it costs me just to email her... I even have to book my telephone calls. While Cassie and I have no money too...'

Lizzie didn't like to think what Antonia continually spent on her horses. Scarily huge amounts, though she was quite sure that in Antonia's mind it was up there with essentials like bread, milk and wine. She thought for a moment.

'What about more liveries? Or could you get a job?'

'May not have the choice,' said Antonia miserably. 'Might have to go and work in the Co-op or something. Needs must, darling...'

God, what a horrendous thought. She'd send the customers fleeing for their lives, thought Lizzie, aghast. And they'd fire her in no time... No. That definitely wasn't the answer.

'No, no, no... not that sort of thing. Something else...' she said, casting around for ideas.

But Antonia sat there looking rather defeated. 'There are a couple more stables – they're filthy dirty and full of junk, darling, but I can't think of anything else...' Her eyes swung over to the painting Lizzie had noticed when they first met. 'I could always sell that – it's an original you know. Might have to, at this rate...'

She took another large swig of wine, thinking out loud.

'I suppose it'll be more liveries. The hunting season's round the corner! Couldn't be better timing really... Have to deal with the owners, of course, but, well, beggars can't be choosers... and once the lawyer's sorted Harry out, I'll boot them all out again.' She sighed, looking slightly defeated.

Lizzie wondered if it would be as simple as Antonia thought, but had to admire her friend, when by the next day, she'd already scrubbed out her spare loose boxes and stuck ads in all the local feed shops.

And at least it was proving a welcome distraction, as far as Lizzie was concerned, from Tom, who seemed to have completely vanished. Far from being upset, Lizzie remained calm and philosophical, though admittedly, still somewhat perplexed. She supposed that he'd succumbed to the charms of the calculating Lucy – so why did it feel like there was still unfinished business?

* * *

It had taken him a while to figure it out, but there was definitely unfinished business between him and Lizzie, reflected Tom. He had found out, too late, that he didn't feel about Lucy the way he used to. His world had fallen apart when she left him all that time ago. Then, he'd have done *anything* to have her back... And now she *was* back it was different. But she had this knack, of drawing him in, planning things for them to do together... And not wanting to rock the boat, Tom had found himself going along with it... but the spark had well and truly died.

But the trouble with history, he thought ruefully, is it complicated everything. It's hard not to be swayed by what you used to mean to each other. Bodies remember – physically he could let himself respond to her. And there was everything you already know about each other... It pulled you back together like the most annoying kind of glue, when really, it would be better all round, if you severed the connection for good.

Not so for Lucy though, who had made up her mind that, one way or another, the next Woodleigh wedding would be hers.

But for Tom, this unfinished business was haunting him. It had been different two years ago when Lucy had broken his heart. But things had changed – he'd changed. He wasn't in love with her, and there was Lizzie. Try as he did to put her out of his mind, she kept creeping into his thoughts.

The more he thought about her the more he wanted to see her. That was the trouble. He'd managed to at least work that much out, though goodness knows he'd taken long enough. Lizzie was so easy to be with. Undemanding... not forgetting heart-stoppingly beautiful without even trying, not like the high-maintenance girls he usually met. All this dashing around with Lucy, meeting this group of friends here, visiting that new wine bar there – 'Everyone's going there, Tom darling...' It was making him crave the peace of Lizzie's back garden with chickens scratching round his feet, and suddenly a cold beer in the Goat was infinitely more appealing than cocktails in the latest, trendiest wine bar in the heart of London. God, Tom, he thought, with a shock. You must be getting old.

Oh, there was no disputing that Lucy fancied him, he'd worked that out, too. The way she cocked a groomed eyebrow at him, tilting her head as she looked sideways, flirtatiously into his eyes. The way she kept touching him, and that smile, so inviting and full of promise... But it wasn't working. He sighed. He knew the time had come.

Back at Lucy's flat, she'd confidently set the scene, believing all her plans were about to fall into place. While Tom was in the bathroom, she dashed around, quickly lighting the scented candles she'd put out earlier. Pavarotti played quietly in the background and there was a bottle of Veuve Cliquot chilling in the fridge. She'd taken her time, and hadn't rushed him, she thought, allowing herself a slightly smug smile as she anticipated what lay ahead.

He came back in, gently taking both her hands, sitting her down next to him on the expensive leather sofa. It's worked, thought Lucy, exalted for all of a split second, before her hopes were dashed for good.

'You dumped me for Stuart, Luce,' he said, only mildly accusingly. 'You didn't explain, didn't apologise, just disappeared, leaving me to find out from Rich, who'd bumped into the two of you having a romantic dinner...'

He shook his head then, and let go of her hands. Hearing the tone of his voice, Lucy dropped the girly, flirty act, stopped tilting her head.

Looking earnestly at him, she said in all honesty, 'I'm sorry, Tom. Truly, from the bottom of my heart. I made the biggest mistake of my life. We were so good together... I really hoped that, well, I could make it up to you and we could give it another try...'

Tom clasped his hands together and looked at her intently. Suddenly there was no choice to make. There never had been. He didn't even know why he was here.

Standing up, he said, 'I'm sorry, it's too late...'

He walked out, feeling a physical need to talk to Lizzie. He really had been an idiot. It was late, but he tried his mobile, which was out of battery again. Crap. Rich was always telling him to charge his phone. He'd try again when he got home. This was important.

* * *

In Littleton, Lizzie stirred from a deep sleep, thinking she could hear the phone ringing in the distance... sleepily she sat up. It had definitely stopped now. Looking at her clock, she saw it was midnight. And now she was awake... She switched the light on and started to read.

* * *

Miles away in London, Tom lay in bed, also trying to read. He'd known it was too late to phone, but he'd had to try. He'd get up early in the morning and try again.

* * *

Next morning, Lizzie was on the way out to her car when the phone went again. Never mind. If it was important, they'd leave a message. Or phone her mobile. It never crossed her mind it might be Tom.

* * *

He let the phone ring until the answerphone clicked in, then changed his mind and hung up. He wasn't sure quite what to say. In fact he was at a loss as to what to do next.

32

The evening of Edward's party, Leo arrived on time for once, as immaculately dressed as before and every bit the perfect escort, Lizzie thought. As long as he kept his hands to himself. Leo, however, fully aware that Lizzie's interest in him had waned, had decided that tonight he'd have some fun.

They were greeted with great enthusiasm by Ginny, already a little the worse for wear, with cheeks that matched the rather revealing cerise cocktail dress she was wearing. Giggling flirtatiously at Leo, she handed them both a glass of pink champagne.

'Don't you dare ask for a beer,' muttered Lizzie through gritted teeth in his ear. Leo smiled disarmingly at Ginny.

Actually, Ginny had carried the whole pink thing off remarkably tastefully in the end. Lizzie had been prepared for the worst, but the fairy lights were sufficiently buried in the trees, and the garden umbrellas that looked so garish in daylight had thankfully faded as it got darker. And the garden, she thought, with enormous satisfaction, was a triumph.

Alice, dressed rebelliously in black despite her mother's best attempts to persuade her otherwise, had been thrilled to see Lizzie.

Lizzie likewise. But she was about the only person Lizzie knew here and after a couple of hours of circulating and mingling with Ginny's guests, she was longing to go home and put her feet up.

'Have you seen Leo?' she asked Alice. 'I imagine he's probably sussing out the talent, but I need to find him. He's supposed to be giving me a lift home.'

Lizzie squeezed through all the guests again to check the kitchen, expecting Leo to be rooting out some beer, when she heard a muffled crash. Then a door burst open, and Ginny practically fell out of the downstairs loo giggling uncontrollably, her eyes bright, her pink lipstick smudged and her dress skewed all over the place. Lizzie boggled. More so when behind her hostess, she spotted Leo.

Oh. How could he...

Seeing Lizzie's face, Ginny winked a huge, exaggerated wink at her. 'Oh Lizzie! Don't be such a spoilsport! I'm having the best time I've had in years!' She gave Lizzie one of her Botox grins and hiccupped, as she lurched slightly.

'Awfully sexy, isn't he? And marvellous at kissing...' Though she'd lowered her voice slightly, it was still loud enough for quite a few people to hear. Heads were turning to stare, but oblivious, she continued, completely trolleyed.

'And it serves Edward right, doesn't it?' she slurred. 'You know... he's such a prick! Oh! Did you know, Lizzie, he's got a teeny little...'

'SShh!' Lizzie hushed her, but Ginny wasn't having any of it.

'Not like that lovely boy over there...' She glanced in Leo's direction and hiccupped. 'But it's a teeny-weeny one...' She held up a finger and thumb to show exactly how teeny.

'Have I told you that before?' she slurred. 'Oooh, I think I better go and find him. It's time to make an announcement...' and she wobbled off, singing to herself as she tottered among her guests, grinning maniacally at them.

Lizzie panicked. With Ginny in that state, impending disaster was round the corner.

Catching Leo's eye and giving him a glare that would have matched any of Dave's slitty-eyed ones, she marched off after Ginny. Leo winced, grabbed a beer and, slinking back into the loo, locked the door behind him.

Lizzie couldn't be sure what Ginny's intentions were, but couldn't help thinking that perhaps a glass of water and some fresh air might be the best plan. Even though Edward deserved everything he got and more.

But she was too slow, and before she could stop her, Ginny had stood next to Edward, silencing their guests, as she started to speak. Too late. Lizzie sat back and watched as the shit hit the fan.

Loudly and unambiguously, wobbling slightly, Ginny raised her glass to Edward, her eyes a-glitter. 'I'd like all of you to join me in wishing Edward a truly memorable birthday... Darling...'

She raised her glass even higher and poured the contents over his head. After spluttering his indignation, Edward stalked off, red-faced and furious.

'Ooh, Edward darling! *So* sorry!' Ginny watched him go, looking extremely pleased and only slightly shocked at herself.

It completely killed the party. The bewildered guests, wondering if they'd heard the last bit correctly before deciding they probably had, made their excuses, some of them embarrassed, some sniggering, which made you question what sort of friends they really were. Lizzie stayed long enough to make sure Alice was okay, which she was of course. Not that she'd exactly enjoyed seeing her father being made to look a complete idiot, but she was secretly proud of her mother, who up until now she'd thought was as weak as dishwater. The other daughters had yelled at their mother that she was 'so embarrassing,' before running upstairs to their bedrooms, slamming doors loudly behind them.

Lizzie extracted Leo from his hiding place, leading him forcibly by the arm, hissing at him that he was totally vile and she never wanted to see him again. When they were safely in his car, she laid into him.

'How dare you come to a party with me, as *my* guest, at the invitation of *my* client, who you then seduce in the presence of her entire family and friends? Not to mention daughters? Oh Leo, how could you...'

'But I was only doing her a favour...' Leo protested weakly. 'Hold on a minute... I was only...' Should he try the puppy dog eyes? He thought better of it.

'...showing her what she was missing,' he continued, but Lizzie wasn't interested.

When she glared at him again, he started trying to explain to her that sometimes these things just happen, before changing his mind. Perhaps on this occasion, it might be wisest to shut up and wait for her to cool down. Had he gone too far? Maybe he'd keep his head down for a while, till it all blew over and everyone had forgotten all about it...

* * *

With the highly efficient grapevine practically going into meltdown, Ginny's public humiliation of Edward was soon the talk of the village, as was Leo. Antonia, of course, was one of the first in Lizzie's kitchen to discover just what had gone on.

'Now,' she enquired nosily, 'what's this rumour about Leo shagging Ginny Whatshername at that party you went to? It's all round the village. Thought he was supposed to be *your* date for the evening? Bit off don't you think?'

Lizzie gave her a look. 'He was my date, as it happens, but don't go getting any funny ideas. I didn't fancy him then and now I don't even ever want to see him again. Leo is appalling, Antonia! Ill mannered, immoral, totally unscrupulous...'

'Okay, keep your hair on... Just asking, that's all. Only... well, you probably don't want to know—' She broke off.

Lizzie, however, was curious. 'You can't not tell me now,' she told Antonia. 'Come on. What is this snippet of gossip you're not sharing?'

'Well, darling... Believe it or not, Leo has been seen since that night. In the Goat no less, and guess who with? What if I said she was quite a little bit older than him and dressed head to toe in pale pink... Ha! I knew you wouldn't know! Bet she could teach him a thing or two! Men are so predictable...'

But Lizzie was gobsmacked.

* * *

'This place is completely bonkers,' said Katie, after Lizzie had filled her in about the party. She was actually staying with Tim for the weekend, with all the dog-walking and sheep-feeding that entailed. 'Have you heard from Darius? Only they were talking about having one of their dinner parties on Sunday, so keep it free!'

Darius had indeed called Lizzie. 'Now then, flower. Sunday, 7 p.m. sharp. You might want to dress up a bit, sweetie... Not that you don't always look utterly charming, but you know...'

* * *

It was a dinner party for about twenty people, rather than the cosy little get-together Lizzie had imagined. Tim and Katie were there, Antonia and Toby, and Susie and Rory, only recently returned from their honeymoon.

'Tom was invited,' said Susie. 'But he's away again. Honestly, he's hopeless.'

Nola and Julia had arrived too, as well as others she knew less well... but in fact all the people who'd become closest to Lizzie over the last year had been invited. All bar one, she thought, spotting an empty chair.

Darius pulled out a chair for her at the head of the table.

'You're the guest of honour, petal! Don't you know the date? Well, not exactly but it was nearly a year ago that you *transformed*, darling, that – that complete bomb-site out there into this oasis of utter bliss... Everyone, be upstanding and raise your glasses to Lizzie!'

'Lizzie!' they chorused as she sat there rather shell-shocked.

'Speech!' yelled Toby, who was already rather squiffy, and Lizzie shrunk in her chair. She didn't do speeches, but then suddenly she changed her mind. She stood up.

'Actually, as you're all here, and before you're all completely legless, I would like to say something. Firstly, thank you. Darius and Angel – you are wonderful friends and I love you!' Rowdy cries of 'hear, hear' erupted. 'But secondly, I want to talk about Hethecote. You see the article in the magazine is about to come out. Miriam's petrified – she already doesn't know how to cope with the numbers of visitors. So if anyone has any suggestions...'

33

Lizzie's phone had rung early the next day while she was still sleeping off the night before. It had been well after midnight when Tim had eventually dropped her home.

'Ah... Lizzie... Just thought you ought to know, only the magazine's in the shops and the phones are jumping off the hooks.' Julian coughed affectedly before adding. 'Um, only I *do* hope you are prepared...'

* * *

'Oh Lizzie, I'm wondering what we've started...'

'Miriam, it'll be fine,' said Lizzie, far more calmly than she felt. 'Anyway, today people are just coming to look around, remember? If they want to handle the animals, they can come back later in the week.'

'Darling...' It was Antonia, with a happy-looking Cassie beside her. 'It is the hols after all and I thought she'd be jolly useful. What shall we do then? Oh golly, just look...'

Darius and Angel were walking into the yard, immaculately

turned out as ever and looking like two fish out of water, with Nola and Julia just behind them.

'Sweetie!' Darius kissed Miriam on each cheek. 'We simply had to come and help... You see, Angel is just *inspired* with interiors as you know. He's just *dying* to branch out into shop-fitting...'

'Come with me,' said Lizzie firmly, before Miriam could turn them away.

'We thought perhaps we could walk around with people,' said Nola. She was wearing lime green Hunters with glitter on. 'If perhaps you could just show us round first...'

Perfect, perfect, perfect, thought Lizzie.

'But darling, it's a barn,' said Angel, looking shocked. 'Do you think she'll mind if I scout around, and see if I can find some props?'

'Of course she won't... and I'll shoot over to the gardens and see what's ready to sell.'

'It will be fine,' said Nola, touching Miriam's arm reassuringly. 'There is so much energy here – you can feel it. Oh, what a beautiful cat... Is he one of Mrs...'

'... Einstein's? Yes, he is – Navajo, I call him. He's been with me for years.' Miriam was beginning to feel less anxious.

'This is such a wonderful place,' said Julia softly. 'You must help so many people, Miriam...'

'Well, the children I think, perhaps...'

'Not just the children,' added Julia thoughtfully as Sid poked his nose over his door and bared his teeth. 'Oh, look at the donkeys – aren't they sweet?'

By eleven o'clock, everyone was in place, and with the half-dozen of her regular helpers in place as well as Lizzie's friends, they were ready to open.

'It's rather a bodge, petal,' said Angel apologetically, when he showed her the makeshift shop. Actually it was rather charming, thrown together from old apple boxes and hay bales, and a couple of old doors as counters. Produce from the schools' gardens was stacked up and Lizzie had filled one of the horse's buckets with wild flowers she'd picked in the fields. Piles of the magazine were there too, just as they promised Julian and the boys had chalked the prices on a rough old bit of wood.

'But I'll have to come back and do it properly, flower...' he fretted.

At eleven, Miriam opened the gate to loud cheers from beyond. Someone from the local paper photographed her as the first of the visitors walked in.

'I say, thanks awfully!' Antonia's voice shrilled above everyone else's as she took money and gave out tickets, telling everyone very loudly that she was taking donations.

Nola and Julia were in their element, homing in on the families who needed their help, and Lizzie was in the garden, showing people around and telling them how it had all come about.

'We needed to raise funds,' she explained. 'But the idea just took off. The schools have worked so hard on each plot... it's them who deserve the credit.'

'Smile, Lizzie,' a camera flashed. Then another...

* * *

At the end of the day, when the last of the visitors had left, Miriam closed the gate with relief. Then she went into the end stable where Marble and Hairy Mary were peacefully munching hay and stroked them, while an extraordinary feeling washed over her. It was as though all those years of hard work and grind had been leading to this one day. Lizzie, Tim... they were right all along. She had needed to change things... she just hadn't seen it. And if Lizzie hadn't come along that first day, none of this might have happened.

'Miriam?' said Lizzie quietly behind her. 'Antonia's got something to tell you.'

'Golly, darlings...' Antonia was looking shell-shocked. 'We've taken over two grand in, and tons of donations are promised!'

Miriam went terribly pale and looked as though she was going to pass out.

'Come and sit down,' said Nola taking her arm. 'You've had quite a day...'

A loud popping noise came from the shop, and Darius appeared with a tray of glasses. 'Champers, petals! A toast! To Hethecote!'

'Actually, I'd like to propose another,' said Miriam unexpectedly, getting her colour back and standing up. 'To all of you, who have done so much... But especially to Lizzie, without whom none of this would have happened.'

'Lizzie!' everyone yelled, as one of the donkeys farted loudly. Everyone except Darius roared with laughter. He looked round in horror. 'What was that?'

* * *

After the initial publicity, Miriam was flooded with volunteers and the new programme of opening was a walk in the park.

'I can't think why I ever worried about it,' she confided to Lizzie. 'I think it was just the change that bothered me. I was rather set in my ways...'

* * *

Ginny had invited Lizzie over for coffee. Slightly ashamed of her behaviour, life without Edward clearly suited her.

'I know I behaved appallingly,' she said, as Lizzie took in the untidy kitchen which had always been so spotless. 'But golly! He came off far worse than I did!'

To Lizzie's relief, no mention was made of Leo.

* * *

As it happened, for once the timing side of things was on Lizzie's side, and just as everything settled down at Hethecote, a wonderful new project had come her way. It was largely thanks to Timmy, who'd recommended her to clients of his, the Buchanans, who ran a thoroughbred stud a few miles away. They wanted to restore the formal rose garden at their old manor house. Lizzie had been given a precious collection of old photographs to work from, and in addition, the gardening journals of the elderly lady who had been its custodian sixty years ago. The garden had remained untouched since she had died.

The Buchanans always had guests staying, some of whom she got talking to as they wandered through the gardens. Her handiwork had caught the eye of many of them, but one in particular was impressed.

'I'm actually looking for someone to restore some gardens for me,' he said to her one day in conversation. 'I've bought a place in Devon. Bramley House it's called. It'd be quite a project, but looking at what you've done here is making me see its potential...'

Eric Masterson was in his sixties. He'd inherited money years ago, he told Lizzie, and invested in commercial property at just the right time. Sadly though, with his wife suffering from Alzheimer's, he didn't have the time to oversee such a huge project himself.

'If you were interested, I'd love you to meet my wife and take a look for yourself. I don't want to get just anyone in, but nor do I want to leave it too much longer...'

'It sounds like a wonderful job,' said Lizzie, slightly wistfully. In truth, it sounded like her dream job, but she'd have to move and leave everything here behind.

'I don't know what to say,' she added. 'Would you give me time to think about it?'

'Here's my card,' said Eric delightedly. 'It's probably best if you come down and take a look yourself rather than listen to my amateur ravings. And it's important that you meet Deidre. You'd inevitably see quite a lot of her. Poor Deidre... she's not the person she used to be,' he added sadly.

'I'll call you when I've had a chance to think,' said Lizzie.

'Oh, and did I mention there's a cottage in the grounds for whoever takes the job?' added Eric, as he walked off back to the house.

* * *

Antonia's new liveries were a nightmare, she informed Lizzie that evening as they shared a bottle of wine in Lizzie's back garden, even though the summer warmth had given way to a distinctly autumnal chill.

'Complete nutters, both of them! Really, it's more trouble than it's worth, darling, especially Sid. Complete arse he is – went off for the day and brought the poor horse home covered in mud and sweat. Then he just left it and fucked off to the pub. Of course, I couldn't just leave the poor creature. Got Cassie to clean it up. Suppose I'll have to have a word. I really don't have time to go running round after other people's horses...'

It was on the tip of Lizzie's tongue to remind Antonia that these people were paying her, but she hadn't finished.

'Anyway,' she continued, 'it simply doesn't make enough. Truth is, I'm not sure what I'm going to do. Now, the ball is in a month! Old Woodleigh's donating some beef, and William, bless him, is giving us a load of lamb. The schools' gardens at Hethecote are frantically growing carrots which were hoping to feed to the animals, but Miriam's pulled rank and commandeered half of them. The band are booked – um, Lizzie. Darling, now I've got you down for the table decorations,' she said in a hurry, 'and before you say you can't, think of Miriam. You're doing it for her. We've got some spiffing prizes,' she continued. 'Aubrey's donating his Rolls for a weekend, complete with chauffeur, as well as a week in his pad in Marbella. We've got tickets for football matches, music concerts and the Woodleighs have donated VIP tickets for Ascot.' She frowned. 'I wonder if we can find someone to cough up for Badminton Horse Trials? Haven't been for years...'

* * *

Bella's walled garden was nearly finished. There'd been no sign of Tom the whole time Lizzie had worked there and all Bella had said was that she'd hardly seen either him or Susie since the wedding.

'Susie, as usual, has been whirling around like a dervish ever since she and Rory got back, and Tom's away of course, off in some far flung corner of the globe. I couldn't even tell you what the place is called. He travels so much I lose track of them all...'

Lizzie had felt a shock at the mention of his name, almost a physical blow. She was kidding herself if she thought she'd forgotten him and she realised that half of her had just been expecting him to turn up at her cottage.

'*Idiot*,' she told herself. '*Stupid, naive idiot*.' And imagined an irritatingly smug Lucy lying on a glorious beach with him, in a tiny bikini which didn't quite cover her perfectly tanned body, not letting Tom out of her sight for one single second.

Odd, Bella had thought to herself, when Lizzie didn't say

anything. I could have sworn there was something between those two... what could possibly have gone wrong?

* * *

Thousands of miles away, under a palm tree on an idyllic beach in southern India which he'd just kayaked round a headland to, Tom was sitting gazing across the ocean, listening to the sound of the waves. He loved that sound. The air smelt hot and the sand was too hot to walk on, and with the cerulean sky above him it really was the most incredible place. It should prove popular, especially with the rustic, back-to-basics accommodation he'd ferreted out.

But he was far from loving this trip. For the first time, he was realising that this beautiful place would be so much more so if Lizzie were here to share it. He'd given up trying to get her out of his head. It was like he had a voice in there, saying her name over and over. Okay, he was working, and this was a great holiday they were planning to market next year, but... Even this far from home, she was there. He hadn't given Lucy a thought since they parted. The way Tom saw it though, he had a choice. He could either carry on as he was, thinking about Lizzie, imagining 'what if' for the rest of his lonely days, or he could take a risk and seek her out. He really wasn't much good at this sort of thing. But he'd have to do it, he decided, though he fully expected to be rebuffed, which was probably no more than he deserved.

34

Lizzie detoured via the village garage on her way home. 'Evenin', miss.' Dave nodded to her, pronouncing all three syllables of 'evenin'. 'Can I 'elp?'

'I think I've got a slow puncture Dave... Do you think you could sort it out for me by tomorrow? About nine-ish?'

'Oh aye, aye...' Dave nodded. Lizzie had forgotten how mono-syllabic he was.

'Erm, okay, I'll just leave it with you, shall I?' Hardly believing she was saying it.

More nodding, as Dave just stood there.

* * *

Lizzie walked off up the lane, which took her past Antonia's where she met Cassie on a tired-looking Scout just opening the gate.

'I'll get that,' said Lizzie.

'Thanks,' said Cassie. Her cheeks were pink and her eyes bright. A steaming Scout snorted loudly, spraying Lizzie with horse snot.

'Mum was in the yard when I left,' said Cassie. 'But be careful – she's in the foulest mood ever.'

'Oh,' said Lizzie, guessing why.

'She's biting everyone's heads off, but she might be better if she talks to you,' said Cassie as she slipped off the horse and led him into his stable.

Lizzie wandered through to where she could hear Antonia swearing at the dogs in the tack room.

'God, Lizzie, awfully sorry but I'm having a pig of a day... It's all Harry's doing. This bloody divorce... if I'd known it was going to be such a nightmare, I might even have stayed with the bastard. Do you know—'

But she was interrupted by the arrival of the large, red-cheeked man who came barging in.

'Sidney Livingstone! My friends call me Sid.' He crushed Lizzie's hand in a bone-breaking handshake before slapping Antonia heartily on the back and sending her flying into the saddles.

'Lord, that horse of mine looks good, Antonia. Doing a fine job, girl, damn fine job indeed,' he added jovially, as he marched out towards the said horse, who looked less than enamoured to see its master, skulking as it was at the back of its stable.

Antonia was muttering profanities again. 'Bloody wanker. If only I didn't need his effing money...'

'Are you busy now, or shall I put the kettle on?' Lizzie tried to distract her friend.

'Help yourself, I'll be in shortly. Got to catch Hamish first.' She stomped off crossly towards the gate.

Back inside, Cassie was making a sandwich. She caught Lizzie's eye. 'She still off on one?'

Lizzie nodded, and grinned. 'What's happened?'

'The solicitor. I think she thinks Dad should just keep paying her bills forever. He's not that bad you know. He'd never let anything really terrible happen to us. And I think she's fed up with the liveries already. She'd have me out there doing all her stable work. I did do some, until I got to Sid's horse. It totally trashes its stable and it stinks of wee, so I told her. CBA.'

'CBA?' Lizzie was mystified.

'Can't Be Arsed.' Cassie seemed far more relaxed about it all than her mother. 'Anyway, you can come and watch the end of *Hollyoaks* if you like,' she added. 'We won't have missed much. It's quite boring at the moment – or have you got time to help me choose a dress? Only I've got a party next Saturday. I've been looking online, but it's just not Mummy's sort of thing. She says she's too busy...' Cassie rolled her eyes, trying to look as though she didn't care, but Lizzie had a suspicion that this party might be quite important.

'You could show me the dresses you've been looking at...' said Lizzie, and Cassie leaped up straight away, forgetting all about *Hollyoaks*, pleased that someone was taking an interest.

Lizzie equally was surprised when Cassie showed her some quite bohemian outfits and she had a brainwave.

'Sparkies! I'll take you to Sparkies! Cassie, it's not far, only in Rumbleford, and I bet you'd find something there! It's my favourite shop - I'd love to take you...'

'Wow, that would be cool...' said Cassie slowly. 'Are you sure that's okay? Mummy won't mind, she finds that kind of thing a real bore. The only shopping she really likes is for the horses... Do you know, I have thirteen pairs of jodhpurs and not one single dress?'

Though shocking, that was not entirely surprising. They fixed a date for the following Saturday.

* * *

Next morning, Lizzie was admittedly dumbfounded when her car was actually ready for her. Well, nearly ready, that was.

''Ere, 'ang on a minnit an' I'll just torque yer nuts...' A young lad in greasy overalls with equally greasy hair, bent over the front tyre wielding something resembling a rather butch hairdryer.

Inside the office, in which it looked like all Dave's invoices from forever were piled messily on the floor, he thrust a scrap of paper at her.

'*How much?*' Lizzie was aghast as she read it. 'I had no idea...'

'See it's that tyre a yours miss, right bad it was, and the labour mind... gotta pay young Sam see...'

'Dave. What if I pay cash and you give me a discount.' Lizzie spoke firmly.

Dave cleared his throat. He wasn't used to folks questioning his bills. He didn't get much repeat business, but had failed to make the connection.

'Bit iregilar like, innit?' Then seeing Lizzie's face, he reluctantly gave in. 'Oh all righty...' and he sighed.

* * *

With a spare couple of hours, Lizzie drove over to Hethecote. Though she wasn't really needed in the garden, she loved to follow the latest developments with the allotments. But just inside the gate, Miriam was talking to a man Lizzie didn't recognise, with a scruffy horse standing beside him.

'But you simply *have* to take him,' the man was blustering as Lizzie walked over, trying to make Miriam take the lead rope. The horse at the other end was staring loftily at her.

'Isn't he pretty?' said Lizzie, taking a step towards him.

Intelligent black eyes gazed back at her, then it tossed its head and snorted.

'But he's an Arab,' said Miriam in desperation. 'He's not going to fit in here.' The horse stretched its curved neck towards her. It really was beautiful, with dark liquid eyes and fine bone structure that would make Hamish look like a sumo wrestler.

'Please,' said the man – slightly madly. 'Only it's the wife's. And she's run off and left me. And I hate bloody horses – especially this one...'

'But we have sick children coming here to pet the animals. I'm sorry, he just wouldn't be suitable,' said Miriam firmly.

The man got out his mobile. 'Then you don't leave me a choice.' He dialled. 'Hello? I've got a horse I need to dispose of...'

Miriam sighed. 'All right,' she said defeatedly. 'As long as you make a donation.'

* * *

The size of the donation bore no reflection to the trouble that lay ahead. The horse became known as Dodger, and though he was impeccably behaved with all the visitors, once they'd left he was diabolical.

'I'll kill that fucking horse,' raged Antonia one evening, as she charged round Miriam's yard after it. 'Bloody animal, got out of its stable and raided the feed room,' she fumed. 'Emptied all the sacks all over the place *and* it tipped the bin over. Then it fucked off again. I know it was him though. He left his calling card in the middle of the floor. The nerve of it.'

Antonia was the only person Lizzie knew who could identify a horse by its droppings. 'And some moron left the hay store open, it got in there too. Hay everywhere.' Antonia really was furious. 'I tell you, I've gone right off that horse. Nothing but a pain in the arse,' she shouted after it.

The horse glanced at Lizzie. Slightly smugly.

'Grab it will you and stick it in that stable over there. Make sure you lock it in.' She stalked off into the tack room.

Lizzie gently held a hand out, which the horse sniffed noisily before allowing her to take hold of its head collar and lead it away, docile as a lamb.

* * *

That Saturday afternoon as promised, Lizzie took Cassie to Sparkie's, the latter not at all sure what to expect, as Nola and Julia embraced Lizzie, and turned the open sign to 'closed'.

'So we don't get disturbed,' they explained to Cassie. Cassie was puzzled. Was it a shop, or wasn't it?

It didn't take long though, for the girls to gently question Cassie and then produce a selection of dresses for her to try on, from which she just couldn't make up her mind. Nola turned to Julia.

'How about the pink one that came in yesterday? Oh, you know I think it's just the right size and with your hair... Cassie, you just *have* to try it on...'

This time it was ages before Cassie finally emerged from the changing room. Looking like the cat that got the cream... The dress was quirky, fitted to the waist, with a skirt of uneven layers of pink and black tulle and chiffon. It swung prettily around her as she turned this way and that, admiring her reflection in the mirror. She looked like a pixie, a slightly punk pixie, thought Lizzie, looking at Cassie's expression of glee.

'This is *so* cool!' she announced. Then declaring triumphantly, 'No one will have anything like this, not even that snotty cow Elouise!'

Lizzie bought her a necklace to wear with it, and they left,

Cassie delightedly swinging her precious carrier bag. Then they stopped at the tearooms round the corner, where they had enormous hot chocolates with marshmallows and cream on top to celebrate.

When they got back, Antonia was in quite a mild mood to their relief, and even enthused about her daughter's choice of dress. Which was just as well, thought Lizzie, otherwise she'd have personally murdered her.

'Stay for supper,' said Antonia. 'Sausage and chips, Cassie's favourite.' A touch of guilt there maybe, thought Lizzie, wondering if Antonia was trying to worm her way back into favour with her rather uppity daughter. 'And I've opened rather a nice bottle of red... Not sure whether Tobes is joining us or not...' She sounded rather unsure.

* * *

Tom was jet-lagged. He always was travelling east, and now he was back, it was catching up with him. But, determined to talk to Lizzie, he drove down to Littleton. He hadn't gone to bed since getting off the plane at seven o'clock this morning, knowing that if he had, he wouldn't have woken up again until Sunday. And wouldn't have made it down to Littleton at all...

Having folded the roof down so that the fresh air would keep him awake, Tom was there by teatime. Bella was expecting him, and there was a roast dinner in the oven.

'Darling! Oh dear, you're looking exhausted! Whatever possessed you to drive down here without getting some sleep first? Beer? Or maybe strong coffee?' she added as Tom stifled a huge yawn. 'Go and sit, and I'll bring it in...'

Fatal. The minute Tom sat down and relaxed into the armchair, his eyes closed, and when Bella came in two minutes later, he was snoring. She stood looking at him for a moment, before covering him with a blanket, carefully, so as not to wake him. He'd always slept like a log as a child no matter what went on around him. He'd no doubt be out for hours.

Lizzie and Antonia drove to the Goat that evening, leaving Cassie at home with one of her friends, happily planning party outfits and hairstyles without her mother sticking her oar in.

Toby, however, wasn't at the pub. Antonia seemed rather put out. 'Haven't seen him for a few days now. Not like Tobes at all. Can't understand it...'

'Call him.' It was obvious, thought Lizzie.

'I have. Even left a message.' She was mystified.

The Goat was oddly quiet. No Tim, Leo or Toby. They didn't stay long, getting home early for a change, much to Cassie's annoyance.

* * *

Tom didn't make it to the pub at all, in the end. He awoke finally just after midnight, and reheated the supper Bella had left out for him. He thought about walking up to Lizzie's... but thinking she might be asleep, or the unwanted thought that she might have someone with her, he went to bed. Even though it was Sunday, he really did have to get back to the office in the morning... He'd been away for two weeks and there'd be a mountain of work to catch up on. Thinking of Lizzie, he was furious with himself for falling asleep. When it came to his love life, didn't he just have a talent for screwing it up.

* * *

Lizzie stirred late for her on Sunday morning, just in time to hear a car speeding past down the lane. She rolled over and went back to sleep.

In the Boxster, Tom put his foot down as he pulled out of the village back to the motorway.

35

A change was in the air as September started. The days were still warm, but there was a wind blowing, swishing the leaves on the trees. Lizzie was suddenly conscious of the sound, like waves on a beach, particularly at home at her cottage. After the hot, sleepy summer it unsettled her, making her restless and fidgety, as she thought about Eric Masterson's offer.

Eventually, she decided. It was time. Emptying her diary and taking up Bert's offer to feed Darren and the chickens, Lizzie drove down to Devon. Her mind was far from made up, but something told her she should consider it. And with views of the sea to die for, Bramley House was a dream. Eric had shown her around and listened to her ideas for the acres of garden and parkland, and then they'd had lunch with Deidre. Her dementia was clearly advancing, and it had left Lizzie with an awful sense of sadness, watching as Eric gently helped her with the simplest of tasks and reassured her that everything was normal.

They'd love her to join them, he assured her. Both of them... but she should think about it. Make sure she was doing the right thing.

And so it was that one year and four months after she set out, Lizzie at last reached Cornwall. Stopping her car somewhere along the North Cornish coast, she gazed out of the window at the craggy coastline that stretched for miles either side of her. Taking out the map she'd bought, she'd squinted at the strange-sounding names and eventually locating Spriggan Point written in tiny red letters, a few miles further on.

Lizzie drove slowly, along tiny narrow lanes edged with stone walls that had taken root and sprouted with wild flowers, twisting and turning past farms and the occasional cottage until she wound her way down a steep slope which ended in a stony car park.

Abandoning her car, Lizzie could already hear the sea. Making her way through the gorse bushes, she followed the uneven path over grass tussocks until the short spikes of grass became sand – and at long last, she was there. The place she'd been dreaming of, with white sand and the clearest, most sparkling water which before her eyes turned a vivid shade of blue as the clouds above her parted to let the sun through.

Spriggan Point itself was a small headland of jagged black rocks which jutted into the sea and as Lizzie clambered along it listening to the sound of waves breaking and inhaling the saltiness, it seemed already she could feel the magic soaking into her. The way the air felt alive. Even the sky was bigger here. And as she watched it all, she realised. So much for timing – this was time-*less*. Completely. Unchanging – as people came and went. Calming, reviving, inspiring as was needed.

Magic, she thought. It really is. Invisibly everywhere you look.

Much later, as she drove back up the lane, she noticed a farmhouse and impulsively she pulled in – maybe they could tell her where to find Roscarn.

As she walked up the overgrown path, she took in the peeling paint and gutters hanging off the slate roof. *A property developer's dream...* she thought, imagining with horror how something like this would get snapped up, and primped and preened into a neat, twee little holiday home.

She climbed over more weeds that fell across the path until she reached the door and knocked.

For ages nothing happened. Giving up, she was just turning to leave when she heard a voice shout from somewhere.

'I ain't selling, if that's what you want.'

A man appeared from behind the cottage. In his seventies, Lizzie guessed. It was hard to tell – he had unkempt hair and a grey beard and his clothes looked ancient.

'Oh – no – it wasn't that...' She hesitated.

'Well, what d'you want then? I don't do no scones if that's what you're after.'

'No. Actually, I was looking for a place called Roscarn.'

The man stared at her. Taking his silence as encouragement, Lizzie continued.

'Only my mother came here. Years ago – maybe as long as thirty years ago... her name was Isobel, Isobel Lavender.'

Something changed in the man's demeanour. When he spoke, he sounded gruff. 'You better come in.'

Lizzie looked around the gloomy kitchen. Piles of this and that were heaped everywhere – letters, old newspapers, bottles, china – gathering a layer of dust. The man was filling a kettle.

'Tea?'

Lizzie nodded.

He removed a pile of creased clothes from a chair. 'Sit down,' he said. As though thinking out loud he added, 'who'd have thought, after all this time...'

Whatever the state of the farmhouse, he made a good cup of tea – hot and strong – just how Lizzie liked it. But still he didn't speak.

'So you remember my mother then?' she ventured.

He put down his mug and gave a deep sigh.

'I do all right. She were something, your mum. Came here all those years ago on her own. 'Bout your age, I'm guessing, bit younger maybe. And she was sad, real sad. Her husband had died a while back.' He frowned.

'My father died before I was born,' said Lizzie.

'Ah, that's right. What did you say your name was?'

She hadn't. 'Lizzie.'

A frown crossed his face. 'Didn't know she were pregnant though. Not when she were here. Whippet thin she was.' He stopped.

'She must have been – she said I'd been here too. And that means, either she came here without me which would seem unlikely... or she brought me here when I was a baby.'

Neither of them said a word.

'My son used to help run the farm back then,' said the man. 'When he wasn't at sea, that was. Jago, his name was. He was between trips when your mum stayed. My wife – Jago's mother used to take paying guests, see. Kept this place real nice, she did. Clean as a pin. Always baking cakes and doing washing.' She sounded like Molly, Bert's wife. A look of sadness crossed his face. 'Don't look quite the same these days.'

'When did you lose your wife?' asked Lizzie.

'Ten years ago,' he said. 'Ten years... and it seems like yesterday we moved in here. Just after our wedding up the lane in the village...' He cleared his throat.

'It's hard, isn't it?' Lizzie reached out and touched his arm. 'Doesn't go away, does it?'

He managed a faint smile. 'You're just like your mum, you are. Thing is...' Then he frowned again. 'I'm not real sure how to say this, but your mum and Jago, well. They were close. Real close. Like soul mates. When they were together, you couldn't miss it. It were like they were made for each other.' He glanced at Lizzie. 'I hope you don't mind me talking like this?'

'No, no,' said Lizzie, astounded at this part of her mother's past of which she knew nothing. 'Please – go on.'

'Well, she stayed a good while. Few months, I'm guessing. She had to leave because her father was ill. She promised she'd come back...' He shook his head. 'Thing is, while she were gone, there was a storm, a real bad one. Jago was out fishing. He never came back.'

'No!' Lizzie was shocked. How terrible to lose a son, so young, like that...

'He wasn't the only one. Half the families round here lost someone that night. There's a stone put up – on the hill. A memorial. Real tragedy it was.'

'I'm so sorry,' said Lizzie. 'To upset you, asking all this. But I'd no idea – about any of it.'

'Your mum came back for his funeral,' said the man sadly. 'Heartbroken she was. Held herself together for that service then went to the beach and cried her heart out. My wife went and got her in the end. She stayed a night with us but then she left. Never once came back. She wrote a letter a bit later. Apologising. Said it was all too painful.'

Lizzie was puzzled. 'What about Roscarn? She told me I should find it. Roscarn and Spriggan Point.'

'Come with me.'

They walked through the back garden through a gate into a field.

'Mind them cowpats,' he said. 'It's not far.'

At the other end of the field was another gate and the dilapidated remains of a building.

'Roscarn,' he said nodding. 'Jago's cottage. Completely ruined-like now... but that's what your mum was talking about.'

He stood and watched as Lizzie stepped forward. She reached a hand out to the crumbling bricks, resting it there a moment, then peering in through the broken window. The remains of Jago's furniture was still there – damp and rotting. Then she looked towards the sea, rippling eternally below.

And at that moment she understood.

'You haven't told me your name,' she said slowly as they walked back.

'I haven't, have I. Forgetting my manners aren't I. It's Joseph. Joseph Talan.' He hesitated. 'My wife's name was Eliza.'

36

It was cutting it a bit fine by the time Lizzie arrived home. Preparations for the ball were nearly in place. Aubrey had come up trumps and the marquee that had been put up on his lawn was spectacular.

'Absolutely no point in half doing a job,' he'd said firmly.

But there was still much to do and Antonia was tearing around like the proverbial blue-arsed fly, overseeing everything except the tables.

'Now, Lizzie,' she'd said bossily, having given her a good telling-off for disappearing. 'You've got a budget. Don't mind if you do it yourself or pay someone else. Don't give a bugger. Just make sure it looks impressive. Okay? I want everyone spending shedloads of money.' Not waiting, she added, 'Good show. Now Katie can meet all the VIPs, and I'll set up the auction...'

* * *

Toby had reappeared. It seemed his father had suffered a heart attack, and in a panic, Toby had rushed to his bedside without a

thought for anything or anyone else. But after the initial shock of
his disappearance, Antonia seemed to have adapted quite happily
to life without him, and their reunion had been far from the joyous
one Toby had been hoping for.

Antonia, in fact, had been out of sorts for some time.

'It's the bally money, darling,' she confided miserably to Lizzie.
'The truth is, the horses cost a bomb, and I'm not sure how long I
can keep it up...'

'Something will come up,' Lizzie reassured her. Having been at
rock bottom herself, she remembered only too clearly how things
had an uncanny knack of 'coming up' when you needed them
enough.

'I hope you're right,' was all she said, not sounding terribly
hopeful.

But something had indeed come up. Two days before the ball,
Toby had asked Antonia out for dinner.

'I'll have to cancel this evening, darlings,' said Antonia. She,
Katie and Lizzie had been going to start on the table plan.

'Don't worry – we can make a start. Is everything okay?'

Antonia looked far from happy. 'Just Tobes, darling. Says he
wants to take me out somewhere special to make up for leaving me
in the lurch. Trouble is, Lizzie, I think I'm going to have to break it
off with him. It was awfully good fun, but it's run its course, don't
you think? Golly, I suppose I'll just have to come out with it...'

* * *

'I've put my flat on the market!' announced Katie.

Lizzie nearly dropped the plates she was carrying. 'You what?
Why? Where are you going to live?'

Katie grinned. 'Do I really need to spell it out?'

Lizzie's jaw dropped open. 'You mean...' she started incredulously '... you and *Tim*?'

'Is it that much of a surprise? He asked me last weekend! And do you know, I really think he might be the one...'

Just as she dropped her bombshell, the door was flung open and Antonia burst in, clutching her hands.

'Oh my God... he only bloody proposed, darlings... I... I didn't know what to do...'

There was a stunned silence and Lizzie poured Antonia a stiff drink which she gulped down in one.

'Phew, that's better, darling. I think it's the shock, but I really do feel a little odd...'

'But I thought you were going to end it,' said Lizzie carefully.

'I was, I was...' said Antonia agitatedly. 'But then he gave me this.' She unclenched her hands and flashed an enormous diamond at them. 'Isn't it utterly heavenly? And it would solve so many of my problems...'

'And create a whole load more,' said Katie bluntly. 'You don't love him enough, Antonia. It wouldn't be fair on Toby.'

Antonia looked crushed.

'Look, you told me earlier you were going to end it,' said Lizzie. 'That it had run its course. Antonia, really, it's simple...'

'Oh, darlings, I know you're right...' She hesitated. 'But d'you think I'll have to give it back?'

'YES,' they answered in unison.

'It's probably a family heirloom,' said Katie.

'And you'd only feel guilty,' said Lizzie.

'Oh Lord... I might not, you know.'

* * *

Then, the day before the ball, the letter arrived. The position was hers if she wanted it. And oh, what a dilemma that left her in...

She talked to Katie about it, who leaped up out of her chair. 'Wow, Lizzie! It's a fantastic opportunity, but you can't! You have this wonderful life here, your business and so many friends, and I'm about to move here too!' Then she added more seriously, 'But this offer's too good to be true, isn't it? A dream job in a gorgeous place... and your friends will still be here, of course... I really don't know what to say.'

And Katie was right. Life here was wonderful in so many respects. And more than that it would forever be the place that had helped her find her way forward. But should she stay? That was the bit Lizzie couldn't work out.

She thought and thought about it. Sat down and wrote lists of pros and cons... No closer to making a decision, she donned her trainers, and went for a run, going miles further than usual, running twice as far as usual in her efforts to seek the clarity she was desperate for.

But secretly, part of her felt that this was an opportunity not to be missed. And if she let it pass her by, that door would be closed for sure. Someone else would get the job, she knew that. And she had this newly discovered connection to the West Country. She'd promise Joseph she wouldn't disappear the way her mother had. If she took this job she'd be so much nearer to him.

She wouldn't lose touch with her friends, but it wouldn't be the same, she knew that. But maybe, also, it was time to give up on the last of her hopes about Tom.

* * *

Everything was set. Looking around the marquee and the tables she had decorated with ivy, flowers and candles, it did look wonderful. The guests were due to start arriving at any minute. The weather had been kind and a team of smart young waiters were out on the newly mowed lawn in the evening sun, holding trays of champagne to welcome them before the fabulous dinner that awaited them inside. Antonia had absolutely insisted that they use top-notch caterers, even though the quote had been well over what they'd budgeted for. Then there'd be the auction, followed by dancing for the rest of the evening with The Bozo Dog Doo Dah Band, already tuning up. It really was all most impressive – Antonia hadn't compromised on anything.

Lizzie had splashed out on a dream of a dress, which Nola had ordered in specially. It was the deepest turquoise silk which shimmered as she moved and made her feel like a princess. Taking a deep breath as she stood there, she couldn't help but feel how amazing this was. And a little proud too, about what between them they'd put together.

Just then Antonia shouted, 'Lizzie? Katie? Cars are here, darlings!'

If anything could have swayed her decision about Devon, it would have been this evening, Lizzie reflected, feeling a mixture of love and sadness as she watched so many of her friends arrive. One of the first was Tim, smartly dressed in a dinner jacket as were all the men. He anchored himself at Katie's side, not budging for most of the evening. Miriam too was early, looking surprisingly elegantly turned out, with one of her sons on her arm.

'I can't believe you've done all this for Hethecote,' she said to them, looking utterly over-awed.

Eucalyptus wafted in, looking shabbily glamorous in a faded taffeta creation that Lizzie hadn't seen before, and startlingly rather happier than usual. And with a familiar-looking figure beside her. Lizzie's eyes widened with her first shock of the evening. She'd never in a million years expected to see Jamie here! Nor had Katie, who was over there like a shot to get to the bottom of it. Jamie and Eucalyptus? Maybe it wasn't as odd as it seemed...

Poor Toby strode in dejectedly, gazing love-struck at Antonia for a second before seizing a glass of champagne and disappearing. Then Leo, with his hand resting in a most familiar way on the expensively clad bottom of Ginny, who was resplendent in pink silk. Looking slightly sheepish as they spotted Lizzie, Ginny sashayed over, her face looking much less stressed and rather more wrinkled than Lizzie had ever seen it.

Ginny kissed her resoundingly on both cheeks. 'I expect you think I'm having a midlife crisis,' she giggled coyly at Lizzie, 'and I have to admit, I probably am! But honestly, Leo has been such a sweetie.'

Leo winked over at them and Ginny blew him a kiss. 'He's been *so* good for me. I feel wonderful! Oh, I know it won't last, but it's the best fun I've had in about twenty years!' And she wiggled off in her heels back towards him.

As Lizzie watched them together, Katie flew over and filled her in.

'Apparently they met at an art gallery! They got talking, probably about some lah-di-dah crappy piece of art, but when Jamie found out where Eucalyptus lived, and that she herself was an artist, he realised he'd seen one of her paintings in your cottage! Is that true, Lizzie? Only I've never seen it...' Katie sounded slightly puzzled.

'I don't put it up usually,' said Lizzie. 'It's a little too, er, modern for my taste...'

'Oh. Well, I'd imagine Jamie loved it then!'

'It looks as though he did! Aren't they just the strangest couple? You know, this place is full of them.' Lizzie indicated over to where Ginny was giggling flirtatiously at Leo, who looked positively adoring. 'You'd never in a million years imagine those two together either...'

'Hmmm, see what you mean...' They tried to stifle their laughter, turning to glance at Euc and Jamie hovering uncomfortably by the bar. 'And it's not her kind of do at all is it?'

'Or his,' giggled Lizzie, enjoying the spectre of Jamie on unfamiliar turf.

Nola and Julia were here, looking exquisite in stunning dresses, which Lizzie was certain had never graced the rails of their shop. They were accompanied by two gorgeous men who could have graced the pages of *Vogue*.

'Oh Lizzie, this is wonderful! Everything is! And you know there's a full moon this evening... the park will be at its most perfect...'

'*Flowers*...' Darius and Angel were behind them. 'How *adorable* to see all you all here...'

Then, as she spotted Susie and Rory, who she'd known were coming, and Susie's parents, who she'd also expected, Lizzie got her next shock. That was definitely Shar, hand in hand with Rich... Lizzie's heart started to thud. There he was. Right behind them all. Tom.

'Lizzeee,' Susie squeaked, dashing over as fast as her slinky black dress would allow. She flung her arms round her. 'I'm so happy to see you! Oh, come and join us, please... I love what you've done to Mummy's garden. She is *so* thrilled with it...' Susie chattered away.

Shar came over too. 'Hello again, I can't believe it's been so long... that thick brother of yours wants his head examining,' she told Susie bluntly, then turned to Lizzie.

'That cow Lucy had him in her clutches for a while, until he got round to extricating himself. She's not here,' Shar added, seeing the look on Lizzie's face. 'Honestly, didn't I warn you he was *hopeless*?'

Tom stood looking round a little awkwardly until he saw her. There was no avoiding him this time.

'Hi.' He bent to kiss Lizzie's cheek. 'It's good to see you again. Really good.'

His expression was serious as he continued, 'Um, there was something I—'

But just then he was rudely interrupted by a deafening announcement of 'Dinner, ladies and gentlemen' and a request for everyone, please, to take their seats. Jostled by everyone filtering past, Tom gave up. He'd had it all planned out, every last word he wanted to say to Lizzie, and there was no way he was not going ahead with it. But right now it was impossible. 'Perhaps we can talk later.' He raised his voice hoping that Lizzie had heard him.

Seeing Tom right now was not helpful at all. It didn't help either, when Leo nudged her elbow, saying, 'Finally got it together with lover boy then!' before dodging just enough out of the way as most uncharacteristically she tried to kick him. But as she did, something jogged Tom's memory, and in that split second, he was transported back to a crowded underground train during the wettest summer in years. He remembered exactly where he'd seen Lizzie before. It was that look on her face as she kicked Leo that did it. Someone had been feeling her up on a train. It was all coming back to him, as was her embarrassment when she'd noticed him watching.

* * *

'Darlings, you've surpassed yourselves!' Angel was wafting around most impressed. The food really was every bit as sumptuous as the tickets had advertised, which was just as well, given the cost of it. Katie had successfully negotiated a deal on some excellent wine, which had gone some way to redressing the shortfall in the budget, and which the guests were clearly enjoying, if the copious bottles they were downing were anything to go by.

The well-heeled among them were feeling most magnanimously disposed by the time the auction came round, and that part also went with a swing. Antonia was deep in conversation with a man Lizzie didn't recognise, until he'd winked at her, when she realised with a shock that it was William. In a spotless dinner jacket and striped dicky bow, a far cry from the scruffy farmer Lizzie was used to. Toby, however, was somewhat quieter than usual. In fact, the poor man looked like he'd just been sentenced to death. Catching him alone, she sat down in the empty chair beside him.

'You okay, Toby?'

He shrugged his shoulders, looking thoroughly dejected. 'Told you, did she? Oh...' Then, 'Damned fond of the old girl,' he said in a most forlorn voice, making Antonia sound more like a Jersey cow than the woman he wanted to share the rest of his life with. 'Thought she felt the same way,' he added glumly.

Lizzie's heart went out to him. 'She's awfully fond of you, Toby... But you know, her last marriage wasn't so great. You can't really blame her...'

Toby was silent. When he spoke, he was desolate. 'Thing is, a chap gets to a point in his life where he needs a wife. Someone to warm his slippers. Darn his socks, keep the home fires burning, know what I mean?' No wonder Antonia had run a mile.

'Toby, if it doesn't work out with Antonia, I'm sure you'll find someone else. You'd be a catch...'

Toby brightened momentarily. 'I don't suppose...' He looked at Lizzie, then lowered his head. 'No, course not, sorry, old bean. Just thought I'd ask.'

'Toby. Thank you. I'm flattered, truly,' said Lizzie, 'but there is already someone. I think...'

'Oh jolly good, well done.' Toby slumped back in his chair and lapsed into silence. Let's face it, thought Lizzie, the poor man had just been dumped. He was bound to be a bit down in the mouth.

'You'll be okay, Tobes.' Lizzie gazed earnestly at him, as, getting up, she patted his hand. 'I promise. I'll see you later.'

She bumped into Antonia almost straight away.

'What did you say to him? He's heartbroken,' Lizzie muttered at her.

'He'll be fine, darling. Needs to man up, that's all. Now come and talk to the Wainrights, darling. They've really been exceedingly generous. Be a darling and take them some free champagne…'

In fact, it seemed that the happiest couples among them were the newest. Tim whisked Katie away to the dance floor, where Leo and Ginny were already putting on a surprisingly dazzling display. Finding herself alone, Lizzie was grateful for a moment to catch her breath and think. But not for very long, as Shar came over and collapsed into the chair next to her.

'Come and have a drink with me and Rich?' she suggested, a twinkle in her eye. 'We're outside – there's a bench under one of the cedars. It's a bit quieter away from this lot! You go on. I'll just collect another bottle of wine, and I'll join you.'

Lizzie wandered outside and looked across the park. Nola and Julia had been right – a huge round moon was rising behind the trees, brightening the dusky sky. It was a beautiful night. As she breathed in the scent of damp grass, she heard a voice behind her.

'It was on a train. Actually, the Tube. You were annoyed with someone, erm, extremely annoyed I think.'

And in a flash Lizzie remembered too. Slowly, she turned round. It had been Tom's coat she'd been staring at, and Tom who'd winked at her when he'd got off the train after she'd stomped on that horrible man's foot.

'Oh…' was all she could say, completely dumbfounded, as the memory came flooding back to her. Then she giggled, adding with feeling, 'That was a really bad day! One of the worst!' Then she suddenly thought – that was the day. The day that all of this started...

Feeling bolder, she asked him, 'Why didn't you call? I really thought you were going to...'

Tom sighed. 'I think I made a mistake. No, I know I made a mistake, Lizzie. A big one. We were together for two years, Lucy and I, until she ended things. I found it very difficult afterwards. When I saw her again, that time with you, I didn't really think. But later, when I couldn't stop thinking about you, I realised...'

He looked sheepish. 'Seems we've been set up. My so-called friends, I assume... they seem to think I need a kick up the back-side!' Rich had told him as much earlier. Taking Lizzie's hand, he led her across the grass.

Lizzie sat down on the bench, still not sure where this was leading.

'I finished with Lucy about two weeks after the wedding. I did call you then, several times, but you were never home. I didn't leave a message, because I didn't know what to say. I wasn't even sure you'd want to talk to me.' He laughed ruefully. 'I'm really not very good at this. I've also been travelling a lot, and back and forth in between, of course, but, I don't know...' His voice tailed off. He wasn't very good at selling himself. Anyway, he'd been an arse.

But Lizzie was not going to make this easy for him. Why should she? And did she even want to start anything with him when she might be moving anyway...

'You know,' she said eventually, 'I'm still not sure what you're saying...'

But his face told her the answer.

Her face fell. 'Oh, Tom. You see, I've just been offered an amazing opportunity...'

So Tom listened as she told him about it.

Then there was a bit of a scuffle, and the sound of voices as Rich and Shar joined them, looking inordinately pleased.

'Okay, chaps?' Rich bent down to look at Lizzie, then Tom, before grabbing Shar's arm and saying, 'Shara my dear, would you like some more champagne?' as he waltzed her back to the marquee.

'Oh, definitely a set-up!' Lizzie looked at him. 'The question is, where do we go from here?'

Tom leaned forward and took her hand. 'You know, sometimes decisions are best kept on hold, just for a while, while you mull them over. That's what I do, for what it's worth. Things have a funny way of working out.' He paused, quite pleased with what he'd said, for once. 'Come on, why don't we go back and have a dance?'

* * *

Rich nudged Shar as there, as in the middle of the dance floor, Lizzie and Tom at last held each other closely. Katie caught Tim's eye and winked, Darius clutched Angelus's arm – even Eucalyptus sniffed a tear away as all of them noticed.

Lizzie and Tom suddenly looked at each other. Both feeling something that they couldn't identify, before looking away. But that electricity was stronger than ever and just as the thought came into Tom's mind, so what if she does move to Devon? It's hardly very far away, Lizzie was thinking exactly the same thing, that even if she did take that job, why shouldn't she and Tom have a future... Barely perceptibly to anyone who might be watching, their arms tightened around each other, as they found themselves for the first time ever, perfectly and absolutely synchronised.

37

Just the right time later...

'Tom, we're going to be *so* late' wailed Lizzie from the bathroom. 'I feel so sick. Everyone will be there before us, and I so wanted to be early...'

'Lizzie, can we just get going? We can always stop on the way if we need to.'

'I can't do my zip up!' came the plaintive voice from the bathroom. 'Honestly, last week it fitted fine...'

'Wear that floaty thing that Nola sent you then,' Tom replied, starting to lose patience. 'It looks gorgeous, now *come on...*'

* * *

Inside the tiny church in Littleton, a crowd had gathered for the wedding. It wasn't as lavishly decorated as it had been for Susie's about eighteen months previously, but it was simply and elegantly done, with white narcissi and candles on every surface, lifting the gloom of a grey February afternoon.

Lizzie and Tom just made it in through the door, only seconds before the organ fired up with Mrs Hepplewhite's admirable rendition of Wagner's 'Wedding March' and Katie, elegantly resplendent in ivory slub silk with a fitted furry bolero to keep the chill out, took her father's arm and started her walk down the aisle.

* * *

It was *so* good to be back. Like coming home. Lizzie hadn't realised until now, just how much she had missed everyone. If it hadn't been Katie and Tim's wedding, it might have felt like her own welcome home party, she thought. She couldn't wait to move back here. In the event, she'd had less than six months in Devon before discovering she was having Tom's baby. Eric Masterson had been sorry that he had to lose her, but had been most understanding, asking her to stay as long as she could to help him choose her replacement. And together they'd drawn up plans for the future of the gardens there, which Eric was determined he'd see through to completion.

'How are you feeling?' Tom was concerned.

'Okay... I think...' Lizzie sounded doubtful. Truth was, she was feeling a little odd today, but she wasn't missing this wedding for anything. Not even if... she banished the thought. Just not today... *please* not...

The reception was being held at Aubrey's house. He'd enjoyed hosting the Hethecote fund-raiser so much that he and Antonia had gone into business. Only in a small way, but it was proving rather lucrative, solving Antonia's financial worries. She and Cassie had moved out of Apple Trees. William had offered her free grazing for the horses, and Miriam had rented half of Hethecote Farmhouse to her, in exchange for some help with the farm. Dave had become a local celebrity with the visitors, being far too old to be eaten.

'Would only be good for stewing now, darling. He's too bally old... Be tough as old boots! Such a waste,' she'd said resignedly, when Lizzie had asked after him.

'Awfully glad to hear you're moving back though, Lizzie! It hasn't been the same at all... I say, have you seen William? Bit of a dish in that suit, isn't he? Actually, I'll let you into a little secret, darling... he's quite a surprise in the kitchen...' She winked at Lizzie. Not the only surprise by the look of it.

The size of Lizzie's belly was the cause of much consternation. Antonia and Cassie couldn't take their eyes off it.

'Good God you're fat! Are you absolutely sure there's only one? You're enormous!' Antonia told her in her usual tactless fashion.

Cassie was fascinated, especially when the floaty dress rippled as the baby kicked around underneath.

'Doesn't that hurt?' she asked Lizzie incredulously, tentatively touching then whipping her hand away in fright as Lizzie's belly stirred again.

'Nothing like as much as when it comes out,' muttered Antonia darkly, under her breath. 'Couldn't sit down for weeks after you arrived,' she told her daughter, which wasn't exactly what Lizzie wanted to hear at that moment.

Cassie had caught Lizzie earlier, as they arrived at the reception. 'Is it really true? That you're moving back? Only I've missed you, Lizzie... Mummy's been driving me mad. You will invite her over won't you, when the baby's born?'

Lizzie laughed. 'Of course! She'd better... I'm counting on it, and you too! I've got you down as my chief babysitter...'

Actually, Lizzie couldn't wait. She and Tom were moving into Owl Cottage, a little further down the lane from where Antonia and Cassie used to live. Her own beloved cottage that she'd moved into right at the very beginning had been re-let, and in any case, would have been on the small side, now that there would soon be three of them.

Tom worked more from home these days, and had started to get involved with his father's farm. Though he still travelled, it was less and Lizzie went with him when it was possible. She was looking forward to her new garden. The only trouble was, at the moment, with the difficulty she had walking even the shortest distance, she certainly couldn't imagine digging it.

Toby had a new girlfriend in tow. Cynthia – quite a pretty girl except for her incredibly big teeth and a laugh like a donkey braying. But he was completely smitten and Lizzie was relieved to observe that this time it appeared to be mutual. Maybe things would work out better for him, and Cynthia would be the lucky one charged with the enviable task of keeping Toby's home fires burning.

Leo had long gone, banished to the wilds of Ireland, where he'd found a job in a large bloodstock yard. After his brief fling with Ginny, during which she'd kept him relatively out of trouble, he'd gone on to disgrace himself spectacularly by having it off with the wife of one of Tim's longest-standing clients, finally getting caught with his trousers down, quite literally. Lizzie had laughed like a drain when Katie told her. Tim had been livid and fired him, saying he'd rather work twice as hard than put up with any more of Leo's embarrassing behaviour. In any case, since then he'd found another locum who'd succumbed to the magic of the village and looked as though he'd be staying.

Eucalyptus was there, still, unbelievably, with Jamie. She came scurrying over to Lizzie as soon as they got to the reception. She seemed a lot less twitchy these days. Less straggly and neurotic – vaguely pretty even. Maybe Jamie had found someone who suited his controlling ways.

'I'm so *very* pleased to see you, Lizzie. Erm, actually we both are...' Lizzie glanced over at Jamie, who managed an awkward wave in her direction. He was sporting rather a natty tie, thought Lizzie, with amusement. Quite a departure for such a stick in the mud.

'You never told me you had an Einstein,' he said to her, disapprovingly, later.

'But I don't,' she'd said, puzzled.

'That painting in your kitchen, Eliza... didn't you know? It was an Einstein...'

Slowly the penny dropped. Mrs Einstein, the breeder of the creepy cats, was none other than Eucalyptus all along! Who'd have thought it?

An unfamiliar tightness spread across her belly. *And the pain...* Lizzie winced.

'Oh, dear, oh dear, oh you're not... are you?' fluffed Eucalyptus, jumping up in alarm.

'Probably just a false alarm,' Lizzie lied, before Eucalyptus added, 'Oh, my, I rather think maybe you are,' watching disbelievingly as Lizzie's waters broke. Dramatically.

'Oh... oh... oh deary me.' Eucalyptus just stood there, gaping, rooted to the spot.

'Get Tom,' said Lizzie through gritted teeth, wishing she were anywhere but here. How utterly embarrassing was this.

* * *

An ambulance came and rushed them off to the local hospital. Katie had desperately wanted to go too, but Tim had gently but firmly persuaded his wife of a few hours that as in fact it was actually her own wedding that she was planning to abandon, it might just be better if she stayed behind and let Tom go instead.

The reception went on as planned. If it had been anyone other than Tim and Katie getting married, it might have been different, but they took it all in their stride, with Tim throwing away the speech he had spent hours preparing.

'Lizzie has made quite sure that we'll never forget our wedding day,' he began, to the applause of their guests. A radiantly happy Katie giggled at his side, both of them knowing only too well that Lizzie herself would be completely mortified.

* * *

Lizzie felt as exhausted as if she'd run one of her marathons. Carrying four extra stone. And just as elated, when a little while later, Tom carefully passed her a small, shrieking bundle with a very red face. Sophie Isobel Lavender Woodleigh... curiously it had been Tom who had suggested the Isobel, and been quite adamant about it too, as he gently stroked his daughter's tiny head.

* * *

During Lizzie's first week in Owl Cottage, it was as though she'd never been away. The stream of visitors was never-ending – Darren had installed himself under Sophie's cot, monitoring the flow through one eye.

'Quite sweet for a baby,' said Antonia, clutching a small stuffed horse. 'Cassie was hideous. They do get prettier, thank God.'

'Oh darling, she's *divine*...' The fairy godfathers, as Tom had re-christened Darius and Angel, arrived laden with so many presents you could only tell by the aftershave who was standing at the door. 'Look at her nose, darling... her fingers are so tiny... *she's perfect*,' they cooed, smitten.*

A week later, Lizzie took Sophie to Sparkie's. She wanted to introduce her to Nola and Julia, and ask, very tentatively, if the girls had any idea where she might find the cutest baby clothes.

The bell gave its familiar tinkle as Lizzie went in. And stopped. The shop looked completely different. Nola's face lit up as she saw her.

Embracing both of them warmly, she explained. 'You see, we're moving, Lizzie.' Nola eyes had looked earnestly at her.

'Sparkie's will still be here, but someone else will be running it for us.'

A familiar pink head popped up from behind the desk.

'Lizzie!'

'Tilly...?'

'Tilly's going to look after it while we go and start our next shop. We're going to Brighton, actually. Julia found the most perfect little shop in the Lanes, and we signed the lease yesterday! It felt like... the right time...'

Timing. There it was again...

They sat in the office, drinking raspberry and vanilla tea, as, in turn, both Nola and Julia held baby Sophie. They marvelled at her peachy skin and the pale wisps of hair... Were entranced even when she screwed up her face and wailed. But they were quieter than usual. Their mood was different, as if something no longer troubled them.

'I shall miss you both terribly,' said Lizzie sadly.

'We won't be gone forever,' said Julia. 'And it's different now, Lizzie. You've found your way. Of course there's more, there always will be. But you'll be able to figure it out.'

'Can you see it now, Lizzie?' said Nola.

'See what?' asked Lizzie, puzzled.

'All of it! How you came to be here, and bumped into Tom, and all the events that happened since that meant you finally ended up together... There was a reason for everything. If just one part of it hadn't gone before, everything would now be different. Even going away for a while was right! Because it's all worked out perfectly.

Your circle is complete! And you have this little darling one, and so it all begins again...'

But it went back further than that. It had all started with one of her darkest days ever and the pervert on the train... But actually, *if* she hadn't stumbled across Littleton... *if* Jamie hadn't been the wrong man... *if* her mother hadn't left her that letter...

'It was always your destiny...' said Julia quietly. 'All you had to do was recognise it...'

And Lizzie didn't say anything. There was a certain kind of logic to their words. Destiny, fate, chance – it existed, whatever you called it. Just because you couldn't see it, it didn't matter. And anyway, who was she to question the ways of the universe?

ACKNOWLEDGMENTS

Time to Take a Chance was my first ever novel. I wrote it when my life was in a state of change. I'd just lost my mum to brain cancer, we'd moved house, work was off-the-scale busy. Writing became a way of taking some time out – and channelling my grief.

But I didn't want to write about grief per se, though inevitably it's part of the story. What I wanted to write about is living. About the life-defining moments that shape us, when we dig deep to find as yet undiscovered reserves of strength. The moments and meetings that challenge the way we think. And moreover, what this does to our lives going forward.

It's a book about love and friendship, particularly those unexpected friends who come your way exactly when you need them, the quirks of small communities, the twists of fate that set us on a different path. Set in a small village, it's also about the beauty of nature and the countryside.

I'd love to thank all the friends who read this back then, for being so generous with their encouragement when I was so nervous about putting a book out there! My family, too, for their endless support. Each and every one of you made such a difference!

Huge thanks, too, to the fabulous team at Boldwood Books. I'm thrilled you are publishing this! And so grateful, too, for your creativity and energy, both pre-publication, and after. To Isobel, my editor, Nia, Claire, Marcela – and to all of you, a heartfelt thank you.

Huge thanks, as ever, to Juliet Mushens, who is the best agent a writer could wish for!

And to you, my readers, for reading my books and making it possible for me to go on writing. I hope you enjoy this one.

ABOUT THE AUTHOR

Debbie Howells' first novel, a psychological thriller, *The Bones of You*, was a Sunday Times bestseller for Macmillan. Fulfilling her dream of writing women's fiction she has found a home with Boldwood.

Sign up to Debbie Howells' mailing list for news, competitions and updates on future books.

Visit Debbie's website: https://www.debbiehowells.co.uk

Follow Debbie on social media:

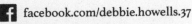 facebook.com/debbie.howells.37

 x.com/debbie__howells

instagram.com/_debbiehowells

bookbub.com/authors/debbie-howells

ALSO BY DEBBIE HOWELLS

The Life You Left Behind

The Girl I Used To Be

The Shape of Your Heart

It All Started With You

The Impossible Search for the Perfect Man

Time to Take a Chance

LOVE NOTES

LOVE IN EVERY CHAPTER

WHERE ALL YOUR ROMANCE
DREAMS COME TRUE!

THE HOME OF BESTSELLING
ROMANCE AND WOMEN'S
FICTION

 WARNING:
MAY CONTAIN SPICE

SIGN UP TO OUR
NEWSLETTER

https://bit.ly/Lovenotesnews

Boldwood

Boldwood Books is an award-winning fiction publishing company seeking out the best stories from around the world.

Find out more at www.boldwoodbooks.com

Join our reader community for brilliant books, competitions and offers!

Follow us
@BoldwoodBooks
@TheBoldBookClub

Sign up to our weekly
deals newsletter

https://bit.ly/BoldwoodBNewsletter

Milton Keynes UK
Ingram Content Group UK Ltd.
UKHW041320201223
434684UK00005B/90